THE
COMMON
HEART

❖　❖　❖

ALSO BY PAUL HORGAN

A Distant Trumpet
Far From Cibola
Humble Powers
Main Line West
The Peach Stone
The Saintmaker's Christmas Eve
Things as They Are

Visit WWW.CLUNYMEDIA.COM *for these and more titles
from the Catholic literary tradition.*

❖　❖　❖

The Common Heart

A Novel

MOUNTAIN STANDARD TIME
BOOK THREE

Paul Horgan

✿ ✿ ✿

CLUNY
Providence, Rhode Island

CLUNY EDITION, 2025

This Cluny edition is a republication of *The Common Heart*,
from the 1962 Farar, Straus and Cudahy edition
of *Mountain Standard Time*, a collection of
Main Line West (1936), *Far From Cibola* (1936),
and *The Common Heart* (1942).

The Foreword to that collection, which describes
the stories' common foundation, the American Southwest,
prefaces each Cluny edition of the novels;
the Afterword to each is also taken
from *Mountain Standard Time*.

For information regarding this title
or any other Cluny Media publication,
please write to info@clunymedia.com, or to
Cluny Media, P.O. Box 1664, Providence, RI 02901

ONLINE AT WWW.CLUNYMEDIA.COM

ISBN: 978-1685954161

Cover design by Clarke & Clarke
Cover image: Gustave Baumann, *Three Pines*, 1925, color woodcut
Courtesy of the New Mexico Museum of Art
Museum purchase with funds raised by the School of American Research, 1952
(933.23G). © New Mexico Museum of Art. Photo by Addison Doty.

THE COMMON HEART

Foreword

THE zone of Mountain Standard Time reaches in the American southwest from western Kansas to the California line and embraces, from Canada in the north to the Mexican border in the south, the great spine of the continent, the Rocky Mountains.

In a diversity of character greater than that of the other time zones in the nation, it includes the great prairies of Kansas; the plains of eastern Colorado, eastern New Mexico, and West Texas; the continental upsweep of the land into the flanks and pinnacles of the Rockies; and finally the high mesalands of New Mexico and Arizona with their buttes and canyons.

In such a land of great visible distance and openness of light, Nature seems to stand forth direct under abstract passions of vast acts of weather. And so too in that country human passions seem to show forth in direct power and effect, through the variety of people in its immense neighborhoods.

It is the land of the prairie farmer. If his world is flat, so too may be his spirit, his voice, his private containment within a human horizon of drought-like shrewdness, all of which must affect his family and they in turn their society. It is the land of the little caboose-red railroad towns some of which grew into wayside cities along the transcontinental rail systems—cities laid out in grids reaching at right angles to the tracks in magic alleys of neon light if seen at night, and two-to-four storey perspectives of drably colored commercial fronts if by day. The land of the cattle or sheep ranchers, and the farmer of irrigated fields, who come to town once or twice a week for gossip and supplies and connection with a world otherwise lost to them where they live and work hidden in the open plains.

Land of any town with forty houses set about an intersection of two state highways which cross like a plus sign in the flat wilderness. Of windmills at far intervals calling the water of life out of the earth on which rain falls so scarcely. Of mountains always visible either close to or far off. The Great River rising in the Continental Divide in Colorado and flowing down through all of New Mexico and then turning southeastward to make a vein, in places containing only dust or gravel, which ends at the Gulf of Mexico. Land where the voice of the wandering evangelist uses all the accents of the people who hear him—echoes of the south, and the prairie midland, and the Plains Texan, and the town settlers from anywhere else. If the evangelist's effect can be called regional, it is suggestive of a civilization delayed for a few generations in arriving at an expression of life which to be civilized must represent the highest collective style of its component people rather than the average, or the lowest.

Above all it is the land whose human history, traceable for tens of centuries, seems of all histories which compose the nation's character, the most immediately recoverable in its environment, and yet the most alight with the quality of legend—just as its landscape, made of hard mountains and cruel distances, seems touched with fantasy. When trail-makers from the east first saw the Rocky Mountains shining on the far horizon, they thought they were seeing clouds.

In those land spaces of the southwest, great as they are, a person stands in relief like an earth feature, small, perhaps, but strongly lighted and as strongly shadowed.

In something of the image of this, I saw the people of *Main Line West*, *Far From Cibola*, and *The Common Heart* when I first unfolded their stories; and because the main action of many of their lives, and the climactic episodes of all three books, occur in their part of the country (to which I have belonged for much of my own life), I gathered them under the title of *Mountain Standard Time*, under which their hours are reckoned.

P. H.

To

PEG AND BARRY DUFFIELD

BOOK I

The Family Story

I · PETER AND THE COUNTRY

I

One winter day, in the nineteen-twenties, the physician Peter Rush was driving carefully through a cold sandstorm that was blowing off the mountains, across the mesa, and down upon the town of Albuquerque. He could hardly see. His huge Packard touring car had the side curtains in place, but the sand whined through the cracks on the bitter wind and stung him in the eyes. The storm moved with rolling scrolls of yellow cloud that turned the sun blue and sent a pale chill light over everything. All his life he had known such days; even early chronicles of New Mexico had mentioned them. He knew how the change of light under the hurrying cloud of earth could make your heart sink. It was common enough for patients under his care to have "setbacks" on such an afternoon. They said they felt depressed, and that they could hardly catch their breaths. When they looked out the window, all they saw was that steel-blue light, and far off on the mesa, that sandy veil being dragged by the wind.

He rocked slowly along the dirt ranch road in the big car. Soon he would reach the highway, and then he could probably go a little faster. He was on his way back to town, where he would meet complaints on all sides about the weather. He could hear himself replying, as he had many times before, "You ought to've been out *in* it, as I was." He knew this wouldn't satisfy anyone, because they could all tell from the way he said it that he loved being out in the blowing cold sandy day. There wasn't anything that took place over that land which he did not enjoy.

But even a day like this? they would ask.

Yes, he would reply, even a day like this.

He had grown up in the town. His father had been a rancher, his mother a doctor's daughter who had come West to try a year of school teaching after a polite graduation from a young ladies' seminary in Washington, D. C. She had never gone back. But her only son's desire to become a doctor represented to her a triumph of her own heritage. The rancher father had accepted their son's vocation with a plains-born silence, and after the youth's college years were over, had sold his ranch and cattle, moved into town for good, and there died of inaction. In this his wife saw a landsman's willing bow to the cycle of life in its seasons, and found solace in helping with the struggles of her church in the raw little railroad town on the middle Rio Grande plains. She died out West during her son's internship in a New York hospital. When he came home for good to practice medicine, Peter Rush saw his boyhood country with the love of a man who knew what he came from, was able to respect it, and wanted to help make it good in his own time.

As the blowing curtain of sand thinned out momentarily, he saw the valley far below him, and he thought "There it is." He meant the town. It lay with its many facets of board and brick down toward the Rio Grande.

The river drew all things toward itself as tributaries. It drew whatever water lay in the sandhill furrows after storms; any green life of the wide valley; the line of the railroad that sought the water level; the cluster of houses; the thoughts of people, their very lives. It was one of four large facts of nature in that part of New Mexico. One was the mountain range to the east. One was the vast plain of the mesa just above the town. The third was the river itself, toward which these lands fell in grand steps. Lastly, across the river, there was a wilderness of white sand, from which arose three extinct volcanoes, sand-hued, and charred brown at their craters. Peter Rush remembered his mother always calling them the "Siamese cats" because that was what their color suggested. When he was old enough to think that it was an odd thing to call a dead fire-mountain, he was so used to the notion that it didn't strike him as strange at all.

His father loved and accepted the country without comment. His mother thought much about it and never got over the private feeling that she was there in exile. But the son had her speculative interest in the land as well as his father's native ease and sense of replenishment from it. His mother's letters to him while he was a student in the East inadvertently betrayed again and again her eagerness for the Eastern life he was living. When he came to realize it, to know what she had longed for all her married life, he promised himself to give it to her as soon as he could afford it. But she died first. He never again lost a sense of compassion for the private dreams, the inner dignities of people; anyone at all; and this was her legacy to his adult life.

As he came toward the town now, through the grainy air of that bitter afternoon, when it blew sand instead of snow, he bore toward what he saw an attitude that said,

"There it is, the whole stuff, and every grain of it has its own value. If I were a painter—and sometimes I feel sure that if I took up a brush and color, I could put down what I see exactly as I see it, I don't imagine it would be very much more delicate than some of my surgical tricks—I would paint everything about this town that I see every day. The trains coming in over the plains all day and all night, and red and yellow and green lights and steam and evening filtering down like blue dust. Paint the muddy river running sweet with sunshine. The long aisles of cottonwood trees on the streets. The yellow light of a day like this which sweeps all of it, the mountains, the mesa, the river, into one bitter blur. I would paint the viaduct over the tracks, and its rickety red wood burnt black with locomotive smoke. The saloon on the corner that is closed since Prohibition came last year, but I would get in my picture the sulphur color of the mistakes of men. The backside of the hospital with the rose brick and the silver smokestack and the feather-blue sky. The

YMCA building of gray stucco there by the tracks, and I would get the comical virgin morality of little boys and earnest youths. I would set down what the American flag looked like on the front of the Commercial Club the day the Armistice was signed. My heart was in my mouth all day afterward, because it was over, and my little boy would have a chance to help work out Wilson's world, a job that will be worth some doing. If nobody has ever painted a picture of a small-town drugstore, and the country-colored men and women that come in off ranches to buy their needs, I would do it, and I would make it magical. If I got good enough, I would make a picture of my wife, and answer some questions in my heart with it. Is it possible to make a picture out of a memory? My boyhood? But my son is doing that every day of his life, right before me, and in a more precious medium. I have decided, anyway, that it is a very good thing for every man to have a great untried talent—like my painting—which will sustain him privately when his day's job doesn't go so well."

2

The Doctor always seemed to be so busy that nobody took him for a reflective man. Often, far beyond anyone's knowledge, he suffered for the troubles of his patients. They seemed so poor sometimes, in the face of the anonymous powers of disease. They all had the same fears, and what could dissipate these on the one hand but the feeling of health returning some sunny morning; or on the other the assurances that lay between the words of the priest when death was coming? The Doctor could say so little when they begged it of him to say. They touched him most when they were most courageous; for then he felt the continuity of spirit which really did take the present back into the past.

He kept a standing order with a bookseller in Boston to send him whatever he could find in the way of original editions of early-day writings by explorers, travelers, army engineers, who had come to New Mexico long ago. He had never seen the bookseller, but between them there had sprung up an alliance that, far beyond commercial concerns, served their passion for the history of the early West. If a particularly good item turned up that was very expensive, the bookseller wrote him first asking if he cared to spend that much. Sometimes the Doctor scribbled "Yes, of course" in the margin of the inquiry and sent it back. But sometimes he would ask his wife Noonie how much they had in the bank, and she would have a pang for what she considered his dreamy extravagance, and assure him that this month there wasn't a cent for any more of those dusty old books with the elaborate tarnished gilt and the ribbed cloth of the bindings ready to turn to powder. At such times he always grinned at her for what *she* read: huge piles of magazines which she read all afternoon in her upstairs porch, which was glassed in and dancing with light. The print traveled by under her eyes without making any impression at all, except that of a sort of visible passage of time. She read with fever. Her eyes sparkled, her cheeks turned rosy, and she seemed to hunger after the romances she pursued so hotly. Of what the words were about, and the people they described, she never retained any memory. That a word on a printed page ever could arrest something of life itself, and keep it alive as long as it could be read, she never knew. Seeking escape into love, she escaped those who really loved her.

What her husband "did" with his books would have given her genuine and admiring surprise, if he had ever told her. But loving her as he did, he was afraid to see just how wide the gap might be between his mind and hers. So he let her think the books simply kept coming in order to be lined up on a shelf upstairs, in his third-floor study, where he could look at them "between calls."

Some of the calls took him to the country (like this one today, out to a barren little ranch on the mesa, where the ranch hand had broken his arm in a fall off the windmill ladder). And when they didn't, he would go to the country anyway, bringing along his latest book, if it had a trace in it of activity hereabouts in the early days. He would search until he found the very place which the old words described; and then—alive to the past because he felt so keenly in the present—he would see again what had taken place long ago.

What he would see always made him conclude, even in that landscape made of such durabilities as mountain and plain and river, that the one constant thing was man's spirit.

But though he did not know it, it was himself he was seeing in those terms.

He was coming down the hill through the cold wafts of the blowing sand. "The color of everything today is the color of the fur on the belly of a mountain lion. It is a cat-colored storm. The whole world has come into harmony with the volcanoes across the river. Thank God there's a little bit of green left here and there, even in winter."

He alluded to his own piece of public folly, which he nevertheless admired. Next door to his own three-story red-brick house he owned two vacant lots. There he had planted an evergreen nursery, with three varieties of pine trees, standing in strict ranks. As often as he could he tended them himself. There seemed to him a happy correlation between this matter of setting out trees in a barren country, and letting them grow just for the pleasure of it, and the pursuit of how this country looked to those who saw it new, generation after generation. To the successive waves of travelers in the West, the land presented a new meaning each time, for each was looking for something different from what his predecessors had sought. He remembered that to the end of her days, his mother had missed "the green" of the East.

Across town, from the hillside, where Central Avenue began to drop down to the river plain, he could see the green blur of his nursery.

When the sandstorm was over, the trees would glisten in the sunlight again, and he would look down on them from his third-floor windows at home.

3

He decided not to go by his office but to go home. If there had been any calls for him downtown, they would've been phoned out to the house. He drove through the streets many of which were not yet paved, and the blowing wind picked up the sand. He came home by streets far out on the edge of town. He always liked that point where the countryside and the town could be seen together. He didn't reflect about it, but what pleased him in the sight was the recollection of how it had been in his boyhood, when from almost anywhere in the town you could see the plains opening out at the ends of streets. The city was growing these days. He avoided the "metropolitan" look of its downtown as much as possible. He was unimpressed by what everyone else hailed as "progress." But he never felt it polite to say so. He allowed his fellow citizens their zeal and their ambition, which he described to himself as a kind of forgetfulness of man's real virtues.

At home he found a scribble on the tablet by the phone in the white-paneled closet under the front hall stairway. It told him to call the office. His downtown nurse answered and said that he had a call to go see a patient, a newcomer, who had been urged by Doctor Treddinger, of New York, to get in touch with him. The patient's name was Mrs. Foster. Her address was 1 Highland Parkway. She wanted to see Doctor Rush this afternoon, if possible.

He still had his hat and coat on, and when he hung up the receiver, he simply sat in the phone cubbyhole, as they called it in the family, and looked out at what he could see of his home from this narrow prospect. It was a spacious house, and everything about it was square and clean. But it sometimes seemed to him empty, in a curious way. The only place in it where he felt at home was his study on the top floor. He wondered if his wife Noonie was upstairs; if his son Donald was home from school; if Cora the cook and Leonard the houseboy (both Negroes) were out in the kitchen. He couldn't hear anything.

The living room had white painted pillars dividing it from the hall. The carpets were green. There was a brass and prism chandelier hanging in the hall, and another in the big front room. There was a lot of mahogany furniture. The stairway over him was of mahogany with a green carpet. The windows had loops of lace curtain and he could see the stern of the grand piano before the wide windows of the front room. He was hungry. But if he went out to get a glass of milk, he would have to listen to Cora complaining humorously about Jacob her husband, who couldn't let other girls alone; or if Cora weren't there, he wouldn't be able to find anything. He considered having a small icebox of his own put into the study way upstairs; and then stood up, impatient at his general discontent in his own house, which made him feel guilty.

He went to the foot of the stairs, and called up:

"Noon? Are you there?"

There was a stir, first, and then an answer, from the big glassed-in sitting room where she did her mending, and loved to read, over the front porch.

"Hello? Yes?"

They both waited in silence a moment, considering each other out of sight and reach.

Then he said up the stairs, with his eyes shut,

"Are you all right, dearie?"

She paused again, long enough to let doubt into her reassuring words:

"*Perfectly* all right, dear.—Are you going out? Or coming up?"

"I'm running out for a few minutes, there was a call for me downtown. I have a million things to do. I'll be back for dinner."

"I should hope so," she said, bridling slightly in her tone.

He waited another moment, but if she was going to be habitually reproachful, there was nothing more he felt like saying. He went out to his car, climbed in and set off again, cruising through the bitter blowy day with the sand rattling on the isinglass of his side curtains. Mrs. Foster lived at 1 Highland Parkway. He knew the place, a large rambling house on two levels, built of logs against the hillside overlooking town. It was often taken by Easterners who came here for their health. If Doctor Treddinger had sent Mrs. Foster to him it was most likely a case of something respiratory. There would probably be a letter one of these days all about it. Willie Treddinger was always late with that sort of thing.

II · THE FAMILY STORY

I

After he went, Mrs. Rush sat still with her mending all about her, looking after him down the street. She was tired. She wished she had gone downstairs to see him. Every time he left her, she wished she had done more, said more, to give him comfort. Yet she could never explain to herself why she had been graceless with him. How much she loved him he did not know; and when he was patient with her, and forbore to rebuke her when she was remote from him, she had a positive passion of resentment in her heart which tasted bitterly to her thought.

How could it be that what had begun rapturously fourteen years ago was now, at times, so doubtful?

2

One week end in the winter of 1906, her cousin Willie Treddinger brought Peter Rush home to Rochester, New York, for a visit. They were both interns in a hospital in New York City, and shared the same small bedroom. They had been together in college, at Cornell, but their intimacy grew only after they had been graduated and sent to St. Luke's for their last two years of training. Peter was then very slim, with what everybody spoke of as a Western figure, with his flat wide shoulders and thin legs and narrow hips. He tried to look older than he was by wearing a heavy brown mustache. His hair was thick and formal above his merry face, which kept a dark tan from a boyhood on the plains. At a Saturday night dance he was introduced to Susan Larkin (whom everyone called Noonie from a childhood rhyme about "Susan-Noonan") and danced waltzes and two-steps with her all evening. There was said to be a half-understood arrangement between young Doctor Treddinger and his cousin Noonie Larkin, but nobody was surprised when the new young doctor from New Mexico seemed to take the inside track. Treddinger was a pink, round young man with infinite good nature. He watched his friend flirt with Noonie and even seemed to encourage him. Noonie was "furious" with him at first for giving up so easily, "froze" him with "looks" for a couple of week ends, and then as happiness began to steal into her heart, she could only remember that it was her cousin who had brought Peter Rush into her life in the first place; and she ended by kissing Willie on his fat cheek in front of everybody at a supper party in her house, and whispering to him that she would always be grateful to him, and would love him like a *cousin*.

She was the prettiest girl of the year, according to what everyone told her. Her eyes were dark and her hair was darker still. She often said she was as blind as a bat, and couldn't see anything ten feet away. But she refused to wear glasses, and her nearsightedness gave her a blurred and dreamy look about the eyes which (all her female friends told her) "broke" many a heart. She was as lively as a squirrel, and had many darling little tricks of gesture which made a man feel protective and hulking and a willing fool. She could sing adorably, played the piano at all the parties, and never missed a concert by either a visiting artist or any of the local musical societies, such as the German-American Saengerverein, which gave a choral concert every year with an expensive imported soloist, like Schumann-Heink, or Otto Goritz, or Reinhold von Warlich. (So much of that upstate culture reflected the "free" Germans who had fled the tyrannies of Prussia in the mid-century.)

Rochester's winters were gray and damp, and unless you were happy, or didn't notice things like that, you were likely to be chilled to the bone on more days than not. But Noonie seemed to give out light and warmth all that winter, for Peter came down every week end that he wasn't on duty at the big New York hospital. He even came the week end he had news of his mother's death way out in New Mexico. Noonie held his hand, and pressed his fingers, and her heart was in her mouth for what he was suffering, so far away, so lonesome in the name of the childhood which had just ended. He told her how he always meant to go home and get rich and give his mother everything she had always wanted, chief of which was an annual trip to the East. Now it was too late. They called off a party she had arranged for that Saturday night, and nobody was there with them but her brother Roderick, who turned the pages for her when she played and sang songs after dinner, to cheer Peter up. It was a quiet and almost tender evening, and it met his sorrow with another emotion almost as filling. He loved her. He saw a lifetime of such evenings with her. He could hardly wait to be in a position to offer to marry her. He went back to New York by the night train on Sunday. He hardly slept in his Pullman, for thinking about her, and all women, really. A few words spoken late at night in the creaking Pullman car by a woman who got on at Utica suffused him with sweet torments and sterling vows.

3

It wasn't long until he was acknowledged as Noonie's official beau, though they were not actually engaged. During a week end in spring, a friend of Noonie's came from Albany, N. Y., to visit. Her name was Elizabeth Kleitz. She was a hazel-eyed, bronze-haired girl who saw herself as a fascinating scamp, a troublemaker, and had earned a reputation for originality. Elizabeth set herself to break up the match which everyone took for granted. She wore dashing clothes with low-cut bosom, and put her face close to the men she talked to, and let her eyes rove up and down their faces; she had lace cuffs on her sleeves that came down to her knuckles, and she tangled her fingers in her radiant hair and let her eyes fall out of sight in what she believed to be the manner of Sarah Bernhardt. She was never quiet, saying "H-h'm, hm—him, 'm, 'm, 'm," all the while anyone was talking to her. Everyone was sure that she kissed everybody, but her vitality and assurance were so great that she was much admired. She asked everyone to call her Lisette.

She stated that she was scandalized at what she found Noonie up to, and promised everyone else that she would save the situation at no matter what cost to herself. Everyone had felt that Peter and Noonie made an attractive pair, up to now; but Lisette seemed to bring a new viewpoint with authority. Noonie's brother Roderick, especially, seemed to cast off his complacent acceptance of the love affair.

The night Lisette arrived from Albany, there was a concert by Eugene Ysaye. Lisette, Roderick, Noonie and Peter all dressed up in their grandest clothes and went. When the great violinist came out on the stage, the audience rose and clapped. He bowed. His dark golden hair, which reached to his shoulders, fell forward as he bowed. He went on bowing as he walked to the piano carrying his violin, which was the color of an oak leaf in winter. His accompanist followed him. The artists made a quiet moment of business about getting settled in their black and white clothes, under the yellow rain of the concert lights above them. Behind them was a painted stage curtain representing a woodland glade with a tiny marble temple in the blue and gold distance. The violinist took his violin aloft and settled it into his rolling chin, lifted his bow with his large white paw, closed his eyes and nodded faintly. The piano began to sing. The bow came across in a deliberately beautiful arc, and began to woo the strings. Ysaye told the lovers all the things they thought no one else knew. Noonie was enraptured. Peter caught her enchantment, and did not even marvel at being elevated by music for the first time in his life.

Beside them, Lisette, like a superbly intelligent cat, spoke to Roderick about them with her hazel eyes. She had the property of seeming to keep up a running commentary even when she said nothing. But all her other means—hands, eyes, shrugs, breaths, sharp little teeth on lower lip, toe taps—were also articulate. No one was ever left in doubt as to what Lisette thought; or that she "thought" constantly. Her ambition was to have people turn, and look after her, and say, "Who is that fascinating foreigner?"

In the intermission, she seized Noonie's hands and said with a champagnelike glance from her yellow eyes,

"Ach, Noonchen, how could you ever give all this up?"

She often affected tender little Germanisms, having studied German at a fashionable convent-school on the banks of the Hudson River.

Noonie laughed.

"Give what up? I'm not giving anything up."

Lisette gasped softly and put her white-gloved finger tips on her lips.

"Na, what have I said! Am I not supposed to know *anything*?" Even in her rages, she remembered to be "foreign."

She turned and rustled off down the hall in a fury. Noonie went after her. Roderick and Peter drifted together and lighted cigarettes, watching the girls in their elaborate costumes, with long white gloves, high-dressed hair, bare backs, long lacy gowns with loops and rosebuds and velvet ribbons and harsh silk petticoats and dragging trains.

Lisette let herself be caught up with, and her pale eyes blazed at Noonie.

"So: you will never confide in your oldest friend? What do you give up if you marry that nice young rancher from out West? You give up evenings like this, and friends like me, and brothers like your darling Rod, he is so handsome and distinguished, and the best young lawyer in Rochester, how often do you suppose Ysaye plays out West, would he ever risk his beautiful blond hair with the Indians?"

Noonie blushed at this outburst, and took Lisette and kissed her lightly.

"Don't be such a goose, Lizzie, he hasn't even asked me yet!" The gong rang to bring the audience back to the auditorium.

As they went back to their seats it was almost visible on Lisette's face (on which there was a hint of paint, which was meant to be daring) that it was an official relief that Noonie and Peter were not engaged. During the last half of the concert she ignored Roderick beside her and turned to Peter, leaning on his arm, enjoying the music exaggeratedly, brushing his cheek with tingles of her magnificent bronze hair, and losing her eyes upward in desperate emotions caused by his presence as well as by Eugène Ysaye's exquisite playing of the violin.

Peter maintained his composure as well as he could; but at times he had to bite his mustache to keep from laughing right out at her. But he knew Noonie was fond of her, and would be offended if he made fun of her.

They left the concert in a carriage, and the four of them being in the satin-padded interior, with the horse's hooves making a remote sound of progress on the pavement, gave them all a sense of privacy and grandeur. The young men held their silk hats on their knees because the carriage roof was too low. The street lamps as they passed fanned yellow light over their faces. The other three all found themselves watching for Elizabeth's face at every lamp. Its confined but expressive antics always rewarded them.

4

Noonie's brother Roderick Larkin was black-haired and black-eyed. His gaze was black and white, and he had a mannerism of gazing intently at people, mostly women, without speaking, under the illusion that this made him irresistible. It would've made him unbearable, except that deep in his eyes there was always merriment, a kind of spiritual good health, which made people excuse his mischief. Noonie adored him, and he suffered her worship rather regally. It was he who had given her her nickname, long ago when they were both children. For years, he had to approve everything she did or wanted to do before she was satisfied. He worked in a rich law firm, and was always in love with a new girl, but the wise mothers of Rochester were already saying that he was an eternal bachelor, meaning by it that the most constant thing about him was his vanity; such as no girl would ever be likely to measure up to.

He was now amused to be Lisette's ally in the game over Peter Rush from New Mexico.

He had always treated Peter with a clubman's airs, using expressions like "old fellow," and "chappie," and in general contriving to make the young doctor from the West feel that he was dealing with a vividly presented character in a book by Richard Harding Davis rather than with a real man.

Noonie was quick to feel this difference between her brother and her suitor.

She resented the silent good manners of Peter's behavior toward her darling Roderick; and when she was alone, she felt like crying with disappointment at the courteous disdain which Roderick revealed by his exquisite attempts to conceal it, when he dealt with Peter. She tried all sorts of little tricks to bring them together, and Roderick behaved with almost creaking courtesy; the while his inner glance told her that it simply wouldn't do, the fellow was simply an outsider, and he would do all he could for him, but like him he simply could not.

Nothing was ever said openly about all this. It was plainly too dangerous. But in ways that were to reach far into the future it would have been better if brother and sister had come right out and quarreled bitterly, and cleared the air.

The fact was that neither knew the depth of feeling involved, and in some instinctive restraint, did not want to plumb it, for fear they might hurt each other too much.

All their lives they had been able to come laughing out of their little differences, and with a sense of being united against a stuffy world in which nobody else saw the colors, the jokes, or the beauties which they saw.

The Larkin house was an old square building of yellow sandstone, holding aloft a cupola, and trailing a carriage house at the foot of the gravel driveway in the deep garden. It was peaceful, comfortable, and thanks to the character of the parents, a house without "scenes."

It was only when Elizabeth Kleitz came to visit from Albany that there was an impish spirit in the old place. Her mother and Mrs. Larkin had been schoolgirl friends, who always referred in their letters to each other to what a comfort it would be when their daughters should grow up in their turn, in similar friendship.

But Lisette was far more bent on being fascinating than friendly, and this meant, first of all, for better or worse, unremitting liveliness.

5

All day Sunday she kept up her campaign against Peter. Roderick kept asking for certain songs, which he would turn for Noonie at the piano. Noonie watched herself drawn into a temper as the day advanced. She began to hate Lisette, and she was becoming annoyed at Peter's attempts at politeness and attentiveness to the visiting beauty. Finally, late in the afternoon, when Mr. and Mrs. Larkin returned from a series of Sunday calls, and they all sat before the fire at the marble fireplace, Lisette's restless duty had its assuagement.

She had a bunch of American Beauty roses at her waist. She broke one away from her satin sash, and put it by her mouth. It was startling and effective on her white cheek. They all looked at her. The elder Larkins smiled. They remembered a whole cycle of years of young children's parties at which Lisette Kleitz always had to be the leading lady. Lisette let a hazy smile drift across her face, faintly shadowing her lifted cheeks. There was never a greater image of innocence and charm than her face when she asked Peter,

"And when you finish at the New York hospital, Doctor Rush, where do you mean to live?"

He answered readily,

"Why, I shall go back to the West, of course, where I came from. I would never want to live anywhere else."

Mr. and Mrs. Larkin exchanged startled glances. They had often wondered what his future was to be, but they had never actually prepared themselves to hear that. They looked at Noonie, who seemed to be so in love with him. She smiled ardently at Peter, and said,

"I thought we had almost naturalized you."

He laughed.

Lisette sat back in her chair, and cupping her hands, held her rose as if it were a beloved face, to which she was confiding lovely mysteries. She had put into the spoken awareness of them all the things that she instinctively knew to be the sole difficulty facing the two young people, who were so sparkling and alive with love for each other.

Roderick bent his glossy head over a cigarette in his hands, to conceal his amusement over Lisette's wickedness. From that bent position, he glanced blackly and whitely at his sister. A pang hit him in the breast when he saw her eyes full of tears. His disloyalty to her was suddenly plain to him. He lost his airy feeling of indulgent superiority, and went over to Lisette. He took her wrist and brought her to standing.

"Come along, we'll go for a little walk in the park. The ice on the lake is breaking up. Sunset is very pretty over melting ice."

In a few minutes they were gone, Lisette bearing an ermine shako on her dazzling hair, and an ermine muff with black tails on her right arm. Her coat was of dark-green velvet. Noonie hated her out the front door. The elder Larkins went upstairs soon after, and Noonie faced Peter by the fireplace.

"How could you pay so much attention to her!" she said.

"I was only trying to be nice to your friend.—Actually, she made me nearly burst with inside laughter."

"Oh: she did!"

"Yes."

Over things they could hardly touch alive into clarity, their wills were at battle.

"You needn't make fun of my friends!"

"I won't, ordinarily.—Besides, she wants to make trouble.— What else do you suppose all that elaborate acting meant?"

"She is simply being loyal to me, in her way, which I admit is rather odd."

"Don't defend her, Noonie, dear."

She colored at the last word.

The strain of putting up with Lisette for the past twenty-four hours made her lightheaded now that her emotions need not be politely concealed.

"You don't mean that."

"Mean what?"

"What you called me."

"—You mean 'dear'? I do indeed. With all my heart, Noonie dear."

"If you did, you couldn't've said what you did before."

"When:"

"When she asked you where you meant to live."

"But I only said—"

"That's just it. You evidently don't mind going off and leaving—leaving *me* a thousand miles away."

"Oh: that hellcat of a redhead!" he said, laughing full of love, and reaching for Noonie's hand. Noonie put it behind her, longing for him to make her tremble and cry with the tenderness she saw in him.

"You are speaking of my house guest," said Noonie stiffly. She was making a fool of herself. She didn't know how to stop. What was in the way. Dignity? Pride? Hunger?

"Oh, nonsense. Look at me, Noonie."

She turned away.

He sighed.

"Well, then, *would* you come with me, when I have to go back out West?"

She turned and all of Lisette's most idle prattle now seemed full of wisdom and foreboding.

"You wouldn't *consider* staying here, I suppose, not even if you *loved* me?"

Her anger which was more than half love begot the same thing in him. He stiffened. He bit his teeth together. His jaw lumped.

"Turn the coin over," he said. "If you loved me, you wouldn't even *consider* coming with me?"

She stared at him. Tears rose and welled over to her cheeks. She was ravishingly pretty in the firelight. Her spirit danced with exasperation and baffled sweetness. The quarrel was as foolish as any of its kind, and while he saw her adorable desirability, he could see too the aching selfishness of love. He remained stubbornly silent and motionless. She wanted to bring his head down to her hot face, and tell him she was his, anywhere, forever, but instead, she bit her lips to be silent, and ran out of the high marbled room dim with Sunday afternoon quiet and twilight, and up the stairs.

When Lisette and Roderick returned, Peter was gone.

He sat in his hotel lobby all evening, staring out the window at the traffic. It had begun to rain. The carriage lamps and the few automobile headlights were like gold blooming flowers reflected in the wet pavements. The clerk called over to him once that someone wanted him on the phone, but he refused to stir, saying he was out. At eleven he got up and paid his bill, and went to the station to catch the Empire State Express. It was snowing by that time; a late winter storm; the ice on the lake in the park would be frozen again by morning. It would be, he thought bitterly, something for someone to take Miss Elizabeth Kleitz to see.

6

There were a few weeks of official estrangement, during which Noonie was almost plainer to him in his misery than she had been during his week ends of good times in Rochester with her. For the only time in his life he was overtaken by a fit of laziness, or lack of will, or something that made him cloudy in the head when he was at work. He slept more than usual, and never seemed refreshed. He was haunted by her when he dreamed. He sometimes stared out the window over the telephone wires and roofs of 1906 New York, and looked at the pale sky where it was full of light over the invisible river. There to the West was his home. He longed for the sight of the plains, yellow in the winter, under the sky as blue as a bluebird's wing, with those white feathery clouds that seemed to capture the sunlight. That was where he was born. That was where he belonged. They were probably laughing at him up in Rochester for being routed by a red-haired chatterbox from Albany.

And at the same time he knew that he would never be cured of this slow poison, this weight of defeat in him, if he didn't see Noonie again. He knew almost numbly that there would be an issue over where they might live after they were married. One night he awoke startled and sat up and stared at the dark room. Then he smiled with a triumphant certainty. Once they were engaged, and married, and everything, he would love her so much that she would *see* how *anywhere* he went she must come with him. It was a surge of strength and new resolve that flowed through him.

He was suddenly full of ideas again. Before he fell back to sleep, he had the most brilliant idea of all, which he would execute the following evening.

The following evening he walked seven blocks to a drugstore far enough off from the hospital so that he would probably be unobserved by any of his cronies on the staff. There was a telephone booth of heavily carved walnut with glass door panes etched in an ornate design. He closed himself into the booth and asked the operator if a long distance call to Rochester was possible on a commercial phone like this. She said it was, but would probably take about forty-five minutes if he cared to wait. He replied that he would wait all night, if necessary, and gave her Noonie's number. The operator said not to leave the vicinity of the booth. He went and sat down on a wire-backed soda fountain chair and leaned his elbows on a marble-topped soft-drink table. There was a copy of *McClure's Magazine* lying before him, and he turned through its pages, carefully looking at everything, and reading nothing, three times, before the phone rang at last. He dashed to answer. It was his call. His heart was pounding. Through the receiver came a steady roaring noise like Niagara Falls, but he could also hear someone saying "Hello?" and he recognized Roderick's voice.

"Rod? This is Pete Rush. I'm calling from New York. Is Noonie there?"

"Yes. Do you want to speak to her?—You are talking from *New York*?"

"Yes, it is what they call a long distance call.—Can you get Noonie to the phone?"

"Wait a minute, old chap. Say, this is remarkable."

He waited, and at last here she was.

She marveled too, and then appeared to recall the reserve which had not yet been officially dispelled between them.

Peter asked her if she could hear him plainly. She said she could. He answered then that he was glad, because he had something enormously important to say to her. The roar of Niagara Falls could not drown out the falter in her voice when she said "What is it," and he said to her that he begged her to forgive him his temper, and to marry him in June, when he would be through at the hospital.

There was a long pause in which only the electric roar of the phone line kept up.

Then she said yes, but they had so very much to talk over first. He replied that there was nothing they could not settle between them. The important thing was to be together again, didn't she think so?

"Oh yes!" she cried into the phone. Her voice rang clarion over the wire, and turned his heart over.

He told her how much he loved her, and said he would be up the following week end. The operator cut in to announce that the time was up. Noonie delayed them a moment longer to ask if the expense was not simply frightful? making a call from New York? He laughed at her adding to it by asking about it, and they rang off.

7

The following Sunday morning he was at her house as if nothing had happened. They were together in the drawing room about eleven o'clock when a messenger boy on a bicycle came up with a package and rang the doorbell. Noonie herself went to answer. She came back bearing a square basket of wicker, dyed purple, and tied with a purple satin ribbon.

"It is for me!" she said, reading the card as she came to sit down by Peter again.

"Open it," he said. He was blushing and there was a stinging in his eyes.

She opened the wicker lid. In the basket was a huge bunch of violets. Their damp, frosty fragrance seemed to fill the big old room. In the center of the mound of violets was a sparkling jewel. Noonie looked at him and then leaned over the violets and took the jewel up to see it. It was a ring, made of a large violet amethyst surrounded by a circle of diamonds. It sparked and spoke in the sunlight that poured through the windows upon them. She looked at him again. She saw his darkened cheeks and the fire in his eyes.

She began to tremble and fell against him dizzy with happiness. He took the ring from her and put it on her engagement finger, and kissed it there. She threw her arms around his neck and hungered after him saying his name softly.

It was many minutes before they were composed enough to discuss the enchanting ingenuity of how the ring was delivered. All the rest of the day she told the story to everyone who came in. Her family's house was always full of people. The bleak ruin of love which had shown there for weeks was now replaced by the highest happiness.

8

When he next came back it was springtime. They went out for the afternoon in a hired rig which Peter drove. They went to the park and gave a boy half a dollar to watch their horse, and wandered over the grass among the fabulous lilac bushes which had come into bloom. Noonie said the city was very proud of the display. There were over seven hundred varieties of lilac represented. The air was cloudy with fragrance. Everything from pure white clusters to black purples was represented on the grand dome-shaped bushes. The afternoon sunlight was like gold embroidery on the grass. They walked hand in hand. She found a lilac whose color exactly matched her amethyst engagement ring. He looked at her sometimes and could not believe anyone could be as pretty as she was, so animated, so full of meaning when she looked at him. And yet there she was, and she was his. He felt ten years older than the year before, and grateful for the feeling. After he left her each time, he wondered how he could've been such a fool for years up to now. When things went well between them, he had the sensation of being wise and penetrating at his work, as if he came to know all sorts of *other* things simply through her; having her in his life; in his heart.

He told her this as they went back to the buggy from the lilac garden. She made him pause, and turned to him and set her hand on his arm.

"No, there is one trouble, Peter, dearest."

"What is that?"

"You are much cleverer than I am."

"Nonsense."

"Yes, you are deeper than I am."

"Nonsense, I simply had to learn a lot of things that you will never *need* to know. That isn't being deep. Merely wide. Or *wider*, anyway."

"I am really such a goose about a lot of things… Or I was, until I met you…"

He hotly defended her against her own depreciations.

She let him rave, as she called it, and then astonished him by saying, "But after all, I don't think I want to be cleverer. I only want to be really a woman. I hate clever women.—Don't you?"

"Like Lisette?"

She was able to laugh with him about Lisette now. They had telegraphed Lisette their news, and received in reply a wire which read "Amazed thrilled heavenly news when wedding saw it coming always." Secure, they agreed that they could relent and let Lisette come to the wedding.

It was such a warm afternoon that they didn't want to turn homeward. They took the dusty, sunlit road that led to the lake. The fields were beginning to green and yield earthy scents. They saw Lake Ontario in the distance, sparkling soberly. They could see one or two sails leaning before the wind.

"Why don't we stop at the boat club," she said, "and perhaps we'll find someone who will take us out for a ride."

"It is rather late to start."

"Just for a little ride."

"A little one."

At the boat club they ran into Roderick Larkin and a girl he often took out. Her name was Evelyn Warner. She was called Evvie. She was a calm blonde who wore starched shirtwaists and held her beautiful head with a classical lift. She played the violin and was famous in local recital circles. Ysaye had heard her the afternoon before his concert in Rochester that winter and promised "great things" for her. She and Roderick were sitting on the pier, dangling their legs and squinting at the late sunlight on the water.

"Have you been out?" asked Noonie.

"No," said Roderick. "We just wanted to sit here."

"We wanted to go for a sail. Is anyone around?"

"I haven't seen anybody all day to go out with. I have the use of the Rogers's sloop, if you want to go."

It was agreed that they would all go. Roderick knew how to sail. They said they wouldn't be out long. The boathouse keeper helped to push them off. Their sloop was called the *Affinity*. It had a tiny cabin with cherrywood fittings and scarlet velvet cushions. But they all sat in the cockpit, with Roderick at the tiller. The wind was keener and brisker than they had thought. He kept the *Affinity* close-hauled and she leaned over considerably, and spanked a heavy spray off the very waves that had made the lake sparkle from a distance as they had approached the shore in the buggy. Evvie sat statuesquely lifting her Athenian blonde profile into the wind, and holding her flat straw hat on to her golden head with her hand. The shore grew smaller. Some white gulls flipped and sailed like chips of sunlight itself. They were all rather chilly on board, but also they were enchanted with the boat moving over the water, and the tickle of the spray, and the fact that when they wanted to say something, they more or less had to shout it, because of the wind and the thundering of their bows against the waves which came rolling, rolling "from Canada" which was way out of sight over the horizon.

They sailed parallel to the shore for a while. The sun was falling. They could see (far back it seemed) the birth of a few early lights in houses among the hills. Roderick said he would come about and they would return, before darkness fell. The twilight was the finest hour of all for sailing, he shouted. They enthusiastically agreed with him. The sloop came about and headed back. But the wind was not so favorable. The vast lake was glistening silver as the afternoon failed, and its depths began to seem black instead of deep blue. Roderick called out to them to be ready, he had to come about again, and make his distance by a course of short tacks, whereas they had come down the lake before on one long superb sweep. As he came about this time, he realized that the wind was riper, and the *Affinity* heeled sharply before he could steady her. As the boom swung over the cockpit, the others ducked and made for the high gunwale again. In their movement, they did not realize how far she had really tipped before she seemed steady again.

There was last daylight now on the very crest of the horizon, and the qualities of the shore became coolly blurred in shadow. The sun was just about to go down. It was making a magnificent tossing path of red gold in the water, and they were sailing more or less in it. As they looked back to the *Affinity*'s wake, they could see the lake water tumbling and swirling blackly as if night were already there.

"Once again," called Roderick. "We'll be late getting home, even if we don't have to take a reef!"

He meant to test it again on this tack, and if the sloop was too nervous under all that canvas, he planned to come into the wind and drop sail, and put everyone to work taking a reef, or even two, so that if maneuvering would be slower, it would also be safer as darkness came and they worked back to the boathouse. He bore on the tiller, and the sail clapped and the pulleys sang. The wind seemed to disappear entirely for a tiny moment; then it took hold. It slammed the sail like a door, and the boom chattered. The *Affinity* kicked. She rose up and came back. She went over on her side. The boom shuddered and hit something and swung wildly. The sloop capsized. It was twilight. The sun was gone. The water was almost icy cold. For a few moments there was a frantic silence, and then Peter called out for Noonie. She answered him from the opposite side of the *Affinity*, which was sluggishly afloat on her beam ends, keel and spread sail holding her more or less steady. He called Roderick and he called Evvie and there was no answer. He swam around to Noonie. She was clinging to the tangle about the mast.

"Where are the others!" she asked. Her teeth were chattering.

"I don't know. Come on, darling. Let me help you on."

They struggled to the stern, and around to the other side where the keel made its elegant curve into the hull. He managed to hug her to the *Affinity's* side, and then lift her up so that she could crawl to safety on the elevated and rocking boat. The light was going fast.

"Evvie!—Rod!" he called.

Noonie suddenly cried to him from the boatside,

"Look! Peter!"

She was pointing. Astern the drifting wreck was a figure, barely floating. It was Roderick. He swam to him. There was blood on Roderick's forehead. He was unconscious and rolled slowly by the waves. Peter hauled him to the sloop and with Noonie got him up out of the water on the precarious refuge of the *Affinity's* speed-modelled flank.

"Hold on to him till I look for Evvie!"

He called and searched. There was no answer. The waves lifted and fell and the shore was merging with night. He saw what he had to do. His heart gave a wrench for Noonie's part in it. He swam back and told her there was no sign of Evvie. Roderick was evidently hurt by the last swing of the boom as they capsized.

"Can you hold on to him, Noonie, while I swim ashore to get help? Are you all right, dearest?"

She nodded, and said,

"You have to rest a minute first, you've been swimming everywhere—"

"I will. I'll hold on here for a second and get my breath. But it'll be too dark, soon, darling. I have to go soon. Noonie, no matter what you think, how long it seems, *hold on*, darling, *will* you? It will seem terribly cold and late and a long time once I am gone, but I will be as fast as I can. There's a launch at the club. I'll come right out. Rod couldn't manage alone."

"I know. Of course. Do go along when you're ready. I'll be here."

"Are you cold?"

"Yes."

"I know. Poor darling Noonie. What a thing for you."

"Poor Evvie.—The poor Warners!—I'll be all right, Peetsie.— Are you going now?"

He gave her a look she never forgot. It was like a kiss. His face was kind and anguished and determined. He pushed away and began to swim slowly toward the shore where the lights were innocent beams in a darkling world. She watched him as long as she could. Her heart was full of longing and prayer. She clutched Roderick by his coated shoulders. There was a moving equilibrium she discovered between his weight, the lift and fall of the hull, and the way she must counter the movement with her own weight and will. She could not see Peter. The wind dried her coldly. It came in a wide angle off the shore. The capsized sloop was drifting outward.

9

Peter rolled slowly and almost lazily from side to side as he swam. He knew he would have to walk and search for help when he finally reached the shore. He was of course tempted to race, thinking of Noonie alone out there, holding on to Roderick, with the drowned Evvie somewhere near by gone forever. His heart felt warm with pity for the desolation he had had to leave her in. He prayed with his unformed words that she be saved; and by him.

It was pitch dark when he at last felt the sand under him. The waves were large, and trundled him in a grand swell on the beach. He lay breathing shallowly with his head on his arm for a moment. The cold struck him now that he was inactive. He had worked off his shoes and trousers and coat in the water. Now he stood up and took off his shirt and tied the arms around his waist and started up the dunes toward the road that ran parallel to the lake, inland. There were farms here and there. He could see lights. He began to run; and then he fell down in exhaustion. He became furiously angry at his own weakness. His heart was ripping away in his breast. But he forced himself to rest. He breathed gently and deeply. He was surprised to feel that his mouth and throat were dry. In a little while he felt that he could go on again; but this time he walked, and kept telling himself that the important thing was to get there. If he hurried too much, he might never make it, in time. All he could think of was the black water out there and Noonie alone saving Roderick.

She must be in terror. He often thought of her as like a kitten. She had that sort of exquisite animation, her small face was as touchingly pointed and set as a kitten's, and she seemed as fastidious and pretty in her movements and tastes.

He came over a hill and ran into a rail fence in the darkness. He hung on it a moment, and had a charge of relief, for there across the field was a lighted farmhouse. He climbed the fence and felt he could risk running now, and he ran to the back porch and beat upon the door, calling aloud.

There was a speculative silence within, and then cautious steps came across the kitchen and the door was swung open slowly. The farmer was there, with his head forward, his eyes shut down to peer carefully. When he saw the shivering, half-naked young man, he slammed the door and cried out, "Hallelujah, amen: The Lord deliver us!" Peter knocked again, and cried "Help!" The man opened the door again, and began to laugh, and said to come in, he was just startled at first, but it *was* a sight. He was all sympathy now, and he called his wife to come in with a blanket. They poked the fire in the range, and wrapped Peter in the blanket while he told them what was needed. The farmer went out to saddle his team to the buckboard. The woman heated the coffee in the big pot which stood never empty all day on the coal range. In a few minutes he felt desperate for action again. The kitchen was a cavern of comfort, its oil lamp smelled somehow dear, and the clinking bustle of the hotted-up range gave him new energy. The floor was covered with strips of tin nailed in a neat pattern and scrubbed until they looked like pewter. There was something heartening about the flavor of the place. The wife brought him a pair of trousers and a bulky old sweater of her husband's. They heard the team out back then, and the farmer call for Peter.

In the cold spring darkness they rattled and champed along the country road. There were a few stars showing and the trees as they went by seemed like shadows against the stars. They reached the boat club in half an hour. They turned out the keeper, and got the launch warmed up. They brought lanterns and blankets. The farmer said he would wait right there until the launch returned.

It took two hours of cruising to find the wreck. At last they bumped gently up to the overturned hull. They lifted their lanterns up. She was still there, and Peter could hardly recognize her. She was haggard and numb. She seemed to be paralyzed. She seemed to be asleep, with only one purpose alive in her: to hold on. She was holding on to Roderick and staring at the lanterns. They reached both of them and brought them into the launch. They were so far out that the boathouse light could not be seen. Peter went to work as a doctor, doing what he could, as the boatman put the launch about and headed them inshore.

He gave her some of the boatman's whisky. She was inert but awake in his arms. He held her like a doll wrapped in the blankets. Presently she felt a little warmer. She moved in his hold, and looked at him, and said,

"I am all right, darling."

Then she fell asleep on his breast.

She never said anything afterward about what she had suffered. Not a word of what she must have felt. She seemed resolved to dismiss the horror of the night from her memory. She exhibited fortitude that amazed everybody who knew her, that frivolous, pretty, delicate little bit of a thing?

Roderick recovered from his concussion.

Evelyn Warner's body was found two days later on the beach far west of the boathouse. They all went to the funeral, at which Evvie's violin teacher played Bach's Air for the G String.

10

Peter marveled at the—the: what did he want to call it?—the *quality*? fiber? valor? of the girl he was engaged to marry. It was evident that nobody else had ever suspected her great strength and character, under her famous gaiety, either. He felt that he knew Noonie's essential self, now, and that nothing in the world could ever make him forget it.

He regarded her as perfect.

It was a foolish and dangerous, even a disloyal thing to expect anybody to be:

She asked him sometime later if he wouldn't consider living here, and joining up with the eminent Doctor Donovan, who for years had been everybody's pet physician. He was an old man now, and must soon think of retiring. It would be a perfectly splendid arrangement. Her father, Mr. Larkin, had even had assurances from Doctor Donovan that he would be glad to see young Doctor Rush, anyhow; just for a talk; nothing binding. What harm could come of talking?

Peter's first impulse was to refuse.

He had a struggle with himself, when he made up his mind to go to see Doctor Donovan. It was one of those days in late spring when the softness, the trivial sadness, of pussy willows could be felt in the parks and gardens of that gray and green city. The sky was gray. It was raining lightly but steadily. The limit of the world seemed to be the next block *that* way, and the gates of the park the *other* way, and the sky was right there, heavy and forever gray, and outside the city were those beautiful but ever so close green hills. And yet the people he knew in Rochester were agreeable and nice. Doctors got rich in the East. It was just that he longed for a lifetime of vision that went out over the plains as far as the eye could see. Far mountains, and fabulous vistas of sky and cloud, and the reach of the Rio Grande from Colorado to the Gulf of Mexico…

He was in a state in which poetry and experience were the same thing.

II

Doctor Donovan saw him at half-past five after office hours. He was an elderly Irishman, very tall, with silk-white hair and deep-blue eyes in a gaunt, pink face. He had a curiously soft voice, deep in his throat. His hands were slightly palsied, and he sometimes looked at them with a thin humorous set of his lips, as if to admonish them to cease of their idiot betrayal. He had a brother who was a priest. They had inner qualities in common.

"You are engaged to that Larkin child?"

"Yes."

"She has always been my kitten. I've taken care of them all for years."

"Yes sir."

"There seems to be some talk of your settling here."

"Some talk, yes sir."

"Do you think you would like general practice?"

"I think so, if I had some surgery too."

"I have always been happy, and very much occupied, with g.p. But I know: I know.—Well, I don't mind admitting that I've looked into you."

"Oh, really?"

"Yes, Ted Larkin and I are good friends. I've known all this for months."

"I see."

"Don't be stiff about it. Everybody acted fondly, whatever they did."

"Yes.—Thank you, sir."

"I believe, all things being equal, I'd like to have you."

There didn't seem anything to say, yet, so they both sat still. Then the old man said,

"However, do *you* think you can settle down here?"

Peter was startled. His misery was much deeper than he had himself admitted. He couldn't help smiling at how the old man had got right straight down to the one point that mattered.

"Why, I suppose I could live anywhere if I was happy in my work."

"Yes. And is there a reason for your wanting to come here to Rochester?"

"Oh, yes.—A very good one, I guess."

"Yes.—And is the reason yours, or hers?"

Peter laughed and shook his head as if in defeat.

"Hers."

The old doctor spread his shining pink fingers before him and gazed at their delicate trembling. He silently scolded the sight of them for a second, and then he said, looking at Peter with the craggy look of a blue-eyed eagle,

"Then you go and think it over again, Doctor. You can come back and tell me, if you like, whichever way you decide."

Peter got up and walked out, knowing that this had decided him.

He felt a surge of affectionate respect for the honesty of that old man who wasted no time with elaborate debate. He knew that he was going back to New Mexico; he hoped with all his heart that she was coming with him.

He need not have worried about that, even though she cried and doubted and rather elaborately "made the best of" how things were. He was like a virus in her blood. She knew that no matter where he went or what he did, she would follow him, for his very touch upon her had become a condition of life itself. Her reason, as she believed, told her what folly it was to leave everything she knew and was fond of, and go away, to an outlandish place, and she agreed with all her family's protests academically, and helplessly. When they said that if he really loved her, he would not take her away from her own country, the only thing she was certain of was that he did love her; but even if that had failed her, the last and most important truth was that *she* loved *him*, and that was what decided everything for her.

The wedding went forward as planned, in June. Doctor Willie Treddinger was best man. Elizabeth Kleitz came, with a somehow rapid effect, from Albany, and all through the quietest moments of the ceremony could be heard murmuring "H'm-h'm, 'm, 'm, 'm—sweet, exquisite—" They had an enormous party afterward, with champagne and toasts and an orchestra concealed but not silenced by palms.

Everyone expected Roderick to shine brilliantly when the time came to make the toasts, but suddenly they discovered that he was nowhere to be found. He had disappeared. It was the one cloud on the proceedings for Noonie, but she knew him so well that she hit upon the very reason for his disappearance: Lisette Kleitz had been industrious in her pursuit of him through the whole cycle of the wedding festivities, and it would've been just like her to *do something awful* right then and there, at the breakfast, as a consequence of which, Roderick might be maneuvered into the position of getting engaged to her. Her possessive and glittering antics of the past few days might well have scared off an even more adroit man than Roderick.

Just the same, his absence disappointed Noonie deeply, though nobody knew this. She buried some of her strongest emotions. Now she wanted her escape from her family to be granted to her by the brother she loved so well. She turned to her husband all the more ardently in her thoughts.

Great hilarity attended the moment when the photographer arrived and set up his box. He was like a ballet master, making little poses and steps, to cause the bride and groom and everyone else in the picture to make themselves attractive before the lens. He took one of Noonie alone, one of Noonie with Peter, and at Lisette's request, one of her with Noonie. Peter wore a Prince Albert coat and gray satin tie with his striped trousers. Noonie was in a cloud of white tulle and lace. They left for Watkins Glen. The carriage which took them down to the station was studded with bouquets of orange blossoms. "How awful!" cried Noonie when she saw it; but actually, she was pleased. She wanted her sweet news to be as public as possible. It was Peter who tried to act as if this were no extraordinary occasion at all. He held one eyebrow higher than the other and looked if anything almost bored. This gave her a pang of pity for him. She felt suddenly as if she had invaded his life and was now hung upon him forever. Would he hate her, when he found out that she would *always* be with him? She began to cry, and he thought it was just happiness and nerves, which was exactly right.

12

By midsummer, they were in Albuquerque. It was one of the hot summers of local memory. There was hardly any water in the Rio

Grande, the streets were dried and cracked by the sun, and in the small house where they lived at first, there seemed to be no corner where they could be cool. But they didn't mind. He watched her to see if this was too different from the life she had known at home. She seemed wonderfully happy. He wondered, remembering how she had refused to refer to the tragic endurance of that night on the wrecked *Affinity*. He felt she had places to which he had no access. It was either that, or she was made happy by the smallest trifles. He worked hard, and his practice began to take hold from the minute he got home, for everyone knew him, his father and mother were well remembered, and Albuquerque was just beginning to be known as a haven for sufferers from tuberculosis, and all the doctors in town were busy.

Noonie didn't seem much interested in knowing anybody else. She wanted to be with him every possible moment, which suited him, too. Two years after they were married, a disaster befell them. It came from a quarter they could not have anticipated, and it was cruelly allied to the love they bore each other: Noonie gave birth to a son. The common ordeal, which she had awaited with excitement and devotion, nearly killed her. She was barely alive for weeks afterward, and when she began to take hold again, and climb almost consciously breath by breath back to life, she was not the same woman. It wasn't long before they secretly wished, as sinful as they felt in doing so, that their Donald had never been born.

It was as if their love story had already been told and finished. What it wanted in length, it had had in intensity for them both. It was a calamity which Peter, as a doctor, could understand, however little that helped his suffering. The child was strong and grew well. As Noonie slowly recovered her physical semblance of health, just as slowly and as certainly they realized that she was afraid to think of having any more children. A fear so central filtered through everything else about her. She was afraid to be embraced. She was afraid she was ruining Peter's life. She adored her child, and was afraid that he did not really love her, as if the baby could perceive her inmost desolate unfaithfulness to the very springs of his being.

Now for the first time, she felt as if she were in "exile," but it was an exile of the spirit, and it made life paradoxically more precious.

Instead of joy, there grew up habit between them.

Noonie was sometimes spoken of as "not very strong," though nobody knew how the illness of her fear seemed a new thing every day; as if the illness came and came.

They themselves wouldn't admit it except in tender, exasperated moments.

He tried to get her to go home for a visit. He knew it would help her. But she felt she "couldn't face them."

Above all, he kept reminding himself, he must never think of what had happened in terms of blame. It was not her fault. Whose fault was half the sorrow and trouble and illness in the world?

Feeling the love in her husband which had once made her breathlessly happy, she wrought misery for them both by her helpless refusal of the love she remembered and now would only let herself imagine.

An almost elfin kind of heartlessness grew within her, the more she lived in her imaginings. She presented to the world an appealing picture. Her face was still shaped like a kitten's, and under her little chin a great big silk bow would have looked appropriate. She often wore a spray of starched ruffle there in accordance with this style. Her cheeks had high color on some days, and on others they were pallid. Her eyes were dark. Her trim little figure looked best in little coats that matched tight skirts, and she was fastidious and extravagant about her clothes. The world might think the Rushes an ideally married pair.

Peter prospered. They built their big three-story red-brick house. The town stretched out over the plains between the mountains and the river. The boy Donald grew up properly. When the War came, Peter was accepted as a captain in the Army Medical Corps, and was stationed at the Walter Reed Hospital in Washington. Noonie stayed out West. It was her habit to live there now. She wrote him three times a week, full, attractive letters that made him believe she was recovering. But it was simply his absence which made her feel that she need not reproach herself so constantly. If they were separated, it was not her fault that she was a poor wife to him.

Her brother Roderick was an officer in the artillery during the War, and was killed in France. She was alone when the news reached her, and the letter she wrote to Peter telling him about it was brief but quiet in its tone. He knew she must have suffered a heavy blow, but with that same unexpected fortitude, she sustained it almost grimly, as if determined to bury the things that troubled her, deep, down, deep. She worked hard at the Red Cross workshop. The ardent qualities which used to stand for something between her and Peter were admired by the other women she worked with. They said she seemed almost tireless. No drudgery was too great to ask her to do. When the War ended, and Peter came home, they found each other almost strangers.

Sometimes she would almost burst with desire to ask him if he had any idea how much she reproached herself for her compelling weakness. He knew, well enough, and his eyes would cloud up with thoughts of the pain and the folly to which they were both locked; for to neither of them had the idea of divorce ever seriously occurred.

He picked up his practice again, and confessed that he was glad to be home.

She had no further need to work all day long down at the Red Cross, with the War over.

Life at home became a system of good manners for them all. They were astonished to realize now and then that you could get used to almost anything. And then they would discover that things continued to change, however smally.

III · THE NEWCOMER

I

"I feel sure it is really nothing," said Mrs. Foster. "Doctor Treddinger made me promise, though, that I would get in touch with you as soon as I arrived. I suppose he has written to you?"

"No, actually, he has not. But he will," replied Peter. "—I know Willie awfully well. He was my best man years ago. He barely got there in time for the wedding."

"I know men like him," said Mrs. Foster. "You're supposed to be annoyed with them, but I always find they're doing ever so much more important things than the things they're late for."

The day was settling outdoors, the wind was falling, and the sandstorm was keening far away down the valley toward Socorro.

Mrs. Foster had a little trouble in breathing. Peter watched her lift her shoulders now and then for a heavy breath. She looked down as if in apology for making such an exhibition of her asthma. The sandstorm had stirred it up. Everybody had said the high and dry air of Albuquerque would do her good for a few months this winter.

The second day she was settled in her house, here came the sand, which appeared to set her off right away.

When the professional part of the visit was over, Peter stood up to go. He was sorry. There was almost a holiday sort of feeling about sitting in this room talking to Mrs. Foster.

"You know this house?" she asked, looking around the long room dark with twilight.

"Yes, a number of people I know have leased it before now."

"I simply wrote my needs, and an agent found it for me. I must say I never expected to be living in a log cabin—a furnished one, at that."

"It is hardly what you ordinarily mean by that."

"I know.—It is very comfortable, and I love the views."

The house sat on a hill overlooking town. Each end of the long living room had a huge plate-glass window, one looking west to the river, the other east to the mesa. Downstairs the dining room had a big western window too. The rest of the house ambled along the curve of the hilltop among some young cottonwood trees.

"The house never looked this—this pretty before," said Peter.

"I brought a few 'things,'" she replied, making it sound slightly comic.

He smiled at her.

She was evidently impatient of convention, and yet lived with an almost exquisite observance of it. She was younger than he by about ten years, he guessed. Her hair was pale soft yellow, almost silvery. She had a very pale face, but her cornflower-blue eyes and her mouth rouged with pink carnation had plenty of color. She was slim and delicate. Her bones were small. She sat almost like a doll, so relaxed and "lost" she seemed in her corner of the huge Spanish red velvet couch which her landlords had set before the rough stone fireplace. In the rustic elegances of the house, which affected a combination of sturdiness with luxury, she seemed amusingly out of place. Peter was thinking all this and regarding her when a third person came in, a younger woman in a tweed suit and a green hat with a feather.

"Oh, hello Judy. This is Doctor Rush, who came to see about my wheezes.—Doctor, this is Miss Bridges, who is *with* me."

"Hello, everyone," said Miss Bridges. "I am frozen. Are we going to have some tea?"

"I hadn't thought to offer any to the Doctor, but if he has time to stay for a cup—?"

He nodded.

Mrs. Foster nodded to Miss Bridges. Miss Bridges said "Thank God," and strode out to tell the kitchen. When she returned, she pulled the red velvet curtains, and a maid came in with a tray of tea-things. Miss Bridges put another log on the fire. It was suddenly warm and local and pleasant around the tea table. Mrs. Foster served the things and between her occasional careful long breaths, said that living in that house with all its red velvet and gold gesso'd candlesticks and carved refectory tables and parchment light shades and heraldic andirons and white plaster and smoked wooden beams, she felt like someone in a Douglas Fairbanks movie. She said Hollywood was in its scenic stage at the moment, and already she said you could find evidences all over the United States of what the movies were doing to public taste.

"I expect we'll be having garages with moats around them before long and crenellated battlements."

Miss Bridges went to the front door and opened it and whistled into the bluing twilight. In answer, a honey-colored spaniel came galloping floppily in, and climbed in an agony of pleasure up to Mrs. Foster on the red velvet couch.

"And this is my Brisky," she said, introducing the dog. She took the dog's head in her small white hands and made a comedy of gazing into the honey-colored face. "And did you cry your eyes out, Brisky? Spaniels always look to me as if they've been weeping."

The dog settled happily down with flutters of its silky fringes and upward glances of love from its lowered head, so that much eye-white showed.

"Do you often have times like today, Doctor?" asked Miss Bridges. She was a thin dark-haired girl with large violet eyes. She just missed being beautiful. Or perhaps, Peter thought, it was because Mrs. Foster was there. And yet she was so quiet, where Miss Bridges was rather muscularly active and vital. Miss Bridges made Mrs. Foster seem frail, and yet he would bet anything he knew about people that the stronger of the two was the smaller, the milder, the one who was ill.

2

But not very ill.

The tea seemed to've helped her shortness of breath. The wind was hardly moving.

"We have sand blows all winter and spring," answered Peter, "but they are usually brief, and they don't happen every day of the week.—You'll be sorry to hear that there is something about them I like."

"Appalled, if not sorry," murmured Miss Bridges. Mrs. Foster smiled at him.

"No," he said to her, in reply to her smile, "I really do. But then I love this whole country, and everything about it—I grew up here."

"That is what does it," she said. "I find it, myself, and on only the shortest acquaintance, almost a *shocking* country."

"That's a funny word for it."

"So vast. So immediate, I think that's it. It is all right *there*, and yet the elements are so grand, I mean the mountains and the desert —you call it the mesa?—and the river, and heavens! those skies! I mean you have to be a sturdier creature than I to swallow it all so easily the first time you see it!"

Miss Bridges said, "I told Molly we should've driven out by car, and then we'd've gotten it all gradually. But we came by train, and woke up to find ourselves *here*.—Except that I hate motoring. I must say all this affected me the same way. Only I'd say it was a cockeyed combination of desolation and rather useless grandeur."

"Well," said Peter, wondering if he liked Miss Bridges at all, "people have made something out of that desolation for several centuries, now.—In small ways, of course, but somehow sufficient. And as for grandeur, the only kind I believe I could ever stomach would be the useless kind."

"Of course," said Miss Bridges, and her voice became almost deliberately musical and she smiled with a perfectly frank intention to be disagreeable, "there is a *cult* for the *West* which I simply cannot abide.—All that *pioneer* talk, and so forth. I get so *bored* with it. What's so damned *wonderful* about it?"

"It was quite a job in its day," said Peter. "The early West was no picnic."

"If there's one thing more tiresome than the *modern* West, it is the *early* West," she replied, smiling with a strange kind of high spirits which, he saw, was her version of anger.

Peter barked a little laugh. He was irritated, and yet he saw beyond her contentiousness into the vague hint of something desolate far, far within her.

"Well," he said, "maybe everyone has a kind of 'early West' within himself, which has to be discovered, and pioneered, and settled. We did it as a country once. I think plenty of people have done it for themselves as individuals."

"Of course there's a new snobbery for psychology, too, isn't there," declared Miss Bridges levelly.

"Lord, that's only a *word*. What it's *about* is as old as—as

Sophocles; or Shakespeare," answered Peter. "Anyway, you'll find me hopelessly satisfied here."

Miss Bridges flashed a "keen" look at him, as if to say, "Is anyone? anywhere?" This disarmed him entirely, for he saw that her whole nature was wry and pessimistic, and he lifted his chin at her in a droll gesture used by the Mexicans, to mean anything speculative and insinuating.

"You see, Judy," said Mrs. Foster, leaning forward with a hint of dismissal in her attitude, and yet of great kindness too, "you've blundered into someone's house and been unpleasant about it.—I think I'm on your side, Doctor Rush. Or I will be if I ever catch my breath."

He stood up.

"You will.—I'll probably drop in next week unless you send for me sooner. I imagine the altitude and so on: everybody feels it: you'll be drowsy for a few days. That's all."

The spaniel rolled sideways and began to wave its flaggy tail.

"Brisky is saying good-by."

He leaned down to pat the dog. There was a faint drift of scent, a lilac, as he stood over Mrs. Foster. It made a thump of the dimmest reminder deep down inside him. Lilacs and rolling lawn with silver sunshine and an old happiness, the ghost of habit, and he was stirred as he had never hoped to be again, but ever so faintly.

Mrs. Foster smiled and gave him her hand. She had a surprising smile, for her teeth were not precisely regular. But their slight oddness—a trifling lift of one over its neighbor—added something witty, something special, to her expression.

"Tell me if that fat little Doctor Treddinger ever writes to you about me. And if I get into trouble I'll call you up."

"Good-by.—Good-by, Miss Bridges."

"Good-by, Doctor.—I'm sorry. I'm famous for being clumsy. I never *mean* it."

He laughed.

"No, I'm a victim of local patriotism, I suppose.—But I always got a tingle or a chill when the other children in school would sing the line about 'Land where my fathers died'—you know."

Miss Bridges took him to the door.

"It's a wonderful thing," she said soberly, "to know you *belong* that much.—I'm one of those post-War females."

They shook hands. He thought he might like her. But it was Mrs. Foster he thought about all the way home. He couldn't help smiling at the unaccustomed airs of afternoon tea, here. He felt that Mrs. Foster sought to seem anything but special or superior. You simply couldn't miss inflections of the world of fashion and all that went with it which she showed simply in the way she spoke. He was a little shocked that anybody should refer to Willie Treddinger, the most celebrated younger man in the country on respiratory diseases, as "that fat little doctor." But there was that about Willie, too, at the same time, if you stopped to think, regardless of Willie's offices on Fifth Avenue in New York. He found himself regarding Willie with her eyes.

He had a lift of spirits when he reflected that he could write to Willie that he found nothing much out of sorts with the Mrs. Foster he had sent out to the dry air and sunshine. He had noticed—but what an absurd thing to write to Willie!—that she seemed rueful, at moments; briefly; and that in her expression, her blue eyes, there was some energy in betrayal of consuming fires within.

He supposed everyone who knew her referred to all this as "charm."

He wondered who she was.

BOOK II

The Ages of Man

IV · THE BOYS

I

Donald Rush, at twelve years of age, could not possibly say what was wrong at home.

He could forget it only when he was with his friend Wayne Shoemaker, who was in his room at school, and who lived eight blocks away at the other end of the same street as the Rushes.

They rode to school together on their bicycles, crossing the viaduct which went over the railroad tracks on that side of town. They never failed, at the top, to stop and gaze each way into the railroad yards below. The engines were as black as coal dust and as richly dull, and their white steam rose into the gold light of the blue sky. They could see where the tracks vanished far away into the earthen blur, and they had a sense of ownership over all they looked at. This viaduct was made of timbers painted and weathered to a dusty plum red, held together with long iron bolts capped with rusted nuts. They would speak of it as "ours," and crossing it on their wheels, they would simply regard it as their property, a fact which they often said to each other would surprise everybody very much if they only knew it.

On sunny Saturdays they would sit down and watch the tracks below, and the cars and wagons going over the viaduct, and one day they found a nut end of one of the iron bolts in the planked floor sticking up through the dust and dried manure and splinters that were packed along the sidewalk edge.

"Look here," said Wayne.

"That seems very careless," replied Donald.

"I think I ought to tighten it."

"I think so too."

He tried, and it seemed immovable.

"You can't tell, if this nut ever came off, what might happen."

"That's true."

Then they both sat back and looked at each other in glorified silence for a moment.

Then using the nickname he had evolved by spelling his friend's name backward, Wayne said,

"Say: Noddie:"

Don knew what he was thinking of, and he said,

"It would crash and go, the minute we unscrewed it."

"The whole thing, ka-froomb!"

They surged with power. The bridge which they owned had betrayed to their imaginations the vulnerable spot of its structure, of this they were certain, and they began to laugh, knowing with one half of their judgment that this was all nonsense; but with the other half, perfectly, exquisitely certain that if they chose, they could cause this whole bridge to creak and split and totter and fall, amid clouds of dust from wrenching timbers, to boy's music of crashing destruction.

"My changle-wrench will fit it," said Donald, pulling an imaginary tool from his pocket, and handling it in pantomime with a professional air.

"Then I believe," said Wayne with a certain sternness and righteousness that had them both convulsed inwardly with amusement at how grownups behaved, "I believe we should tighten it some, the trains rumbling underneath must jar it loose, and if we don't inspect it pretty often, no telling what:"

They set to work repairing the grave weakness in the viaduct, and as they were finishing, they heard a train whistling long to the east, and regarded each other and nodded, exchanging assurances that they had managed the job just in time; if the Limited had come through and had this faulty engineering not been corrected, at least temporarily, there would have been a disaster.

So they got on their bicycles and rode on down the other side, the masters of all they saw, and aware of their virtue. They had reached that degree of friendship at which things that would require hours and possibly days of explanation to make them plain and plausible to other boys were, between the two of them, instantly so. They were citizens of the world of the imagination.

2

In a way he could not describe, that world seemed to Donald to fill the rickety bungalow where the Shoemakers lived, out on the sandy edge of town, as it never seemed to him to exist in his own house eight blocks away, that high red-brick house with everything in it. He never wanted to hurry home when afternoon was falling. But if he was with Wayne, it was always exciting to come back to the Shoemakers' from the sandhills, or the mesa, or the river, side by side on their bicycles, through the darker dusk of town.

Ordinarily, their ways parted on the homewood outskirts of town, at a street corner where a single electric light hung high up. Donald and Wayne always debated whether they had time to "ride home with each other," an observance they kept whenever possible. Donald would ride halfway home from the corner with Wayne, and then Wayne would ride back halfway of *that* distance with Donald, and then they would separate, until next time, when whoever had the long ride tonight would have the short one then.

On this evening the winter twilight over the plains fell in waves of chill, and the boys rode faster the colder they got. Wayne called to Don,

"Come on all the way home with me."

"Why?—I can't."

"Come on and stay for supper, and we'll study."

"I'll catch the dickens."

"We'll call up your house from Mr. Daingerfield's."

"All right.—You call the number."

Their voices were like horn music in the quiet streets.

Cottonwood trees were overhead, bare and shapely for winter. The streets they approached going home were not paved, but instead were of packed red sand. On a corner two blocks from Wayne's house, was Daingerfield's neighborhood grocery store. They went in and asked if they could use the phone. Mrs. Daingerfield, who tended the store in the evenings while her husband went "out back" for his supper, said they could. Wayne called the Rushes' number, and when the connection began to ring at the other end, he handed the phone to Don.

They looked at each other soberly until the phone was answered. Then Donald looked into the phone.

"Hello, Cora?—Is my mother home?"

He waited a second.

"Hello, Mother? Can I stay at Wayne's for supper, and study with him afterward, if I get home by nine o'clock?"

They watched each other while Don listened.

Wayne began to laugh silently, which affected him like a pain in his belly. He felt so excruciatingly amused and enchanted by Donald's question because he knew that to ask to be out till nine was preposterous; he also knew that it was a *deliberately* unreasonable request, and that Mrs. Rush would agree to his staying for supper if he would promise to be home by eight. Ask more than you expect to get: this was a principle with them.

"Well, all right," said Donald waving Wayne to shut up and not choke with laughing that way, in case it could be heard. "I'll be there by eight, I *promise*. Good-by, Mother. And thanks. Thank you *ever* so much, I will do anything you want me to on Saturday morning."

He hung up.

"Goll, what did you get to laughing for? It might've spoiled everything."

"I couldn't help it. Can you stay till eight?"

"I have to *be home* by eight."

"Come on.—You won't believe it when you see Martha."

"Why? What's she got now?"

"She's got her hair funnied up now. I told her it looked very madamo-zell, meaning it as an insult. She took it as a compliment."

"My God."

They pedaled fast, their hams in the air. It was after six o'clock. The moon was out in the twilight blue sky. The boys felt happy in the cold early moonlight. They were full of ruthless energy. When they slid up to the front of Wayne's house in the sand lot where it stood, his mother could hear them inside. There was a citrous yellow light in the small window, from the pressure gasoline lamp that hung in the middle of the front room. In the late day-blue air outdoors with the sweet pallor of the moon in it, that yellow window was like a magic casement to the boys. The happiness in them seemed to gather suddenly, and knot up in the pits of their stomachs, and they crashed through the front door together, struggling shoulder to shoulder to see if they could go through at the same time.

"No, no! Wayne! Don!" cried Mrs. Shoemaker, turning fiercely on them and clapping her hands together rapidly. She was scowling and her hair was in strings down her cheeks, her face was flushed, and she was like a mother sparrow, gray, furious and whirring. But the two boys ran up to her and put their arms around her waist, and she hugged them back, still scowling, abating her fury, and saying "Well!" with a snort and "Goodness!" with a breath, until she was smiling at them and smoothing her feathers back into order and calm.

"I brought him home for supper," said Wayne.

She looked at Don's dark small face, and a pang hit her under the breastbone. We haven't got much! she cried inwardly, and I have eleven cents in my purse and it's too late to go to Daingerfield's and buy some hamburger, these children will be my death yet, they never think of what it costs to live! All this went by in a streak, her habit of worry, at the same time that she smiled to Donald and said,

"I am so glad, Donnie, if you will eat all your crusts, which are good for your teeth, you are welcome to stay.—I'll tell Martha."

But Martha was only a few feet away, because the house was so small that her labors at getting supper in the tiny shallow kitchenette at one end of the room were not separated from the rest of the life of the house.

"I heard them," said Martha, not turning around.

"See!" whispered Wayne, poking Donald. "What did I tell you."

They looked at Martha, who held her back very stiff. She knew the two were in league against everybody else, including her. Her hair was a great cloud of small wiry ringlets, standing out from her head and neck.

"Oh, Madamo-zell," called Wayne gently and with exaggerated accent.

"Now, then, Brother," said his mother mildly, but with far more impact than her sparked fury of a few minutes ago. "We need some coal. Wait? I waited hours for you to come home and get me my coal. I'd've got it in myself but for the life of me I can't see why I should haul coal with a strong son like you in the house, only he's practically never *in* the house, where he spends his time the good Lord only knows, and at what, I am sure I never could say *on the witness stand*, if I was asked.—But to go back to *me*, I nearly had a *lank fit* today I's s'tired. And if you stand there and think I am going to haul coal in day in and day out, you are just ever so very much mistaken and you might's well know it this minute!"

3

All this while, she was setting the table, and the boys were gone long before she finished. She was very small, and every move she made seemed made in earnest. She had a worn, thin, but appealing little face; her hair was graying; her pale eyes always looked worried; but she kept her prim mouth in a smile and she put a little rouge on it when she was working downtown at her job, just to brighten things up for the customers. She was a waitress in the Harvey House dining room down by the main line tracks of the Santa Fe railroad. Her energy and her pride made her the favorite waitress of half the people in town who went to the big gray stucco hotel that sprawled among patios and arcades by the tracks. She had one evening a week off, and this was it.

"Now Sistie," said Willa to Martha when the boys were gone, "don't start it again. He's just *getting there*."

"Very well, but it all seems one-sided. If he can treat me like that, I ought to be able to treat him *back*."

"No," said Willa, her eyes watering at the almost foolish glow of youthfulness and freshness about her eighteen-year-old girl, "you're older. You simply must not laugh at him, just because he's young and your brother."

With everybody else, Martha was a young lady; but with her little brother, she was still a girl.

It was one of the details that made them a family, and gave their frugal and wind-trapped little house its climate of use and comfort.

Out in the back yard, there was a waist-high shed in which the coal was dumped…huge lumps of bituminous coal around which the sand had blown in miniature dunes. An ancient cottonwood tree stood in the back yard, so old that some of its branches were dead. But others held on to their bronze leaves all winter, and in spring, dropped them for a green skin over the silver-gray bark. Under this tree Wayne grew up. They could all see it from the one room that housed their kitchen, their dining room and their living room. A glance at the tree which filled so much of the small window would tell them inside how the time was outdoors. It was a venerable and beautiful possession to measure the outdoors by. It refreshed Willa Shoemaker simply to look at it. She was used to having "her boys" (by which she included Donald) live in the tree. The last time she could remember punishing her own son was for breaking off a little branch of the cottonwood while scrambling his way through its upper reaches.

Outdoors, the boys filled a scuttle with hunks of the coal. Some of the coal dust arose and when they breathed it it made their windpipes tickle.

"I have a word for you. After supper I'll get my dictionary. It's a word about the way to *be*."

"What is it?"

"I'd rather you *looked* at it, the first time."

They came back inside with the coal. In the center of the front room stood a big base burner. It was like a personage in the little room. In the winter when the sand cried against the walls on the cold wind off the mesa, they had to keep the stove positively dancing in its tracks with a roaring fire. The mother never failed to recognize with a pang how much each big lump of the black dusty coal was costing as it went into the bulging stomach of the stove, with its glowing little windows of layered mica.

"All right, throw in two of the middling ones," she ordered. The boys clanged and scraped at the stove.

One day that curved bellyfull of tiny windows had made Donald Rush think of the gorgeous gallery in the poop of a Spanish galleon, of which he had seen a picture in his pirate book. Ever since, they had called the stove the *Spirito Santo*.

They liked to name things when they found resemblances. The little kitchen was called the "diner" because Willa said it was like the narrow galley in the dining car which she remembered very well from the journey seventeen years ago when she had come out here with Mr. Shoemaker in the first place.

She promised to prove this to them "When we go home." By this she meant that someday, somehow, she was going to take her two children back to Michigan for a visit to her own old home.

"Now! That's just about it!" said Willa, looking over the table, her eyes snapping at the four places laid out, and the food partly on, and her hungry ones waiting. "Come on, Sistie, bring the rice and the stew from the diner, and we'll sit down."

4

The greatest treat in young Donald Rush's life was to be asked to stay for supper with Wayne, on Mrs. Shoemaker's day off, when the sensation of festivity and happiness was so great in the little clattering house that he loved to help create it, and would wonder ruefully why, in his father's three-story brick house with two Negro servants and a lot of elegant truck like stained-glass lamp shades and thick green carpets on the mahogany and white stairways and a mahogany pianola in the living room that they didn't play any more because they were sick of it, why there was so rarely this feeling of the Shoemakers' that everything was simply *right*.

They waited while Willa bent her head and said Grace. The Shoemakers were Catholics. Donald sometimes went to Mass with Wayne.

He knew this prayer now and said it silently with them just as if he were a Catholic too. Then they raised their heads and Mrs. Shoemaker served them.

Martha resolved to be kindly, and offered Donald a piece of bread with such visible courtesy that he began to laugh, choked on his rice and turned a deep pink under his swarthy cheeks. They really thought he was choking to death (as they said later) and Wayne began to laugh too, knowing it was the ridiculous manners of his sister which had caused the whole thing anyway. They made an uproar, Willa helping and scolding, the boys gasping, and Martha making cool and miserable remarks full of scorn; for she knew what they were laughing at, they were laughing at her, and it broke her heart, which was both more and less than a heart. It was a vessel, a cup, and it was empty, and perishing to be filled.

When they recovered, they were so exhausted that the rest of the meal went off quietly, and the boys had to do their share by clearing the table and drying the dishes, which Martha washed. By then they were friends again and all three together did a popular song called "Taxi!" in which Martha sang the words—"Oh, taxi!"— and the boys whistled a response—"Phwee-phwaa,"—and knocked the rhythm on the drainboard with their knuckles.

"Now get to work with your books," said Willa.

She had left the table cleared and brought them a kerosene lamp. She regarded herself as a well-educated woman, which, indeed, she was, but all she knew had come to her out of activity; not books. She was profoundly reverent of books. She often said if she ever caught either of her "two" mistreating a book, she'd take and spank the daylights out of him. She sent the two boys out to unstrap their schoolbooks from their bicycles, and set the dictionary on the table for them, and a jelly glass full of pencils of all lengths which she kept handy.

"Oh, yes, what is that word?" asked Donald when they came back and settled down.

"Oh, yes, I nearly forgot.—Here it is," said Wayne, finding it in the dictionary. Donald looked; it was the word inscrutable.

"H'm."

"Don't you see?—That is what *we* are."

"That's right. Nobody else knows a thing about what we think and work on."

"You see?"

Mrs. Shoemaker frowned. She didn't know what they were saying, but it certainly didn't have the perplexed energy she believed proper to the act of studying.

"If you're going to work, then *work*," she said to them. "And if you're going to play, then *play*. But if it's *play*, then off home marches Mister Donald Rush, one-two-three."

They closed the dictionary, and got their books of American history open and began to resemble, for her benefit, that image of studious children which, as they read, slowly became the truth about them, within and without.

Willa dwelled on them with her eyes for a moment.

5

Her son Wayne was light-haired, with a thin little face and a long neck. His cheeks were frosty with a sort of young lint, and under the skin were patches of dark color which made him look very intense. He had blue eyes, and his forehead was always ribbed with intention or belief or doubt, though he made a point of looking at ease. His mouth was sober and full-lipped.

He was the exact opposite of Donald, she reflected. Don was a little smaller than Wayne, but a little older, much solider in the body, and dark brown. He had black eyes which sparked and flashed with light, so intense were the whites. His head was round, and his hair was like blue-green-black cock's feathers, shiny curved spikes of elegance that fell across his forehead. He had dimples up under his eyes.

She knew the two boys were twins for energy, however different they looked, the one tall and rangy and wheat-haired, and the other a young black cat whose quick head swifted toward everything new. One was a rich boy, as wealth in the town went, the other as poor as "respectability" could possibly be there. Neither of the boys knew this; but Willa did, and so did her daughter Martha.

Martha went to business college during the day. She had graduated from high school the year before, and though she knew lots of young people, she worried her mother because she seemed so "alone." Night after night, Martha sat here, at home, doing her practice or sewing (she sewed beautifully) or simply lying back in her chair with her eyes closed, but not asleep. She was dismally unhappy, but could not tell anyone so. She was certain that she was hopelessly plain and unattractive; and her reveries were all concerned with hopes for beauty. The discontent of this was reflected in her face, and her own mother couldn't be sure whether Martha was pretty or not. Sometimes she seemed so, and then again—

Willa believed it sinful, almost, to imagine that you could *hurry* life. It was of God's disposing, and let there be an end to wicked rebelliousness in the heart!

She was a widow. The children's father had died when Wayne was a baby. All he left her was the remains of a chicken ranch out on the mesa five miles from town. He had died of tuberculosis, for whose cure they had moved here from Albion, Michigan, with just enough money to buy the mesa acres, and put up the long chicken house of adobe, with corrugated-iron roof, and front entirely built of small glass panes. Willa had thought for a while of returning to Albion; but nobody bought the ranch, and the very energy that drove her for the sake of her children also dictated loyalty to the vestiges of her husband's poor efforts; so she decided to keep the ranch, and get a job, and someday, Wayne should run it, and be his father's son. Already he was good about earning money when he could, doing odd jobs for Mr. Jensen, the Stationer, on Saturdays or after school. Sometimes when Willa came home Saturday nights aching from the extra crowd at the hotel, she found his money, some half dollars, quarters, nickels, pennies, and dimes, cleverly stacked into a tapering tower and surrounded with her silver spectacles, on the table by the base burner, by which, he knew, she liked to sit and rest for a few minutes while she read the Albion *Evening Recorder*. She indulged herself with this home-town paper, though the subscription price would have given the family a trifle of the luxury which they fiercely did without. But she was proud of her home country, and as the years went by, she read about boys and girls she knew back in Michigan and always saw them just like that, as they were when she'd left them; and she was her girlhood self as she wandered among the personal items and the revelatory little advertisements and the offices of life as recorded by the gray pages. What she always wanted most when she read about Albion again was to have Wayne and his sister Martha go back with her just for a visit. They had never seen that green country. And she would be so proud to show them off, her Western children, both so good and both so handsome.

One reason Willa was so positive about working for her life and her children's was that she knew that Eternal Life awaited them all; and to earn it by being faithful and busy on earth seemed to her, in conviction beyond thought, the very least anyone with a scrap of dignity could do.

She was never too tired after a hectic Saturday night at the Harvey House to get up early for Mass, and to see that Martha and Wayne got up too. They hurried to the autobus on the corner when the sun was barely fingering the top branches of the huge cottonwoods in their end of town; and were almost always on time for services in the big church on Sixth Street, with its embossed tin roof, its wooden towers with slats in the belfries, its painted plaster statuary, and the high mist of blue shadow that Wayne used to squint at in the ceiling, to make the distance up there seem farther and farther off.

Here abided the one reality that united all the others, and made them her servants, not her masters. Every act of her daily life was unconsciously released into energy, generosity, affirmativeness because she loved God and believed in his Son. People did not see her as an essentially religious person. She made few enough gestures and displays to prove it. But her furies, her worries, her determinations of will all reflected her belief. Her children knew it. Her will was righteous. They never would dream of trying to cross it, or cheat it; for long, at any rate.

She would work till she dropped to see that they got everything the other boys and girls in Albuquerque had. And the fact was, they missed nothing essential. That's what it was, to live in a small city, and know everybody, for everybody grew up together. Lately she had seen in Wayne little valorous furies which she believed were connected with his new rage for being big and strong. She found him several times in the sandy back yard "practicing not to be clumsy." Sometimes his voice sounded as if he were talking through a comb and tissue paper, with more breath than tone.

6

The Shoemakers had a clock which was kept on a shelf in the diner. It always ticked loudly, and Donald suddenly heard it.

"Goll, I'd better see what time it is."

"It is five minutes to eight," said Willa, who could see the clock from where she sat reading her newspaper.

"Goll, then I'll have to *scratch*," said Don. "Thanks for the dinner, Mrs. Shoemaker.—I'll be *there*," he added to Wayne, meaning that the next morning he would be on his bicycle at the corner where the street light was, and they would ride to school as usual.

He got up to go out. The moonlight was like silvery blue air outdoors. The huge bare tree in the back yard seemed like a net set out to catch the moonlight. Donald saw it through the back window.

"I wish we had a tree," he said, perfectly seriously.

Willa gasped a little laugh at him, because Doctor Rush owned the lot next door to his house and there as a hobby cultivated dozens of evergreens, in nurserylike rows. But she knew what Donald meant, and was touched by the way he loved everything the *Shoemakers* had, and she said to him,

"Well, you may have ours, you know, Donald, so long as you don't take it *away*."

This struck the two boys as hilariously funny, and Willa, seeing what a funny thing she had said, burst into laughter too, and they all died laughing, until Martha abandoned her musing dignity and said, "Oh, for heaven's sake," and sassied her face at them all, Donald too, which delighted him as a mark of his membership in this family.

He went out the front way, got on his bicycle, slung his books by their strap over his shoulder, and rode off homeward.

V · FIRELIGHT

I

One of the advantages of living in a small town was that you could go home for lunch without losing much time.

Peter liked his house best at midday, when the sunshine seemed to come streaming in everywhere. He would have smiled at himself if he had ever recognized that he now followed a routine every day at noon when he came home. He had a huge red leather armchair in the bay of the front windows of the living room, and he had resisted all efforts of Noonie's to get him to give it up and let her place something a little more "in keeping" there by the lace curtains. As soon as he got home, he took the mail from the table in the front hall, unbuttoned his coat and vest, and went in to his big red chair, on which he always found the *New York Times* lying three days old, and whatever bundle of books might have arrived for him from the Boston dealer. There he settled himself in the sunlight, and glanced at the *Times*, yawning. He yawned tremendously, relaxing in great quaffs of easiness. The headlines swam in his comfortable tears, and he rarely found anything to interest him enough to read it through.

He threw the *Times* down and shuffled the mail, making one pile
for Noonie to handle, including bills, letters from mutual friends,
appeals; and another for himself to take up to his third-floor desk to
work on in the evening, when he did all his personal business at his
private leisure. The best came last. Today, there was a package from
Boston. He guessed it contained only one book. He always opened
his packages last, during his noon ritual, using the little gold knife
on his watch chain. He kept the blade surgically sharp, but always
had to stretch and bend to make the knife reach on its chain. This
was an inconvenience he was so used to that he no longer noticed
it. He cut the strings and made a great scatter of wrappings on the
floor. The book was a War Department report published in the '50s,
describing an Indian skirmish of the previous decade. He flipped
the pages, and came on a section of twenty-two lithographic plates,
done by Messrs. Leuwenthal, of Philadelphia. The first picture was
a portrait of an officer in full dress. His name was First Lieutenant
Aubrey Worthing Barton, 6th U.S. Cavalry. He had thick hair like
carved curls of black walnut, from which sideburns came down on
his round, formal cheeks. His eyes were deeply shadowed. His nose
was short and straight. His mouth might've been drawn by a child,
so artless was it, with full scrolls of lip and shadow. His chin came in
a positive curve down to the stiff white ruffles of his dickey, which
cascaded over his gold-braided collar that stood up sharply on either side to his ears. His breast was broad, and made broader by
the lithographed spread of gold braid that ended near his arms in
gold buttons. He was looking at the artist; which meant that any
later viewer would receive that same gaze, direct, light-plumbed,
the record of a day and of a life. His left arm was bent, to cradle his
sabre against his silk sash. Even within the conventions of its time,
the lithograph was convincing. The young man was admirable and
believable; women must have admired him; and nearly a hundred
years later, what he had set down of what he had done was exciting
to the Doctor because it had happened right here. He promised
himself that after lunch he would go upstairs and read Lieutenant
Barton's account of his Indian fight east of Albuquerque in 1850.

He folded his hands on his book over his belly and lay back and shut his eyes, to review what he had done that morning, and arrange what had to be done that afternoon. He could let down his tensions like an animal. His most lucid and at the same time recuperative moment of the day was this one before lunch. He had got everyone in the house to thinking that he always fell asleep for that fifteen minutes; he never dozed off, but it suited him to have them think he did, because they went softly, let him alone, detoured him discreetly until the bell for lunch was rung by Leonard, the colored houseboy, in the front hall. Three brass chimes hung in the high doorway between the hall and the dining room. Leonard enjoyed making variations within the limits of the three different tones.

Today, Peter heard him go to the hall and ring the chimes in this order: *high, low, middle, middle, low, high,* and then an elegantly final, *middle.*

2

In a moment, Noonie came downstairs, and he saw that she had been busy all morning, for her eyes danced, and her cheeks were flushed, and she had a sort of freed look. His heart rose a trifle as he got up to greet her. She looked up at him, to see, for today, if he was reproachful. He was not, and they went into the dining room. Donald was at school, and had taken his lunch with him, as usual.

They were served by Leonard, a light-yellow boy in his early twenties who had his own ideas of propriety. He set every plate down and took it away with a flourish. His elbows were elegantly sprung from his sides when he toured the dining room. He came through the pantry door as if on to a stage. His white coat crackled with starch. He was a smooth rounded creature whose hair looked like little wavy pencil lines on his skull, shining with oil. He had pale-gray eyes and an irrepressible smile.

When Leonard went out for a moment, Noonie made a reference after him with her eyes, and smiled at Peter.

"What is it now?" he asked.

"Leonard, again!"

"Anything wrong?"

"No, I am just amused, that's all.—I found him boxing in the hall upstairs again this morning."

"*Boxing?*"

"Alone. Dancing and waving his arms around and shuffling.—I heard him sort of *breathing*, so I came out of my room to see, and there he was, I thought I'd die."

"Shadowboxing, then.—I guess he still wants to be a boxer."

Noonie frowned in caution and then cleared her expression: Leonard was returning.

Peter looked at the young Negro and grinned. Leonard grinned back, and said,

"Yes *sir*, Mist' Doctoh," and set down his serving.

"You in training, Leonard?"

"Yes *sir*, always in trainin'."

"What for."

"How you know, sir?"

"Why, you look so in such good condition."

"Yes *sir*. Gon get me one 'em di'mon belts."

"Oh-ho. Prize fighter, eh?"

"Ess *sir*!"

"O.K., Leonard. Then Mrs. Rush and Donnie and I'll all live off your championship purses. We'll never have to go to the poorhouse."

"Hyuck!" said Leonard, vanishing through the swinging leather door with its brass studs. He felt immeasurably complimented and told Cora, the cook, so.

"Don't forget Don's birthday," said Noonie.

"No. Thirteen, isn't it: what shall I get him?"

"Yes, thirteen.—Do you think he's all right, dear?"

"All right?—Why, yes.—Why, I haven't noticed—Have you seen anything wrong with him?"

"Oh no," she said, and he recognized her habit of worry, and crowded down a little flare of anger which it always gave him. "But he's growing so fast..."

"He looks fine. He *seems* fine. God knows I see little enough of him."

"I know. Neither do I."

"When I was a boy, some of my best times were spent with my father. I never see Don."

"If you would *talk* to him—"

He bit his jaws and considered saying that there was nothing he longed for more than to talk to Donald; but the boy seemed so unreachable; so *inscrutable*, he guessed he meant; and he knew it would never do to try to force anything. He knew too that if he said these things to Noonie, she would assume he was aiming them at her; she would meet his uncertainty with her guilt; and off they'd be on one of their exasperations; which always made them both sorry for hurting the other.

He shifted the tack.

"I think it would be awfully nice if you gave Don a birthday party."

"Oh, I couldn't," she said quickly.

"Why not?—Thirteen is sort of a milestone, I don't know why, it always seems to be, though."

"Yes, I know, but—"

He waited. Her first habit was to refuse. Often she brought herself to change her mind. This eternal negative!

"Still," she said, "I don't know."

Leonard came and went again.

"It might be fun.—He might adore it.—How we used to *do* things!" she sighed, but rather happily, he saw. "At home in Rochester our parties were famous. I'll never forget Roderick's best one, it must've been *his* thirteenth, Mamma spent days and days, she made me a costume out of white plumes and gilded palm leaves, it sounds awful, but it was adorable, and I was supposed to be Papagena out of *The Magic Flute*."

"You needn't go to all *that*: but some boys and girls and games and God-awful rich food and jealousies and stomach-aches and fits of shyness and fits of love: it all belongs.—Let's do it. I'll come home early."

"All right, dear, if it would please you."

Her eyes sparkled.

"Not if it would please me, though it *would*, but it would make Don sort of *have a house* to bring his noisy and sticky friends to, as he ought."

"I'll have a staff meeting," she said with humor, "with Leonard and Cora. Don't give it a thought."

He beamed at her.

"What shall we give him?"

"I know," she said with animation, "why not ask Wayne Shoemaker? He'd know exactly what Don wants."

"Well, I will. He's a good little kid. I saw that girl of theirs the other day. She's a young peacherino."

"Peter!" she said in reproof, but she smiled.

"She is. All breasts and wet looks and corn silk hair and awkwardness. Made me feel like an *old fool*," he added lecherously. "She come out sudden, as the farmer said."

When he talked that way, she couldn't help looking at herself mentally, always to her own disadvantage. She changed the subject.

"I've spent the morning going over your suits."

"Do I need anything?"

"Oh, you have them all made exactly alike.—And that beautiful Scotch homespun is always ruined by that dreadful tailor downtown."

"My Italian?—I hate suits to be different. He knows just what I want and gives it to me. He hasn't had to change a thing in ten years."

"*That's just it*," she said laughing. "You're *so much* better looking than your clothes, darling."

"Everyone *ought* to be," he said, trying to sound gruff.

He had filled out since his intern days, when he had looked like a cowboy strayed East. There was an intent animal look in his black eyes, so that his whole head seemed concentrated toward his object. (When they were first married Noonie used to say, putting her hand over the thick hardy dark hair back of his ears, that she believed his *thinking* happened right *there*.) His brows came down over his look and shaded it with meaning. On his generous upper lip he wore a carelessly trimmed mustache.

When she faced his knowledge and directness, Noonie (like other people) asked herself, "What is it? What does he *draw* from?" In his buffed face she saw the plains, yes. But what else? He always seemed ready for what was next; the next thing; we'll do it; we'll manage; people have managed before, and even if they haven't, *we'll* manage.

It was the affirmative spirit that inhabited him.

She could see its likeness most clearly, perhaps, in his hands, which were powerfully veined, the color of sunny clay.

People often looked at his hands set to their tasks of divination and help, and then at his face, to see *what he knew*, and found out there that he loved life, and met it truly.

"What else did you do this morning?"

"I rested, then, and read a little—I read my magazines, that you hate so."

"I don't hate them at all."

"Yes you do, you said they were made up of either commercial or sentimental lies."

"Well, yes, but that doesn't mean I *hate* them, I don't *hate* morphine, or the people who need it sometimes."

"Oh. I see. I am like a drug addict."

"I didn't *say* that, either."

"I warned you once how really and truly stupid I am. You didn't believe me."

"I still don't. My mother was a schoolteacher, and my father never went to school at all, and they were both wise and successful people. They knew how to live where they lived."

"You do love this country, don't you."

"Past, present and future," he said.

"I think you're different, lately."

"I? Nonsense."

"Yes, I can't tell you *how*, but it's there."

He got up from the table and tossed his napkin down.

"Well, I am not aware of it, but I hope it is not unpleasant?" he said lightly, holding out his hand to help her up.

"Oh no, dear, I didn't mean it *was*—happier, some way."

"Oh, good Lord:" he scoffed, and walked upstairs with his new book.

3

But it was true.

He marveled at the intuitions of womankind.

Every day for the past week, in his travels up and down the town, he caught sight at certain moments of the big window of the log house on the highland. Toward evening, the sun, going down behind the volcanoes across the river, would throw a glory of firelight on the big window and he would see it above the dusk which was filling the streets. The sight, the reminder, did make him happy.

VI · OTHER AMERICAS

I

Late one afternoon as Peter was about to leave the hospital, he phoned his downtown office to see if there were any calls.

The nurse reported two things to him from his memorandum tablet. One was to go to see old Don Hilario Ascarete, out in Old Town; the other (he knew it all the time for he had written it himself, but in an obscure search for whatever plausibility might later be comforting, he was calling now to be "reminded" of what he had been thinking of all day)—the other was to "check up" on Mrs. Carmichael Foster at Highland Park.

"Oh, yes. Thank you. Is that all?"

He hung up and went out to his big car waiting in back of the hospital on the circular gravel drive. There were two veins of thought running in him, and as surely as tributaries reach a river, they would come together, he knew.

He wanted to go to see Mrs. Foster, and he wanted to go to the sandhills to search out Lieutenant Barton's battle site.

He decided not to do the first. She was probably perfectly well.

Willie Treddinger would have written long ago if anything had been seriously the matter. She might feel obliged to bring out the tea table again if he dropped in. He had a sort of hanging discouragement in his breast at the thought of her, and there was no better cure for that sort of nonsense than a little action.

He went to the sandhills.

He had Barton's report with him in the car. Peter knew the town so well, with the images of both a boy's memory and a man's, that he bet he knew just the place to go to.

There was a road that led from one of the town streets across the main line railroad tracks, and up into the sandhills, ending at a gravel pit which hadn't been excavated for years. When his car got into the sandhills, and followed the winding road, Peter felt transported, as if he were lost in a desert whole continents away. This was because the hills rose sharply hiding the view of the town below, and alternated with one another so clearly, as if eroded blocks of earth had been set down in a maze pattern something like immense cog teeth. When the rain happened in torrents on the mesa, this winding place became a canyon boiling with pale-brown water that rushed upon the streets of the town and fanned out for blocks.

He could search months for another place like this one, but none other answered the description: "A zig-zag, almost road-like, course between sharply steep hills of gravel, in places forty feet high, and rarely less than twenty. As can be surmised from the nature of the engagement, cover in such a place was sure to be as hazardous to one side as to the other. We therefore, deeming it at least as advantageous, and possibly more so, proposed to keep to the tops of the miniature canyon, and were within a few moments of achieving this objective, when we were sighted again by the Navahoe, all of whom acted in concert to prevent our reaching an incline which would deliver us out of the sandy bottom."

That was what the book said: Lieutenant Aubrey Worthing Barton had written his diary in 1849 and 1850, describing his encounters and observations while a member of a preliminary survey party sponsored by the War Department. There was no mistaking the general locality, Peter knew. Albuquerque was clearly indicated on the maps in the old War Department report. Barton told how the land rose sharply some two and a half miles east of the Rio Grande; and that would be roughly just across the railroad tracks today. He told how the sandy course wound down from the much higher mesa. He said they had ridden parallel to the river, but inland, following the base of the sandhills in a generally straight line. They had camped for the night farther to the north, and leaving at dawn, had come six miles by the time the episode took place.

Peter left his car at the edge of the gravel pit, and walked around the huge crater made by the steam shovel, which still stood cold and rusty in the middle of the cavity. The gravel-haulers had taken away part of the nearest sandhill, but by squinting and leveling his sight about opposite to the top of rise facing him, the Doctor could imagine the terrain as it had been, and though in Barton's account it had been earlier in the day than it was this afternoon, the time of year was pretty close, the mountains way beyond there hadn't changed any, and just such clouds could well have been going over the zig-zag canyon.

The Lieutenant wrote with a bare factuality which made easy his movements to follow, places to identify, and (from their very absence) feelings to supply.

Peter could tell himself what had happened all over again, now looking for the first time at the place.

2

They came along the edge of the hills, and once having been seen they didn't seem to care if they stayed in full view. They were off their ponies. In the same kind of sunlight they looked like little creatures made of baked clay, that earthen color, for they were all practically naked. They had lances and arrows, and Barton had seen sunshine on two rifle barrels, at least, as he turned his horse and backed his men up around one of those jutting cogs of sandhill. A bullet sang out from the Indian rifle. The soldiers wondered where in the hell an Indian had got hold of an army rifle, they could tell by the sound what it was, and the gravel just beyond them on the next turn of the canyon up which they were retreating puffed and fell, scratched by the bullet.

Some of the Navahoe were on the other side of the canyon, too. The soldiers went on up the sand course, riding fast as they could to get in and out of the light. Where the course ended there was a long incline of heavier gravel. They were going to go up it, because to be caught down in the shadow would be the end, they all knew, and Barton rode at the tail of the column to handle command and be the nearest to the enemy. He rode like a toy soldier, stiff in his stirrups, with his head bent around to keep an eye on the Indians. They had got their ponies again, and were coming along the rim like horsemen in a nightmare who rode and got nowhere. It was just because the soldiers below and the Indians above were going at pretty much the same rate of speed.

Barton called ahead to McIntyre, his second in command, to start right up the incline the minute they got there, and take the surveying party with him, five men with the instruments, the records, which they had on two packsaddled horses, and a squad of men. The rest would stand with Barton at the rear and cover the escape, it would mean seven cavalry soldiers and their lieutenant, and it was at the bump of the earth there on the right where the gravel showed in coarser strata that they made their stand.

Any sound in between the sandy walls was magnified.

McIntyre understood and signaled.

The civilian surveyors were willing as anybody else to stay and see it out; but McIntyre swore at them and charged up the slope.

Barton jerked his horse around and wheeled his squad. They hadn't time to dismount. They had no cover from which to obtain both protection and fire effectiveness. So they faced the crest above them on both sides and let go with their little short carbines.

Something happened to two of the Navahoe. Suddenly nothing sounded but the gong-ringing of the shots in the narrow place. Then as the white smoke drifted invisible and the clouds were far off again, and their ears subsided of their blood protest, they heard McIntyre's horses scrabbling on out of sight.

Barton knew what the Indians were doing, anybody would have done it, too, they were riding in a wide ring back from the canyon edge, and spreading out to head off McIntyre and the survey party when they should emerge from the sand on to the wire grass of the mesa.

Barton waited in the gravel for a moment, listening. Looking up, the sand walls framed the sky, which was china-blue with those light-gold clouds. McIntyre was pretty young, but he had been on the frontier longer than Barton, and Barton said to the soldiers with him that he'd bet McIntyre would come out of it, which meant that so would the survey.

It was the survey to which they were all detailed to afford military protection.

They had never been called upon for active fulfillment of their mission until this morning.

It seemed almost as if noon must be right upon them, but Barton's big silver watch with the hair-line Roman numerals and the scepterlike hands angled the hour at ten minutes before ten.

If the Navahoe left the canyon party to go after the surveyors and McIntyre out on the mesa, there was only one thing to do, get up there and close in in another wide encirclement and make a battle diversion.

If the Navahoe on the other hand were still along the rim but out of sight, and coming like little brown animals to the edge of sight but not of visibility, then McIntyre would in due time come around and spare somebody for a counterattack on his own.

It was something that had to be found out.

Barton told the others about it, and gave his reins to his orderly. He said they were to watch closely, and if anything *happened*, they were to mount and ride on after McIntyre and join him, and in general, to get the party back to Albuquerque as soon as possible. A soldier volunteered to do the job but Barton said it was his to do, and left them there in the shadow which was creeping away from them as the sun went on over toward the zenith, so that they felt divested.

Barton went on all fours to the bellied gravel of the near hill, and started up. He went slowly, the ground was grainy and rolled under him in slides. He cocked his heavy pistol and set it down each time with much caution, because the trigger was beautifully ready. Ordinarily he liked nothing better than a nervous trigger; but now when he had to use his hand to help take him forward over the itchy gravel, he did wish his gun wasn't so trick.

But at the same time, he didn't know what might be awaiting him at the top, when he got there and had a look. The instant of cocking might be too long to wait, in some circumstances.

Below and behind him, the men watched.

Nobody could interpret the silence.

At one last forward take of the hillside, Barton paused and shut his eyes a moment. "Well, yes or no," was the sort of thought that hit him, but it meant things more elaborate than that in terms of what was going to happen immediately next.

Then he came on, one more crawl, and he looked over the edge, and he saw at the same moment he heard.

Ten yards away lay a dead pony and behind it was an Indian whose eyes were open and the livest motionless things anywhere. The lieutenant's pistol *did it* just as fast as he knew it would, and he ducked back again, listening. He heard a curious clipping sound, nothing an Indian might make, and presently he looked again, and saw a prairie dog four feet away using its teeth on something. The Indian was out of sight behind the dead horse's back.

Not another thing was visible on all the immense plain.

The wind seemed cooler up top here, and he shivered, for it just then registered against the sweat that was on him all over, and his clothes felt cold and heavy for a second.

He turned around to look opposite him on the other rim of the gravel canyon. There was nothing. He waved down to the troops in the half-shadow below to mount and hurry right up the incline, and he would run to meet them at the top. He heard the equipment squeak and clash as his men mounted, and a fine confusion of thump and scrabble from the hooves of the ready horses.

He went forward crouching to look beyond the dead horse. He had the pistol cocked, of course.

It is something to have it for the first time, he said to himself, this is the first combat I have known, and I sweat hard, and I was vaguely afraid of everything that might happen. But now we are safe for the moment. I believe I made the right decision, which is a notable relief, because many another hide than mine depended upon it, whatever it was to be.

That Indian is dead, behind the horse, I can see him now. His eyes are open, and perfectly dead.

An affectionate sense of the almost comic obedience of the horses made him grin with pride and relief when he and the men reached each other. He mounted his own animal. Standing in the stirrups he led them up the last mild rise to the mesa proper, and there they saw what looked at first like several of those dust devils which traveled whimsically over the flat plain, engendered by heat and the convection of air currents. But they did not whirl in a stately dance, they peppered and popped with speed, and the soldiers knew that galloping horses made the dust rise in so many small plumes.

"Here we go," cried the Lieutenant.

They rode at a charge. All they could hear was the wind of speed and the valiant fusillade of hooves on the spine-grassed earth. But they saw two white puffs ahead of them in the wide circling line of the dusty pursuit. Barton drew his own carbine from its leather scabbard, and signaled his men to copy him. He nodded them to fire after he did. The position in effect was that the Navahoe were sandwiched in between the retreating line of cavalry and a pursuing one. The diversion to save McIntyre was so far a tactical problem, executed with as much precision as if on the blackboard at West Point, under Major Thompson. Barton fired, and his squad followed. They were too far yet for the shots to take effect, even if accurate aim were possible while riding, but they were seen, and the widely scattered crescent of the dust trails ahead was suddenly broken.

The mountains were much too distant to offer any cover.

The mesa was as open as a great book, with a few shallow valleys such as a book made at the binding.

Down below, where the little adobe town of Albuquerque was among its cottonwoods along the Rio Grande, there were many deviosities which could make concealment.

The Navahoe turned into a racing single file and headed toward the wide valley.

At that, shouting like cowboys rounding up a herd, Barton and his men swung broadside. Far beyond the Indian column they could see McIntyre's squad do the same thing. Dappled by the sunshine and the little archipelagoes of cloud that drifted by in the oceanic blue, the three groups of furious figures raced toward the fall of the mesa. It all looked, to a detached recollection, like a rehearsed maneuver, except for the meaning of the white puffs of rifle and carbine fire that were exchanged all the way down the long mild slope toward the sandhills. All of the Indian shots went wild but one. That shot tucked itself with an energetic poke into Barton's left shoulder. He was out in front. He stayed there as the pursuit swung down the hill and the trees began. It was too heavily grown to allow a concerted escape. The Indians separated. Coming down, the cavalrymen could see that there were about a dozen Indians, and scattering like their quarry, scratched their way through the cottonwood thicket. In the cool damp shade the shots rang closer, and suddenly stopped, for they had come to the streets of the old town, and the Indians stayed by their horses, waiting. They were shining with golden sweat on their clay-colored breasts. When Barton came up he took the two Navahoe rifles, and found them empty. He asked for the spare ammunition, and they gave him empty pouches. They acted with neither defiance nor humility. It might have been a commercial transaction for all the feeling displayed on either side. Barton's blue flannel shirt was black at the sleeve where he was bleeding. When

McIntyre appeared, they shook hands, smiling at each other, two youngsters professionally confirmed.

After a brief rest, they all rode into the town, and presented the renegade Indians to the civilian authorities in the Plaza, who received them with a certain reserve, the young officer thought, considering what capricious havoc the Indians might have turned against the town, or the trading wagons that came down the river road from Santa Fe every week during such fine summer weather as this.

At least, Lieutenant Barton hinted as much in his report.

3

The light was going.

Peter returned to the car and rocked slowly down the gravelly course until he was back on the street.

He came back into the present and found his half-mind, like a subterranean place, still coursing with its buried river. He heaved at the huge steering wheel of his car and headed for Highland Park.

He was admitted by the Swedish maid whom he'd seen before. She asked him to wait a moment in the hall. He heard tapping and clicking in the big room down the steps to his right, and concluded someone was using a typewriter. The girl returned and asked him to go in.

It was Miss Bridges at the typewriter, which was set on a cleared desk in the corner.

"Hello, Doctor Rush. I suppose you're expecting to see a patient? She's simply fine. I'll go call her. Sit down."

Miss Bridges made him feel that she would arrange any questions and answers that might be "indicated." With a kindly glance she left him.

I was right, he said to himself. I am a fool to come.

But he didn't let himself off any further than that. He knew that with the Miss Bridges sort of woman, he was worse than awkward. She—what was the new word?—she was sophisticated. She seemed to exist in a sort of slang of the emotions. Undoubtedly she'd "been" something in the War, and was the sort of girl forever stamped by mass association with males. "A bifurcated mind," he said to himself.

Mrs. Foster came back with Miss Bridges, and at once he felt sure of himself. She was smartly put together in a trim little suit with a sweater and a rope of huge Indian silver beads around her neck. She saw him looking at them as they shook hands, and she said,

"I've been the happy tourist since you were here last.—I begin to understand jewels and such ornaments as marks of bondage. These weigh a ton."

She seemed very well. Her blue eyes were free of the look he remembered, the humility and apology of suffering. She was pink from walking outdoors. Her pale hair was ever so slightly disarrayed.

"I've been out walking with Brisky all afternoon.—I saw you drive by a while ago."

"You did? Where:" he asked. There was a remote strike in his breast.

"I was walking out by the hospital, and over the sandhills beyond. It's a wonderful walk to make. It is rather rough country, and I am a frightful lazybones, as well as a fraidycat, and it is just exactly as rustic as I desire to be. And my wonderful galloping footstool, which is what Brisky looks like half the time, will assuredly protect me from rattlesnakes."

"This is rather good," he said. "I was out *in* the sandhills."

"What on earth for?"

Miss Bridges called across their conversation with a cool satisfaction at interrupting them,

"D'you think I'd bother you if I went on typing?"

"Oh: it might, Judy. Why don't you come over and sit with us and we'll have some tea, *now*."

Miss Bridges got up and made a sarcastically gallant gesture of resignation.

"No, I'll send it in, but I believe I'll go up and rip out all that I've knitted so far today."

She came over and shook hands sturdily with Peter, as if she belonged to his club.

Mrs. Foster watched her out.

"Judy's a dear, but nobody ever knows what will strike her how."

"Is she an old friend?"

"Yes.—She was simply heroic in the War. So were lots of others, too, of course. But you do see it sharper when it's someone near to you. She says she has the most fearful dreams, even still."

"What did she do?"

"She was in an ambulance unit. She married a boy from Boston who was killed in the Argonne, and it seems that the only way she could sort of surmount her grief was to take back her maiden name, and make herself a new life.—It's not everybody else's way, of course. But it *is* Judy."

"That's very interesting.—I'm glad you told me. I've been a little sharp, thinking about her."

"She's really a dear."

"—But she did interrupt us. I wanted to tell you about the sandhills."

"My sandhills," she murmured. The tea came and she got busy.

He told her he'd found the site of the first known Indian skirmish hereabouts between an American and the Navajos. He described Barton, and what he was doing out this way, and the diary he wrote for the War Department.

The maid drew the curtains and went out.

The room was dim and the fireplace was alive. When a log fell after a while, Peter, still talking, got up and went over and kicked it back, and came back and sat down, quite as if he were habituated to this, as if this was where he lived. He did it without thinking. Mrs. Foster watched him with amusement and with what else? She was disinclined to call it anything, and she knew how laughably wrong it was possible to be, and there was nothing worse, she could well remember, than to let something aspire within you which might have no counterpart where it desired one, and she wished she did not feel so animated in her heart. But the fact was, she did feel so, and she said to herself that, for a formal person, she certainly felt intimate with an unseemly earliness.

4

As he talked, he watched her, and her responsiveness was something that fed him as wood fed the fire. Over her face there flickered that accompaniment of realization in another which anyone fond of talk is always seeking. He said that Lieutenant Barton was only a boy, really, when this thing happened three quarters of a century ago, more or less, and yet he had handled everything with the resourcefulness and courage of an experienced man. She smiled when he said it, and he paused to see why, and then he laughed, and said,

"I suppose you are amused by the male claim to triumph at any age."

"No, I was delighted by the way it all seems so real to you, just from looking at the sandhills.—And your boy Barton could walk right in the door in his epaulettes and his sidewhiskers and I would greet him like a long-lost brother.—Go on."

"Well, that's about all there is to tell, except that they saw the Indians safely delivered to the authorities."

"What became of Barton?"

"I looked him up at home after lunch after reading his diary. He was a Brigadier-General before he died in the Civil War. He was wounded at Chancellorsville."

"I always think there is something inexpressibly sad about soldiers' deaths. Soldiers and actors. They use *themselves* so to make their livings, I mean, their little own physical presences, and when it is finished and done for, the very *materials* of what they did are gone."

She filled their cups again, and then said,

"Do you know how this land of yours strikes me?—It strikes me as an almost wholly masculine land."

"Now Lieutenant Barton owes *you* a smile."

"No, I mean it. Do you see what I mean? I know dozens of places—in the East, the South, the Mississippi country—even California, the West Coast—which don't strike me just that way. They're soft, close, narrow, compromisable lands. Any girl or woman is her own boss if she feels like it, in any town or city, generally. The sun shines, yes, but in such places, it doesn't enter everywhere. The *shadows* out here are burning with light. The country is so great and the jobs that keep us alive on it are so close to the first simplicities that it takes men to do them, all of them. It is Adam's own land. Isn't it?"

"I'd never thought—Let me tell you something," he said, his eyes illuminated by memory. "When I was a boy, one day riding out on my pony by the river, on a Saturday morning, I met an old Indian, he seemed old to me at the time.—Have you seen the Indians?"

"'m: they're so far from being really picturesque that I quite like them."

"He was, too. He was all faded and wrinkled and marked by work and had dried earth on him, in one form or another. He was watering his horse. I asked him where he was from. And what he answered I have never forgotten, and I think what you've said today may tie up with it, I mean that there may be several meanings coming together for me."

"What did he say:"

"I asked him where he lived, and he made signs and seemed to cover the whole space here, from the river to the mountains, East to West, and he said, 'I live in the house of the sun.'"

"How beautiful."

"Yes, but he didn't *mean* it to be *beautiful.*"

"I'm sorry."

"No, all I mean is, that he was exactly describing where he lived and it had that real spaciousness for him.—And besides; this is what I didn't know then, as a boy: but the sun is the male source of life to the Indians. It is also the holder of fertility. The power of life itself. They use it in ceremonies and paintings and symbols to mean all these things.—I mean, you have arrived at the same answer as the Indians, if you see what I mean. I'm very clumsy."

"I'd hate for you to be as dry and as fluent as an archaeologist.—My uncle is one, so I can say that, can't I.—I do think that is a charming episode though. And I see exactly what you mean.—It is a man's country, and of course, I think any woman who is a *proper* woman, would be content there, for that very reason."

She saw a shadow fall over his face for a moment, and said nothing. Then he smiled and looked at her, and said,

"You might be describing my father and mother, by inference, as you talk about this country. He was a rancher. She was a school-teacher from Washington, D. C. You might say that most of her life was spent at something she never had educated herself for. But she was a wonderful wife and a charming mother. After she moved into town, long, long, after I was a boy, she got in *her* licks for the church and the ladies' clubs and the first struggles of a public library. The only thing she ever missed was the green trees and fields of the country she came from."

"That early root is never really gone, is it."

"No, but some places it strikes deeper than others."

"I think the *place* is more in the heart than in the land."

"I guess so. I studied in the East, and would do it again, if I had to decide all over."

"But you came back here."

"I came back here."

"You know, I can't imagine that people of other countries have quite the same—what is it: the same *at-homeness* in so many different kinds of their own country as we have, in the United States? Do you?"

"I've never been in Europe. But I imagine life is very local and intense there, wherever it may be.—I think *we* are essentially *at home* in an idea, a climate of belief, maybe you could make a case for our being the most *philosophical* people in the world, with *all* our rawness and our movies and our habit of being raucously ashamed of our lack of foreign culture. I mean, if we are at home in the idea of being Americans, it is related much more to why this country was born than it is to where we live, actually.—This is odd, right on top of my passionate speeches about my own square of earth. But you know what I mean."

"Of course.—It has occurred to me before, that all our best works of literature have had the vitality of that idea in them, rather than strictly a local color."

"And we're always traveling all over our own country. How it looks and sounds and feels everywhere else. We all know that.— We all want to live in just one place, the best place for us, but we all know the other places too. I don't think a writer or an artist (or someone like that) can do us any good if he doesn't know more than his own little place. He can write about it all he likes, but he must have a sort of *versatility of the spirit* and bring home other Americas than his own. Then when he gives his own special America back, it will mean something widely."

The fire broke a log in two, and their thoughts broke with it.

He stood up.

"I've stayed much too long. I have a million things to do."

"But the time has simply flashed by.—I wonder what time it is?"

5

She went to the window and pulled aside the red Spanish velvet and looked out.

"It is nearly dark," she said. "You can see the barest daylight left on the river."

The house was on the hill. They looked down across town and out to the wooded valley where the river gleamed in opened turns of its course.

"You ought to drive along the river," he said. "In winter it is almost more magnificent than in summer.—The trees are made of beaten gold and silver. Groves and groves of cottonwoods with winter leaves still on the branches."

"I'll go. My car has arrived. Judy and I'll get around a good deal now. But she hates motoring."

He made a surprised face, and said,

"Yes, and we've forgotten entirely about your health! This is a professional call, after all, I was to check up on you."

"I'm glad we forgot it. I am perfectly fine. It was just something the sandstorm stirred up that time, and I must've been tired from the trip. Trains always exhaust me."

He told her she did seem perfectly well again. He said he was sorry, in one sense.

"But you will surely drop in again?" she said. "I'd like to read some of your old books about this part of the world, if you could ever bear to lend them."

"You would?"

They shook hands. He promised to bring some books. In an odd little way, they were now less than intimate. She said if she was out, just to leave them with Helga, who would take care of them. He said he hoped she would not be out, but in any case, this afternoon had been extremely pleasant. She thanked him and said it was awfully nice to know *someone* here, though she actually had come to rest, and didn't *want* to meet a lot of people. They parted with these valedictory trivialities; everything they had felt was still alive; but put down, deep, soft, spirited away.

VII · THE WIDOW

I

The sandy chill air made them all grateful for the warmth of the *Spirito Santo*. It was Willa's evening off, and (*for a wonder!*) both her children were home with her this evening. She was sewing. Wayne was supposed to be studying at the other side of the table. His sister Martha was at work on a letter to a friend of hers who had gone to school with her the year before, but was now living in Walsenburg, Colorado, and going to high school there. Martha's stationery was lilac colored, with a silver monogram that she had lately decided was much too elaborate; too childish; she would buy a "severely plain" paper next time.

But the conviviality of the family interrupted their separate tasks time and again, until Willa was ready to *admit* that there was nothing in life so sweet as having your children by you, harking to what you had to tell them.

It was all about Daddy, again, but they thought tonight she had a new power and animation in her remembrances that used to embarrass them slightly, and make them feel obscurely guilty. What had happened was that both Martha and Wayne had grown up enough to feel, at last, the truth and the depth of their mother's love for their father, and her fierce refusal to lose him even though he was dead so many years now. The children had a glimpse of far storms and glories in their mother's drab life for the first time; not from what she said so much as from the eagerness of the way she said it. She looked rosy and her eyes danced and there was a stab of girlish folly now and then in her gestures. In their two ways, the children were inspired and moved.

2

"—so the day he bought that chicken ranch out on the mesa, I hardly spoke to him all day. I said to myself my, he is such a fool, *imagine it, your daddy, how could I think that for a minute!* But he came home with the deeds in his pocket, and pulled them out and showed them to me, and he said, never mind Will, you may think me a visionary and a fool for doing this but someday you will bless the day. So of course I broke down and cried for thinking so meanly of him, and he hugged me, and he kissed me, and he fiddled his fingers behind my ear, this way, the way he always did when he wanted to please me, and nobody knows what that always meant to me, some day you kiddies will know what I mean. Your daddy was the kindest man that ever lived, I used to wake up at night and lie there and lie there, wondering what I had done to deserve such happiness.

"—and the thing he was always working for and thinking for was the future. When you were born, Waynie dear, I'll never forget how he came in as soon as they would let him see me, and he took my hand, and he rubbed his thumb across my fingers, he was trembling, and he said, Never mind, mother, no matter what happens to me, or anything, you have a fine strong son to protect you now, and he picked you up and held you for a second, and I remember, I thought it was the *strangest* thing I ever saw, he blushed when he held you that time, and the nurse laughed, too, because she noticed it.

"—and it *is* true, he *did* make money. He was just's clever's a barrel of monkeys, and if he'd kept his health, we'd all be *rolling* today. But he never let on, and *I* never knew, but after he died, the doctor told me he'd never had a chance from the minute he come here, but you think he'd let on? No siree. Not on your tintype. And when he was so weak he had to be in bed those last few months, he used to write down things for us all to do, and one day, Waynie, he watched you playing in the yard, the way you used to do? making your boats out of old planks and pushing them on the ground? he wrote down on his pad that perhaps you ought to be a midshipman at the United States Naval Academy? He told me how to get in touch with a Congressman if the time ever came. He said anybody at all had a perfect right to get in touch with a Congressman and get him to help to get their boy into the United States Naval Academy. He said the Government was the engine, all right, but he said the people, any old people, you and me, and your grocer and your banker and your doctor and your cripple that sells the papers by the bank on the corner and your druggist and your old nigger yardman, said the people *ran* the old engine, and never forget it.

"—I tell *you*."

She shook her head vigorously, but really had run out of things to tell them, and what she meant was that the dead father from whom their life had come was even, larger in her thoughts than he had been alive.

3

Wayne was hot-faced and packed with pride in her ramblings. He could hardly remember his father, but his throat was full of a lump of love and resolve. His eyes were glistening with wet light, and he breathed with his lips open, staring at his mother until she returned to the present and *saw* him. She leaned over and rubbed her knuckles in his silken bristly hair.

"What dear?"

"Nothing, Momma. Only:"

He stopped, and she waited. How far could a boy go without

seeming foolish, he wondered. Would she laugh at him for what he was performing in his mind? Or would she see that he was only fulfilling his father's promise to the future?

She began to talk again, about the time the Rio Grande flooded many years before, and how Daddy had put on hip boots of rubber which he borrowed from the duck-hunting neighbor next door, and gone out wading to help the rescuers in the west end of town who were saving Mexican families by the light of oil lanterns. The sound of the water was what he talked about most when he got back, for in the dark, the rushing muddy waves seemed to roar and crash louder and louder with every moment. He had such a cough when he returned that she was furious with him. But from inside his shirt he brought out and handed her two glasses of jelly that had been rolled off their shelves by the water, and she reminded Wayne how he always used to laugh every time she told him, when he was a *little* boy, about the glasses of jelly rolling along in the flood, such a strange thing for jelly glasses to do...

They were borne along by her voice, and by the remote cracking and gasping of the fire behind the poop-deck windows of the earnest iron galleon that stood on a tin matting decorated with a border of stenciled vine leaves.

The children had escaped; Wayne, to the future, Martha, to love.

He almost lay on the table, with his pointed chin on his open schoolbook, his sweatered arms curled about his face, and his eyes shining above them like windows in a battlement. There were simply no terms to describe the goodness and the power of the father whom he had heard about. Such things as weakness, aimless imagination, lack of vitality, all held together by a touching sweetness, played no part in his image of Mr. Shoemaker, yet these were true of him. Wayne was clothed with the grandeurs of executing a mission; a dedication laid upon him as sure as fate; and in his imagination he moved superbly out upon the bridge deck of a great battleship, that rode the waves without creating spray or a wake, but glided grandly like a wonderful plank of wood crossing a lawn of grass, toward a distance where a bank of clouds loomed in the late sunshine, revealing in silhouette the array of an enemy fleet, whose guns suddenly began to cough and charge the air with spurts of fire. He was fired in his heart by all the things which his vision tried to make clear to him, and he felt, but he did not know, how he was compounded of love.

4

Martha's letter was abandoned.

She seemed to be listening to her mother, like her brother Wayne; but she too was lost. She was dreaming of her lover. She knew how they danced together, his arm around her, so; his body coming upon her with every step, and hers eluding his exquisitely; his whisperings while the orchestra seemed farther and farther away. She knew also how he sounded on the telephone, when he called her up to ask her for a date, or perhaps just to tell her something inexpressibly funny and at the same time perfectly darling that had just occurred to him; and how they would sometimes let the phone rest silent, and simply hear each other breathe—a thought which made her tongue tingle as if she tasted a flashlight battery, which she hadn't done for years. And she knew how it was when he came to call for her, riding his horse, and leading hers, and how they went to the wood where the sunlight struck through the shadows to a bank of moss and ferns, where they alighted and where they kissed. His hair felt like the cushion on the sofa in the corner, a golden plush, except that it was long and curly. What she could not make herself sure of were the things her lover said. Her heart was in her mouth at the breath-taking sweetness of how she felt and what she was *sure* of; but this lover of whom she knew so much was a youth she had never seen. She lived with him and longed for him, and knew nothing about him. But everything he meant, and everything she meant by inventing him in mind so urgently, was somehow already present in her mother's prattle of remembrance. And it was this that had sent Martha's thoughts where they went.

5

"—and all you have to do to see what a fine-looking fellow he was is look at my children. Wayne has his eyes, and Martha his mouth, and of course you have *my* hair, but he had, and you all have, beautiful foreheads, anybody'd know you anywhere for his children, if just only by that one little thing, so wide, and high, and such fine smooth bone at the temple. No wonder I'm just so happy, and willing to work, work, work, though I am sure he never expected me to *have* to. But he would've known how I'd've *done* it, if I'd had to, as it turns out I *did* have to, after all, and he couldn't but *approve*."

The children were shining in wonder, though not at the same things. But their mother thought she knew why, and was content with them.

VIII · RIFLETIME

I

Wayne Shoemaker sometimes made a little money by working after school in Jensen's, the stationery shop and bookstore. He would drop in and ask Mr. Jensen if he needed anything, and Mr. Jensen would say the shelves all needed dusting today, and set him to work. Mr. Jensen had pale-blue eyes, which always seemed to be watering with some kindly weakness, as if he could never refuse anything that anybody asked of him. He carried an enormous stock of supplies, and was the rabbit transfixed by the snake eye of whatever salesman came along. He did a good business, but made very little money. Everybody in town knew him. The chances were, he liked that better than being rich. He felt sentimental about small boys of any kind, and in them, he saw the cartoon values of such symbols as the ole swimming hole, freckles, a can of worms to go fishing with, a loving cur dog, bare feet with a dirty bandage on the big toe, stolen watermelons and other comic attributes of small boys more rooted in folklore than in actual modern life. Wayne, with his sober

blue eyes and his standing silky yellow hair, was sure of anything he
wanted from Mr. Jensen.

Wayne liked his occasional job. He enjoyed handling the stationery supplies. There was a fabulous plenty about so many hundred
dozen pencils, such ranks of ink bottles, such pyramids of paper. He
dusted the piles of writing tablets with a dreamy pleasure in their
spotless beauty. A bare page of paper always did something obscure
to him, it made him want to set down something there; a drawing,
a line of words; echo of life in some fashion or other.

2

He was working at the long center table in the store for some minutes before he glanced up and recognized Doctor Rush up front
at the book counter. The Doctor was turning through a book. He
seemed blurred with daylight all around his edges, as Wayne looked
at him against the front windows of the store.

Wayne went on working.

Peter went on reading.

They were aware of each other.

Peter had seen him out of the corner of his eye. In a little bridge
of truth and feeling between them, which had nothing to do with
their relative ages, they felt shy of each other. Each denied it to
himself, watching the other circumspectly. Each inhabited a world
of Donald Rush's that the other knew little about.

Finally Peter put down his book and took up another, and in
the act, "saw" Wayne, and nodded to him.

"Hello, Wayne. Are you working nowadays?"

"Just now and then.—H'lo."

"You're the feller I've been wanting to see."

"Well, sure," said Wayne.

"Can you slip out and have a drink with me next door?"

"I'd better ask Mr. Jensen."

"Well, you go ask him. I'll wait."

Peter watched the remote interview. Mr. Jensen appeared to
meet Wayne's request with a toughness he did not really have.

Wayne returned and said he could go. They went to the Mint Confectionery next door and sat in one of the booths and ordered. Peter had a Coca Cola, and Wayne took a marshmallow fudge sundae on chocolate ice cream, with ground nuts and a maraschino cherry on a dome of whipped cream, studded with slices of banana.

"You see a lot of my boy Don, don't you?"

"Why, sure."

"I know he is always making plans about doing things with you.—You knew he was going to have a birthday pretty soon, didn't you?"

"Why, I guess so."

"Well, his mother and I are hard put to it to know what to give him for his birthday. Mrs. Rush said I was to find you, by hook or crook, and ask you for a suggestion. So here we are, meeting in a sort of folk gathering place, imbibing the fashionable indigestibles of the day, while I lay my problem before you."

"Well, I *see*."

"Can you think of anything he wants? Has he mentioned anything?"

"Well, goll, I don't know. Right off, that is."

Peter lighted a cigarette, sat back, and waited. Wayne went on with his sticky delight, spooning the sundae with a steady pace. They sat in silence for perhaps five minutes. He could see that Wayne was dying to say something but didn't know how to, and let him wait. Pretty soon the metal sundae dish was licked clean by the spoon, and Wayne sat back and stared out into the shop, whistling silently. Peter crushed out his cigarette.

"I won't offer to buy you another of those frightful confections. My professional integrity inhibits my natural generosity. It is not often that a general practitioner can intervene so effectively between a potential patient and the source of acute indigestion."

Wayne looked at him, and he saw that the Doctor's kidding was all really on his side, and the sparkle in his eye when he made those ridiculous sentences was rather youthful. He burst out laughing, and wondered why he had felt so tongue-tied. He wished he could talk that way. Maybe that was what the dictionary was for. He suddenly loved his dictionary fervidly.

"Well," said Peter, "I just thought I would *ask* you, anyway. We really want to give him something he really *wants*."

"I know," said Wayne, in the mildest and most natural voice in the world, "he wants a .22 rifle."

"I see. That's the sort of thing I wanted to know. Thanks, Wayne. We'd better get back to work, both of us.—A .22? Do you think he'd be careful with it? Would *you*?"

"Oh, sure. *Surely*. We would exercise extreme caution in operating the gun," replied Wayne, and blushed. Nevertheless, he felt a little flare of success in dealing the Doctor's conversation back at him. How excellent it was to be educated!

"Well, that sounds like *it*, then. I'll tell Mrs. Rush what you said.—I believe she is planning a party, but don't you say anything about it to Donnie."

"Oh, no, indeed."

Indeed was a good one, too.

They parted with a handshake. When Peter had disappeared around the corner, swinging in his energetic walk, Wayne felt older, taller, and more gifted than ever before. Doctor Rush made you *feel like somebody*, he reflected, and went back to his job furiously.

3

That afternoon, Peter left his office a shade earlier than usual, in order to reach the hardware store down the street before closing time. He just made it. They let him in the door, and then locked it after him, and drew down the striped awning shade over the plate glass of the door.

Ed, the clerk, was a man his own age with whom he had gone to school years ago here in Albuquerque. Doctor Rush wondered if *he* looked as old as that now. Good Lord, they used to go hunting together, way back then. The river on Saturdays, the mesa where the jack rabbits leaped up from behind unlikely bushes, the sandhills way over the river where quail speckled the memories of September…

Ed handed him one .22 rifle after another, now, and a host of simple joys returned to life in the Doctor as he handled the guns.

What a thing happened to a man when he took up a gun to hold! Atavism, he said to himself, but he couldn't dismiss the—the *basic* sense of rightness he felt at hefting a rifle in his hands. A gun made him want to be alone. How enormously simplified the terms of life were, if you thought along this line. Some sky, a wilderness, survival the first and last responsibility, mind bound to earth and earth's caprice its governor; how tempting, the lordship over the animal kingdom; what trials of innocence by the innocent; what wisdom in the impassive mountains, what justice in the fatigue of a body tired by the earth; to lie down when darkness fell by the chill mountain lake, and not stir until sunrise crept down the opposite peak...

He smiled and humorously gritted his teeth at the nonsense which welled up in grown men at times. Let the boy have the rifle. Rifletime was a season in any man's life. He laid his cheek on the stock and squinted along the sights. It was an expensive present, and a dangerous one, too, of course; but if he bought it for Donnie, he would also be buying the memory of his own boyhood, that he could put it from him, in the name of his son.

"This one's a beauty."

"Boy, sure is prettiest little rafle in the house."

"I think this's the one I'll take, Ed."

Ed didn't look *that old* any more. He was just a ruddy, skinny and familiar figure, who hadn't changed in any essential ways since high school. The streets were none of them paved, then, years ago, but *all* made of sand, and Peter remembered how Ed used to ride to school on an old mare who was tied all morning to the cottonwood tree out on the edge of the recess playground in back. It had seemed such an original thing to do when they were both boys in high school that he always expected Ed to be a famous and "successful" man.

"O.K., Doc.—Will you take 'er?"

"No, send 'er out Friday morning. It's Donald's birthday, and Mrs. Rush's planning a little party that evening at suppertime.—She'll hide it while the kids're at school. Thanks, Ed.—Glad to've seen you."

Ed winked at him, and let him out the door, and watched him a second, reflecting that this was a mighty lucky town to have a doctor like him, ol' Pete, and proudly he recollected going to high school with ol' Pete, who would ever've thought *back then* that ol' Pete'd amount to something? Just a litto biddy ol' *kid*, used to hunt *jack rabbits* with him, she-oot!

Ed dropped the canvas shade in its place and put the rifle into its flannel sock and tied a tag on to it marked for delivery. He expected that would be one happy ol' kid when he got aholt of this litto rafle.

IX · ANOTHER COUNTRY

I

Within the very fabric of the little family of Willa Shoemaker, something was going on which might have been whole countries away, for all it concerned them jointly. It was something like that that Martha herself felt about it; another country; another spirit; alien to her busy mother and laughably foreign to her little brother Wayne. But in her own heart, there were perceptions and vistas which were so new, so troublesome and so breath-taking that she concealed her state by an air of sullenness "not at all like her."

Martha wore her silky hair in a heavy fall beside her cheeks. Her eyes were very blue, and full of silver sparks. She rubbed her cheeks, whenever she could remember, to make them look highly colored; all the rubbing she could manage never added anything to their crab apple glow. Her mouth was rather large, but its lips were sweetly modeled and could hardly take the shape of anything but eagerness, a smile, the appetite of happiness. When a little younger, she had played a game with Wayne of being grown up, and severe, comically critical of everything; and then her mouth had pursed ridiculously, as if in a distasteful kiss, while Wayne had saved up his laughter until she too could drop her acting, and the two of them explode with mirth.

Now the expression of kisses, unspent, lingered over her mouth, and gave it a first ripeness that made people look after her when she passed. She said to herself often enough that she wasn't pretty; her fresh dresses and crisply laundered white collars that she wore to work at business college gave her a smart look, she knew that; her attempts to walk with grace and dignity instead of with the comic exaggerations that had convulsed Wayne so short a time ago as a year—this bearing she was learning by habit; and all her impulses to foolishness that had been part of her character in the family now seemed to sink deeper into her heart, and become part of the inner delight that she must keep the world from seeing, until she knew what it meant.

She supposed everyone would know, and speculate, and try to *influence*, soon enough.

She was suddenly in love with a boy she'd known in high school. He was a class behind her, so that now, a graduate and already ahead in business college, she was dating him even though he was still only a senior. He still had to ride his bicycle up the hill to the big redbrick and white-stone high school every morning at eight-twenty. His name was Richmond Summerfield, nicknamed "Bun." His father was a druggist, and the son worked in the family drugstore after school and on week ends. He was a year younger than Martha. She wondered sometimes whether this mattered. But when they were together, it never seemed important, and she forgot it as often as possible.

And it was an endless source of doubt and wonder to her that for years she had known Bun casually, simply as a boy with merry dark-blue eyes, and the face of a ripe peach, and dark hair combed in deep shining rakes that set off his handsomely shaped head, and the energetic harmonies in his body that made it seem powerful as well as young. She had never given him a second thought, any more than any other boy she knew. Instead, she had dreamed awake over her imaginary lover.

And then what: then like turning a page of a story, as cleanly and sharply as that, and as easily, she had been smitten by his look, across the counter in the drugstore, one day, while she was buying some foot powder to take home to her mother who was on her feet all day, as they'd heard her remark a thousand times, and the world was a place in which one great secret existed, and it lay in Martha's heart, driving out forever the foolish image which she now knew had been so unreal and even shameful. For days she avoided Summerfield's Drug, as it was known in town.

What if he would "merely look" at her?

It would break her heart.

She crossed the street to the opposite side to avoid the chance of encountering Bun, and of having him see her simply as some ol' girl.

When she was alone, she would shake her head as if to scatter the thought of him apart.

But it did no good.

She wept at night and stormed herself to sleep with angry scoldings of her foolishness at allowing anything so implausible as the hope that he might love her too to inhabit her days and hurry her nights.

But the trouble became too great to deal with halfway. She resolved to go into Summerfield's and contrive to get any other clerk to wait on her, and if Bun were there, she'd simply wave casually, and complete her purchase, and walk out.

2

It went according to plan. There was a clerk named Rollie Glovers who looked more like a drug clerk in his tan-colored linen jacket than Bun did, and his pale face seemed vaguely medicinal. Down the aisle behind the heaped counter she saw Bun, looking at her with his dark eyebrows up in a surprised smile. He came toward her. She nodded. He asked if Rollie was taking good care of her. She answered him, Yes of course, but her voice croaked and itched in a dry whisper and she coughed over it, and looked down, hating her heart for beating so fast, and her cheeks for coloring so deep.

When she looked up again, she had what looked like tiny lights in her eyes. Bun's face changed as he regarded her and he gave Rollie a comedy poke in the ribs, to send him off down the aisle to wait on someone else, and the two of them were left, looking at each other across the pyramids of powder boxes on the perfume counter, until the immediate betrayals they had both made began to embarrass them, and they went confusedly back to the foolish excuse of purchase she had begun to make.

Her fresh, starched, frilly aspect and her long blonde hair and her lips pressed close together looked entirely new to him. His hands trembled when he snapped a rubber band around her little parcel and handed it to her. She looked at his hands and her throat began to beat, and she knew she could not say a word if her life depended on it.

He came around from behind the counter and took her to the door. He fancied he could smell the laundering of her clothes.

What the heck, he thought, at this extraordinary thought.

Then he asked her if he could have a date that night.

At once, an ease plumbed her deeply. Gone was the terrified, unhappy child within her who had made her days so heavy. She felt almost elaborately at ease, and with a curious kind of grandeur, she said "Let me see," and went through the parody of remembering whether she had an engagement or not. Then, to her appalled heart which only asked to say *yes*, urgently, and at once, she heard herself tell three lies, saying that she was engaged this evening, and tomorrow, and tomorrow, but the day after that, it would probably be all right.

She watched his face, to see if she had ruined forever the very terms on which her future life depended. But he smiled with what looked like humility, and his dark-blue eyes made little stars of thought deep inside which she said to herself later looked simply "gallant," he took his disappointment so dearly. He said if three nights off was the best she could do, it was still prob'ly better than he *rated*, and he asked her if he should come to get her at home.

He said he had no car, and was never sure whether he could get his father's, anyway. She didn't want him to come to the little house so far out on the sand street where the street lights were so far apart on every other corner.

She said she had some books to return to the public library anyway. Why didn't they meet there? He said that would be fine, and took her hand to shake it, rather formally.

Their touch together was like a miniature jolt of electricity. Neither of them, as they said so often later on, felt that they could let go, *you know*, the way electricity does to you, when the current gets into you, they say sometimes you never *can* let go, and the shock keeps on going through you, and *going* through you, until at last somebody or something turns the power off, and there you are, weak as a cat, or dead, or something, never knowing what hit you…?

That was how she felt, making her way up the street alone. Her mouth was dry, and her eyes felt as if they were shining and hot and stinging. There was a gulp in her throat. How tall was he? He was taller than she, and so deep in the breast and so broad in the back. She now felt her pulse racing, and she said to herself that it was the most awful risk she had ever taken in her life, what if he had simply raised his eyebrows and said, "O.K., I'll ask you some other time," which of course he would forget to do—why—and if he did, why, she would die. Her heart beat so she felt a little giddy and breathless. The only way she could feel what had really happened to her, was by suffering an imaginary tragedy. Tears for what might have happened came to her eyes, and drowned her happiness over what did happen.

Watching her disappear among the walkers of the sidewalks he felt ageless and very well, turning his big gold signet ring slowly on his knuckle. The ring had been his grandfather's, and was made to represent three ropes braided together, wound around a fancy capital S. His grandfather had been a medical officer in the Civil War. Bun meant to study medicine in college. The ring was an inheritance and a dedication.

He was a believer in the body, as an athlete. He was astonished at falling in love, and wondered where he'd gotten it—from her eyes, how she looked? Her voice, trying to speak? He went back into the store, came up behind Rollie Glovers at the counter, reached around his side and took the clipped pencil from the upper pocket of Rollie's starched jacket, passed it around his body and dropped it into the lower pocket on the other side, and chucked Rollie under the chin, and ended with a jazzy tattoo of drummed knuckles on Rollie's skull,, saying, "O.K., babe," and passing down the counter to the back of the store and out of sight behind the swinging half-door to the prescription room, which smelled powdery.

3

Hovering up and down behind the counter, which had its masking battlements of merchandise, Rollie had enviously watched the two of them. He wished passionately that he would explain to himself why he never could seem to *win*. Every time he got into situations with other people, he never seemed able to make an impression. He knew perfectly well what was right and what was wrong; he was as sure of that sort of thing today as the day four years ago in Amarillo, Texas, when he had been converted during the revival meeting the spring of his graduation from high school. He was very careful in what he thought of as *personal habits*, too. He bathed twice a day and kept his clothes pressed and when a necktie he liked got shiny he would go down to the boiler room at the YMCA where he lived, and steam it and then flatten it overnight in the atlas he had bought two years ago for the purpose of memorizing five geographical names a day.

He loved his books, and often sent away more than once a month for a new one. He was *developing his memory* that way; and he was learning how to make *deft, ready conversation*, too. And—a shy, sensitive person, "like many thousand others"—he was also finding out how to be *never at a loss* when *thrown among strangers*. As for getting up and making a speech, nothing was further from his natural abilities; but he decided that the occasion might come up when he least expected it; and there was another book with diagrams and sample selections for him to study, so that people might one day say, "Listen to Glovers! We never *knew!*"

Was there anything simpler than training yourself to make a habit of having *one pleasant thing to say* every single day to every single person you met? And yet how startled people would look, at times, when he would try it. It was like the sort of thing he found out from those other books that came in plain wrappers, and which he approached in *scientific interest,* to have a well-rounded knowledge of the facts of life. There were chapters on *courtship* which told how to do, and yet when he had a date with a girl, and tried *how to do,* she mostly often would make sounds or gestures that meant, "Um-*hum,* but let's—let's just watch the movie," or "Why, Rollie!" and giggle.

And yet he was sure: the books all insisted, and so did the things he read more than anything else, the advertisements, he was *sure* that it was only a matter of *using spare time wisely*…there was actually a "boy" he knew in Fort Worth who learned to play the piano from the advertised thing, and was able at the same time to *avoid hours of tedious practice!*

And his health! How careful he was, and how regularly he took his various doses of medicine, so that *Nature's delicate balance* would not get out of whack! That last book, *Adding Ten Years to Your Life,* had a series of charts of the human body, with things to check every day that had to be done to *keep vigor.* He checked them carefully, and looked at himself for traces of the *perfect, radiant health* that was sure to result.

Sometimes he thought he found them, and at other times he was miserably discouraged.

Because what it all came back to was that *people* didn't seem any different toward him; and there were actually moments when he faintly thought that trying harder might not be of any use.

And yet if that were going to be true, why, what about the things that *everybody* believed? You couldn't tell *him* that all that millions and millions of dollars spent on advertising was spent for nothing, why, everybody knew that wasn't so. Everybody *did* what they read about, and bought, and that was how everything helpful got discovered, after all.

So he would fiercely clench his thoughts and (though he never admitted it to himself) actually he would pray that his faith be sustained.

Oh, forsake me not, for that I am *thy* child.

Oh, I want everybody here tonight to *know*, I want them to know that I have *been* weary and sick *at* heart, *oh*, I want to *say*, I want everybody to hear me *say* that I have been trying to find the way to the Vineyard, I have searched among the devious paths, I have humbled myself before the gods of offering, *oh*, grant unto me that *I* find the *way*, in six easy lessons. *Oh*, how to keep regular, do *you* need the answer to the secret of how to make an impression? Oh, there *is* a way, for every smile on your face there is another smile waiting somewhere in the world to be smiled right back at you, did you know that, *Oh*, Lord? Oh, amen, *amen*, I say unto you, why did she turn and snicker? *He* didn't know, but all the rest of them did! *Oh*, hear me. Ha-ha is what they said behind their hands, what makes our friend look so listless, no pep. Oh, did't you know, he is not *regular*?

Where is the Pretty Girl who will give the word of advice about This New Way?

How do they get to smile in the pictures of After? Oh I know all the pictures of Before. What has not been vouchsafed unto me are the sweetnesses, the powers, the winnings, of After.

Do you want to be attractive?

Check the answer yes or no.

Someday the coupon, the *right* coupon, will come along, guide me to the paths of the righteous that I may know it when it appears, and I may enter into my kingdom by mail, in six easy lessons, in plain wrapper, Amen.

4

And yet Bun and that Shoemaker girl had gotten together just as easy as falling off a log.

Rollie was passionately envious, and vowed he would watch them, and "be in on" what they did, by whatever means he could command.

X · THE BIRTHDAY

I

A kind of sweet fury took hold of Noonie. She had decided to astonish and enchant her child and his father with a revival of the delights of the old days in Rochester, when all birthdays had been festivals lasting weeks. The family would start out weeks before the actual *day*, and prepare. There were forbidden areas in the house where the celebrant could not go. There were sweeps and whisperings of tissue paper. The sewing machine whirred and sang all day. At night there were unexplained rustlings while packages were taken up the back way. Everybody sustained an elaborate pretense that there was nothing unusual going on. But Noonie could remember how Roderick would be looking at her with his black-eyed smile, his head down, his mouth parted in hot-breathed speculation. The family connotations of such intense labors came back to her here, now, and she was tireless in her preparations.

To have her small mystery was wonderfully good for her. She had rosy cheeks, her eyes sparkled, and her conversation was arch and endless, since she had to keep them thinking about everything except the thing that was going on in the house.

Donald would surprise her in intent conference with Cora, the cook, and be whisked out of the kitchen with his glass of milk and plate of sandwiches before he could even ask for anything. He found large piles of department store boxes out in the alley refuse cans. He saw names and telephone numbers written on the hall pad, and heavily scratched out so as to be illegible. One afternoon he deliberately tested the atmosphere of secret and ecstatic labor by going up to his mother's bedroom and sitting down and fiddling with everything on her dressing table, while she worked hard, over by the sunny windows, in front, to seem idle and patient. He could tell that she was bursting with something. He had one of his rare desires to go and put his arms around her and hug her. She didn't even seem tired. He saw the lid off the sewing machine in a corner of the room, and he recognized snips of crepe paper of bright colors on the floor, where Leonard had not really swept up.

"What are you doing with my things?" she asked idly, threading a needle. He noticed that there was no completed darning anywhere on the sewing table. She was just pretending while he was there.

"Nothing."

"Look out for my rings."

"Where are they?"

"In that little Dresden china box with the three cats on it."

"Oh. Can I look?"

"You've seen them a million times.—Yes, go ahead. What a funny boy. You always loved sparkles."

He took the lid off the box. It was lined with mauve velvet. There lay three rings, with big diamonds in them and one with a large amethyst circled with diamonds. He picked them up and walked to the sunshine of the window, and held them up and squinted at them, and was needled by their fiery stabs, and he saw magic in the jewels.

"Why don't you ever wear them, Mother?"

"Oh, I don't know: I don't *feel* much like diamonds, nowadays."

"Why not, Mother?"

"Oh, I don't know.—You wouldn't understand."

"I would too!"

"Darling Donnie!"

She reached for him, and now that she wanted to kiss him, his desire to hug her disappeared.

"What's the matter?"

"You do know I love you, don't you, Donnie, I am such a poor mother to you!"

"No you're not!" he said. "*No you're not!*" he cried again, and refused the obscure doubt that he had known for so long.

She kissed him on the cheek, and sat back again, and let him go, and he turned the rings in the light.

"Will you wear them if—if we ever *do* something?" he asked.

"What do you mean: *do* something."

"I mean, like a party, or anything."

"Party?" she said, with an airy laugh. This was exquisitely the kind of close shave that made the secret preparations ever so worth while. "Who said anything about a party: don't be such a silly-billy boy."

But there was the most cunning laughter in her voice, it came from her heart, so full of devoted and clever plans, half of which were already carried out. Wait till he saw the enormous drum, made of crepe paper, cardboard and gold cord, which she and Cora had slaved over, and which was filled like a huge pie with presents for everybody. It would be brought in and set on the dining-room table and then the sliding doors would be shut, and locked, till the party. Then each child would be given a golden cord to pull, and out would pop the most adorable presents for everybody... And the paper hats: none of your cracker kind: she was making every single one of them. Paste, scissors, sewing machine, colored papers, fringe, tassels, seals...out of them all came the most beautiful shakos and fezzes and helmets and tiaras and busbies and "Merry Widows" and "Toscas" and "Gainsboroughs," which the children would never have seen the like of. And Cora was going to decorate the cake with three colors, and it was coming in on a large new wooden palette because Donald loved to paint and someday might be a great artist, and use a thing like this instead of that battered box of water colors. And she had got a number of games together, which the children would all play, and even planning the order of the games was something of a job in itself. Nobody would ever expect such elaborate and ingenious things as were in the making besides.

"Party?" she repeated. "Why should there be a party?"

"Oh, I don't know. It just occurred to me, as a remote possibility."

"—Where on earth did you learn to talk like that.—Honestly, growing boys are like magpies, they hear something and pick it up."

She was certain that she had handled it just right. He didn't suspect a thing. She said,

"Aren't you going out this afternoon? Or do you want to sit downstairs and read.—You ought to rest more, darling. Drink your milk and take a little rest. You never know when you will need your reserve of strength! Look at me!"

This was in her habitual style of worry. Sometimes she felt Donald's strenuous life was a burden to her; a rebuke to her own weariness; proud of his furies of ingenuity and activity, she was unnerved by them, too, and was always advising him to rest, be more quiet, drink more milk, stop *racing* so, as if she could store up in her child what she lacked herself.

He could not bear these advices. He could remember, if he could not explain, how divided they often felt, in that house. They all really loved each other; and their exchanges ranged widely from overly thoughtful attentions to bursts of black-eyed anger and scorn, which were never patched up by apology, but allowed to be dissipated through two or three days of slowly thawing silence among them. Noonie would make some remark that if taken up tactfully could weld them together again. "How are the trees doing, Peter?" or "What are you and Wayne doing this Saturday, Donnie dear?"—and they could then talk about the lot next door with the evergreen nursery which was the neighborhood's smiling folly, or about how the boys would take a pack of lunch, and maybe ride out on the mesa for the day, and see what they could see, perhaps at Wayne's old abandoned chicken ranch where the adobe walls were weathering under the wind into rounded edges, and the mountains seemed so near, and there was supposed to be a snake pit full of rattlers which they had never yet found but would surely find someday.

Donald went back and put the diamond rings away, and stood in the middle of the room, looking at her, smiling with a frown, with his head a little on one side, like his father.

She laughed fondly, and said,

"All right, go on, do anything you like, only don't stand there and *diagnose* me."

"Are you trying to get rid of me?"

"What in the world *for?*" she asked, lyrically, and once again, the charm and excitement of a surprise in preparation was implicit between them.

"Then I'll go," he said, and she remembered how her brother Roderick always used to do the same thing; publish for his own the reason for anything he did.

2

The Doctor got home a little after six the evening of the party, and found his wife in the green-carpeted hallway of their large, comfortable and ugly house, watching the birthday party in progress. There were a dozen boys and girls in the living room. The player piano was going. The light was harsh and bland, falling through the crystal prisms that hung from the brass discs set near the white ceiling. The children were flushed and unconscious of themselves. A game of pinning the cloth tail on the printed donkey was under way. Some of the boys had lost their tissue-paper hats. Some of the girls wore theirs with conscious style. Noonie's eyes were dancing, and her breath came in little hot wafts through her lips. He thought she looked pretty, and he hugged her with his hat and overcoat on, standing spread-legged around her and laughing privately on her cheek.

"Don't, Peter, look out, do you think they're having a good time?"

"They're O.K.," said the Doctor, ignoring the roomful of busy children.—"You look's'if it was your own party yourself, Noonie, look at me."

"I'll be dead when it's over, I've worked all day. But I do think he's loving it.—I've saved your present till you got here."

The Doctor was suddenly shy. He dropped his arms away from her, and took off his hat and coat. He wanted to say that he wished he didn't have to give Donald the rifle in front of all those children. They never looked really aware of anything as it really *was*, and he dreaded their jumping staring acceptance of a present that it had given him such delight to buy and bestow with his imagination and his love upon his boy.

He walked to the white-pillared doorway between the hall and the living room. Donald and Wayne sat side by side on the piano bench, watching the Truman boy from the other side of town stagger in blindfold toward the sheeted donkey tacked on the closed mahogany sliding doors of the dining room. The Doctor's heart sank. If he had ever seen an image of boredom it was his own son, with those big, staring eyes in that brown face with its excited color but blank expression. The other youngsters were full of noise, and seemed oddly so much younger than those two on the piano bench. The player piano was puffing and clanking out its tune. Nobody listened. Edward Truman pinned the tail on the donkey's very middle, and pulled off his blindfold, while they all screamed at him, and he made an idiot face, crossing his eyes, hanging out his tongue, and wabbling his fingers under his chin, to make his own point of how gloriously he had failed. Then they all fell silent, looking at the Doctor. He smiled at them all. Donald looked up at him with his face lowered and smiled back. Nobody did anything. The Doctor felt suddenly angry. After all her work, he thought, and these little devils won't help to make it a party, it's dying on her hands. Valorously loyal to his wife's helplessness and her hope, he turned and took her hand and pulled her into the living room with him. He didn't realize it, but it was his arrival that had changed everything. They were now all self-conscious, it was the Doctor, when you were sick they sent for him, he gave castor oil, he smelled like the hospital, let's get out of here, there wasn't enough ice cream anyway, "h'lo Doctor Rush"—for he had greeted them all. He went to the corner bookcase which had glass doors behind which were curtains of stretched pongee silk. He unlocked it. There stood the long package. He got it out, walked over to Donald, and handed it to him, saying, "Happy birthday, Don."

It was such a big package that they couldn't get close enough to see, while Don unwrapped it. He knew by the weight what it was, the balance of it, and when he got to the gray flannel sock in which the rifle was finally protected, he was dumbly reluctant to open it further. He looked up at his father.

"Goll, Dad, thanks."

The others cried for him to go ahead, and open it up, what was it, was it a gun, gosh.

Doctor Rush noticed that Don looked as if he might suddenly cry, and his own heart melted in him at that, and he leaned down and took the gun off his son's lap, and knelt there and gently opened the flannel sock, bending down to hide his own face. He got the gun out and handed it back to Donnie now, and stood up rushing air out through his mustache.

"There you are, son.—D'you like it?"

"Goll, Daddie:" but he simply could not talk any further, struggling to preserve his calm and powerful interior. He lost his battle when the gun had to be handed around to the other boys. He charged like a football player into his father's middle, and butted and hid his head against the Doctor's vest, hugging him around the pockets frantically, not caring who might be looking, all those kids, and girls, what of it. Somehow foolishly, the gun ended up in Noonie's hands, where it looked like a large spoon, the way she held it. But her face was what they all were drawn by, and in the midst of this heartless and noisy young public, the Rushes had one of their united moments.

3

Shortly after that the children went home, leaving Wayne and Donald and the .22, in the middle of the green carpet on the living-room floor. The gun had a rock-gray barrel, shining along the myriad rings of its tooled surface. The stock was a beautiful leathery brown, which felt smooth and cool under the palm. The bolt sounded simply beautiful when it was clicked open and closed, riding its element of oil, which smelled sharp and almost sweet. They both knew that Donald would sleep with it tonight on his sleeping porch upstairs. They all knew that his thirteenth birthday, and the party, and the present, were all points of history for them in the family...even to what happened just before the Doctor and his wife sat down to dinner. Don came and said Wayne had to go home, now, and he would like to ride home with him; which broke the harmony so lovingly born among the family half an hour before. Peter said he might at least stay home this one evening, on his birthday, and Noonie was exhausted enough to murmur that he never took time to sit down and *talk* to them, after all the work she'd gone to, but if that was how he felt about—why let—and if it meant no more than—still, the boys *had* had their supper, the party supper was at five-thirty...

Wayne was there, and said it was just so he could give Don his present, it wasn't much, so he hadn't brought it here to the house.

Don told him never mind, to go on home, he'd see him tomorrow. Wayne thanked Mrs. Rush for the party, went out, got on his bike, and rode as far as the nursery, and paused there, sitting his saddle, and hating the change over everything in the big house.

In a few minutes, Donald came out the back door with his new rifle, got on his bike, and rode along the sidewalk past the evergreen nursery. Wayne wheeled around to join him, calling in a loud whisper.

"Can you come?"

"Y'p."

"Is it all right?"

"I guess so."

"Gee, I'm sorry."

"We simply have to be superior to disturbances of that kind."

Then they both laughed with pride at this statement, and were at once together in their private world of authority and power. They charged on their bicycles, riding like the wind down the sandy dark street where the intersection lamps showed the way far ahead like diminishing stages of a tunnel.

"I can hardly wait to see the gun."

"I'll let you have it the minute we get there."

Their tires spurned the loose gravel, and sang.

Presently they were there, coming to rest under the big cottonwood out in back of the Shoemakers' house. Wayne got off his saddle, but Donald didn't, so he waited. But Donald said nothing. What he wanted to do was apologize for the trying episode at his own house. He was so happy to be away from it that he felt guilty, and thought he could fix it up if he said something to Wayne. But that was not possible after all, for it would seem disloyal.

The evening was chilly, they shivered, turned and saw the moon beginning its ride up from behind the mountains to the east, on the mesa. It would be fully spring before long. This was simply such a moment as they would remember forever; the pungent cold night smelling deeply of new leaves on a wind from the loamy river; the heavy rise of the thick old cottonwood trunk from the swept bare clay of the back yard; the bower of leaves and stars overhead as the branches opened and grew so slender and airy; the wonderful, common moon which they had known for so long in thoughtless mystery; the sense of home in the yard, the street, the town, the plains, and each other.

"I sneaked out," said Donald, finally. "I'll go back soon. I had to see what you had for me."

"Come on in, it isn't much.—But it *belongs*."

They went into the back door of the canvas house. There was another surprise waiting for Donald. It was Willa Shoemaker, who had taken this evening off instead of her regular Wednesday, to be there when Wayne brought Donald for the second birthday celebration. She had heard them ride into the yard, and had lighted the candles on the cake she'd made. The *Spirito Santo* was hotting with a windy fire and trembling on its cast iron claws like a tremendous amiable dog. She hugged Donald and wished him a happy birthday, and he blushed with unbearable guilt and delight at this party. They were all excited, she most of all, and proud of the event and her family's contribution to it. Wayne went to the sewing machine in the corner and from the top drawer he took a small package which he thrust at Donald.

"Here it is, and happy birthday, Noddie."

It was two boxes of .22 ammunition.

They talked about it then for some time, while they ate the cake and the ice cream Mrs. Shoemaker had ready for them. The rifle lay on the table between them, shining in the kerosene lamplight. They both spoke animatedly but often without making sense, Mrs. Shoemaker thought, smiling over them behind her newspaper in the corner. She almost wished now that she had invited Doctor and Mrs. Rush to the party, too, there was certainly enough food for them all in ordinary portions. She reflected that she had little enough chance to *entertain*, working as she did all day and, seemed, all night.

Her thoughts took flight comfortably.

She saw them come, what charming people, she had always liked the Rushes, our children are such friends, do come in, Martha, here're the Rushes, come say hello to them, my, what is that that smells so delicious, why that is my famous fricasseed chicken which I know you'll enjoy, my mother back in Michigan taught me the recipe, you add just a pinch of curry powder, how handsome Doctor Rush is, some people wouldn't think so, but I do, shall we sit down? Doctor, you here on my right, it does seem such a long time since we've had a chance to *talk*, everybody is so busy… The daydream was a mixture of the facts of this little house and the enormous resources of the Harvey House dining room, and her vision tickled her with its outlandishness as much as it comforted her with its wishes.

"And yet, I'll bet, if I asked them, they'd come," she thought, coming back with a humorous frown to the present.

When the ice cream and cake were gone, the boys insisted that she pull up to the table with them to play the card game of Authors; and all three of them took pleasure in the succession of faces on the cards, famous to them out of their schoolbooks. At the end of the game, Donald said,

"Here's Washington Irving," and made a face.

"Here's Emerson!" cried Wayne.

"Bryant!"

"Who's this!"—with a scowl and a mustache made from a curled-up lip.

"Mark Twain!"

The stove was quieter. The mica in the poop-deck panes nicked with a little sound of cooling. It began to feel late. The party was over. Wayne rode halfway home with Donald, and then added an extra block because of the birthday.

4

After the birthday party, late at night, Peter awoke to hear Noonie weeping, and when he asked her what was the matter, she answered that it was one of her headaches, the pain was unbearable, and made her feel so dreadfully sad in addition to hurting her head so.

He got up and turned on a shaded light in the far corner of the bedroom, and she winced at the faint glow that dawned on the white wallpaper with the silver stripe in it. He went to their bathroom and mixed her a powder and brought it back. They could hear the clock downstairs in the hall, and it sounded as if it were walking slowly, rocking from heel to heel, up and down the polished hardwood floor, all night long.

"Here, drink this. You'll fall asleep."

She wanly shook her head.

"It'd only make me more nervous."

"Nonsense.—Come on, Noonie."

She turned away.

She put her fingers over her eyes.

She was exhausted looking, and the petulant suffering in her face reached out and touched him. He had a thrust of desire at her white and fainting prettiness, with such shadows around the eyes, and at the same time, he wanted to strike her.

He loathed the weakness that fed upon itself which he had gradually come to admit in her.

He bitterly conjugated "to love" in his thoughts, and he wanted to shake her by her white, lovely shoulders until she should cast away the headache and the futility which had produced it, and begin to live on being a woman again, instead of on the dreams of fear and disdain which had seemed to be her growing substitute for feeling and thought.

But he simply stood by her bed, looking down at her, scowling almost professionally, and controlling himself with his habit of lumping the muscles of his jaws.

It would do no good, he reflected, if he added his anger to a situation already without much sense.

In a moment his perverse hatred left him, and he took her hand, and squeezed it, and she let him do so without looking at him.

"Look at me, Noonie," he murmured, and she came around at him with her eyes which were dark and mysterious to gaze upon. She saw him ruddy, his hair tangled and his eyes dancing brightly, his nightclothes outlandishly youthful with broad stripes, heavily wrinkled from sleeping in them, and he was a warm presence beside her, and his dearness smote her out of the years in which she had failed him, and her guilt, her intolerable burden of refusing him his children, made her want to take him in her arms and forgive herself over and over through his love.

But her head throbbed and her mouth was rueful, and she believed he was full, and justly so, of silent reproach. So now out of unworthiness, she lost once again, between them both, the thing they both desired.

"I must remember," he said to himself, watching her eyes kindle with these thoughts, and then stream with tears again, "I must remember that weakness can visit anyone. What if I judged here, at home, the very thing I try not to judge anywhere else?"

He patted her arm, and tucked the satin covering up to her ears, and went to turn off the light. She was proud of the bedroom, its crystal lamps on her dressing table, the silvery elegance of the wall paper, the soft white fur rugs thrown over the morning-glory blue carpet, the long mirrored doors, the clouds of filmy curtains at the bay window that looked over the street.

As soon as the light was off, he knew that he was wide awake. He didn't need much sleep anyway, and was used to being called during the night. He rubbed his head and stood in the darkness of the room a second, and she listened for what he was doing.

"What?" she said, apprehensively, as he didn't move.

"Nothing. I think I'll go out on your porch and read a little while. I'm not sleepy."

"Now I've kept you from going back to sleep."

"No-no. It doesn't matter.—Get to sleep yourself, Noonie. I'll be quiet coming in."

He put on his bathrobe, a richly habitual garment that she often said was a disgrace, it was so old and rubbed, and went to her sunporch and closed the door and then switched on the lamp. He found heaps of magazines on little glass tables, and piles of mail, circulars and advertisements and booklets which she had sent for by clipping and filling out coupons from her women's magazines. He smiled at such evidence, and sat down on her gray satin long chair, and took up one of the magazines she had left there. It was long after midnight, by the way he felt, if that was any way to tell, and he began to turn the large colorful pages quizzically. What a world of health it was! How everybody smiled in the illustrations! What pretty girls, all of them exactly alike, what modest and muscular men, all of them brothers! Here his wife sat day after day, living, with such innocent companions, the risks of rivalry, the penalties of misunderstanding, the rewards of virtue. He began to read one of the stories, it was well enough written, it moved easily, he knew every moment what was coming; but as he read, he seemed to perceive Noonie between the lines, and his heart began to burn at the pity of her life, and its search for answers here, in the lifeless conventions of these pages.

Poor Noon, he mused, closing his eyes, the happy ending can't be handed to you, I'd do it if I could. It's worth more than half-a-dollar, anyway. *Anyway*, you can't buy it.

XI · PERSONAGES

I

The next time he went to see Mrs. Foster, he had a pile of books, some of the Spanish letters of old days, reports from early American venturers, and a volume called *The Western Attorney*, written by a young Missourian of the 1850s, Elias Gray, who had come over the Santa Fe Trail to serve the Territory of New Mexico as assistant to the United States Attorney.

"Now you can begin to get some sense of the past, because the settled life of our time has made hardly a scratch on the spaces here. You can have the sense of how things really were, for those older struggles."

"I was saying to Judy only yesterday that you do really get the most extraordinary sensation, sometimes, of stepping from one time into another, when you go poking around the country."

"I know. I have felt it for years. The land itself keeps telling us."

"Yet I could not say how."

"Nor could I. I only know that when I find evidences of how other men, older men, in forgotten times, loved the land and worked here, I am confirmed in what I feel now, in my own time."

She then said something which startled him.

"Are you anything of an artist? I mean, do you draw, or paint, or try to write down how you see things?"

"Why, no.—But this will possibly amuse you, and it may even make you think I am pretty conceited. But I have always had the feeling that I *could* paint, I mean that I have always *seen* things exactly as I could *fix* them, for good. Some days it seems to me that everything has a crystal clarity, and that I have too. And I say to myself that if I had time, I would make pictures of everything that appealed to me. I don't see how the job could be much more difficult or skillful than what I do up at the hospital in the operating room."

"Provided you *see*," said she, "I don't see why you couldn't either."

"Why? Why did you ask?" he said.

"Why, simply that I get the impression that you *do* see as an artist. You have the kind of respect for things that an artist has. A sort of mixture of goodness and yet a sort of detachment from formal morality. And I think you see, and get so much from, the past, that it makes you full of all kinds of little head starts on understanding the present."

"Well! this is all news to me. But if you get that impression, I am of course flattered and glad.—How do you get it: are *you* an artist?"

They both looked a little surprisedly at each other. They had never made plain between them how little they knew of each other; and yet they felt intimate. They both knew what it meant; they both told the truth with their eyes, if not their lips.

"Oh, yes," she said, offhandedly, "I write, now and then, there is no virtue in it, but then one has nothing to say as to whether or no.—I sound like something in Mother Goose."

He had to go. He left her the books, and said they would talk them over when she'd had time to read them. He thought she looked "hard" when she spoke of writing, and he wondered why.

2

It was Noonie who told him really who Mrs. Foster was.

She said that here for weeks they'd had a celebrity in town, and nobody knew it, and he asked who. She said the novelist Mary Carmichael was here, was staying in that large rambling log house on the hill, and the public library was having a run on her books. Noonie went to the library one day and the librarian told her that Miss Carmichael was in town, was writing a new book, had come to find high air, sunshine, and peace, and would undoubtedly produce another best seller right here and everybody in some splendid if unknown way would share in the virtue of that local act.

Peter was dumfounded.

He felt sold out.

He had heard—who had not?—of Mary Carmichael, but he never had connected "Mrs. Carmichael Foster" with her.

Noonie said that Mrs. Foster was a "divorced" name. Carmichael was her maiden name, and when a woman was divorced, she kept her husband's last name, and used her own maiden name, that is, if she was fashionable. She was delighted and eager about Mrs. Foster's fashionableness. She had found out that Mrs. Foster lived with little accents of style and circumstance quite unusual in the town as it then was. She kept a small car and had a chauffeur who had brought it from New York. Her cook had come with her, and a housemaid. She had a secretary along, too, who typed her manuscripts every day.

This explained Miss Bridges.

Peter felt an unreasonable want to hear no more. He hated hearing anything about Mrs. Foster from Noonie. It posed them too closely side by side in his thoughts. But Noonie was fascinated and went on.

She said they said Mrs. Foster was seeing no one. The librarian had tried to call, when the news got around, as it *would*, but Mrs. Foster, or Miss Carmichael, as you liked, had sent word that she was "seeing no one," having come to take a rest cure, but sent an inscribed copy of one of her books to the library, and in general tried to indicate that she was grateful for interest, if unable to meet it with gestures on her own part.

The librarian said Mrs. Foster saw no one but her doctor.

"Yes," said Peter, "Willie Treddinger sent her to me."

"What! To you!" cried Noonie. "You never told me."

"Well, Noon, (a), I didn't know who she was, and (b), as you know, I never say anything about my cases, even here at home."

"That's true. Well: anyway:"

She said they lived with great style in the log house. Mary Carmichael was worth mints of money, from the way her books sold, and the gossip around town was that she disliked the way the house was, and the dishes, and all the *things*, so much, that at incredible expense, she had had the whole place done over, and had barrels and barrels of china and boxes of silver sent out, and kept a whole flock of expensive and delicate dogs, and in general lived like an actress or an opera singer, with fresh flowers by the dozens, every day, and long distance calls and heaps of telegrams, and so forth and so on.

"Don't you think it would be nice if I called," said Noonie, "inasmuch as you're her doctor, and we all know Willie?"

"Do as you like, but I don't believe I would, if she really wants privacy. She never said anything about it to me."

"Isn't she *well* enough?"

"She's well enough to do what she likes, but if she wants to be left alone, I think that's that."

"Of course. I certainly wouldn't *throw* myself at her.—You'd die if you could hear the kind of thing everyone is saying about her. — They say she is simply exquisite, a blonde, and that she could make a fortune in the movies if she wanted to, and that Douglas Fairbanks offered her the leading part in one of his pictures, and she refused. Imagine."

"She's very pretty," he said, with a heavy heart, because something was expected of him. "I don't see why the town should lose its head over her, to quite this extent."

But he saw the animation in Noonie's face which everyone else would have, who made of Mrs. Foster's fame and presence a really pleasurable event.

3

He went out presently, feeling cheated, somehow, and yet he laughed at himself for feeling that way. He had always felt she was a very special person, and to find out why he had felt it, in its common terms, from the legitimately interested prattle of his wife, made him conclude that he was a graceless clod. He had asked her if she were an artist. She had probably thought he knew all along who she was. She might consider him the worst of all snobs, the snob who makes a point of ignoring in any relationship with an eminent or gifted person the very gift and the eminence it yielded. He blushed at the idea. He hated any distortion of honest interest. He felt that Noonie was far more natural now in her cheerful outpourings about Mrs. Foster than he was in his suddenly readjusted view of her.

Well, anyway, it revealed to him the true nature of the attraction she had for him.

He said to himself that if she was a famous novelist, and a public figure, and a local tradition already, then he would excuse himself from her orbit in the future. He had enough to do without pursuing her. There was a kind of bitter peacefulness in deciding that. He was spared a harder decision later on, he felt, by making this one now.

He turned his car toward Old Town, where he wanted to go to see old Don Hilario Ascarete, who in his late eighties had reached a kind of tentative survival that could afford to deal only with concerns in life which had connotations of eternity.

4

Old Town lay down by the river bottoms. Its streets wandered like the ditches that fed the cool green fields. Peter often wondered whether the original lanes had not indeed followed the ditches, which all year long needed to be traveled to supervise repairs, and see that robber farmers had not broken the ditch banks to conduct water wrongfully to fields that were not allotted irrigation. It was very possible that a hundred years ago, and more, when there were no streets, but only the Plaza, the town network was made up of the scattered houses, and the paths which connected them came less from design than from habit. So a pastoral town never had the grid pattern of a railroad town, where everything was laid out at right angles to the tracks.

The Old Town was made of the very same substance upon which it stood: the river earth, adobe. Walls, streets, barriers, were all of the pale dried mud which even in the sunshine always seemed to have the palest lilac shadow of color over it.

Some of the buildings were older than the oldest giant cotton-woods that crowded the low roofs and the wandering walls. They were so old, Peter thought, that they seemed eroded rather than just worn by human occupancy. A corner of a house would look like an old man's shoulder, bent and drooping from carrying the weight of years; but still vital with duty's residue. The ever-renewing process of plastering with mud after hard rains gave those houses a sort of organic life, in which they put forth new parts when old ones wore away. Nothing delighted Peter more than to see, in the early summer after a violent rainy spring, a little colony of weeds and grass growing out of the tops of adobe walls or earthen roofs. It seemed to him like a compassionate arching over of the earth's life, to cover as well as support the life of man. It was not a gloomy parable to him, a living grave; it was evidence of the vitality on which all living creatures drew mindlessly, most of the time; but which, he was certain without knowing just how or why, could be explored and used in conscious self-renewal by men if they would only look for their own true natures and find peace within them.

But of the complexity of those natures, he had of course seen plenty of evidence in his professional life.

Peter brought his big car along the dried ruts of the road running past the Old Town church. On his right was a long wall of a house that looked like the road itself lifted on edge and rising and falling in roadside wavers with the contour of the ground. It had deep boxed windows. There was a double door of aged paneled wood from which all paint had long since peeled. It must be one of the oldest houses around here. Don Hilario would know.

He turned into a lane across a field, and came to the Ascarete house, which was set on the broomed packed earth of a courtyard. The house made a right angle. One side cast a long triangle of shadow on the other side. Where the triangle hit the ground, old Don Hilario was sitting with his back to the warmed wall. Crouched over his stick, his knees brought up by his middle because he was sitting on a low bench, he resembled a votive clay figure in a funerary deposit such as were brought out of the pyramids of Mexico. But when he saw his visitor, he pulled his hat off across his face and half arose from his bench. Incomplete and crippled as it was, the gesture had the politeness of real pleasure in it. His voice was like a broken old tune-pipe, a country flute. He spoke in Spanish, and Peter answered in Spanish.

"Why, how delightful, my young friend the Doctor. Come in, come in, sit down, sit down."

"You're looking fine this morning. What a pretty place to sit and look out over the meadows to the river over there and the sandhills way beyond."

"I've been following some blackbirds that sat up there in our tree. They went over the field and tried another tree. Since then they've never made up their minds. Back and forth, back and forth. Like my grandchildren."

This was a joke. His tiny black eyes and the folds of wrinkled face around them were always squinting, as if to see and estimate shrewdly. His name suited him in a fascinating inner harmony. He always struck Peter as being a highly humorous man, and a very good man, essentially.

He had many children and grandchildren, and a galaxy of great-grandchildren.

"They are strangers, to me, you know?" he said to Peter, squinting.

"Who?"

"My relations.—Oh, in and out, in and out, I see them, they have no idea at all of what I know, how much I know, they come to speak to me respectfully, and I can look at the youngest ones, the boys and girls just growing up, and I can see right straight inside of them. No wonder they blush when they look into my eyes. There is nothing they do and want to do which I don't know. To forgive: this is half of life. To do: this is the other half.—Such pretty children, they come and look at me."

"I suppose they just belong to their own times, and they hurry ahead in the present."

Peter knew how the cheerful young Spanish-Americans lived with enthusiastic observance of current styles. Their repainted Fords, their soft drinks, their Saturday movies, their United States slang, exiled old Don Hilario in a fixity of the past.

"Let them go," he said, as if he were a fixed point in life, and they but wanderers. "They all have to find out that everything I have told them is true. When they are old enough to know that, they are ready to tell their own children. I have seen many things; but all you have to know are a few things."

"I want to ask you about something."

"Something to remember?"

"Possibly."

"It takes me a long time to remember, but if you will do me the favor, I'll try."

"Of course. Take as long as you like."

Don Hilario reared back and made a noiseless laugh, a little round black cave of mouth in which the joke of his having all the time in the world, with one foot in the grave, was relished by his tongue, curved up like a chicken's. This was not morbid. Going to die was like going to a party, for anybody so old and so full of what might be called death's health: peace and readiness and completion, on earth. Peter resumed.

"I would like to know all you can remember about that long house, coming down the lane, this way. That is a fine old doorway, and such deep windows.—There's a grocery store at the front end of it. You know. The Sanchez's place.—Was the house standing when you were a boy?"

Don Hilario shut his eyes. Two streams of liquid, not tears, but little runnels of sunshine strain from his weak old eyes, coursed down beside his nose.

"I will have to meditate," he said. "The next time you come back I will have it all ready for you. When I sit down to remember something, I like to have it in order. Give me some time."

He glanced up at the Doctor, an arch old look of pure nonsense. They both knew he was being contrary. But it was as if the old man had a comic propriety which meant much to him. Peter sighed with satisfaction, as if over a curing patient, and took his leave. Years ago, half a lifetime, Don Hilario had been a lawyer, a man of cultivation with a voice in affairs. He had been wealthy and had lived like a grandee. His two oldest sons, now long since dead before him, had been educated in Paris and in Spain. He had known everybody of consequence in this part of the country, and had had a voice in Territorial matters of any importance. Not many people remembered such things about him now. He didn't seem to mind. Neither did he seem bored or discontented. Only those who had never given everything at their disposal to give away, such as ideas, talent or power, ended up by being bored in their declining days, Peter decided. Anyway, the courteous privilege of past grandeur could be allowed Don Hilario now. Out of what his imagination could dig up that would be true to the past, Don Hilario would spend weeks in making a tale for his young friend the physician. Peter thought that it was worth while from everybody's point of view. Few enough people found living value in the old man nowadays.

BOOK III

Adam's Own Land

XII · WANDERING BARKS

I

They did meet at the library that evening. Martha brought her books back, and left them at the loan desk, exchanging a word with the librarian who was a good friend of hers. Then she turned around and surveyed the reading room with a deliberately hard look, standing something like a fashion figure in *Vogue*, a shoulder up, her legs elongated by a feeling of elegance, her mouth faintly disdainful with expression and brilliant rouge, which she had put on after leaving home. She wore short white gloves which made her bare arms look brown. She was trying to look much older, and independent, and private. Her second self was alive within her again, that smaller girl who seemed to tremble within all her limbs, and make her heart seem low and heavy, until he should come. Like a lady of great fashion, indifferent to onlookers, she drew out her heavy bone-rimmed glasses and put them on, looking around the room for him.

He came up to her from behind.

He had been standing among the bookstacks watching her. His face was furiously red, which made his eyes flash with blue and white light. He imagined everyone in the reading room was watching them. He took her elbow with two fingers, which she disliked for its tentative, clumsy possession, and without a word, steered her to a table in the far corner where nobody else was, and sat down with her at a yellow oak table.

He was dry in the mouth. All his street-corner lore left him. She could neither look at him boldly with her rouged mouth ready, nor greet him idly. Their constraint made their hearts sink. It was a mess, a mistake, he was a year younger, she was an impostor, made up like that, trying to be older than she was, when they both knew that inside, she was a child yet, and he was only a thickening cub with dreams in his eyes that were merely embarrassing and had best be lived through as quickly as possible.

What would save them?

He put his hand out on the table, and she looked at it; the look of it restored her; she took off her glove and put her own hand beside his; it was a fragmentary portrait of their two selves; and in a moment, he covered her hand, hiding the neat, small, clever, white hand with his large mild hand, which felt warm over hers, as if the sunshine which had tanned the relief map of his veined fingers and hand-back were still in his flesh.

She remembered that looking at his fingers had first made her feel so much.

Now she began to blush, and he smiled, losing his extra color.

"Now I am glad I came," she said.

"So am I."

"I nearly didn't."

"I's afraid of that."

"But I couldn't go back on my word like that."

"I knew you couldn't."

"We'd better not hold hands here."

"Let them look."

"No, someone might know us."

"O.K."

So they separated, and searched for things to say.

It was possible for them to smile knowingly, because they knew that boys and girls on dates always went somewhere where it was dark, a patch of grass in the park where the bandstand was, or someone's automobile, to make love. They had kissed other people at dances.

They knew what to do.

But it wasn't what they wanted to do now; not that same way; they felt in their bones that if they went out now, one of two things might happen; either too little would come of it, or too much. It was too soon. They had some hovering wisdom that respected what they were feeling more than *that*.

And yet they knew too, that until they felt each other, and drank from one another's words, and heard one another's lost breath, they would be miserable.

Tomorrow night, maybe; the next night, perhaps; perhaps he could get the car from his father; they would then be free in a private world. Meantime, let them simply look.

2

Talking was discouraged in the reading room. One or two older people had apprehensively stared at them as if to frown on their first attempts at conversation. They whispered a couple of commonplaces. Martha looked around. There was a bookshelf with casual volumes in it, selected for browsing by the library staff. She nudged Bun, and he went over to the case, and got several books. They spent the first evening of their passion leafing through books, sitting side by side, commenting in croaking half-voice on whatever struck them as interesting. They were picture books…one of them contained colored photographs of scenery in the Southwest; another held plates of art masterpieces from the museums of Europe, where they met their counterparts in painted lovers by the grand masters, and found no reality at all in arrested attitudes of passion or in the elaborate nudities of heroic bodies; and another volume was an edition of Shakespeare's Sonnets, with illustration for each poem, in black and white lines, which made no sense to them. But when they came to this book, Bun took charge with some vitality, turned the pages until he came to something, and then put his finger down on certain lines, and looked at her direct.

She looked back, never caring if she ever saw the printed words, for the look on his face, which was all the poem she cared to read.

But he insisted with a nod, and when she bent her head down, he saw in her look what she had seen in his; and a rush of something in his blood made him swallow, he widened his thighs apart, and put his hand over his hair, and bent down with her to look at the printed words which for some reason he had never forgotten when his grandfather's books had first been unpacked, years ago. He must have been only eleven or twelve at the time. The big wooden boxes had come from Kansas City, after the old man's death. The day the boxes were opened, Bun had watched everything as it was unpacked, and the one book it had been his fortune to clutch for a few minutes, right away, was a much pencil-marked copy of Shakespeare's works.

"*It is the star to every wandering bark.*"

That one line was all he retained, but he suddenly knew what it meant, after a childhood of confused, attractive images established within him by the words.

3

So their first evening together was prim: leaving the library shortly before closing time at nine-thirty, they walked down the hill toward the tracks, and passed the YMCA, and stopped at the Mint Confectionery for some ice cream. Then he put her on a bus that would take her to the corner near her house, far out on the edge of town, and after watching the bus turn the corner, out of sight, with a sort of a *lump*, he guessed it was, in his throat, he put his hands in his pants pockets and walked down the street to the White Elephant where the click of billiard balls sounded past the open door, and went in to see what he could see. But it looked curiously sordid to him, the same scene where he had often breathed the smoky air with delight, and he felt now older than those boys and men bending over the green tables which were islands of light in a general gloom. Smiling absently at the proprietor, he turned around and started home.

He sighed deeply, as if something within him had awakened to make demands which he could not recognize, or appease.

Then a memory of his married sister's baby appeared to him for no reason that he could pin down, and how he'd held the child, and seen its nodding face so near his own, and how, holding the baby under its arms, he had let it trundle and dance on his lap, and at the memory of that gleeful striving without aim, Bun turned hot with what felt like joy and shame both, and entirely bemused at intimations of his next time of life, he began to run easily along the dark sidewalk, observing beautiful form, and once again becoming a power at the muscular art he knew better than anything else, so far.

XIII · THE DESTROYERS

I

Around ten o'clock Saturday morning, Wayne and Donald set out for the mesa on their bicycles. It was a warm spring day, like summer itself, and they had summertime in their veins, so that they had no idea of what they wanted to do, but had to go and do something. They spoke very little as they rode across town and approached the viaduct. Don carried his rifle across his legs. As they crossed Silver Avenue, they began to feel invisible, and squinted relentlessly at the sights of the streets. They could hear the trains working on the tracks over to the left two blocks away. They suddenly had a surge of delight in anything at all. They bent double and began to pump hard; their threadlike spokes made a silvery music and twirled with the blaze of sunshine.

A couple of blocks away they could see the old red sooty viaduct begin to rise between the buildings on the corners. One of the buildings was a bottling works. Its bricks were painted tan. Over the windows were carved cornices of blue stone. Built long ago, the edifice had an antique dignity. The boys always thought of it as a château, from a resemblance it had to a picture in their geography book. Only châteaux really had towers like the one that rose from the corner of the bottling works, a tin dome with a wrought-steel lightning rod and miniature dormer windows, where pigeons lived in irrelevant splendor. The second-story windows were blind with boards behind their dusty glass. The boys vaguely believed that suites of rooms elegantly furnished were hidden there, where crimes of passion, as they declared unknowingly, had been committed, by Monsieur le Vicomte, a generally useful character whom they had distilled out of the novels of Alexandre Dumas. Actually, years before, the building had been put up by a Missourian "from back East" to house himself and his family on the second floor; while below, he set out a line of general merchandise. He was a rich man for his time, and of polite tastes. What the château tower stood for, in him, cost him his fortune. As a little railroad town years ago, Albuquerque was not ripe for grandiose investments. Business moved along other streets. The Missourian sold his building and went back home. What he did and who he was Donald and Wayne had never heard of. "History" had nothing to do with *their* lives.

They charged around the corner past the château and began the ascent of the viaduct. It rose across the tracks. At one point of the climb, the mountains far across the mesa seemed, if you squinted, to be exactly on top of the viaduct's highest level. It was another of those days when the engine steam was golden with sunlight, and the sun was hot and comfortable on the bare head and the leather-jacketed back. The shadows of all the things they looked at were sweeps of rich black, and the lights of the day were sparkling with color in everything. Up on the mesa they could see the sand devils spinning in miniature whirlwinds before the pale-violet screen of the rock-crumpled mountains. Sweeping their sight from left to right, or north to south, they encompassed the immense plain and longed to be on it, lost and secret masters of such land.

They gained the summit of the viaduct, and saw there again the bolt which they had declared to be the one indispensable in its structure. They slowed down. The warm wind blew through their hair. Donald turned his hot black and white gaze on Wayne.

"There it is."

"I see it."

"I believe it is time to make an end of this wretched viaduct."

"Perhaps you are right. Certainly they could not follow us if it went."

"We would be miles away by the time they repaired it, or found another pass."

"It will take perfect timing."

"I have a perfect sense of timing. I know exactly how much time to allow between the last turn of the nut and the escape."

"They could see us from the château."

"Ha-ha. Much good that would do them. The tower stairs are steep, and we should be gone before they reached the courtyard. I should be willing to notify them first, even, and challenge them to prevent us."

"You recall that it was my calculations which betrayed this weak central point in the structure?"

"Indeed I do, mon cher confrère. You shall be decorated for your discovery.—Well?"

"Let us dismount."

They left their bicycles and bent down over the bolt.

"Seventy thousand pounds of frugal pressure, as I estimate it."

"Correct. I calculate that twelve turns will bring the last thread of the nut to the top. I believe that the adjustment will be so delicate that the least vibration to follow will release the nut and the bridge will fall."

"In other words, the very attempt of anyone to follow will bring it down?"

"Precisely, my dear Doctor."

"Ah, Monsieur le Vicomte, allow me to congratulate you."

"And now?"

"To work."

They pantomimed the reversal of the nut.

Their eyes were scowling and glowing, and their whole belief in their drama depended upon the intentness and the technique of their actions. They never mistook the imaginary for the real; they interchanged them deliberately.

"There!—Quick: careful!"

"Mount!"

They flew down the other side of the viaduct with the wind in their mouths, and as they reached the street, they paused and turned, and making with their mouths the sounds of wrench and crash and crack and splinter, they completed their imaginary destruction of the viaduct by agreeing that it was falling, it was breaking up, clouds of coal dust and slivers and drifted dirt were bellying up into the lovely hot sky.

And then for a moment they were abstracted and they gazed idly at the street, the occasional car going past, people down the block, without seeing them.

2

Then they started awake again, and turned their wheels around and headed up the long hill before them at whose summit they would find the mesa. They were hungry but did not know what for, and perhaps would never know. Long assuaged by play and dream, like the affair of the viaduct, they owned powers that were rousing toward acts.

They gained the crest; rose through the scattered streets of the town way out there where the wind blew so close and the tumbleweeds danced so free, and they paused to look back. Below them in the golden clarity lay the town of Albuquerque; far at the end of its streets went the river. They could see the silvery skeins of the water that took up so little of the wide sandy river bed, which was edged with the fragrant boskage of the *algodones*, the cottonwoods, so fresh and green in the baking forenoon.

"I wisht we had gone to the river instead. It is warm enough to go swimming."

"We'll go next Saturday."

"The current has changed the bank where we always go, did you know that? It moved right in under old man Rhodes's fence and took the ground away. There are the posts and the wires just hanging there."

"So much for old man Rhodes."

Above the river rose the sandy cliffs of the other side, and then the sand plains, and then the three volcanoes with their blackened cones that powerfully suggested the fires that had flowed there so long ago, and had died into rocky ash and turned to sand.

"Where shall we go now?"

"Let's ride out to the ranch."

"It's too far."

"No it isn't. We can eat our lunch there. We can look for snakes. You've got your .22."

"O.K."

They rode out the highway that reached through the mountains. Halfway there, they took a straggle of sand toward the left that made a lane through the dusty sweet-smelling desert bushes. Once on the mesa, which looked so flat from below in the town, they found all sorts of variations in the levels of the plain; riding up and down long hills, now buried in cool drifts of blue shadow, now emerging into sunlight where the rancher's road wound along the easiest slopes of the shallow hills.

3

Before long they could see the abandoned ranch. It consisted of a single-room dwelling of adobe and the long chicken house out in back, with its face made of dozens and dozens of little square panes of glass set in wood. The buildings stood on a raised table of windswept ground. Long easy slopes fell away to the common level of the plain in all directions. It was like an open stage, standing under the sunlight in the fragrance of noon on the mesa. Tumbleweeds were blown to the house and the long shed. Miniature dunes of sand swept up to the adobe walls. It was a forlorn place, yet to the boys it represented a rich property of which they had the control. Neither of them could remember it as it had been when Wayne's father was alive. If they could have recalled how it was then, they'd have been obliged to admit that it was a foolish venture, this chicken ranch, way out here away from everything and everybody, and no wonder the widow had been unable to sell or lease it when her husband died. She hadn't been out to inspect her property for years. She always thought of it as a valuable resource, and felt earnestly secure in the hope that if there were ever a costly calamity in the family, why, they could "realize" something on the ranch to tide them over. In time, she came to view the worthless investment as a piece of farsightedness on her husband's part, and would reflect devotedly that "Daddy was a very very clever man when he bought that place out on the mesa, never know when it'll come in handy." Meantime, it was left to the wind that blew away its adobe edges until they were rounded and flaked off in the drying heat.

But here the boys had a sense of property. Here they were alone in the midst of the teeming plain. The humble shed and the house could be a palace or a fortress to them; and after toiling so infinitesimally over the baking distance, they would have all the pleasures of reaching haven when they came to Mr. Shoemaker's investment.

They always watched for rattlesnakes, having heard years ago that there was a snake pit on the property somewhere. How far their land went nobody could say, because there were no fences. The boys were free to own as far as they could see.

Today, they set their wheels in the shadow of the house. The door was of solid boarding, and was padlocked.

"I didn't get the key from Mother."

"We won't want to go in, anyway."

They looked in through the window at the shadowed end of the house. It was all there, safe, a table with an oilcloth top, a broken rocker, a rusty stove. The other window was covered with tacked burlap on the inside.

"Shall we lunch yet?"

"Let's find some snakes first."

They put their bicycle padlocks on their wheels, and set out, walking to the east. Ahead of them the mesa was furrowed with lines of blue shadows from the high clouds, which made the ground look like a series of parallel valleys. They would imagine that in the next few minutes they would reach the nearest band of shadow; but they never did. The bright sun was on them all day.

They kicked up a little dust as they went, and they crushed the plants they walked over; they breathed the dusty fragrance of bruised desert grass, it smelled warm, part of the day, reminding them of what they had always known and owned of the country. They felt hollow with pleasure at the unconscious reminders of their freedom, their triumph of existence this near the earth.

They longed for a sight of the snake that was their superb foe.

"I believe we are coming into snake country now."

"Come on, we'll go more slowly."

They bent double, and went ahead peering at the roots of all the grassy clumps where in the noontime shadow they *might* see the clay itself begin to move and flow across their path, emerging from the cool blue into their dazzled vision as the clay-colored diamondback.

They were full of hope and yet of dread. Today for the first time they were armed for such a hunt.

"You'd better load 'er up."

"She is."

"Then cock 'er."

Click.

"May I try one, if we see anything?"

"S'sure."

Their teeth were almost chattering in the baking day.

"There's one!"

They went to their knees, staring, with their mouths open. But it was only a prairie dog's movement which they had seen, as the little thing scampered down into his hole. But their hearts beat and their spit dried as if they had seen the great snake itself; and how they viewed it in their thoughts came forward out of a long darkness of inherited fear and desire, so that each was a young Adam, hunting for the symbol he was at the mercy of in Eden.

Presently they came up to their crouching walk again and went ahead through the hard-caked dust of the ground.

"Listen!"

They froze and cocked their heads; but what had sounded like the first flicker of the rattles was the beginning of the upward grind of a locust, saluting the hot zenith with its song.

They grinned at each other and nodded, and went on. They felt superbly fit. The very agony of their caution made them sure of their prowess and their hunger for danger and destruction.

"There is a hollow place, look at the shadow on the side of the rise. I'll bet that's it."

"We'll come down on it from above. We could shoot right into it and beat a retreat back over the hill."

"If we had to."

They hurried in a wide circle to the top of the low rise where the silvery heat wavered in the air and made the deep-blue sky seem to glisten slowly. They had a bowel-hollowing excitement and were perfectly sure they had found the pit. They came down on their bellies very slowly and silently, looking on all sides for the enemy, for this was just such a hillside as tempted him to lie in the speckled shade of a hot sweet-smelling tuft of dusty grass. They must not dislodge any of the white alkali clay that was caked into little clods like chalky stones, for they might then roll down the shallow slope into the mouth of the snake pit, and stir up that terrible music which at one of its stages did sound so much like the shelled song of the locust.

4

Now they were so close that they had the flaking crust of the ground in their nostrils as they breathed. Right there below them was the pit. They could see its downward rim, and the bushes that grew there. There seemed even an old pathlike place which led down into the pit from the other side. The shadow hung immediately under them in the stand of noon. Tumbleweeds had blown into the pit, and the sand was modeled by the wind into body-looking shapes.

"Listen:" whispered Wayne.

They laid their cheeks down on the ground and closed their eyes to hear. There was a slight stir down below them, a whisper of movement, they could feel a faint hot breeze wander over their faces and wrists, and could not decide between sound and movement as to what they heard and felt.

There was that little faint hushed whisper or slide or scratch of something moving down there, and now they were terrified. They opened their eyes and looked at each other, and knew it. Donald's brown jaw was shaking his whole head because he had his teeth clenched. Wayne knew exactly how he was feeling, and why, and that they both agreed on what to do, regardless of how they felt.

"Let's go," he whispered.

They had one more pause for the savor of courage, and then more scared than they had ever been in their lives, they nevertheless scrambled around the edge of the pit until they could look straight down to behold what it held. When they saw, their eyes began to smart, and they felt their hearts beating for the first time, in big, slowing thumps. Tangled at the bottom of the sand pit was an old flag of newspaper which the hot quiet wind was moving against the weeds. There was nothing else there but the rounded sandy beds made by the sheltering rim, and the shadow of the miniature cliff lay there coolly.

Wayne slid down into the pit and took a box of matches from his pocket. He lighted the paper and danced back to the edge. The fire caught the tumbleweeds, and blew upward with hollow fury making black oily smoke in which the silvery heat and the orange flames spiraled together. It was like the relief they both felt, and it also burned away their disappointment.

"I bet they can see this smoke from the city!" said Wayne.

5

"I haven't shot my rifle yet."

"Save it for something good."

They started back. A vagrant noon wind was whipping up around them. They were nearer now to the sand whirlwinds which danced at freedom on the plain.

"I'm hungry."

"So am I.—Let's get our lunch."

The long shed of the chicken house concealed their bicycles from them, to which their lunch boxes were strapped. They hoped everything was all right, and still there, and began to trot toward the two buildings which from a distance were like little blocks of hot blue shadow set up on a disc of pouring light. In a moment, by silent agreement, they fell into a run, and raced across the undulating plain. They got hotter and hotter, and when they came around the chicken house, they were panting. The bicycles were there, safe, the boys stood in the enormous quiet grinning, and the wind gusted at their feet. One of the sand devils of which they had seen many all morning as they had toiled over the mesa came shooting dust ahead of itself and while they stood transfixed to see how close the thing would come, it came between them with a miniature blast. It funneled the dust high into the air and went shocking across the separated clumps of grass, and faced into the chicken house. There it changed its course and went rattling down the length of the shed, banging the loose panes in their faded white wooden frames. It was like a scale in music. The glass was all loose. One of the panes at the other end of the shed fell out and broke. In a second, the wind was gone. The sand devil left the earth and its funnel cloud simply drifted into the blue as a fading lift of dust.

The boys laughed at the wind, and spat the dirt out of their mouths, and rubbed their heads to free their hair of sand. They were charged, as if the whirling cone of sand had charged them electrically. Their eyes were blank and a little wild. It was the way ponies acted in funny weather, all stirred up when the wind pranked viciously down on the ground near them and screamed around in circles that would strike they never knew where.

They could smell the sweet hot ground, and they felt the sweat tickle and run inside their clothes.

"I'm going to shoot!"

"What at?"

"Anything!"

"There's a can."

"Here, you try it."

"No, it's yours."

"What'll I aim at?"

"There's a board sticking up on the chicken house."

"Hey!"

It was a command to watch. Donald set his rifle and laid his cheek down on the nut-smelling wood of the stock. He aimed at one of the panes of glass in the face of the chicken house and shot. The glass cracked and went.

"Hey!" said Wayne, but at the same time he did not know whether this was an objection. He put his hand out for the gun, and Donald gave it to him. Then he too took aim and fired and another pane of glass crashed to bits in the most instant reward. They fell on the ground on their bellies and rubbed themselves into the hot earth until they had comfortable hollows made and they set out to destroy the glass front of the empty and sand-blown shed where the glass was so loose that it rattled when the breeze blew.

An intoxicant wave of destruction swept over them. The gun cracked and the smell of the powder was like something that could make them drunk. Their faces got hot and their eyes glistened. They licked their lips and held the .22 shells in their teeth until they were ready each time. They traded the gun back and forth after each shot. It was a single-loader, the oily music of the bolt was a delight to hear, and they felt happier than they could ever remember. The glass began to lie all along the base of the shed, pale, water-colored splinters shining in the sun. They could hardly wait for their turns at the rifle. As long as they had any shells they must continue to break the glass. Their sense of power was a seasonal force; it had so long been latent; it was now so free.

6

They knew all the time that what they were doing was wrong. Their eyes told each other that when they looked to exchange the rifle. It was clear to them that they were destroying something that cost plenty of money, and that did not belong to them, and whose loss would trouble someone very much.

They fired and the glass crashed. The recoil of the gun was like a blow in return for what they did.

But they knew exquisite freedom in the act, and they went down the rows and rows of the little square panes until in a surfeit of wreckage, they were finished, and ready to think again, and not a whole piece of glass remained in the faded wooden squares of the chicken house.

They rolled over on their backs and stared at the sky. They still had the electric taste of the copper shell cases and the oily feeling of the lead bullets in their mouths.

"We're out of shells, about."

"Y'p."

"Do you like the little ol' gun?"

"She's a beauty."

"I wish we had something else to shoot at."

But this was not true, they both knew it, and said no more. They tasted folly now. They were shy about looking at each other, or the wreckage they had produced. How would they ever face Mrs. Shoemaker now; and where might they ever get enough money to replace the glass; what was such fun about breaking all those panes, now that it was done? Why did they have to go and do something so stupid for? Why had it seemed so different while the gun was shooting and the smoke was drifting so blue and so sharp-smelling in the hot day on the mesa?

"Are you h-hungry?"

"Are you?"

"Oh, sort of.—Not very much."

"Neither am I."

They went over to their bicycles in the shade of the house, got on, headed back toward the highway, and returned to town. Neither of them had ever thought much before about being good or bad, they had simply behaved one way now, another then. Now they were filled with and committed to knowledge of their own acts. They spoke very little; but they were dimly tried with recognitions of how people *were*, that they had always heard about, and neither of them knew what to do about it, and each searched for himself in the criminal foolishness of the mesa, and knew obscurely that something had happened *to* him rather than that he had *done* something.

When they got near home, they slowed down to separate, and before they parted, they impulsively shook hands, to preserve their league, after disaster.

XIV · THE EMPEROR'S NEW CLOTHES

I

What was guessed about life as it went past in the streets of a small town was often wrong, and hurtfully so; but sometimes it was true, and no less hurtfully.

Noonie heard that her husband was "seeing" Mrs. Foster. The gossip was as usual rather late; for by the time it had currency, Peter had given up going to call on Mrs. Foster. But it was almost as if there were a kind of collective intuition in the people, and as if they had become aware of something almost by waking up to it. Nobody really told them. Noonie got it by hints and solicitous comments and moments of false charm in which one woman would say to another how fortunate it was for such an interesting person to be in town, and to have met the one person who could probably speak her language here.

But it was all so vague that Noonie couldn't be sure. And even if she were sure, she said to herself, how had she the right to rebuke him?

What had she given to him which she had promised so long ago in Rochester, when everything had been so gay, and even a clever and outrageous creature like Lisette Kleitz from Albany could not swerve him an inch from his path? No, no, no, stormed Noonie to her heart. She wept when she was alone. She knew that the worst was true. She would castigate herself for daring to expect him to be more true than any other man could have been, and in a humility which exhausted her by its self-punishment, she would find a

certain peace at last. But it was always coming back to the realization that things were "not the same" that made her head throb with
pain, and her heart rise into her mouth, and her whole life seem a
shocking waste. One shred of determination she did cling to, and
that was that she would never let him see that she "knew." If he ever
found out that she "knew," then he would surely hate her for having
no more spirit than to suffer what was going on without proclaiming her rights.

The curious mixture of truth and nonsense; suffering and illness; something sweetly staunch and at the same time feebly hate-
ful; brought to the situation a focus of everything about Noonie as
she was at that time.

2

Peter hadn't seen Mrs. Foster for weeks. He was absorbed in forget-
ting all about her; the consequence was that everything reminded
him of her. He had no idea of the gossip that was going around. It
had gone around before about him, as it would about any other personable man who was also a physician, much in the public awareness,
his car recognized everywhere, his comings and goings at all times
of day and night both explainable and debatable. He was attentive
to Noonie, and was surprised to see how sometimes this seemed to
grieve her. (She was certain that he was concealing things by being
especially sweet to her.) He was working hard. Vaguely troubled, he
knew that every year had some times in it when a man didn't feel
his best, or up to himself, or confident and powerful. Times like
that passed. Nobody saw the effects of them. He had no patience
with a human temperament he often ran up against professionally—that which demands as some sort of obscure but tyrannical
right the optimum of happiness, health, or achievement, day in and
day out. Many invalids crippled themselves further by their rage
against fate when many of them could have accomplished a life's
plenty by demanding less of life. Nobody had a *right* to happiness,
he believed. Everybody had a right to try to *earn* it. He wished,
if there were to be happy endings for him and his, that they be

granted as the results of their own decisions. Decisions as to what to give and what to keep; what to value and what to sacrifice, the one compelling the other. Such a frame of mind reflected the position of his life now. The letter from Mrs. Foster brought back something he had given up.

3

Dear Peter Rush,

I am now out of reading matter. You brought me the most extraordinary things, and I am hungry for more, if you have the time and the inclination to lend them. I've been working very hard, and I am sure you have too, but if you can drop in any afternoon, I'd love to take on over a passage in one of the books you left with me... *The Western Attorney*, by that master-prig of all time, Elias Gray. I have been hugely amused at his airs and his judgments. He came out here nearly a hundred years ago and saw everything with the sniff of a Missouri intellectual. I'd like to know whatever became of him! He is detestable, and yet he is so sure of himself that he writes quite fully and frankly of himself and the result is, I feel I know him *well*. And knowing him *well*, *I* cannot help liking various little bits of him. Do you ever have this odd sensation? From reading, I mean?

I had the most casual note in the world from Dr. Treddinger, who wonders if I am prospering under your care. I do think you ought to come and tell me how I am feeling, so I can answer him properly.

Yours sincerely,
Molly Foster

When he folded the letter up he laughed at the fragility of certain resolves. She was vividly before him. He was still angry at her for never telling him who she was. But that meant he was cross at not having known on his own, and was just blaming *her*. He saw her repose, the white, faintly pinked cheeks, and her little mouth which she kept rouged, and which sometimes looked sad, he thought, when she was not speaking. She was so small, he remembered, when she put herself on the couch in front of her fireplace. But all this sounded very pink and white and frail and colorless if you left out her eyes. What blue fire he saw in them, deep down, the jeweled energy of thought and feeling, speaking to him, he was certain, of the same thing he had carried concealed since the very first day he'd seen her. Her eyes were large in her small face.

How on earth could he believe he knew so much about her when they'd met so little, and then spoken of everything but themselves?

He made up a package of books from his shelves way upstairs, and the day after getting her letter, he took them to her. There was every legitimate excuse for such a course; and the fact that he told that over to himself made it clear again that he was a shyster, dwelling on the plausible aspect of everything but truth.

He did make one concession to his resolve; his pique, actually. She'd said to come in any afternoon. He stopped at her house about eleven in the morning. If she were working, he would simply put the books in the hands of the Swedish maid, and leave them with a message. It was a hot morning, the light stood golden everywhere. Above the town, he could see the roofs glisten. Approaching the front door, he was stopped when Molly called to him from the shadow made by the living-room wing of the house. She was sitting in a deck chair, wearing black glasses, and she was holding a sheaf of typed pages on a lap board.

"Hello."

He turned.

They both knew instantly that they were cross with each other. She hated being interrupted at work. He hated being caught violating her conditions.

"Oh. You're there. I brought some books, but I thought I could simply leave them with Helga."

"Do come over. I'd be glad to take them.—I look frightful and I am furious with you for catching me this way."

"I'll run along. A million things to do."

"Million?"

"Dozen, then."

"What have you brought?"

She reached for the books.

"Some more diaries and so on. I don't imagine any of them will amuse you like Elias Gray."

"That man!" she said, setting her papers down on the grass next to her, and putting the books on top of them. "Will you stop for a cigarette?"

"I'm bothering you."

She slowly took off her glasses and set her small mouth in a speculative line. It was very deliberate, she looked prettier than he had ever seen her, this way, with her hair breezed about her face, and her cheeks reddened by the temper she saw in him and felt in herself. She got out her own cigarette and lighted it before she answered him. Then she said,

"There's something the matter."

"No there isn't."

He smiled grandly upon her.

"We've been frightfully polite before this, but today we're as polite as cats getting ready to fight.—I wish I knew what to say. It is true I hate to be disturbed when I'm trying to work. Maybe *I've* been rude."

He scoffed at this in a brief laugh.

He squeezed his eyes almost shut, looking at her. He wondered where the doctor and his patient had disappeared to. This was a new atmosphere today. He decided to be honest with her, and at once, he felt easy and unconcerned about what might happen.

"Well!" he said, nodding his big head slowly at her, and settling down on the warm grass, "I am furious with you."

"There! at last.—Why!"

"I suppose I feel duped."

"Duped?"

"Yes, duped. Here you let me come here and fumble along, talking to you about things that you probably see instantly, or know by intuition, and parade myself as a special soul who enjoys looking around *in back* of life, and one day I am told quite casually who you are, and what you do and how famous you are, and I suddenly feel like a schoolboy caught making up his recitation as he goes along."

"My *dear*," she said softly, leaning forward, her face waved over with blushes and misery. He was amazed at this reaction. "How frightful for you! I know how *vulgar* you must consider it. I couldn't very well hand you a brief autobiography, on arriving. It never occurred to me that:"

She broke off, and looked slyly at him. It was an urchin's face she made.

"—This will make it even worse," she said, mocking herself. "It never occurred to me that you *didn't* know all that, whatever it's good for. I thought you were being well-bred with me, and sparing me any direct reference to my sordid livelihood."

"I see. Well. Anyway, I didn't. And I suppose I felt clumsy and foolish when I found out."

"How?"

"My wife mentioned it. She was all of a dither."

"Oh."

"The whole town is."

"No, really?"

Her cool detachment irritated him again.

"And I feel with them that they have a right to be.—I certainly wouldn't begrudge them a little flurry of excitement if someone distinguished and beautiful and mysterious comes to town."

She threw her cigarette inexpertly on to the driveway. He said to himself that women should never throw anything. Then she leaned down toward him.

"Now please pay attention," she said. "Once and for all, let me say what it is *really* like, this trying to write books. I know, simply because I've had a share of popular success, what people think, and how they have a strange, almost silly awe, of anyone who, as they say, is a 'creator.' I had it myself when I was a child, going to sleep with my first scrawled notebooks under my pillow, and imagining how it would be to meet Marie Corelli. I've since found out. Actually, it is an arduous business, which makes hags of females, and short-tempered blusterers out of males. They are always having to question life in themselves. They often fear they haven't the answers which contain both truth and beauty. They beg their works to reveal likenesses to those of great masters who have gone before them, not remembering that a good book is first of all like no other by anybody else. They measure their successes by their own doubts, and their failures by their own certainties. They are wretched away from their works and plans, and they are ruthless and selfish and wretched *at* them. There is no more glamor or distinction about it in their own view than a plumber has, whom they envy because he can forget his plumbing when he's off the job. Their enchantment, and their rewards, come from something about their work which nobody else ever mentions, if they ever see it, and that is an occasionally granted sense of the universal in both beauty and evil. To sing a song, or to tell a tale, and so somehow tap that universal thing in the response of other people—this is about as close to giving thanks as an artist can ever come; for all great works of art are thanksgivings, in one way or another, for life itself. If you knew, too, how often people like me felt like swindlers when receiving applause and admiration from good people who have made a mystery out of the things we do! They have made it for their own delight, I know that, and often I have tried to believe what they have expressed so kindly and with such radiant virtue of association! How *moral* they have made me feel, at the very moments when they have enjoyed seeing me and my kind as escapes from morality, the morality of habit and duty and father and mother and children and kitchen and hope! So if all of this seems to you anything to have been impressed by, so that you had to be sulky over its discovery in my own hard-worked person, then I hope I have changed your mind.—Do you see, Peter?"

She sat back and looked at him.

He reached for her hand and squeezed it and began to laugh. He spread his legs out on the grass and rubbed his hair and sat up. He had diamond lights in his eyes from the tears of amusement over which he squinted in the sunshine that had moved over them shallowing the shadow of a while ago.

"Well, I'll call you Molly, too.—I am black and blue. If I'd never made you mad at me, I don't believe you'd ever've stopped being fragile and refined and exquisite with me. You're a fake. There's nothing delicate about your health. You're as strong as a horse. All writers are swindlers, then."

"They all invent ill health from time to time, so they'll have an excuse not to work today. The good ones never get away with it, to themselves."

He stood up.

"Well, I'll never ruin your morning again, but I'm very glad to've done it today."

"You might as well stay to lunch, now. I'll never get anything more done before noon.—Or do you have 'a million things to do,'" she added, smiling.

"I can't. I'm expected at home."

"Of course."

She looked at him quietly. She never mentioned his wife, in any way, inquiry, reference, anything. He vowed that next time they met he would deliberately talk about Noonie. He didn't like the idea of having one door leading to Noonie, in his mind: or heart: and one to Molly. Just as certainly, though, he knew Molly would prefer the two doors.

"Come in. I'll give you back the other books."

4

They went into the cool, dim house. She found the books on the long table behind the red velvet couch. He stood next to her. How cool. How gentle the air here, after the blaze of sun outdoors. He looked down at her. He was moved to her. His heart gave a thump. A cool, sweet lightness came into his arms. Oh, Molly, he thought. She turned and held the books to him, and looking into his eyes, she said,

"I never showed you the photograph of my Betsy, did I!"

She took up a silver frame from the table. The picture showed a serious child of fourteen, with straight silky light hair, standing in sunlight before a big tree, dressed in riding clothes, with a big collie in front of her slim boots.

"Your daughter?"

"Yes."

"Where is she?"

"At school in the East.—She's a darling. She writes me every day."

"I suppose her name is Foster?"

"Yes. She sees my husband's family in New York a certain number of times a year. I—Dickenson Foster and I were divorced four years ago."

"Isn't he terribly rich?"

She laughed.

"Westerners!" she cried. "I'll never get used to them. It's what so many want to know, but nobody else ever asks, right off.—Yes, he is. But it doesn't have anything to do with *my* life. Or Betsy's."

She said,

"Oh, there was one place in Elias Gray I wanted to point out to you: where is it: about the time he went to Chihuahua, and was taken to the *salon* of a famous female gambler. What a prig! My heart went out to her, after the way he spoke of her."

She ruffled the pages until she found the right one, and then she began to read aloud with a superior tone to suggest the character of the author of *The Western Attorney*:

"'I had not been long in Chihuahua City, whither I had traveled from Albuquerque in the company of an American trader in a train of six wagons, when I was informed that one of the sights of the place—otherwise a pretentious dust-heap—was a certain Doña Catalina Anonciación de Gutierrez. This female functionary, who would elsewhere have been notorious, was the chatelaine of a famous and elaborate house of ill repute, and was in the flower of her gifts as a gambling proprietress. With a certain temerity I will confess in the face of my reader's judgment that I agreed to go one evening in the company of my trading friend to observe the laws of social life as exhibited under the guiding genius of Doña Catalina, a confession I make thus boldly since her establishment housed, in addition to its other blandishments, the seat of such simple social commerce as one might otherwise find in the home of a leader of society.

"'Madame Gutierrez, because of her rumored proficiency many years before as a music hall singer, was given the soubriquet of "La Voz." This has the touch of the underworld, even in the States, where low characters are often said to be designated by nicknames illustrating capacities, traits or physical peculiarities. "La Voz," then, was a small female of uncertain age, fantastically painted as to face, and outlandishly garbed as to person. She was a past-mistress of those arts of insincere cajolery whereby wretched men are flattered into risking their money at gaming, and their souls at immoral traffic. She moved about her premises with a self-possession which I must confess impressed me at first as suggesting a certain grace. But her hands which I chanced to notice as they operated at one of the gaming tables were those of a greedy bird of prey; and any sympathy, or more properly, should I say pity, which I may have felt start up in me, at her self-condemned plight, lasted only so long as her pretensions to ladyship. She was evidently most popular with her visitors, who attended her *salon* in great numbers. I caught glimpses of her all evening, now (detestable habit which even respectable females share in here) smoking a cigarette with this man, or again, imbibing a potion of brandy with another. Our acquaintances of the evening all spoke of her with admiration, and seemed to base their regard on the oft-reiterated assurance that "La Voz" lived a life of the strictest propriety herself, and was never even known to look at a man save as an adversary at the gaming tables. When we were preparing to depart, we were given our *congé* by "La Voz" herself, quite as if we had been guests in a home of the most irreproachable *ton*. I am told that because of her wealth and general style of living, which is lavish, though hardly tasteful, she is one of the most influential and respected figures in the local society. The perception of such social differences as this, between our own fabric of decorum in the United States, and the essentially looser, less moral-minded scheme

of society in the Western provinces and Mexico, has, in itself, repel-
lent as some would find it, been of sufficient interest to justify my
foray into so inconvenient and unenlightened a region.'"

Molly slapped the book shut.

"The self-righteous fool!" she said. "Doesn't he make you furious?"

"I remember that book.—La Voz was a famous lady. She was
here, you know, for a while."

"In this town?"

"So they say.—Nobody knows where, or exactly all about it, but
when the American Army came here in the forties, she was supposed to've been here. I've wondered about her. Elias Gray certainly
allows her very little, doesn't he."

"Well, the proper fate has overtaken him.—Anybody who sets
out to raise himself at someone else's expense, even by complacent
contrast, like Gray with Madame Gutierrez, ends up by looking
very cheap in the end.—When you write novels, you have to be so
careful about taking sides with your characters. They have the odd-
est way of confessing what your vanity would conceal.—Children
sometimes fail to see our happy disguises, too. They don't see the
Emperor's new clothes at all. My Betsy was like that when she was
younger."

Peter took up the frame from the table and looked at the young
girl again.

"I have only one son," he said.

Because of the sound of his voice, she was moved to put her
hand on his arm, briefly. She said to him, in her mind, You will
never be able to conceal anything, will you? This made her heart
tumble, for the betrayal, the honesty, the innocence it carried about
him to her. She saw herself acting "forwardly," and she began to
color again, in her cheeks, and she took her hand off his arm. Her
hand was trembling. She was powerfully moved. She felt a little sick
and dismal, to be so at the mercy of—of him, or anyone. He looked
gravely down at her. He knew he had given away more than he'd
meant to.

He said silently, What a mess.

Out of nowhere, it occurred to him to fend off this moment by saying,

"Have you ever driven up to the cliff ruins of Hano?"

"No.—It was one of the places to which Judy Bridges and I had planned to go after my car arrived from the East. But we never've done it. Judy hates motoring, ever since her ambulance days in France, in spite of everything I can say to her about setting out to *tour away* her dislike of it.—For the wrong reasons, you know, she keeps all sorts of troubling things alive. But she won't go."

He watched himself think it up, and savor it in imagination, and conceive how she would do about it, and say to her then,

"Would you go with me, someday, pretty soon, when I get sort of a gap in my schedule? We could leave in the morning and be back by dark, or even a little before.—It is a fascinating drive, by back roads, mostly, but when you get there!—I couldn't possibly describe it. I haven't been myself for years and years. I'm about ripe to go again."

Yes, he thought, perhaps doing things, and having something to show off, and lecture about, would be the way. He meant that it might be the way to skirt the sweet peril he was sure of now.

"I will go," she said. "Even if Judy won't. Yes. It will be fascinating."

They were then at some sort of delicate peace, agreeing to be together again, and having made no avowals concerning that which they both felt sure of, that it existed; but which they were unsure of, as to what they must or must not do.

He nodded and said he would let her know. Arming his books, he went out and drove off downtown. The hot noon wind rippled the pages of her manuscript on the grass outside. She suddenly remembered it, ran out to gather it up, and was smitten in her breast by the way she spent hours inventing what happened to people. She made almost a prayer that her inventions might come close to the truth of such things as she was feeling now, and that they have the courage to betray her very self, if need be.

XV · THE KISS

I

The young lovers met again at night, under a street lamp on the library corner, with its globe up among tree branches, lighting the leaves with the freshest green, and sending down to the grass and asphalt ground a ring of pale light in which they stood, waiting for the bus that ran up the hill toward the mesa. All around the tree, and themselves, was nighttime; and in the very center of that vague dark world were the ring of light, the emerald canopy of leaves, and their two figures.

They said they would not go into the library this evening; rather, ride out to the end of the bus line, and take a walk.

The bus ground its way up the hill, past the hospitals, the tuberculars' bungalows with canvas curtains inside screens, past the buildings of the university at the crest of the hill, and out a way on the graveled highway that led to the mountains.

At the end of the line, they got out. In silence, they began to walk down a street toward the darkness. There were a few houses scattered around on the mesa. If they turned to look toward town, the lovers could see the skillet of light that lay down on the plain that led to the river. But they did not turn. They saw a street lamp, a single globe of light hanging from a wire strung between diagonally opposite poles, at a far corner. This was their objective, by common agreement. The night was warm. Far beside them as they walked lay the rocky shadow of the mountains. Over them were the stars. A car went by now and then. The silence in their heads was about to break of their desire and their desperation. Martha knew that the higher courage had to be his, when the time came; and so she spoke now, and it cost her a heavy beat at the heart, to hear herself making trivial words, clothing passion, as it were, with propriety.

"—I spent the afternoon writing letters."

"You *did?*" he asked in disproportionate surprise.

"I certainly did. I must've written half a dozen."

"I think that's *perfectly remarkable.*"

"Oh, no it isn't, not at *all*, I often write eight or ten a day. For *that* matter."

"You *do*!"

His tongue almost cleaved to his mouth.

"And I typed them all, without looking at the keys."

"Not at *all*?" he asked with ghastly roguery.

She felt her jaw tremble as if she were icy cold.

"Well, just enough to be *sure*, when I was *doubtful*."

"Oh, I *see*."

Bunny laughed uproariously. She pinched his arm.

"Sshh! People will *wonder* what—"

But she herself began to laugh, and took his arm, bending over as if she were choking.

Nobody was around.

They had walked into the influence of the single street lamp, and looking around them, they saw no houses. It was a new real-estate development laid out in hope rather than in cash.

In the light, he looked at her.

She looked off into the darkness.

The street ended where they stood.

As if pushed by the idle little wind on the mesa playing in the evening, they went on past the end of the street, where the country faded in, and the sandhills were undisturbed, and the starlight began to make its faint show.

2

Neither of them ever forgot the place. Years later, when the streets were paved out there on the mesa, and families lived in the houses set so near to one another, and radio music drifted from one window to the window of the house next door, and the big planes heading for the airport came beating their way over the houses leaving a wake of tumbling sound, and children of tonight were citizens then, years later the edge of the sandhills in the starlight would come back to them in dreams or reminders in their experienced lives.

He first of all did a delicate thing, which made her heart beat, but not from fear. He took her fingers and one by one set their tips on his lips, as if to acquaint her with him. He could not have said why he did this. He hardly knew he was doing it, in the sense that he would know his own more prosaic acts. It was a poetic animality that moved him.

Then he knew in the pulse that they remembered how they looked, he and Martha Shoemaker, whom he had seen for years in perfect indifference; and he set his legs and put his arms around her sloping back, and bent down and kissed her on the mouth, and took what he gave.

She seemed to faint in his arms; and as if to bring her back against him, he pursued her with his lips, and she returned, never able to tell him or anybody else how far she had fled, and how swiftly she came back again.

In the whole evening they hardly said fifty words.

When he let her go, they were shaking, and she took his hand and pressing it urgently, and keeping it by her in the darkness, by her side at her breast, under her arm, she hurried them along, walking back to the highway, where the busses ran, which they must find, and on which they must ride home at once, coming into the area of electric light and peopled streets and cars going around corners making their tires whine.

He wanted to know if she was sorry, and she could do no more than squeeze his hand in anguished tenderness and look at him and then look away again.

He wanted to hold her again, and kiss her no matter where they were; her puzzling behavior was entirely unlike anything he had ever known before. He worshiped her for being so agitated; he sorrowed to know if he had hurt her; and from her hand on his, he knew how much she loved him. Her maidenliness tormented him as no practiced loving ever had with some of the girls he knew.

They rode to her corner, and he got out with her; but she wouldn't let him come to the house. She kissed him on the cheek and whispered that she would be at the library tomorrow night, and left him. He was dizzy from what she gave him. It was actually less than many another encounter he had known; but the feeling she conveyed—this was something entirely new.

He was longing and content in the same breath. He shook his head and said to himself with comic sobriety that he sure had it bad. He wanted to take her head in his hands and stroke her hair softly and vow that he would take care of her. At the idea, tears came to his eyes, and a plunge of rage in his breast made him suffer for what he would do to anybody who knowingly or unknowingly should ever hurt her.

3

When Martha got home, Wayne was in his bed, and called to her, but she ignored him, which was nothing new. She went to her room, and pulled the curtain which was all the privacy she had in her own little doorway, and lighted the kerosene lamp by her mirror. She had framed the mirror in pleats of white cloth with large green satin bows at the top corners. She was still trembling. She looked at herself. She said to herself that she was almost *sickened*, she could taste it yet, she could feel it now, the wetness of his mouth, the *otherness* of it, the invasion it made of her strictest self. On her breast she could touch the depth to which she had been stabbed by her heart when he had kissed her.

She went to her washstand and took a glass of water and some mouthwash and rinsed her mouth out and sought to recover herself from what she had done in the darkness on the mesa, saying to herself that it was only a kiss, dozens of kisses, and nothing like this, they had meant nothing, why should this one?

Unable to answer, she sat down on her bed which also had white pleats and green satin bowknots, for which she had saved up all she could afford for seven months last winter, and asked herself what he had seen of her in that moment; for it seemed to her that she had given herself wholly, and shown herself entirely to him; to a man; and that the Martha Shoemaker who had ridden in miserable eagerness up the hill on the bus was a child, and indeed, not even related to the Martha Shoemaker who had come home with his hand in hers, and his flavor and essence on her lips and on her fate.

Whatever he had seen, in the knowing blindness of lovers, it was his, now.

Was it only last month that she had spoken to him in Summerfield's?

How much can happen in so short a time! she mused. She felt wise, womanly and passionately dedicated to a privacy that was almost the same thing as virtue; and would defend what she now knew against anyone's *wondering*.

And then she was ashamed of washing her mouth out, and decided that it was the final act of the girl she had once been… She would never, never tell him, or anyone else, about it; of that she was sure.

XVI · HALF WAS LEARNED
AND HALF WAS DIVINED

I

Willa Shoemaker saw little enough of her son Wayne, and had to come to her late knowledge of him by flights of intuition, at moments when she was home from the Harvey House dining room. Every time there was something troubling him, he took the most elaborate pains to conceal it, and usually resorted to carrying on his puckered brow a series of bored wrinkles, and to whistling a little tune without making anything but a musical whisper. These measures gave him away. Willa had come to know them as signals of distress in her boy's inner life. But the time had long since passed, she knew, when she could take him on her aching legs as she sat before the *Spirito Santo*, which in lieu of a hearth was the family center, and rock him on her thin breast, and enfold him in protection from whatever it might be that troubled him.

One night she came home late, as usual, and found her house asleep. The children had left the lamp turned low in the living room, where they also cooked and ate, and she settled down to the Albion *Evening Recorder* with her glasses and a box of crackers and a mug of milk, preferring these things to eat at home over the "menu" food she could have had free at the Harvey House. It was a fine night out, glistening with moonlight in early spring. She had caught the last bus home. She was tired but richly and virtuously so, and let her weariness hang on her limbs like a rug. She thought she must have dozed over her week-old news from "home," the Yeager place had burned down on the edge of town, Martin Yeager was away at the time, and Grace and the three children were alone in the house, the paper said, when the flames cracking awakened Tommy, the youngest, and he aroused the rest of them, and they all got away safely, but the house was gone. She remembered—red brick and a white square tower full of cobwebs, they used to go up into it in the summertimes, Martin Yeager was at school with them all, and the rich man's son of the bunch, and now without a house, but's not's if he couldn't build four more just like it and *never miss it*, still he was a good boy, she remembered exactly how he looked twenty years ago, and saw him in her musings as he would return home from his trip and find his red-brick house blackened to the ground which was so green all around, a stocky and merry-faced boy, Martin, with black hair, and something in his eyes which even now made her stir and imagine she was blushing, for the way she used to think of him and the things he would say, and *mean*:

But of course long ago, when she was a girl, she had never had any doubt about who it was she loved. It was Freddy Shoemaker, from the very first. Martin was Freddy's best friend. He was like an old pillow somebody kept around, a comfortable boy, always merry, and watching everyone cleverly to see what they would like to do. And when he knew, why, then he was ready to go and do it too. When Willa and Fred were married, Martin Yeager thought up all the jokes and the hectic things for everyone to do, and she had always been certain that Martin had kept Freddy from getting drunk ("spiflicated") the night before the wedding, for which she had always been grateful. How could she ever explain some things?

When she and Freddy ran away to the buckboard, the last thing
she did was hug Martin and she never forgot how the tears came
to her eyes, and she laughed, and the tears ran down her face, and
she cried out that she was so happy! Then she and Freddy drove
away to everything that had happened because it was meant to
be...

An odd thing! she would sometimes think busily, with no
pangs, how much she thought about Martin Yeager later on! She
never felt disloyal to Freddy's memory in doing so. She never felt
that way about Martin. He was simply a very old friend who was
now married, and had his own family, and was keeping right on
being rich and taking care of the money his father left him back in
Albion and being a good Catholic citizen. She sometimes imagined
how it would be if they were ever together again, and she freely felt
critical of Grace, the woman Martin had married, and all her do-
ings, though she hadn't seen Grace *since* then....

And yet, at the very same time when she would be living with
animation an inner kind of life over Martin Yeager—and yet whenever she thought of happiness or hunger, worthwhileness or doubt,
it was always her poor dead Freddy she thought of; for it was he
from whom she'd learned tire meanings of these words. His flesh
had taught her so, and his notions, too.

But she could not help dreaming of what might have been, or
might someday still be, through her daughter Martha and one of
the Yeager sons.

It was, this double life of memory and desire, the compact in
her self of the timeless and the placeless: half was learned and half
was divined, and the whole was a dear possession.

2

The paper slid from her lap with a hard whisper, and she came out
of dozing to hear something else. It was Wayne, muttering in his
sleep, and she tiptoed to look at him on the sleeping porch, where
the moonlight bounteously lay upon him through the screens. He
was moving obscurely under his blankets, and his face was ghostly

with distress, his mouth open, his fingers walking under his chin. He made no words, and she was frightened, yet as she stood there, she calmed her heart and said to herself that he was Wayne her baby, and not to be afraid of this visitation that made him seem so far from her as she stood and watched him; and her eyes swept his length on the bed, and she could hardly believe he had grown so big, and she asked God to let him sleep in peace. It was simply an answer to what she held of him in her heart that, hardly had she made the prayer, than Wayne seemed serene again, and cheeked heavily down on his bed in long exhausted breathing.

She watched him for another moment, then left him, and said to herself that she had seen for days how disturbed and warningly indifferent he had seemed at home. The little incident had exhausted her, too; and she made her way to her bed in the built-on lean-to at the street end of the house, and without lighting her lamp, she laid herself down, and fell asleep.

A dialogue of dream selves asked her for Wayne. One said,

"Never change, you are my baby, you must never leave me. What would I do without my baby? Everything you need I am here to give you, do not betray me, do not change the look in your blue eyes, do not hold your little hands away from my breast, I know each one of those ten little fingers, and they have hurt me but they have needed me."

And the other said,

"*Let him go.*"

"No, no, he is my baby, he will suffer so if he grows up and goes away to life."

"*It is the only way to let him know anything. He must pull out his roots and take them along with him, and that will hurt. But his legs grow long and his jaw gets square and his fingers are big and tender; not little and ruthless any longer.*"

The one cried on in her dream,

"I did not bear him to have him grow and leave me."

Replied the other,

"*He has already left you.*"

"No, no."

"Yes, he is already a discoverer, and kicks in his dreams against what he now knows. Standing to watch him as he slept you already knew this too."

The one within her seemed to sigh, and say,

"So it was. I sorrowed to see him weep in his sleep, and I could not reach him to comfort him."

The other within her said in a victorious and easing power,

"You will give him to joy as well as to trouble, when you let him go. Remember that. It is a worthy thought to awaken on."

She awoke, the moonlight was white outside, and lay like snow on all it touched. She had a dim memory of what had possessed her before she awoke, and she felt her face where she had wept silently asleep. But she couldn't imagine why she had wept, and concluded that she had yawned, for a deep peacefulness lay over her and she felt no longer tired. Listening for Wayne again, she heard nothing, and she smiled and meant to herself that he would run into troubles soon enough, but he would have to learn to handle them himself, and besides, think of all the joys of growing up and being a man and knowing life and having a family himself some day, they would all be pretty children, and *he* would know then what it meant to lie awake nights and worry, and *worry* over your children, bad enough to have to work hard all day, back and forth, back and forth, still, worth it, when you would fall asleep like this, and be oh so happy, with everything secure about you, *how Martin Yeager used to laugh without making a sound, like to bust, Grace always was crazy about him.*

She slept again.

3

By morning, there was no memory left of what had possessed her during the night; and she was brisk, a little breathless, comically sharp with her children, getting them both started for the day.

XVII · AN OLD ENDURANCE

I

The hospital of which Peter was senior surgeon had been established long ago in the eighties by an order of nuns who still ran it. It was a faded, rose-brick building of three stories with a white pillared portico. On its hillside above town, just below the mesa, the sisters had coaxed green grass and shady trees out of the sand. It had walnut window casings, many of them rounded at the tops, and its rooms were old-fashioned with plaster moldings and high ceilings. The public reception halls and rooms were caverned with shade, and were now furnished with a sort of itchy elegance of the period of 1910. Every ten years the rooms were done over completely. It was about time for another refurbishing. The objects that would not change were the enormously enlarged photographs of the Archbishops of Santa Fe, in full canonicals, which hung in the reception room, and the framed illuminated parchments with papal blessings from the successive pontiffs, sent all the way from Rome.

The nuns were efficient. Their hospital made money. A fund was lying by which would soon be large enough to build a completely modern annex to the institution. Meantime, they did with what they had. Doctor Rush was given anything he asked for for the operating room. He got on famously with the sisters, and they felt they owned him, and often spoke of him as "such a *boy*, to be so *able*," which had been true of him say fifteen years ago. But the sisters were always long on traditional matters, anyway, and he would be considered boyish as long as he worked under their auspices. He was not of their religion, which they forgave often in arch little pokes of humor in his direction, a wistful recognition that God's goodness extended everywhere. For his part, he often said that if he *had* a religion it would be that of the hospital where he spent so much time. He understood well enough what a priest said to him once: "You have a religion, all right, Doctor. I doubt if you and I would quibble over anything much more than vocabulary." They laughed heartily, and meant to each other that all services to the proper affirmation of life eventually met in a philosophical perspective.

The sisters were proud of Doctor Rush. He had been identified for so long with Saint Joseph's that they always assumed as a matter of course that he would be a part of any great occasion, such as the silver jubilee of the Sister Superior, which was held this year.

A whole day was set aside for the celebration, which was made august by the presence of the Archbishop of Santa Fe, who came down in his black limousine the night before, spent the night in the rooms always reserved for him at Saint Joseph's, and pontificated at a solemn high Mass early the next morning. The Sister Superior was crowned with a silver wreath, which she wore all day. Presents and telegrams arrived all day long. Her married sister from Des Moines was there, and was much made over by all the other nuns. An atmosphere rarefied by the simplest joy and charity filled the staff all day. Irritations were forgiven, and favoritisms erased. If Sister Superior sometimes did seem cold and distant it was today understood to have been simply the nature of her position which made such an attitude inevitable, at times. Twenty-five years! Think of it! And the long distance calls from the Mother House in Chicago, and the purse sent by the school children of the parishes, and the rosary from Rome, and the morocco leather album of testimonials from classmates at the convent so long ago, and the moving picture camera to take pictures with *yourself*, and the machine to show them with, and the set of altar linens made by the children at the orphanage and presented to Saint Joseph's chapel in Sister Superior's name, and the garland of Masses promised by Sister Superior's brother who was a Jesuit missionary in Alaska, and most exciting of all, the banquet in the evening at which the Archbishop presided, with "Sister" on one side of him, and Doctor Peter Rush on the other...

The patients' dinner hour was set ahead thirty minutes so that the big room with the white pillars and the opalescent glass bay window with the ferns banked in it could be made ready for the celebration dinner, which was ready at seven-thirty.

The nuns outdid themselves in the arrangements. The table was one continuous plateau, making a large m-shape with square corners. It was lighted by candles dipped in silver paint, and held by silver sticks. A mound of roses made a bank down all the table, which glittered with silver dishes, icelike crystals, gnarled silver knives and forks and spoons, all the treasure which the nuns reserved for only the highest occasions. There were heaps of candies and nuts and there were place cards hand-painted in water colors. At "Sister's" place a silver basket held all the telegrams of congratulation which had been coming all day. Selected ones were to be read aloud later by the Archbishop himself.

At his place there was a throne chair upholstered in red velvet, and topped with the arms of the archdiocese. A velvet footstool was waiting for him under the table. His napkin was tied with three yellow roses. Everyone else had pink ones. The papal colors were yellow and white, and everyone, except the Doctor, understood and commented upon it. The tone of the occasion reminded Peter of a cross between a children's birthday party and a wedding jubilee. He was a little embarrassed at first by the innocent exuberance of all the sisters, and amazed at the labors they had expended. The ceiling was tented with streamers of white and yellow satin ribbon. The walls were hung with sacred sodality banners glittering with silver-gilt embroidery and fringe. The air was full of little cries of simple joy from the nuns, whom he knew better in their other selves, quick, determined women who did their best to lessen suffering among the living.

2

But if he was embarrassed at first, at what seemed to him in a pang of pity an over-organized expression of joy, he lost that feeling when he saw the look on the Archbishop's face. The prelate was a tall, heavy man with a big face and a big nose and a big mouth, and light-blue eyes. His hair was graying, but he looked only middle-aged. He wore glasses. This evening he had on his purple moiré mantelletta and white lace surplice, and his magenta skullcap. It was a full dress affair. Peter was in his squarely cut tail coat which he had not worn since 1915 when he had read a paper on thoracic surgery in St. Louis to the American Medical Association. What Peter saw in the Archbishop's big amiable face was an amused and yet grati-fied look of agreement with how everybody felt. It was as if he, too, was touched by the enthusiasm of the occasion, and yet wise enough not to despise anything that innocently made anyone happy. His eyes were shrewd enough, Peter decided; and yet they were also full of liveliness and tolerance. And he had the friendly knack of taking homage at its true value, and that was, according to the pleasure it gave the giver; not the receiver.

After a little while of an official grace by the Archbishop, and flurried exclamations with table neighbors about the "exquisite" ap-pointments, and exchanges of clever place cards, the party settled down. The speeches were to follow the dinner. Peter had a sinking of the stomach when he thought of his, and what he would manage to say.

"Do you ever get over feeling awful before you have to make a speech?" he asked the Archbishop.

"Nev-er?" said the Archbishop, turning on him with light-blue recognition. He spoke with the flattest and slowest of accents, Mid-dle Western and somehow disarming, in a man of power. His words rose and fell in a sort of arch simplicity. "Now I have made? myself a the-ory aboutt-it."

"What is that:"

"I belieeve my stage-fright is *always?* use-ful. It makes me give a better speech? to the exact de-gree of how? frightened I am, be-fore."

"That could certainly be. Maybe I can kid myself into that, too."

"I often kid myself, Doctor,? but I al?-ways admit it to myself when I? do so."

"Sister, did you hear that? The Archbishop admits that he kids himself, at times."

"Oh, Doctor, how can you say that!"

"He'ss right, Sister? but I ad-mit it privately? first."

They laughed politely with each other.

The Archbishop then said,

"I love slang. It is a relief? to use it, the Americans are won-der-ful with it."

This had a faintly foreign timbre to it. Peter smiled at him, and said,

"Did you have foreign parents?"

"Yes, I did. I was born in Chi-cawgo. Bohemian stock. How did you know?"

"Just a little hint, in your speech, somehow."

"Is that your hobby? Most interesting."

"No."

"What *is*?"

Well, what was. He hadn't thought of it as such. Probably it was his collection of books and—and *places*, in the history of his home town.

He told the Archbishop that.

"Places? Yess. History is always? alive, isn't it."

"I grew up in this town, went to school here, and when I came home from interning in New York, I was so glad to be back that I said to myself there must be something behind all the way I felt. So when I began to have a little time, and a little extra cash now and then, I began to get books. I mean the old ones, as many as I could find, and afford, by the old fellows who wrote what they did them-selves, when they first came to this country."

"Wouldn't it be? fine," said the Archbishop, "if everybody loved his homeland as? much as you do. My! What citizens we would have! wouldn't we."

"Oh, I don't know.—Yes, I imagine so.—But in the places where I was a boy, somebody long ago was a man, working to use the wilderness."

"M'm."

The two men, both powers, in their way, were a little shy, for a moment, at the almost poetic terms their thought was taking. Then the prelate went on:

"You know? We are gathering all the parochial records in all? the little churches of the archdiocese."

He added that he was having a vault built for such precious records in Santa Fe. It was a work that should have been done long ago. But there was still time to save a lot. And who knew what they would reveal of the intimate life of the Spanish generations when scholarship was able to study them?

There was one little scrap of brownish paper, the Archbishop declared, that was to him the most remarkable and touching document in the whole lot so far catalogued. It was a letter, written in the winter of 1598, in Spanish, of course, from an encampment somewhere near here: somewhere in the vicinity of Albuquerque itself, as a matter of fact: written on Christmas Day in 1598, by the father of a child born the night before. The letter went to the Captain-General de Onate at the pueblo and capital city of San Juan, telling of the birth, and the quality of omen it had, Christmas Eve, mind you, the anniversary of the birth of Our Lord Jesus Christ, and so far as anybody knew, it was the birth of the first child among the new settlers who colonized New Mexico that year.

"I have often? wondered ex-actly where the place was!"

Peter was stirred by this discovery. His eyes sparkled and he illustrated by his enthusiasm what the sisters always meant when they called him "boyish." He asked if he might see the letter some time. The Archbishop answered that if he came to Santa Fe, he could see it any time. Or better still, meantime, a copy could be sent down by the first post after the Archbishop's return to his office.

He said it would interest the Doctor especially, from a medical standpoint, too; because the letter reminded the Captain-General that the writer and his wife, their servant, and a soldier, had been left behind to camp because the woman, in a difficult pregnancy, could not travel any farther for fear of dying. She was not strong, and they all preferred to risk the strangeness of the country than continue the racking journey by oxcart, with its day-long discomforts. So they had stayed behind for several months, and the child had been safely delivered, and as soon as they could travel again, they would overtake the colony at San Juan, where the baby could be baptized, and the Captain-General himself could be its godfather, which the writer prayed he would agree to do.

"If you will send me the letter, I'll go and find the place, if there is any description at all in it of where they were."

"There might be a hint?"

"I'll find it. It must've been somewhere on the road to the north, there are only a couple of ways the old road could've gone."

"You find it for me. I will be much? moved to know where the first soul was born not a stranger to this land."

<h1 style="text-align:center">3</h1>

A rustle in the banquet room brought them both back to the occasion. Something was coming. The nuns knew it, and stirred at their places. They were like pupils in school, sharing a charming joke which excluded the teacher. They bent their hooded faces to each other, and the sibilants of their speech made a little flight of bees through the room, as they cautioned each other to "watch S'st' S'perior" when the doors opened and the cake came in.

This proved to be an enormous dome of pastry, borne by four orphan girls on a huge breadboard wreathed in smilax. Twenty-five silver candles blazed away on the iced dome, which was garlanded and studded with sugar sculptures, and the date, and the name of the recipient. Everybody stood up and clapped, and began to sing in fervent stridency:

> "Holy Day, with joy we rise,
> And sing our praise to thee.
> Let our song reach to thy skies,
> And let us happy be."

After that there was small chance for further conversation. Speeches followed, the reading of the telegrams, the playing of jokes, and finally the staff's gift to their head, a sumptuous silver crucifix mounted on an ebony base, and draped with a little rope

of fresh violets. This reduced Sister Superior to happy tears. The
woman before whom they all trembled in official life, in tears, like
anybody else! It was almost too much, as a spectacle, and the emotions of sympathy changed the tone of the party. The Archbishop
turned it all to laughter again when he rode over them with his rich
voice, saying that they must watch out, or they would have him
weeping too.

Peter, when it was all over, said to himself that he was glad he
came; not only for the conversation with the Archbishop, but also
because if he had sent regrets, which he had considered doing, he
would have put a blight over the party by not realizing how important it was to the fifty or so women in the room, all of whom seemed
so full of joy. He preferred not to think of his own part in the pro-
gramme, the speech he had given through six foolish minutes, as
he recalled. But they had applauded him fondly, and he supposed it
could not have made much difference what he said, they just wanted
him to *take part*, they were all tipsy by then, anyway, with excitement, and food, and candy; candlelight; the break in the discipline
of hospital routine.

4

Two days later, the letter came from Santa Fe. The Archbishop sent
a translation into English of the original letter, and also included a
fairly clear photostatic copy of the old document.

> To the Captain-General and Governor,
> Sr. Dn. Juan de Oñate, at San Juan.
> Excellency:
> In the name of the Father and of the Son and of the
> Holy Ghost, Amen.
> On the Feast of the Nativity of Our Lord, in the val-
> ley of the River of Our Lady, near the black mesa which
> you will recall, we have all stayed since our company left
> us to pass onward to the North, owing to the feeble con-
> dition of my wife who has now been happily delivered

of a son, last evening, with much trouble, but eventual safety. My servant will bring you this news by his hand. I will keep the soldier Ruy Martinez de Quevedo whom you so well ordered to our protection. We have had no worries from the inhabitants. We are almost at home here; having set up walls of earth against the weather, which comes off the black mesa above us. But the fall of rocks where we all encamped together provides natural protection. There are many trees which we can use for fuel. My wife is weak but safe. My son is your first native colonizer, surely. I pray you with my wife to act as godfather when we are able to set out to join you and the rest. We are in a fine place for a city, details of which I will report. When I am able I intend to return here and set up a shrine to the Holy Nativity on this spot where our fears have come safely to such blessed issue. Nearby there is a protrusion of yellow soft rock from which blocks could easily be cut. Our horse and our burro forage freely, but suffer from the cold which has been extreme for two days, with snow falling above us on the mesa, and at times blowing down over our shelter. But I have kept the fire alive for weeks, and have traded for extra bedding with some Indians nearby, who have let us alone otherwise, though I believe we are watched from a distance. They are good people, and I have the idea that they have been waiting for us to come, with the word of God. It was snowing at dawn this morning when we awoke. I, my servant and the sergeant all knelt together by the bed and recited prayers to celebrate the Nativity. When we looked out it was but a curtain of white that we saw. But we were never prey to the terror of solitude, for truly we were not alone, but in the company of God, who mercifully blessed the life we all attended here since November. I am restless to join you and resume my duties. I hope my steward is attentive to my wagons and possessions, upon which at your will you must surely and freely draw as suits the need of the colony. We will come to you in about a week, unless reverses visit us, which God forbid. My oxcart is now in good repair and excellent comfort for wife and infant. We have made a covering of skins. There are many beavers on the river to the west of us, about two miles. Given in homage, this 25th day of December, 1598, in the kingdom of New Mexico, at his camp, by

José Diego de Nájera
Captain of the Governor's Army
and Commissioner of Deeds and Titles,
by Patent of His Majesty the King.
(Flourish)

They must have marched north along the river road, passing right through the site of Albuquerque and continuing by the riverside as far as possible. But there came that point where the river cut through volcanic terraces, and any road would have to abandon it, and strike inland, holding due north as far as possible. Peter believed that the little family must have gone about twenty miles beyond where the city was today. He reviewed the country where the black mesa was, and where the rocks cropped out in yellow ocher, and where there was a heavy forestation of cottonwoods. There were many places that he thought of. But while making a call in the country village of Atrisco, which was on the highway to Santa Fe, he had an impulse of recognition.

5

They had telephoned him from the grocery-and-filling station store on the highway to come at once to see Señora Aguirre, who was very painfully sick and was believed by all who saw her to be dying. They gave him directions, you come out the main highway to the gas pump, turn right on the dirt road that crosses the big ditch, follow the fence and the trees to the first turn, and go right on past it, until you come to the second turn, which you take, to the left, and there are four houses, of which the third is where the sick woman is. There is a Ford touring car in the yard, and a row of hollyhocks. He should bring medicine with him, to give right away, since she is extremely ill, and cries out momentarily, with the sweat pouring down her face. Her whole family are with her, except her second son, who is "working for the State" (that is to say, a prisoner in the penitentiary). All others are at hand, and much grieved. This is a neighbor speaking. Please hurry.

It took him about forty minutes. He wasted no time, nor yet did he break his neck to get there, knowing the temperamental liking of those people for the social opportunities of crisis, which led them to interpret every megrim as a last illness, and celebrate it with enthusiastic grief. When he reached the shady lane from which the sounds and smells of summer were baking upward in sweet drowsiness, he certainly could not miss the house of pain. The yard was animated by chatting neighbors. Babies played on the packed earthen floor about the house. Two wagons and the Ford touring car illustrated the focus of importance in the village. The sunshine dwelled whitely over the pale lilac mud color of the house, the dark-green alfalfa field out back with lacy black shadows under the plants, and the colors of the hollyhocks which cupped the light in silky shades. When his huge car was sighted coming down the dirt lane, rocking magnificently like a landship, Peter heard a chorus of pleasure, relief, anticipation come up, and he arrived in a triumph.

As soon as his eyes were used to the darkness of the house, he began to examine Señora Aguirre. She was fat and had a sort of grand doleful prettiness about her face. His first guess was acute indigestion; but he made a very careful examination before he came back and confirmed it. When he was able to risk it, he gave her some medicine, and explained the tortures of flatulence to those by the bedside who held positions there by family precedence. It was true that *Mamá* already seemed better, able to lean up on one elbow, and command the middle daughter to bring the Doctor a piece of chocolate cake from the table there. He nibbled at it enthusias-tically, but sparingly, as if to make it last. Weak with reassurance, Señora Aguirre guessed that it was the orange fizzes she had drunk on top of the *frijoles, atoles, enchiladas, tamales* and cherry ice cream last night at the party she had gone to in Los Griegos, that might have brought on this infirmity today.

She next commanded the same daughter to bring her the rose-painted china teapot from the shelf above the stove in the other room. With a gesture of the greatest propriety and charm, she lifted the lid off and drew forth a thin clutch of dollar bills, asking the Doctor what his fee was for restoring her (already!) so much to that peaceful health she was accustomed to enjoy. He replied with instant good manners that his fee was one dollar, but she need not pay it now if she cared to wait; he would have his office send her a bill. This caused her to hesitate a moment; it would be possibly more refined to receive a bill, through the mail, stamped, addressed, deliv-ered to Atrisco. But she was first of all a woman of great good sense, and she shrugged, and selected the cleanest paper dollar from her supply, and handed it to him forthwith, to save him further trouble.

He closed his bag and stood up and shook hands around the room, and was almost carried to his car by the friends who were now planning to stay on for lunch, since they were here, and Lo-lita was feeling already so much better, they would all have a bite together, a few beans, some coffee, somebody would make a pan of cornbread.

He asked if he could eventually get back to the highway by con-tinuing on the lane in the direction he had come from. They said yes, but he must watch the little wooden bridges over the ditches, with that heavy car of his. The place to turn to the right the last time was at the yellow stone slab, which he would see to the left of the lane. Four squares of yellow rock, so, that stuck up a couple of feet. The road couldn't go much farther, anyway, because the cliff was there, so it turned south again. They used to say there had been a shrine there, long ago, but that was unlikely, since there was no reason for it; no highway, no house, no church.

6

When he was by himself, driving along in low gear and rocking on the rutty dried mud of the path, he shook his head again over that experience he had known so many times in his country; of taking one single step from the golden present and knowing so sharply the feeling of the golden past; the focus of thought or vision didn't even change; simply a step into that other time, where he—or anyone who made it—could see the edifices of the imagination.

He had to leave his car presently by a bend in the ditch which fed the alfalfa field to the right. The road crossed the ditch at a sharp angle, such as mules and a wagon could negotiate, but not his enormous car. His certainty began to fade a little. Nothing really looked like *the place*. But he wandered ahead on foot, through the shade of the big green trees with their softly clattering leaves, the applause of summer in the river valley. Now he could see no houses. The field of alfalfa was behind him. Somewhere ahead, he knew, were the main line tracks of the Santa Fe railroad; but they were hidden by the wild grass and the cottonwood bosques.

He knew how this place must be in winter.

And that was his clue.

Now he could begin to see.

The trees would stand silvery thin to the washed pale sky. There, ahead, what now looked like a shadow in the distance, was the face of the black mesa, and through winter's trees, it would be very plain and near. He began to walk faster. The weather often arose in the mountains which were way back out of sight across the upper mesa, from where he was now, and it swept forward and down over the black cliff on the wind. If there was shelter to be had, it was to be had right near the mesa fall; that black volcanic rock that looked like velvet from even the littlest distance.

The road was full of grass.

In winter, the snow would blow along and lodge in the ruts. But long ago, there were no ruts. There was supposed to be a tumble of rocks protruding from the ground; he knew how they would look; squares of yellow stone like magnified clusters of crystal shapes.

All about him were the three stages of river forest. He saw dead trees, which looked as if they'd been polished by wind until they had the sheen of old silver. Mostly he counted the mature trees crowned loftily with domes of green shadow. And scattered everywhere were saplings of the heroic line of descent, tender whiplike stands which in their turn would make the river groves endure.

The family of José Diego de Nájera saw very much the same aspect. What they had experienced near here, somewhere, was familiar enough to Doctor Rush.

He saw the wild grass rising ahead of him, losing the lane. The lane turned to the right, heading south. No doubt in time it found a straggling way to the main road. He came out into a little clearing of sunlight. He saw something he believed he almost remembered, as if he had seen it before. There was a body of rocks grown up with grass, and the stone was yellow. The black fall of the mesa was almost misty with blue shadow. In the tall grass where he stood he saw a small platform of the yellow stone, four squares laid together. Whatever their purpose, they had been so laid by men, how long ago nobody could prove. Peter had no doubt at all that in 1598 the son of José Diego de Najera had been born on this spot; and that the father, keeping his promise to himself, had come back when he was able and had built a shrine to give thanks for the happy issue of his worries. But the Royal Highway didn't come by this way. The motor road of today was a couple of miles to the west, across grove and field and water ditch.

With the aid of three men, and a fire they'd kept going for weeks, and with woven pieces bought from the Indians, Señora de Nájera bided her time. Her husband was a man of education. It was possible that she was a well-born lady, and it was known that she was not robust. Her education would not of course match his. She had no particular need of learning off the page something that her body would know by inheritance. What they all learned most usefully, probably, was what they heard in church. Time and again the factor of survival was spiritual. Any doctor had seen plenty of evidence of that. The weather could drive like a bird through the air, and enter everywhere. Three men could make a go of it, ordinarily, one a servant, another a soldier, another a civil administrator. It was hardest to wait for what was going to happen. As Christmas Eve drew nearer, it occurred to them all that there might be a true and exalting purpose in the trial they were enduring together. But perhaps they did not think it a trial? There was no hint of such an attitude in the letter the father wrote when it was over. Life, then, was never a burden? It was a mission to be executed, no matter what the conditions of the moment.

The day before Christmas, probably in the early morning, for the Señora, a frail and suffering woman, the intimations of pain had begun. Nobody could do anything helpful at such a time but keep the place warm; it was snowing, remember, and the smoke blew along the ground. The gray light would fly with the clouds over the empty reach of the trees. Risk, of course there was risk, the men would be more aware of it than the woman. Pain and forgetfulness and resolve drifted in and out of the woman's mind all day long, one purpose alone inhabiting her. The men would smile at her and promise her safety when she was able to see again after a bad time. It wouldn't matter to her where her baby was born. At home in Mexico City, in a stone room hung with curtains and woven pictures, and busy with women, and scented with medicines, there would have been essentially the same thing to suffer and complete. It might have been a lucky thing that Señora de Nájera had no real picture of how far they were from everywhere, the four of them, with their oxcart and the two oxen out in the grass.

But the husband knew, and he knew too that if she should die, and her baby with her, he must leave them there. She was not a strong woman, they had always felt. But she was stronger than the wilderness, and the distance, and the cold, and the anxious fellows there, and the tradition of poor health, and the crippling modesties that attended so much of life.

It must have been over before midnight, and the firelight wavered over the five of them.

No wonder they had the instinct of commemoration, and

vowed, after this prosaic prodigy, a thankful stone. An honor, the rebirth of man which was the first chapter of the life of Jesus, had visited the family in the river wilderness. That they should be simply one with the Holy Family was clearly the intention behind the fall of the birth upon Christmas Eve. A devout man could hardly conclude anything else.

For the rest, the Spanish letter was full of worldly responsibility.

Captain de Nájera was a busy man, by temperament, and the land, the resources, the *chances*, all preoccupied him, once the hazard was past. A place for a city; the kind of rock; the animals; things to do as soon as he could get at them, when they rejoined the main colony.

It was entirely likely that in a week or so, they had gathered up their things, and started on again.

But Nájera evidently meant what he said, as a general rule.

7

Peter stood up on the yellow stone platform and glanced around. The land was generally level, and the oxcart might have gone right on north from here, for a little distance. But the black mesa jutted out sharply about half a mile up, he could see the dark profile through the trees. He could see too, standing on this small elevation, a silver pole with a painted signal arm and red and amber and green glass, and he said of course, it was the railroad.

As he went back to his car, he heard the whistle of an engine far down the line.

It spoke to him as it always did to Americans. It told of distance and speed and of going somewhere. It unerringly found the boy within him, as in every man. He did not feel obvious or banal when he contrasted it in his mind with what the little Spanish family had endured and brought to triumph so long ago, in a wilderness. The oncoming train was a symbol for all the complexities, the ease, the accustomed powers of comfort in his own day.

He next said to himself that in re-enacting the events of the Spanish letter here in this sun-latticed grove, the birth of a child

in hazard and love, he had answered out of the past the longing for
more children which the trouble in his family had denied him.

He wished for Noonie something of the wilderness challenge
of survival or death; to give life to others rather than harbor it for
yourself; and he knew that if she was ever to become whole again,
it would have to be at the risk of crisis; of just what kind, he could
not say.

Things changed.

The spirit endured. Find it, recognize it, respect it, share it. He
scowled and nodded, alone, and vigorously, as if to justify himself
for such meditations; how embarrassed the people he knew would
be if ever called upon to hear this sort of thing spoken by one of
themselves! "The happy materialists," he murmured, recalling what
bad form it was, among the Americans of his time and position, to
acknowledge the soul and to question the laws of the speak-easy
and the country club.

The train now came charging upon the embankment in a triumphant harmony, like some creature of tremendous music. It was
the California Limited, demonstrating the beautiful curve of the
land at the base of the black mesa, and its shine and sing, its plume
of smoke capturing the sun in gorgeous turbulence, its roar and
glisten, its length and passage and clickety elegance, swept over and
past him, and on through the sandy distance toward town, and back
to today.

8

He wrote to the Archbishop in the evening, upstairs in his attic
library, announcing his discovery, and arguing circumstantially for
its recognition.

To this the Archbishop replied that it was gratifying that he
had possibly identified the spot where the first native-born child
of the colonists had seen the light, and added that he for one was
not astonished to learn that the evidence of such a lonely birth had
been a moving experience, since after all "it was a beginning. Any
birth, any time, is the greatest of all beginnings, for it is the life of

a new soul, the confirmation and the hope of all the immaterial knowledges which men have always been certain of, in the face of demands for proof from the more material-minded of our diverse and fascinating fellow mortals."

XVIII · HEAR ABOUT LOVE

I

One afternoon Peter came home unexpectedly to pick up his black looseleaf pocket notebook in which he jotted memoranda about his cases. He ran upstairs to his third-floor retreat, found the book on his desk, with his lump of cleanly sheared obsidian on top of it, and hurried down the stairs again. Down the hall, the door from Noonie's sunporch was closed, but the afternoon sunlight was caught in a film of curtain behind the glass, and he wondered if she were there. He went to the door, and tapped, and opened it.

There she was.

He was pleased at the picture he saw. She was reclining in her gray satin chaise longue, doing Don's mending. The light came in and flooded her with a golden diffuse pour. She was smiling like a child full of mischief. She had deliberately kept silent to see if he would come to find her. Her cheeks were flushed with pleasure at the little game, the little echo of courtship they made. The glass of the many windows was dazzling. The scent in the room was leafy, from her boxes of plants that lined the front wall. He had a glimpse of the girl she had once been, and he was lifted by it.

He came in and sat down on the end of her long chair and she dropped her sewing and leaned toward him and kissed him. She seemed full of gaiety. Her eyes danced and her lips were hot and shining.

"Darling, what are you doing?" she asked.

"I ran in to get my famous black book, I've been without it all day, and I've needed it a dozen times, so I decided to take a moment and really get it.—What are *you* doing?"

"—These shirts of Donnie's. He is pushing right through every-thing he owns."

"You look very sweet, sitting here like a little puss in the sunshine."

"Do you know I have never gotten used to the way your coats always smell? Medicine."

She shuddered with comic fastidiousness.

"Do you mind?"

"Of course not.—It's *you*: isn't it?"

"Come here."

He kissed her, and asked her silently, by his eyes upon hers, whether she had come back to him. He never tired of asking this question, in whatever way the moment dictated.

She clung to his shoulders, and said,

"Don't go now."

"I have to, dear. I'll be home as soon as I can."

"Come back at five, then, and take me riding in the car. It is so long since we took a drive together."

The whole town had the habit of riding around, just to look at things, the streets, the river, the mesa, the mountains, in the late afternoon. The country roads weren't very good, but nobody had the habit of driving very fast. The automobile was just ending its age of innocence.

"Well, I have to operate at five. But I'll come as soon as I can, after that."

She sank back on her satin tufting.

"I knew it."

"Knew what?"

"That you wouldn't."

"Couldn't."

"Couldn't, then.—Oh, I *blame* nothing," she said airily.

He could see that she was being elaborately "reasonable." It was lost, that fond gaiety of a moment before. He saw her forehead cloud with the expression that always meant "one of her head-aches."

"Really, Noonie:" he said soberly, to indicate his desire to keep the air clear.

"Oh, never mind," she replied, putting her fingers to her temples. "It simply *is*, that's all. You'd better go. A nagging wife is certainly no asset to any man's career. One finds one's place, I am sure."

He had an ironic twist of thought, and wondered what she had been reading lately. This wasn't her native style. His hope sank. How could he've expected it to last? He went out and down the stairs and got into his big Packard and drove off. What: what: what: will help her? His heart came into his mouth when he asked himself that. He was afraid of what it would need: what finality: what ordeal: to help her.

2

After he had left her, she began to cry, telling herself she was a fool. But it did not help her to feel any better. As usual, when she gave way to a troubling emotion, it was as if a sluice gate had been lifted, through which other emotions were free to pour, so that at times she ended up in misery over something far afield from what had set her off.

This is what happened to her now, in the sunny upstairs porch where her magazines were stacked high on the mahogany table, in two neat bastions flanking the silver lamp.

Out of some story or other she had read, in some one of the radiantly printed magazines by her elbow, an idea, a phrase came back to her. What was happening to her? Here she was nearly in middle age; possibly someone would consider her *actually* middle-aged, and what did she *have*? Her tears flowed and her breath blew hotly over her lips. It was true, wasn't it: "love itself was passing her by." No, no, time could never be recalled. No, no, whatever could make the heart feel, seize upon it! Why, love was a birthright, what else did a woman need in her life? Imagine, being "passed by by love itself"! Not Noonie? That attractive little Mrs. Rush?

She stood up and rushed into her bedroom and turned on the crystal lights on her dressing table.

Her mirror had pretty colors and sunlit spaces to show her. She looked into her own eyes, and looked away despising the imaginary creature she saw.

She stopped her weeping, and powdered her face, and smoothed her hair. Her hands were trembling, and she thought it would make her seem more in command of herself and what she was going to do if she put on her rings. She opened the Dresden china box before her mirror and took out her three big rings, diamonds, all of them, and put them on.

She went to the hall. At the head of the stairs, she stopped and listened. Far below, in the basement, there drifted the sound of Cora ironing, the dim thump of the heavy iron when she set it down, and the wisp of monotonous singing which the Negress always gave out when she was content at her work.

Yes, she was there.

Yes, she was another woman. It didn't matter who she was, or of what color. She was a middling-young colored woman who had been with the Rushes for six years. She was married to a black man who was a porter at the Harvey House downtown. Every year or so she left him declaring that she was th'oo with his cuttinups. But pretty soon, without any more said about it, she would return to their union, and her big smile would be like a lamp in the kitchen. The other servant, Leonard, who served in the dining room, and kept the house clean, the lawn cut, the car washed, and the table waited upon, was her vassal, whom she required to address her by her married name, with "Mrs." and everything.

She saw Mrs. Rush come into the basement laundry, holding a scrap of paper which she knew at once was a "list," and she wondered a little gloomily "now what." If there was anything she loved, it was being let alone, and the laundry down here was a nice room, sunny, for a cellar room, that is, and off by itself, and the laundry smelled so nice? and felt so smooth when she ironed a piece? and her voice sounded so pr'tty?

But Cora saw then that Mrs. Rush was *looking that way*, and became fascinated at once. She thought Mrs. Rush looked mighty

pr'tty, but sure did seem upset. Sure did seem *irait*? Cora, like an animal that knows when a human is afraid, knew that Mrs. Rush was
the weaker of the two of them. She set down her iron, and said "Yes,
Maaam?", and believed that Mrs. Rush had just been crying. The
Negress was naturally warmhearted. She wondered if she should go
and put her arms around her mistress, just for no reason at all, but
she figgered maybe not, all them diamon *rings*.

So she waited to discuss the "list."

But Mrs. Rush said,

"Go right on with your ironing, Cora.—Go on."

Cora resumed, wondering.

"I just—You don't mind if I ask you? Are you living with Jacob,
again, now? Cora?"

Cora made a musical sound, laughter and scandal all in one, and
said, yes, she was, she sure was, that *ma*-yan! he never let her be, no
matter what he *did*, no good but to go right straight *back* to him.
Shoo! My oh *my*.

Yes, there it was, Noonie said to herself, there was a woman full
of love, there it was, what was it like? Cora, how ample, how true,
how sure. She licked her lips and put her hands together, her rings
trembling with light.

Noonie's cheeks burned with shame.

"Do you love him?" she asked.

Cora laughed weakly and flopped her hands loosely from her
wrists and let them hang there while she comically wagged her head
from side to side, and said,

"I *guess* 'azz what you call it, I cain't *hep nothin* when he wants
me to!"

"He—he wants you all the time?"

"Shoo! He's a buuull? that ma-yan!—I c'd kill him when he trifles on me, but he *need* more woman 'n jus' one? I honesly figger so,
but I won't *tell* him so."

Noonie began to fold her "list" carefully into little even squares.
She gazed at it as if it were a very important task, and made her
hands stop trembling as well as she could. She cleared her throat

and meant to sound perfectly serene and mistress-like with Cora, and asked Cora to tell her more; all about it; Jacob; what it was like; loving like that; did it really exist; could she stand it; getting loved that way.

Cora was a little shocked, not at the question, any woman might ask that who was a close friend, shoLord, she talked enough and she heard enough when 'm ol yellow gals got together 'thout their black boys aroun to hear what they said and git all swelled up and conceited, hearin thataway. But this was her employer, and a white woman, and don' know; summin funny about it. But there was something pleading in Mrs. Rush's attitude, standing there folding that slip of paper with her little white hands. Lord, honey, thought Cora, if you wan' hear 'bout *love* that much I'll sho tell you.

She resumed her ironing and told her. Her talking voice was silken and gentle, and deeply full of animal music and possession.

Noonie began to tear the little piece of paper into exact little squares and drop them to the floor while she listened to Cora.

Cora was good. She honestly owned what she celebrated. She had no shame. Her pride was happy. She knew her sorrows because she couldn't help being jealous sometimes. Thing is, he never did fail to come back to her, even if he went off cattin sometimes. It seemed to her that there wasn't anything you did that you couldn't talk about, if you saw it where it belonged. When she looked up at Mrs. Rush again, she felt compassionate at what she saw in that composed face, with its downcast eyes, desire and fear both showing through.

The torn bits of paper drifted to the floor.

"You'll be all right, Mrs. Rush, honey? I make you a cup tea?"

She tactfully put them back to where they belonged in relation to each other.

Mrs. Rush shook her head, and said with a smile that she had forgotten *what* it was she had come down to *speak* to Cora about, and pale with her thoughts of what she had heard, she turned and went upstairs.

3

Cora sighed, when she was alone again. She had never understood, and she didn't understand now, how come so many white folks get like that, over *that*. Live in a house with white folks, couldn't hep knowin some things. White folks sure got unhappy lot time when ain't no *sense* to it.

XIX · THE POETS

I

The lovers, separated by going to their homes at night, sometimes knew formless poems of passion within themselves even greater than those to which they tried to give form in their kisses together.

Late at night when the whole house was asleep below, Bun would awaken in his attic den, where his narrow iron bed was. The dormer windows were swung open. The starlight looked cool far out there, and the nights when the moon was swollen with pure light during the early hours before midnight were a third and strange time of day in his room, that light on the floor, on the books tumbled before the bookcase, on his clothes like fallen clowns by the chair, on the single sheet which was all he could bear to cover him, on the long legs he flung free of bedclothes for the need of the cool breath of night and the wash of moonlight on his hard flesh.

It seemed to him sometimes that he raged all night in his bed, with love.

He hated his room then. It was a boy's room. It had those models of locomotives on the neat, narrow shelves that he and his father together had built to carry that miniature display. This bed was wide enough for nobody else; and so it was too often peopled by phantoms of love. The roof sloped to a peak above him, and it was as if a man could stand only in the middle of the room with his head up. There were possessions too trivial and too dear for his present freedom. They reminded him of too much that he wanted to forget, in order to be free with his passion. He blushed to remember the little boy he had been, because he wanted now to outgrow the little boy with acts of creation. Sleep came down upon him only like a wing that was lifted again in the flight of his desires before his thoughts.

Let the moonlight go away.

When the cool air wafts in through the windows I can smell the river sometimes. It is cool, and I smell roots and leaves and the silky dragging of the muddy water. If I squinch my eyes shut maybe I can see the place again where I used to go swimming and all the other boys I knew and we knew everything and we didn't care and we were naked in the mud and pure in the heart because nothing bothered us the way things bother us now.

He would get up from his bed and go to the window and look out to the west to see if he could see the river in the moonlight, way across town there below the highlands. If the moon was perfectly right, distant water caught a gleam and shone there, a tiny wedge of silver among the banks of trees on the far edge of town, which he could look down upon.

It cooled him. It freed him for a moment. It made him forget himself, and the flow of shame that followed the waves of power released by his desirous thoughts.

Now I will go to sleep in her name, he would think, and return to his cot, purified. Across the room in the darkness he passed the mirror on his bureau and he made a silvery shadow in it, going through the moonlight. He ground his jaws at the shadowy mirror.

2

Martha lay awake and could see out through the screens how the moonlight poured on the dark varnished leaves of the huge cottonwood in the swept back yard. The tree was alive with tiny points of moonlight on its dark shiny leaves, moving in the wind which (fantastically) could have been but a veil of air localized to the tree itself, since no stir seemed or sounded in anything else hereabout. Beyond the tree, in the limitless silvery blue of the night sky, there was an immense cloud, miles and miles away. It was so disposed that it seemed to echo the very shape of the tree crown in its imaginable domes and caverns; mighty, towering, fabulous in the pour of white moonlight upon its white cliffs. Regarding it, she was its owner. Nobody else saw it, she felt, just as she did. Traveling hugely and in tremendous airiness, the cloud was some sort of signal for her; a confirmation of the senses just before sleep. So her heart traveled, and so her thoughts arose. So her eyes saw, when far lightning pierced the interior of the vast cloud, and showed her vistas of silver like the very future, in the highly echoing galleries of the thunderhead muttering dimly above horizons too far to see. To the north, even farther than the moonlighted palisade of heaven, she saw a star, troubled by distance so that now and then it lost its beam; but still it shone, when she searched for it; and she owned it as poetry. Purely she loved, so that her whole self was alive to love. She whispered to herself with her eyes closed, seeing the words as remembered shapes upon Bun's own mouth,

"It is the star to every wandering bark,"

and by this she meant the love they held together; and if there had ever been anything mean, or funny, about their two heads over the printed page in the yellow table lamplight of the public library where they had come upon Shakespeare's words, such connotation was gone, and justly so.

The lightning walked vastly in the cloud galleries; the thunder crowned far mountains that were out of sight; the star's beam was dandled by the altering depths of the earth's atmosphere; all faithful to themselves as she was to herself, and true.

XX · THE CLEANSING RIVER

I

"—And now they telephone," said Noonie to herself Saturday morning. She was standing in the hall calling upstairs to Donald to come and talk to Wayne, who was waiting at the other end of the wire. She had forgotten that when she was a child, the telephone was known; but saw it now as an astounding modern invention with which even children could make sense.

In a moment Don came down and she watched him. As he neared her she wanted to put out her arms and stop him with an embrace; but she knew he hated such demonstrations, and she smiled remotely at him, feeling that same odd, lost feeling that her son gave her now and then, and she half-decided for the thousandth time that she had given all her own strength and health to him, and that he was uncomfortable with her as if he dimly knew how much he owed her, and chafed in the debt.

He went to the phone cupboard under the stairs where there were a light, a mirror and a little shelf with the Doctor's memorandum pad.

"Hello Way."

(What's the matter, Mrs. Rush wondered, he doesn't sound like himself.)

Then Donald swung the door of the cupboard shut, and she could hear no more.

In a few minutes he came out, closing the door carefully after him, and started upstairs again. Noonie came out of the living room with her magazine and asked him if Wayne was coming over, and if they were going out for the day, did he want a lunch put up, if they were? Or would Wayne stay to lunch here, it was such a lovely day, she said she was so glad he had such a good time with Wayne, she said she never had a minute's worry about them. But he hardly stopped going up the stairs to tell her no, Wayne was not coming over, and about the lunch, no thank you, he was going out by himself, and wouldn't need any.

"—Need any!" she echoed, "You most certainly shall have some, I'll have Cora fix a box, you most certainly shall not go hungry!— What's the matter. Is anything the matter, darling?"

"No, of course not," he said, and disappeared in the upstairs hall to his room.

She said to herself that he *said* there was nothing the matter, and so she was probably worrying needlessly. But he looked very peculiar, boys *were*, they just *were*.

Upstairs Don knelt down by the window and put his fists and chin on the sill and stared out over the side lot where the evergreen nursery grew. He did not know how he would eventually make it up with Wayne. He would have to find a way to do it. He all but had to hang *up* on Wayne who had begun to insist that they go to the river together for a swim. Donald said this, and that, giving excuses; but Wayne had a ready answer for each one, and didn't believe him. Donald couldn't tell him exactly what he wanted to do, and where, because it wasn't exactly clear to himself, even; but he knew by how he felt that he had to be alone this morning; and it was the first Saturday morning since he could remember that he and Wayne hadn't gone out together, or at least explained what prevented their meeting. Wayne finally didn't say any more on the phone but just stayed there in silence. Both boys held the phone and said nothing. The wire sounded alive and connected, with a little far sound like gas escaping somewhere. Neither wanted to be the first to hang up, or start talking all over again. Finally Donald said,

"Well, I'll call you later on, Way."

"Oh, *very* well. Good-by."

"Good-by."

Click.

He certainly sounded put out.

Don got up from the window and went to his closet where he found the rifle. He put on his blue corduroy cap and got a sweater whose arms he tied around his neck; and he began to tiptoe to the front stairs, listening. He didn't want to get caught and be handed a box of lunch. He didn't *want* anything to eat. He could hear sounds in the kitchen, his mother and Cora; they were rattling waxed paper and fixing him something. Deciding on a dash, he flew on tiptoe down three steps at a time and was out the front door before anybody saw him. His bicycle was out in front. In a second he was riding down the street toward the meadows that lay off to the south through which the great river crawled shallow and sandy in the spring sunshine.

He found the dried mud road that ran along beside the *acequia madre*, the big irrigation ditch from which the little ditches of the meadows got their water. In a very short while he had left the town behind him, and was free in the country-smelling, hot river land. He had his rifle under his arm. People who saw him would think he was on his way to shoot birds. The river was edged with deep stands of cottonwoods and willows. How fresh their green was at this time of year! They gave such a sweet-smelling shade that he loved just to go and lie down in such a clump and shut his eyes and love the trees by not thinking or caring or wanting or doing anything. Maybe if he went today:

So he hurried his riding, and presently came to the place where the great ditch between its high banks turned and ran parallel to the river. A footpath went up the ditch bank and led across the brown rim on a clayed plank. He dismounted and struggled up with his bicycle, for to leave it on this side of the ditch was to risk robbery; and there were always plenty of others around on Saturday—the Martinez gang from Old Town, who ranged the meadows like a revolutionary army, would steal from you and take your clothes and chase you, if they ever outnumbered you enough. He got the bicycle across the plank with exciting difficulty, because a vagrant swing of the front wheel might plop it off into the ditch below; and down over the other bank of the ditch, where the heavy greenery began. He found a clump of young willows that made a perfect blind, and there he laid down his bicycle, locking the rear wheel with his special padlock. He stood listening. He believed that he could actually hear the river, not that it made a rushing sound as it went, for it went too slowly and shallowly on the wide bed. But he could hear the wet life of the banks, and he shut his eyes the better to receive those tiny sounds of suck, and seep, and he knew from what he remembered how the mud was glistening where the river wet it, and how the banks under the trees might be wet from high water that came from melting snow in the mountains to the north. There were insects singing in the radiant green air of the riverside glades. The sandhills across the river were white golden in the sunlight. Far to his left would be the bridge that crossed the river in Barelas, where Borelli's saloon stood on this side, and where all the tin cans were dumped down on the river edge. The cans, when the sun was just right, glittered magnificently from this distance, like a huge pile of enormous diamonds.

2

He wished he could stand like this with his eyes shut remembering everything else until he forgot how he felt.

But he opened his eyes, and pushed on through the green tangle of willow and cottonwood saplings walking in wet ground until he saw the flat bank and then the river and then the other side, and the high blue above it.

A great heron heard him coming and claimed a lift with its wings and sailed inland over his head out of sight above the trees.

He did not bring his rifle to the aim.

He had no bullets.

He went to the edge of the bank and began walking south, as close as possible to the river. Now he could see the whole open riverscape, the bridge, the black structures of the edge of town, one white steam plume from the Santa Fe shops, and behind, the blue mountains.

He kept out a wary eye for other walkers along the bank; but he saw none. Perhaps he could just make out what that little glisten of light might be by the bridge, down by Borelli's; he looked again; it was boys in the river. When they stood up he could just recognize their flesh. He must be done at the river today long before he got that far.

What he was watching out for was quicksand.

Many was the time he had come to swim here with Wayne, and the two of them had recognized what they were sure was quicksand…an extra movement of the shallow current, the little particles of sand rolling and boiling ever so gently, the way a stone would fall there as they threw it, and then begin slowly to shine with the sand climbing around it, and then the polishing work of the water as it closed over the top and went on down stream dragging a little sandy trail for a few minutes and then again nothing at all but the cool pale muddy color of the whole river.

Walking down the edge, he could kick off a clump now and then and by so little change the course of that always changing river.

Ahead of him there was a point of new territory, as he thought of it; the end of old man Rhodes's pasture, which the river had cut into during the last flow of melted snow in the north. Now a fence line hung unsupported between point and point, where the river had cut away a new miniature bay. The uprooted poles and the wire stretching from terminals on still solid ground were collecting driftage. Branches made a barrier there. Donald went inland and climbed through the solid fence and came back out to the bank beyond.

As he thought; the water was shallower here because of the new spread of the river into old man Rhodes's pasture. Here he would be able to go into the river and get across to the dry bank in the middle, and he would cross that, and come to the other vein of the river near the opposite shore. That great land spit was like a miniature desert lying between two independent streams. The quicksand was well known to be more treacherous and rapid over there on the other side.

He sat down and listened again, this time for voices; but heard none. The eleven o'clock whistle from the sawmill way across town blew its steamy music into the air, and he heard it with pleasure. It was a cheerful sound, mellowed by distance. When it died out, he looked around and decided he was alone. The meadows stretched inland, the trees were still, the far bathers at the bridge seemed hardly nearer for all his walk. He untied his shoes and kicked them off, and then his stockings, and then he stood up and yanked off all his clothes. The air felt sweet on his warm skin. He began to feel dread for the certainty of what he must do. He made a bundle of his clothes, climbed a cottonwood that had a lot of low leaves, and stowed his things in a hidden Y of the tree.

He debated a moment whether to take off his waterproof wrist watch; but he decided not to bother. Then taking his rifle, he went to the river and stepped in. The current was warm and pushy as it rose on his legs. Underfoot he felt sliding mud; not quicksand that drank you up steadily. Suddenly he was up to his waist, but the water was still idling, so he held up his arms with his watch and rifle and pretty soon he was coming shallower, and stepping into flowing mud, and then the mud came up to the emerging flat, and lay there, a plain of still wet but baking warm river earth that felt delicious to walk on. Beyond that was the long spit of smooth dried mud, so rich that it was pale purple, and cracked by drying into edible-looking little cakes. On to this he now emerged, and both banks seemed far away. He was happily lost in a wilderness of sunlight, separated from his world by a river on each side of him. Upstream or down, he was alone, and now he wished for Wayne, but he still knew that what he wanted to do he had to do alone.

3

He had gone alone the day before to see the man at the paint store, where they sold glass. The store was crowded, but he waited, whistling silently. Pretty soon, that little skinny fellow with a face like a smiling rat, a rat who was friendly and didn't see anything funny about looking like one, came up and asked if he had been waited upon.

Donald replied that he was interested in buying a pane of glass.

"What size?"

Don frowned, feeling that he must look deliberate, and held out his hands as far apart as the size of the panes of glass in the chicken house up at the Shoemaker ranch.

The clerk nodded.

"'Bout eight by eight?—I'd have to cut it for you."

"Could I watch?"

"Sure."

"How much would it cost?"

"'Bout twenty cents."

"Apiece?"

"Why, sure.—You want more'n one?"

"Oh, no, I was just figgerin."

"Well, come on back. I'll do you a pane that size."

They went to the workshop out in back of the paint store. There were picture frame molding and frames and stacks of paint in cans and sheets of glass in excelsior; and two old rocking chairs hoisted against the ceiling by ropes, evidently just to get them out of the way.

Don watched while the agreeable young man "took and scratched" the right size on the corner of a large pane of window glass. The diamond cutting tool bit the glass with a grind that made him shudder comically. Then the great moment came, of tapping the big pane to make it crack the little one off, clean and astonishing.

"There she is."

"Well, thanks.—Here, I'll pay for it."

"Twenty cents."

"Here it is."

"Sure do thank you. Come back and see us."

"Sure will."

He went out and rode off. He knew what he wanted to know. Twenty cents apiece, and they must have wrecked about—how many?—about three hundred, with the .22 rifle. His heart sank at a new thought. The glass would cost something to *put in*, too. He turned around, rode back to the paint store, and asked what it cost to *put in* a pane of glass that size.

"Just the one? In a window?"

"Well, yes, in a window."

The clerk took a pad and pencil and as he spoke, he read out the figuring he was doing.

"Eight b' eight, twenty cents, time and labor, twenty cents, materials, that is putty and depreciation, ten cents, it'd cost you right around fifty cents?"

"Thanks."

"O.K.—Hurry back."

"Sure will."

He rode off again. His face was hotly flushing. When he reached the park on the way home, he rode up on the lawn and lay down on the grass. He had a scrap of paper in his pocket and a fine pencil which wrote red at one end and blue at the other. He multiplied three hundred panes by fifty cents and it came out one hundred and fifty dollars.

He was ruined.

It was a fortune.

The most money he had ever earned in one week was a dollar and five cents, helping Wayne down at the stationery shop when they were rushed during textbook season, and all the school children came to get their books and pencils, and things.

He rolled over and buried his face in the grass.

It was the first time he had ever realized that the Shoemakers were poor. A hundred and fifty dollars meant the world and all to Mrs. Shoemaker. He had practically robbed her of it. He had never believed sums like that before. It had been easier to imagine seventy million dollars in pearls and radium, the rare treasures of M. Le Vicomte, than it had been to know what a hundred and fifty dollars meant in actual value, of time, labor and pride.

They are so poor! he cried inwardly, in the agony of discovery. That's what that little house meant, and Willa Shoemaker working so hard and jerking so thinly when she walked so fast, and the way Wayne's clothes were always darned and patched and the way Martha cut his hair sometimes, instead of his going to the barbershop…

He hated his big ugly brick house and the servants they gave money to wait on them and the jewels his mother had upstairs in a china box.

He knew of no way to discharge the debt he owed.

But a way of expiation by sacrifice did occur to him. That it would cost him so much gave him a stoic's resolve and strength.

4

He went on walking over the dried river middle toward that other side which brought the desert of the sandhills down to the very water's edge. The dried mud was hot to his feet. Over his skin the sun laid a garment of feeling; when he turned toward it, he was clothed by its touch. He fancied himself turning browner, looking down his breast. He was proud of the muscled plates developing on his body. If Wayne were here, he would run him a race. They could race for as far as you could see, upstream or down, on this wide dry river between the two waters.

The ribbons of sunlight on the other half of the river were beginning to be blinding as he walked nearer. There no trees grew, everything was lifted flat and empty to the sun. There was a miniature cliff of crusty earth a foot high which marked where the river ran. He came to it, and it caved in under him, so he moved back. This was the treacherous side. He began to walk downstream, watching intently for the kind of current, the sort of shallow glisten of the quicksands. He picked up a clod of dried mud in his free hand, to be ready with it. His stomach felt hollow with suspense, and he had his belly muscles sucked in so he looked hard and lean, the color of the dried river land he was trudging on alone and small.

"There it is!" he exclaimed, and leaned down to see. The water was washing almost idly over a glistening lift of river sand. The channel had moved gradually away from him, and was taking the swifter water downstream by the opposite shore.

"I wish" he said, but he had no idea how to say what he wished.

He heaved the big clod of dirt into the sand, and it began to turn dark with water, like a lump of sugar held edgily in a cup of coffee. The sand seemed loose and fat and hungry, and into it the hunk of mud began to sink steadily. In a moment the water was sheeting along over it. Whatever fell in there would vanish that same way. He sat down to look at it. He lay down and crossed his arms over his eyes, leaving his rifle athwart his middle, but it burned him from being in the sun, and he got up again. He had read about people feeling that their hearts were in their mouths; and that was how he felt now.

Now it must be something like an accident, or people would never be able to think well of him again. Perhaps if he began to see how close to the edge he could walk, without breaking down the cut-out edge of the bank, along the place where the quicksand was, he would have to be careful about keeping his balance to avoid falling in.

He began to tiptoe as near as he could. He held his arms out to balance himself. Over the water he held his rifle.

In the sunlight he was sweating and shining.

"Now another step," he thought, "This is a game after all, to see how close I can come without actually falling in and getting caught, there is nothing I would not lose to keep from being caught in the quicksand, *not even my new rifle.*"

He stepped, and the crust of mud gave way under him and he lurched. His right leg went into the water and he felt the cold, fluid, terrifyingly easy slide of the sand up around his leg. He threw himself sideways to solid ground and he called out, and let go of his rifle which flew through the air and landed flat in the shallow water. He rolled himself to safety, far back from the bank, and felt his heart pounding at the narrow escape he had had. His wet leg itched where the sun began to dry it. Heaving, he got up to look for the rifle. It was gone. The water was as idle and unruffled as if nothing had ever fallen in there, and been buried from sight and out of guilt, on that jelly of wet sand.

He sighed deeply.

That was exactly what had happened, and it was what he could tell everybody.

Now he turned and began racing back across the land spit toward the green side of the river. When he came to the other water, he left the run in a long sailing dive and buried his head in the muddy flow and drifted downstream in warm oblivion as long as he could hold his breath. Then he caught at the other bank and lodged himself against some roots and let the current run over him and eddy him gently and with its earthen power, wash him clean of his fears, his remorse, and his actions.

He felt better.

Punishment was done.

Whether the instrument deserved it or not, he did not consider.

Drowsing there, he soon seemed an accustomed part of the life of the riverbank; and all the little things he had scared away now returned and were part of the noontide drone…the water spiders skating near the bank, the mocking birds that had taken a circle in the air before returning to the leaves, the beaver up the way who was examining old man Rhodes's ruined fence where the drifting cottonwood branches were piling up. The air shifted this way from the south; not actually a wind, rather a medium for sound. The boys swimming down by the bridge appeared here by their voices, tiny sounds of Saturday music that reminded him of where they were and how they looked in the sunlight, gold toilers in the golden river distance.

He wondered who they were.

It was enough to get him up.

He climbed from the water and ran upstream to his tree, and by the time he got there he was dried off. He dressed quickly, and started back. When he came to the place where he turned inland toward his willow brake, he aroused the same heron, which bandied its way once again into the air. Through the grove ahead he thought he could see someone, and he stopped to peer, wondering if he would have to fight for his own bicycle, or even to retain the key of the padlock. He came ahead carefully, and then in a plunge of high spirits he recognized Wayne, sitting on the ground beside his own wheel, waiting. Donald ran through the saplings, crashing and eager.

"Where's your rifle?" asked Wayne.

"How long've you been here?—It's gone."

"Gone?"

"Yes. Let's go. Let's ride back by Borelli's."

"Where's it gone?"

"I'll tell you."

They got their bicycles up and over the plank across the great ditch, and down on the meadow path which they would leave for the road running inland from the river, but more or less following its course.

"I had it with me out on the river, on the other side, in case I saw anything, and when I got over there, I was going along the edge watching the quicksand, and she caved in with me, and I just barely fell back myself. The rifle flew out of my hand tzing! it was gone in the quicksand."

They rode in silence.

Then Donald said,

"Don't you believe me?"

"Sure."

Wayne added to himself that if he'd been along it probably wouldn't have happened.

Aloud, he said,

"Are you going to tell your Dad?"

"—I don't know. Sooner or later, I guess."

"I haven't said anything to Mom yet."

"Neither have I."

"Let's speed."

They rose on their pedals and charged down the fragrant dirt road. Pretty soon they came on open land by the river and saw how near the bridge was, and Borelli's saloon. They could hear the boys swimming, and to see them, and who they were, they rode through the dirt street up onto the bridge and came to rest on their saddles, looking down on the bathers who were far enough off to be naked and unrecognizable except that they looked like Mexican boys.

"It must be Joe Martinez and his gang."

"I guess so. They come every Saturday."

"What do you suppose they do down there?"

"They'd show us quick enough if we got anywhere near.—Remember the day Neddie Truman went by there? They practically skinned him alive.—They busted his wheel up. You remember that."

"That's right."

5

A sudden concert of noon whistles began to ascend from all over the town. Their sound somehow made the day seem hotter still. The old bridge rattled its planks under the traffic…an old wood wagon or two, intermittent cars.

Wayne suddenly turned to Don, and said, with an air of coming at last to what was unspoken between them,

"I don't know what got into us that day."

"It was a week ago today."

"Is that why you lost your rifle?"

"It flew out of my hand, I tell you, or I would have fallen in, I would rather let my old gun fall in than get caught myself."

They felt sober.

How childish the pretending of all their past seemed now! That play about destroying the viaduct! It was a sort of anguish to sit here on the sunny old bridge and remember such things.

"Let's go?"

"Where:"

They turned their wheels and glided down the ramp toward Borelli's saloon. It was washed with the tremendous deep cool shade of the cottonwoods that stood around it and above it, and out in back, near the bank, there were some willows. In summertime, Borelli had an open-air beer garden there, with lattices whose paint was faded. The front door was open. The place looked cool inside. The nickel piano was fumbling through a remote tune in the back room. The street in front was of clay, and so were the walls of the house. The boys rode slowly down to the door, and sat, looking in. From the front room there issued a cool draft of air with a beery fragrance that made them blench wondrously, for all it suggested.

They felt lost.

This shabby and comfortable old saloon was like a symbol of a world where the lost retreated.

They longed to enter, in woeful excitement.

Borelli was a blue-faced Italian with a ceremonial belly and a sentimental indignation about the morals of the young. His sixteen-year-old son Nick spent his spare time hanging around the place. Nick Borelli was as slow as anybody they knew in school, to understand what they talked about and liked to think of; and yet on the other hand, Nick was at home in a whole world of which they knew only the scrappiest references. Nick was sixteen, and privy to what the talk about women and what they *did* really was about; he used to tell the younger boys, some of whom did not believe a word he said. Nick's voice sounded as if it were full of crumbs, husky and satisfied. Nobody ever forgot the day Nick had a bottle of beer with him at school. It passed around the tender little mouths still without character and they all swallowed some. He assured them all that down at the "Place," by the river, there under the willows and cottonwoods, he could get them anything they wanted, at any time. His old man was an easy one to fool, and never really knew how much beer, and cigarettes, and stuff he ever really had on hand, so he would never miss a thing.

Nick had brown, softly shining skin. He was always smiling under his curved nose. His heavy black hair grew down to his temples and almost to his eyebrows and under his sweater his shoulders bulked big and round. Everybody liked him because he was so friendly, besides the things he had to tell. He never understood a thing of any importance in the classroom, but was encouraged in such activities as penmanship, at which he would spend hours, making expert and decorative pages full of capital S's, with heavy downstrokes, and light, birdy upstrokes. He was often allowed to decorate the blackboards, which he did publicly and proudly, turning to the class for silent applause from time to time. The boys all liked him; but the girls knew he was just better than a simpleton, and let him alone. He didn't seem to mind. He liked the women in the other house by the river, who worked for his father, and who treated him like a mascot.

The world of the imagination, where Donald and Wayne were so busy, would never be revealed to him.

From the cool vista of the back room, Nick saw the two boys out in the sunshine, peering into the door. He got up from the oil-cloth table back there and came forward through the several doors and the boys greeted him.

"Looking for something, kids?" he asked with his father's ministerial cordiality.

"Nope."

Nick had a face full of innocent friendliness, because that was just how he felt.

"Come on around back, if you want to do a little business.—The old man is in town. Come on."

He jerked them toward the back yard with his shiny black head. He seemed infinitely older than they. It was intolerable not to know as much as that about everything.

They walked their bikes along after him on the hard swept adobe ground.

It was hot and quiet in the yard and they could see glimpses of the river through the long-hanging willows with their new green fingers.

Nick treated them like esteemed customers of no particular age, and sold them two bottles of beer and a package of Egyptian Deity cigarettes. He wrapped it all up for them in a couple of funny papers, and thoughtfully provided a bottle opener.

Nick told them they could go sit down in the back room, if they liked. But they suddenly hated him. They wanted to get away from his oozy good nature. They also dimly thought of cops and raids, for they'd heard of Prohibition. No, they said, and went back to their bicycles and rode across the bridge to the far side of the river. At the end of the bridge, they wheeled down on to the sand, and went around under the bridge, where the old planks above them made alternate bars of shadow and blades of sunshine. The sand was cool. Little ranks of river grass grew there. They sat down and felt private in the midst of life. Overhead the planks rattled and thundered musically whenever a car or a wagon went across. Low down to the ground, the two boys saw a flat world—the river stretching widely afar; little water; much light; land fading into the distance, finally rubbed out by the heat.

With the same question in their eyes, which neither could translate, but which asked if there were no end to folly, they opened their beer, and lighted up their smokes; confirmed by their dismal trophies of indulgence.

XXI · THE PROGRAM

I

There was a rising and falling, and as they spoke of it, eternal flow
of their rapture that made Martha and Bun want to keep a secret
for some time yet. They would meet evenings at the library, as usual;
only now, with a sense of design come into their lives where before
they had only known and been vaguely dissatisfied with a succession of things to do, they embarked upon a program of what they
called "self-improvement." They were sober and inwardly excited
about it. They pulled long faces over their intellects, and this very
attitude gave them an almost unbearable, delicious inner reminder
of their desire, which was now so channeled and controlled that it
became a kind of engine source for their very lives.

If it was worth while to be together, then it was worth while to
make the most serious plans for the future. The most serious plans
for the future meant looking at themselves to see what they needed
to realize their hopes. To realize their hopes meant knowing what
Bun was going to do. What Bun was going to do was become a
doctor.

"The only doctor I know is Doctor Rush. My brother Wayne is
a great friend of little Donald Rush."

"My father says Doctor Rush is the best one in this town.—He
knows them all as only a prescription druggist can. Says Rush is a
deep one, too. He *studies* a lot."

"What about?"

"Oh, I don't know.—Just *studies*."

"Mrs. Rush is not very well."

"I'll bet she has never been in love, then," said Bun.

Martha looked at him in delighted amazement.

"There. That's what I mean," she said.

"About what?" he asked.

"About you.—Two weeks ago you would never've made a remark like that."

"Like what?"

"As intelligent as that, about Mrs. Rush, and love."

"Oh." He laughed airily. She wanted to eat him up, she said to herself, when he looked as charming as that, with his eyes almost smiled out of sight by his smooth and glowing cheeks. "I believe love is health," he added, crowning his first effort with one even more delectable.

"You will be the greatest physician in the Southwest. You already have what very few of them have."

"What is that?"

"Intuitive genius," she said soberly.

"I believe perhaps you're right. Of course, it is a gift for which I can hardly accept credit. My mother always said that my grandfather Summerfield, *her* father-in-law, that is, was a very superior man.—This was his ring."

They regarded it together. In silence he took it off his finger that was like a young branch in spring, with sun-pinked bark, and put it on her thumb. For several moments they did not speak. And then with the dramatic inspiration of their state, she gently took them from the beating impulses of desire and wooed them back to their intellectual league, and they bent again over the book on the table before them—a history of medicine which they were absorbing together, page by page, reading in silence, and nodding when they were one by one ready to turn the next page.

They had a program of further study all mapped out.

One page of German grammar every evening. One page of French essay writing, "because the French were so good at clear argument." This was a sentiment Bun had found in his sophomore notebook in his attic den at home, where Grandfather Summerfield's books had been put. Five pages of *Pickwick Papers* every evening. One § of the medical history, though sometimes they were unable to finish that assignment before closing time because some of the §'s were longer than others. And finally, a book on the care of babies—a subject which they approached with a sort of stern modesty, declaring that there was too much prudery in the world about so wonderful a fact as birth and so delightful a birthright as rearing children.

2

One evening she suddenly faced him during their study, and asked him why he was called Bunny. He said that an aunt came to see him, Susan Leighton, from Kansas City, when he was a little boy five years old, and he remembered vividly that it was Auntie Susan who had first called him Bunny, and that they had all been photographed on the lawn of the house out on South Walter Street, and Auntie Susan had held his hand, and got him to laughing by asking him *whose* bunny he was, he was *her* little bunny, so that when the Kodak clicked in the hands of his father, he was laughing in glee, and on the print when it came back from the developer's in its yellow paper envelope was the record of the moment when they had all started to call him Bunny, which later years and older friends had changed to Bun.

"Bring it to show me tomorrow night, darling!"

"I will if I can find it."

He was suddenly shy. He knew perfectly well where the picture was, it was cornered into the black-sheeted photograph album that lay on the under shelf of the mission-style library table at home. Nobody looked at it any more. Auntie Susan was dead, too, but what fun she had been, how clever she was with her humor and her devotion to him as a little boy. She died an old maid, but if her life had never been full to the brim, she had certainly helped to give others a lot for their own lives; he frowned and tried to remember if this might not in itself have been a fulfilled mission for Auntie Susan.

Anyway, he did bring the picture the next evening, and Martha pored over it, and he thought she looked almost greedy.

She felt like his mother, possessing the little boy in the snapshot with her eyes. She had a sentimental film on her vision which she turned away from him so he wouldn't think her a fool. It was so exactly like him now, twelve years later, by her side, in his always fresh clothes, his pressed trousers, his spotless sweaters, his bulky-shouldered coats. He was the cleanest boy she ever knew, and the strongest-looking, not with bulging knots of muscle, that bored her, but with a harmonious look of flowing arch and staying tension; bone and flesh. And in the snapshot, there was the gleeful little boy, laughing with all his heart, and over him, the bending figure of Auntie Susan, whose face was hidden; all that showed of her was the anonymous attitude of love and protection. To one side, patiently fond, was her sister Mrs. Summerfield clasping her own elbows, as if resigned to awkward usefulness.

"You do. You look exactly like a bunny," said Martha finally, "with such a big-toothed smile.—May I keep the snapshot?"

"It's Mother's," he said.

"Can't you get another?"

"The negative is lost, I guess."

"Then I guess you want it back."

"—It's Mother's."

"Oh: very well."

"She'd miss it, darling."

"Oh, very *well*, take it."

He was calm, because he was right, and never believed in apologizing for being right. He put the snapshot back into his wallet, and reminded her that after all, she had his Grandfather Summerfield's braided gold ring.

She knew what it was that had irritated her. Not the snapshot, which turned her heart to water, but the feeling of having put herself into his mother's place for a moment; this was guilty; poor Mrs. Summerfield; how total love was; some day she would find some way to have Mrs. Summerfield forgive her without knowing exactly what for.

"I am a fool, but I don't care," she said, turning them back to their book again.

They were serene and sure in working this way together. It made the future seem a clever little arrangement of their own devising. They had a sense of movement and direction which seemed to them unique. All other people—such as also came to use the common riches of the public library—seemed to them "little people." A sense of pity suffused Martha and Bun when they looked around them at others. They never knew it, but they were arrogant in their love.

XXII · FORGIVEN

I

When Peter came downstairs from his office and went out to his car late in the afternoon, he was astonished to see his son Donald sitting there waiting for him. Now what on earth: he thought. But the Rushes were so rarely articulate with each other that he simply smiled at the boy, and got in and drove off.

Something was up.

But he would never get at it by asking. He drove in easy silence for several blocks, and said to himself that maybe Don just wanted to ride around with him, and if he did, why, he was more than welcome. It had never happened before. It might never happen again. But if there was anything beyond sense it was what a boy that age might take a notion into his head to do, or want.

Don pursed his lips to whistle, but made no sound. Peter could see a dark shadow along the boy's deeply curved lip. You couldn't call it a mustache, but it was a hint of where a mustache would be, one day. Good lord, already, what do I remember of my own adolescence? Hardly any details. But it all turned up very sharply in the memory of feeling a couple of years back when I was reading that book on rites of primitive peoples. No wonder they mark every stage with a duty or an act of suffering or an ordeal by shock. They make life a series of stages, and simplify what is expected of everyone by making it all cut and dried, perfectly plain. What do we do? We just let our children slide from phase to phase, and nobody can be expected to develop with the same harmonies as everybody else, if there are no clearly marked lines to cross, obligations to undertake, and phenomena to recognize. Our obscenities (and some of them, willy-nilly, are acts of discovery) are all secret. That's where the savage has it over us. His are exposed and even ceremonial, and their purpose made plain and impersonal.

I believe I'd've been abysmally unhappy myself as a boy if I'd had rich parents, or been born in a city, but as 'twas, all this land to charge around in; my horse to ride; my share of work to do to keep the house warm in winter or the field plowed and tended in summer; my Bible lines to learn every week; the cycles of animal life on our ranch; nobody much to be with, even after we came in town so I'd go to school; you wouldn't believe the difference of the two worlds, my boyhood's, and my son's. I may be wrong.

2

He drove to the edge of town on the south, where he had a call to make in a veritable shack, the home of a tubercular patient. He took his bag and left Don in the car and went into the house. Don sat looking out at the plain into which the street opened and vanished, as if it were a river reaching the illimitable sea. The sun was going down and the light was long and golden. There were some towering cumulus clouds far off beginning to look like pink marble in the softening light. Donald wondered if he might someday be a great artist, noted for sunset effects, and have his name printed in books with two dates, in brackets, showing when he was born, and when he died, like *Sir* Anthony Van Dyck (1599–1641). This troubled him only for a second. Should he tell Daddy about the rifle? Or, rather, *would* he tell him?—For that he *ought* to do so, he knew. He knew well enough that the Doctor would never ask anything about the rifle. A lifetime of presents, and his father had never once checked up on what was done with them. His father never came around butting in, he would say that.

The door of the house opened, and Peter came out, followed for a couple of steps by a young woman who was smiling sociably with a white, drawn mouth that would break the other way when she was alone again. He was always reached by the social courage that people tried to maintain when he had to leave bad news behind him.

"Now let's see, where next," he said, turning the big car around and heading back to town. "I'll run by the hospital the last thing. Let's go by old MacClellan's house and see what's wrong with the government today.—He's been a lot spryer since I told him to quit reading the *Literary Digest*. Just did it to make him *start* reading it. Now he gets in a fit over the nation, and forgets to snarl about his liver. Liver's all right, or it'd be a scandal if it *were* any better in a man his age."

They stopped at a miniature copper-roofed castle of red brick and white stone down by the park in town. While the Doctor was within, Donald squinted his eyes dreamily at the deep windows, the towers, and stained-glass jewels in the upper halves of the front windows, and made a king's palace out of it.

A golden twilight was at large in the streets when they drove on again.

After a couple of other calls, they parked up at the hospital, on the graveled circle of driveway in back.

3

The hospital stood on a knoll, and Peter sat at the wheel of his car for a moment, gazing abstractedly out across the sandhills below them. Under the yellow sky, all things on the earth were graying to a dusky black, the roofs of little houses, the lines of fences, the bulk of sheds and anything built. Twilight brushed across these mean structures and their silhouettes came together in one long earth-bound line, rising and falling like a melody. What fixed Peter's eye and penetrated his spirits like a song, clear and sweet, was, commonly enough, a single electric light bulb hanging from a right-angled pole at the intersection of the dirt streets of the sandhills. The light globe hung against the yellow heaven and burned and burned like a clear yellow star. This sharp clarity of the lamp against the grander general clarity of the light-poured sky over the shadowed earth was a sight on the outskirts of Albuquerque that never failed to visit a brief enchantment upon him. It always made him think of the ingenuities of people, bold and clear, against the impassive beauties of the earth's nature. It turned his heart over with affection for the one, and with humility before the other.

He thought of speaking of it to Don, but changed his mind, and got out of the car.

One of the nuns met the Doctor as he came up the steps.

"Good efening, Doctor, who is that in the car vit you?"

"Hello Sister, that's my boy."

"Your cude liddle boy? How sveet!"

"Oh, yes, he and I are great buddies. He rides around with me on my calls all the time."

"Na!" cried the sister softly, at this pleasant marvel of family life, as the Doctor went to the elevator.

Now that's odd, he said to himself, what on earth made me tell such a ridiculous lie?

But he admitted that he knew, all right, and when he came down half an hour later, he felt a little shy of Donald, as if the boy knew the hopeful sentimental imposture his father had made.

So they rode again in silence, but this silent being together was enough for them both, they both being Rushes, as the father mused humorously, and he was deeply happy, and he thought Don seemed at peace, too. At dusk they got home, sure of each other, just because they could ride around together for two hours and not have to explain anything.

Anyway, though he couldn't say why, Donnie felt forgiven.

XXIII · ON THE MOONLIT MESA

I

Bun had managed to get the family car from his father, and was waiting at the library corner when Martha got off the bus. He was smiling like a Chessy cat, she told him, not realizing at first whose car he was standing by. When he told her that he had the car for the evening, she was suddenly embarrassed, and disappointed him by her meager response to his achievement. She got in, blushing furiously, and sat down, hating herself for being so unreasonable; but what stormed within her was pity for them both that they weren't married and independent, with their *own* car. How long would they have to meet this way like naughty children, and suffer the infrequent charity of the druggist who let his son use the car for the evening?

Bun was stiffened with irritation too. He had performed miracles of "logic" to argue his father into letting him take the car, and now she didn't seem pleased. How could you ever know what women would think! His pride in being at the wheel was punctured. He felt like driving her right home and letting her out at her corner, and turning around, and driving back to town, and getting drunk in the back room of the White Elephant, where he had heard liquor was sometimes sold to minors.

He drove out to the mesa, waiting for her to speak. He kept looking out the left side, his side, of the car because he didn't care to look at her.

By the time they reached the open plain he was really angry, and she was frightened. Her heart skipped along in a rapid race with her thoughts. How could she forgive herself, through him? Was it gone? Their carefully built edifice of security? What about the program of self-improvement; the care and feeding of babies; the pledges of their lips and hands?

She thought of kissing him wittily as if to make him realize that she had only been fooling. But he was monolithic beside her, and there had been too long a silence.

"Our ranch is out here somewhere," she said at last, but her conversational sound mocked sincerity.

"Oh, is it?"

She felt committed to a policy of hollow lightness, and with her heart in a squeeze of dread, she went on.

"Do let's drive over to see it, there's enough moonlight, I haven't been up here in ages.—Poor Mumma! She thinks it is a gold mine, or something. My father used to have it to raise chickens on, but his health got worse and worse, and finally when he died the ranch was just abandoned. But we still own it. My little brother comes out here with Donald Rush sometimes on picnics.—I'll watch for the road. It goes off to the left, somewhere, here.—There it is!—No, wait. That's the neighboring place. Ours is just a tiny place, a couple of acres or something. But it has some cute little houses on it."

He drove on, simply looking at the left lane of the highway. Before them were the mountains, lifted as if the surface of the plain had been raised from below, a cosmic tablecloth beneath which unseen hands created a row of mountains.

2

Now a thought began to burn in her head. Why shouldn't she and Bunny take the little adobe one-room house at the ranch and fix it up and live there when they got married, and got started on their own?

She took his arm and with her touch, begged him to forgive her. Her animation reached him. He turned and looked at her.

"All right, we'll go see the place," he said, and she thought it almost as if he answered her excited thought. "But I'm not going to be any more impressed with it than you were with my dad's car."

"I'm sorry, honestly, I am, darling, I am such a fool, Bunny, all my life when people have got me nice things I have been so happy that right away something *else* seemed to happen inside of me, and I acted as if I was *ashamed* of what they gave me.—Poor Mumma has worked her fingers off for me and Wayne, and when I think of it, I want to *die*, but I can no more hug her and thank her than I can *fly*!—About *something else*, I can make her see how much I love her.—I must be an ungrateful and terrible woman. I don't know why you ever looked at me. They say a mean spirit shows in your face first of all. I must have a *hideous* face."

Her humility was so much greater than he expected or wanted that he thought what a bum he had been to say a thing like that to her. He put his arm around her and laid his head down on hers for a moment, still driving.

"Hush yo' mouf," he said. It melted her heart to hear him assume another character for her amusement; he was usually so forthright and always seemed to her as unchangeable as the mountain rocks ahead of them.

"Wait," she said, and sat up. "There's the road."

He turned off into the sandy lane, and they drove, lost and

found among the shadows of the moonlighted foothills, until they came to the little ranch with its two blocks of adobe.

"Here we are.—Doesn't it look *tiny*! I remembered it as a little more like something than *this*!"

"A ranch!" he said, laughing.

"Well, that was the chicken house, there, and—the glass is all broken. Look. It is like snow on the ground, in the moonlight."

"—Not a whole piece left.—Roving kids. What could you expect?"

"Mumma will be *killed* when she sees this…"

Her voice wailed. She was like a forlorn child, feeling what her mother would feel.

"Is that the house?"

"Yes. It has one room. Shall we peek in?"

They looked in, and could see nothing but the pale squares of the window across the room from them at the other end of the hut. The darkness between this wall and the opposite one seemed rich with excitements and suggestions to her.

3

Calling his name softly, she turned and took herself to his arms, shutting her eyes to see them together in such a little house, by themselves, as if night could last forever and this kiss, too.

It was such a pure and beautiful triumph, to erase their little misery over the car in each other's striving embrace.

They denied the vast thoughtlessness of the land around them with their burning thoughts and aching selves. They were possessed. They could not let each other go. No, no, no, she said to herself, and even to him, half-aloud, when she could, her breath skipping in a suffering laugh; but neither would he let her be, nor she him.

She loved him wildly, at the same time trying to call to the rescue such things as "a page of German grammar every evening." It availed nothing.

He rode his passion as if it were a horse of which he was master, yet which he let run where it would.

The night was perfectly still; but a cloud came over the moon and gave everything a chill sense for a moment.

Trembling, they broke apart.

"*Gosh*, darling," she said. She sounded sore-throated with emotion. No poetry if she had spoken it could have tumbled his heart more in her name.

She fell against the adobe wall and put her fingers to her temples.

"We'd better go."

He put his hands on the wall up above her and fell to her and took her mouth again with his. Holding him with her lips, she began to press him away with her hands on his hard belly, which yet caved in at her touch, and this time when he desisted, she ran to the car and waited for him in silence, wringing her hands and shaking her head slowly, as if saying, Oh my, oh my, oh my, and wondering not with mind but with blind ages-old memories of woman, what she had done...

He came back presently.

He was composed.

He was silent. But she knew he was not angry. He was dizzied by how narrowly they had walked, and how willingly. If he had spoken, he could have asked only one thing. He knew how a maiden heart could beat now.

4

Halfway down the hill, when the lights of the city were well spread before them, and the cars ran ahead of them and people were in the streets, he sighed and it sounded humorous, and he reached and took her hand and squeezed it, meaning that they were safe again, and how could it be that it was true that everything passed, except their love itself.

XXIV · THE STRONG TIDE

I

Willa Shoemaker saw evidences of something stormy in her daughter. She saw Martha rarely during the day, and in the recent evenings, attempts to talk to her had been unsuccessful; really *talk*, that is. Martha was "charming," and "considerate," hurrying to help if she was needed, and once she had thrown her arms around her little bony mother with an ecstatic hug, but had instantly withdrawn herself as if sorry to have betrayed something.

"What is it, Mar, dearie, what *are* you doing?"

"Nothing, Mother, I am in a *silly* fit."

"You haven't had a *silly* fit for years, nor Wayne, either, my children are growing up so fast," said Willa, looking at her daughter earnestly, which made Martha sharply angry for its penetration. "I remember," Willa continued, "you and your little brother used to hang out your tongues, and dangle your hands from your wrists, and run around in circles, and when I would ask you *what*, you'd both say you were having a *silly* fit.—I wonder if other families are like ours!"

Martha looked at her direct; with hard, pretty eyes, and with the blazing vitality of anyone young which made anyone older look dowdy and used-up, and said the cruelest thing she could think of, as a protection for what she cherished in secret:

"I suppose all families are pretty much the same, except that ours isn't as *happy* as most, I guess."

Willa looked at her with an animal's eyes, flooded with misery, but she was too well-bred, the mother, who waited tables all day for a living, to reveal her deeply hurt pride and security, and left the selfish girl to go and consider what made her so selfish.

Willa had a pretty good idea.

2

It was part of the texture of talk in such a town that *who went with whom* was sure to be common property sooner or later. Willa had heard about Bunny and Martha from one of her working friends down at the Harvey House, whose younger sister worked at the public library. Willa knew Bun Summerfield, and his whole family, but to refresh herself as to what *kind* of boy he was, she took some time off on an afternoon and went to Summerfield's Drug to make a purchase and see him. He was there. He didn't wait on her, Rollie Glovers did that, with his pale and rather ghastly politeness; but Bun bowed to her, and she smiled back, not without feeling a pang at how much of a threat he represented. She said to herself that he was a sweet-looking boy, with such an open, frank countenance, and he smiled the most honest smile sh'ever saw, he had such beautiful teeth. He was so well-groomed. He seemed to take to people in a lively eagerness that was very likable. Why did he look so beautifully dressed in his tan linen jacket with "Summerfield's" embroidered above the pocket, when Rollie looked like a pillowcase held up at the corners? She took her parcel…more foot powder, for it seemed to her she could never have enough in the house, she got so tired these days…and as she went out the Central Avenue door, she looked again at Bun, and was startled to see that he was just as avidly looking at her. Her heart sank. *She* knew, even if he was not old enough to know, how much people could communicate without words. She went back downtown to the Harvey House grieving for Martha, and yet stirred by a reverie of Martha's time of life.

Who was she, the mother, to deny what her child would reach? There was a lump in her throat when she remembered the meadows of her own girlhood. It was such a green picture, the land flowed with silver brooks, and the trees hooded over young people in the evenings in summertime, and where love first of all came alive was forever the picture of the country where her heart would dwell. How different from this desert country where her husband had brought her! How sweet to plan and scheme and hope for a return to Albion, with her grown children, where they too might find their start in life, as she had!—This boy Bunny Summerfield was like any boy anywhere.—Martha would forget him.—When could she afford to make the trip?

This thought returned her to the present, for she knew they had no money for such an undertaking as the three of them going home to Albion for that long-dreamed-of visit.

As she always did when there was something troublesome to be got through with, she squarely looked at it, and said to herself, We can't go, and that's the end to it, don't be a fool, Willa Johnson—using her maiden name. In many ways she was, to herself, a maiden still. People saw one aspect of this when they remarked on her energy, her eagerness that seemed so friendly.

3

For the next several days she watched Martha and her suspicions stayed alive. Martha was so funny lately, trying so hard to be her old self. Willa didn't know how much to believe, or what to say, and when her thoughts raced along as they could not help doing, with images of Bun and Martha, both so sure of their beauties, so strong and proud and indifferent to anyone else, she would almost lose her breath to *think* that they *might*—what they *might* blunder into, in spite of their righteous upbringing. She didn't know whether she should give up all chances for temporary peace in the family, and come right out with it, and *talk* to Martha, or not.

What if she did that, and what if she was wrong, and Martha and Bunny had nothing to—to be ashamed of?

How would she feel then? How would Martha feel? Wouldn't it kill Martha's love for her mother, forever, not to be trusted any more than that? It certainly would. She shivered at the narrow escape she had had (in thought) of losing her daughter's trust and love.

Yes but.

Would she *ever* forgive herself.

To think of what might happen for want of a sympathetic word, *in time*.

What if it'd've been possible before it was too late—? If for the want of what a mother could tell and save, her daughter should've gone and…?

She worried and worried, and watched. She consoled herself by thinking of Bun, and of how "clean-cut" he was, and of what innocent happiness danced in his eyes. He would never be the one to:

And yet in her heart, in little stirrings, there were likewise starts of obscure wish that love should visit the two youngsters and declare them one. After such hardly recognized seedlings of feeling, she would be doubly anguished, even jealous, at the romance that worried her, and she would scold to herself that no-matter-what, Martha had to be talked to.

But Martha: the *dimmedest* thing (as Willa thought, using her nearest approximation to a curse word), was unapproachable in the most subtle and final way. She couldn't say *why* she couldn't talk to Martha. There was simply something in the way. Martha was like a little *woman*, whose rights would not be infringed, not by any body, not even her own mother. It was all very plain and untouchable.

4

Oh-sigh-oh-my, 'll watch and 'll *watch*, and there's that *boy*, that Bunny, still you never could know, if she'd only come and tell me, just anything, a *scrap*, just say she's *meeting* him, and who he *is*, of course I *know*, but still: what a goose I am to worry-worry-worry, tears in m'eyes, lump in m'throat, has to come to everybody, look at how happy *I* was, do you suppose I made my poor mother Sarah Johnson as miserable as this, yes, I suppose so, we used to get the surrey in the evenings, and four of us go buggy riding, taking a long road around to get to the Yeagers' big brick farmhouse, where all the parties were, where Martin Yeager was, too, *what did Martin have in his eyes*, he had lights that danced, poor Martha, my poor little girl, I hope God keeps you as He kept me, for it is a strong tide that runs in the strict course of love…

XXV · THE TRIP TO HANO

I

It was a day in early May. Little white clouds like flags were whipped out in the scented wind which played warmth over the land. Peter went in his car to get Molly. She was ready and waiting. Miss Bridges was with her in the big dark front room.

"For goodness' sake, don't come back till late," she said. "I can get the most enormous amount of work done if you will keep Molly out of the house all day.—We've promised the typescript by next Wednesday, and I'm having my hands full."

"You're sure you wouldn't like to come along?" asked Peter.

He saw Miss Bridges's eyes flash and her mouth rake downward in an ironical denial which confessed far more than it should've, about how much she really wanted to come, and how much she punished herself for reasons that were obscure to her and everyone else.

"I loathe motoring," she replied.

"I told you that, Peter," said Molly.

"Yes, I asked Mrs. Foster if you wouldn't come, and she said you hated driving."

Judy Bridges shrugged and pursed her mouth looking at Peter with angry humor.

"You should call her Molly, you sound very stuffy being formal with her when she is first-naming you all over the place."

"Ju-dy, hush," said Molly softly, and lightly kissed her on the cheek. Then she turned and nodded to Peter that they might leave now.

Judy had made enough of a comment to make them feel a trifle constrained as they headed out to the country in the big car. He had always liked the way Molly would simply sit and say nothing when a silence fell of its own weight. So many people he knew couldn't bear to let minutes pass without making or hearing talk. But he felt right now as if he would give anything to break the silence which Judy's ironical farewell had led to. It was as if Judy had challenged them to say, to reveal, what was plain to her, that they were in love, that they were escaping together for this day all the just dues of habit, and that to anyone with even half the brains and experience of Judy Bridges, the whole thing had been perfectly plain from the first moment they set eyes on each other.

But for a while he could not invent anything that would let him down easily, out loud, and so he looked at Molly beside him, and believed that for the first time since he'd known her she seemed moody. She was glancing out the right side of the car, her head tilted in its shadowing hat, as if to "see" the country better.

They were driving down the river road, now coming under airy tunnels of arching cottonwoods, and now crossing golden sandy spaces of sunshine. The river was to their left. The road curved near and far from it as it went down the valley. Beyond they saw the mountains, or if the near ground rose to hide the mountains, they saw their effect in the cloud clusters in the sky, faint with golden heat.

Molly suddenly sat up and turned her attention back to him with decision, as if she had sharply finished feeling a certain way, or thinking a certain thing, and was saying "There!" to it. She smiled and stretched her arms before her.

"This is heavenly."

"It's going to be a hot day."

"I shall simply love it. I want to bake like a lizard and simply confess the power of the sun.—You don't *feel* it anywhere else. Whoever really *sees* sunlight back East? You take it for granted. You don't get struck by the flat of it as if it were a sword when you step outdoors there. You don't say to yourself, *My, there it is again, the source of life*, when you step into East Sixty-Seventh Street in the middle of the morning. I could write a whole mythology, with pretty little temples and clever ceremonies and some symbolical but harmless sacrifices, about the New Mexico sun. I suppose this has all been done, but ever so much more seriously than I would do it.—I never feel any charm, I mean cunning, little, daily *sweetness* in the mythologies which professors record in their tall narrow books. Do you?"

"I don't know. I never read any."

"Well, anyway, I would make mine a sort of *darling* system of gods and goddesses and powers and attributes and sins and penalties."

Peter laughed with a sudden idea of what her books must be like, from the way she invented this happy nonsense.

"Is that what your novels are like?"

"Oh."

"Oh *what*."

"Oh, then you have never read any of them?"

"Why, no.—I thought you knew that."

"No, I just thought you didn't know who-I-was in relation to all those books."

"No, I didn't know anything about any of it."

She smiled ruefully.

"I suppose only women read what I write. What a horrid thought."

She was being lighthearted, he saw, but also there showed in her face a suddenly hectored look, and he thought it made her look the way a child does when you get a sudden hint of what the child will look like in old age. It was a flying shadow of the future. He was moved. Whenever he was touched his face became absolutely fixed. It was a stern expression. He was articulate only when his heart was easy. He thought now of anybody's frailty, but it came clear to him in her likeness. He sounded almost harsh when he said,

"Why is that horrid? What's the matter with women reading your books?"

She had no idea of what notions her remark had brought up, either about her, or about his wife, and her habitual sleight-of-spirit which substituted romancing for living.

"Oh, women are so *avid*," she said. "They keep looking for themselves in books. I imagine a man who loves to read is always seeing other people in them, people he knows, and admires, and hates, but rarely himself. He is so sort of *decent* about it that when an author *pinks* him with something he didn't know anybody else ever knew, or thought, or imagined, he is amazed, and says to himself, *Why, how in the world did that fellow know that about it, why, that's the way I am.* But a woman would be reading everything, all along, as if it were all about her, and she would coldly condemn anything that the author had his characters do if it wasn't what she herself did or would do.—This is so silly, all I mean is that if my books have only what women like in them, then I am in a rage."

"I don't think you can make such a reckless accusation about all women. I have known some perfectly selfless women."

"I know it, so have I, I'm just *talking*, of course.—But I do think women in general would admit the *kind* of thing I meant."

"You do:"

"Certainly I do.—Women don't ever shrink from facing and admitting the worst about themselves. I suppose it's their most really clever weapon.—And if anything happens to their children, they're so much better about *managing* than men."

He kept thinking that if she had a chart of what was wrong at home, in his house, she could not've been treading more close to everything that troubled him. He refused to carry it any closer. He pointed to a road they could see rising and fading in the sandhills to their distant right.

"See that road? That's where we turn off on to get to Hano."

The earth and sky met in an almost yellow blur of heat in the faraway.

It was late in the morning.

They felt like runaways.

In a moment they reached the place to turn off from the river road. A rolling desert of sandy hills lay before them, and they had the sensation of being lost in it when they left the green mercy of the river side. Once again there was that sense of going beyond time which Peter had when he came direct to the country. The air was hot and the sandy dust off the road came up after the car in a cloud so dense that it now and then overtook them. They literally tasted the earth. It was oddly bittersweet.

"What is it like, where we are going?" asked Molly. And then a double sense of her words made her turn to look at Peter, and she put her hands to her cheeks and wondered while a throb felt in her breast. Used to using her emotions for what she wrote, she was subject to the power of words, and the question she had asked seemed to her full of the doubt, the possible sweetness, the hurtful guesses which any future held. If Peter too felt the second-thought in what she'd said, he didn't show it. He was squinting slightly as he drove through the desert glare, and she saw his face, brown, a faint glisten on his weathered skin, a shaft of light in his eye, a boyish lift to the tip of his nose, a browner red to his rough mouth, and the round cut of his solid chin, fixed against the background of the sandhills which moved past beyond him.

He ignored her question.

"As for what happens to children," he said, after about two miles of silence and road-eating, "which you mentioned a while back, nothing can happen to them which could possibly be as serious as the things they don't actually see or touch."

She was now sure he was deliberately evading her question; why, she didn't know.

"How? in what way."

"I mean the first important thing for a child is a certainty of being safe. As the child grows, this security from without can be allowed to lessen as the child learns what hazards are and how to meet them from within, until its own security is woven part and parcel into its character."

"Yes."

"But the thing that makes or unmakes this kind of safety for a child is the thing the child feels at home, unspoken, alive in the air, a food for the heart. A psychological security. It has nothing to do with money, or good food, or careful upbringing, or what school you choose, or who your children play with. I have seen families with the shabbiest kind of surroundings and the most careless treatment of all the things the Public Health office would have fits over, and the craziest diet, and the riskiest kind of life for their kids; and the kids've been wonders of health, happiness, proper toughness, and even beauty. Why. Because the father and the mother were in love and truly mated and loved being with each other and seemed to belong together and the children felt it, could know it without seeing it, and the security which the parents felt in each other simply became a climate for the little ones to grow up in."

He was frowning as he drove. She suddenly felt that she must not intrude into his thought with any questions. She decided to be academic with him.

"That sounds awfully arbitrary. I feel that the first thing is decency in the physical life of the child, good food, and proper hours and care, and enough baths and fresh clothes, and you may say all you wish about the charm of love in a hovel, but I'd prefer to have my daughter able to cope with germs if they beset her, which has happened and will again."

"Risks, yes. Preventive medicine and such are grand, and I not only practice but I preach the same. But if I had one thing to rule as a sacrifice, in a given situation, it would be the very things you regard as the more important. I believe that nothing else matters *as much* as that a child shall feel from his first to his last day in his father's house that all is well there, for him, and those in it, between each other. If there is a failure there, the child will know it, even if there's nothing of it outwardly visible. The more I work with—with ailing people, the more I am convinced that the first factor of life on this earth is spiritual, as it is in the next. Any doctor has seen miracles of recovery which could only be traced to health in the spirit."

"You do convince me, nearly."

"That's the sort of health I'd like my child to have forever. I'd never worry about him, no matter what befell him. I've seen plenty of what does befall people now and then."

What is it, she asked him silently. You are telling me something out of your heart, and I am ready to hear it. She became oddly agitated within her outer composure. She wanted to put her fingers to her temples, and for a moment be out of the sunlit wilderness of those baking sandhills. But she knew from how he sounded that he was telling her of how things were in his house, and her heart beat when she believed that he was coming upon discoveries for himself about what he might do in the future for his son. All she knew was that he had an only son. The boy stood before her in imagination now, clearly, and so did the mother, called up in her thoughts by the way he had spoken, as if such bitterness were distasteful to him, yet had to be said by his own lips.

She rode with him in silence, until he said, some time later,

"The country where we are going gets into foothills pretty soon, look, you can see a faint and cooling line of blue beyond the farthest sandhills. Those are mountains, but long before we get to them this sandy country is gone, and we are in winding hills of rock and scrub pine, and once or twice in a dark forest. We get pretty high, and at last we come to a place that winds up to a tremendous mesa, at the foot of which there is a river. Often there is no water in the river, which has cut a deep canyon in the floor of the plain below the mesa. One side of the canyon is much higher than the other. Its face looks out over what seems like a world. Up toward the top of the canyon-side, there is a cliff that stands clear and open like a brow of earth. The closer you get, you will see that there are little places in it, they are windows, and doors, and they are walls of mud-cemented stones, and that is the empty cliff city of Hano, where people lived a long time ago."

"Is there no one there now?"

"A Park Service guide, probably, but probably no one else."

They came into a huge island of cloud shadow which cooled them for a few miles.

He was withdrawn into thought. He felt that there could be no better proof of the intimacy he felt with her than this, that he feel easy about such a withdrawal from casual talk. After a while, as if with a decision in his mind, he said,

"My own boy, for instance. My wife is very dear to us, to both of us, but when he was born, something happened to her, it's hard to explain, and commoner than people know. Anyway, she feels she cannot have another child. It is without sense, and an illness of course, and it has meant a good deal of patience and sympathy. But those are not the same things as happiness. I don't believe grownups have a right to demand happiness. But I think children ought to have it. The kind I was talking about back there.—That's what that was all about, I suppose you gathered that by yourself. I don't mean to be heartless talking about Noonie to anyone else, and I never have before in my life.—It is some sort of relief. If you're embarrassed, perhaps that would help excuse it all."

"Oh, no!" she said. She cursed herself for the readiness of her emotions. They came up and choked her. She said to herself that she loved him, and pitied him, and must not say so to him.

"Anyway, what I've felt for some time is that something big and maybe awful will have to happen before anything can be better with us."

"Oh, I do hope not!"

"So do I."

He turned and looked at her, for the first time on the long drive. He thought she was almost unbearably pretty and that she looked different from when they'd started. He scowled at her which gave a dark band of intensity to his brow, and he ground his jaw forward a trifle, nodded once, with vigor, and then looked back to the road.

It was as if he had said that never before had he allowed to be so plain to anyone else what had been clear to him for so long. He seemed to confess to great tenderness and at the same time to great strength, if these two things should have to be at cross purposes in his life. He had the air of someone who's made a resolve, and would fight forever if allowed to, to keep it. If anything should happen to break it beyond his power, he might become a different person, and meantime, the hardest thing in the world for him to do was to admit to anyone else the weaknesses which he had seen in others, but never before in himself.

She had a habit of irony which appeared more in her books than in her relations with people. It now repeated to her, without any answer, the answer, the question she had asked him before. What is it like where we are going? A rueful look accompanied that sort of thought over her face. Her life had been tranquil for some years, and lonely, and for the most part she was grateful for it, after her marriage to a rich drinking man, and after her divorce, she welcomed what seemed almost an inability to feel things much at all.

Now she felt a pain at her heart, and she shut her eyes for a second, as if in dismay at the power to feel.

"We are coming to the foothills," he said, "look, there is the first scatter of the piñon trees."

2

The road curved and all they could see were the noonday glooms of the pines which made forest on both sides. The air was cooler. The road climbed up and turned back upon itself, crossing a mountain ridge. It dropped down the other side, they crossed a green plain, and entered a wide valley, which turned slowly to the west. As the car came about this grand turn, they were in full sunlight again. The valley became a river bed to the west, full of pinkish sand. Above the river hung the cliff. Peter let the car roll to a stop, and they both stared at the upper face of the cliff, where the empty dwellings were, with windows and doorways shadowed by the bright sun. It was quiet. The dust of the road settled back to the ruts.

"We're about two miles away still."

"—Do we want to go closer?" she asked, turning to him with a sudden reluctance to see this ghost of life which stretched along the upper cliff for a mile. She was uncertain of her feelings; but it seemed to her that these were almost like open graves, these dark little caverns in the clifftop.

"Why, of course. It doesn't *mean* anything till you get right up into it."

He drove on.

They came along the valley until they were at the foot of the city. They left the car in a clump of piñon trees, and by a weathered silver cottonwood bridge they crossed the river bed, which was dry. A board shack stood at the other end of the bridge, bearing a sign which read "Custodian." But it was closed, no one was to be seen, and Peter led the way up the path which began to climb from the river's edge. It was a sandy trail. The sun was like a hot iron on their backs. The trail was steep. They had to stop for breath many times. When they paused, they turned their heads in the silence. They were almost pressed by the silence, which made the blood beating in their ears seem like little thunders.

"We'll have to climb the ladders, the last stage of the way," said Peter.

"I get dizzy."

"It looks harder than it is."

"Do we want to go on top?"

"Oh yes, you won't get the lift it must have been to live here, long ago, if you don't see the world as they saw it."

His eyes were sparkling. He was open to yesterday, she saw. His imagination was kindled by the memory of this long-empty town in the cliff. She had a little current of misery and irritation at finding herself so moved by the empty cliff houses still far above them. They began to climb again. They could not talk. It took all their breath to proceed.

The trail finally brought them to a sort of shelf, where weeds grew in the rocky crevices, and the first of the houses stood in the dust of rock and time. The walls of the house were made of flat rocks mortared together long ago by mud plaster, of which none now remained. Yet the walls were worthy, and the windows and the doorway, with its high stone threshold, and its rock-colored wooden beam, were shapely. The room within looked as deep as a well and as cool. The floor rose in rounded sweeps to the inside walls. Opposite the door was another doorway, half-high, leading to an inner room.

"Here is where they lived."

"Who were they?"

"The Hanos, the sun children, you notice that their city faces east. Turn around."

She turned and looked over the valley. Far away at the horizon the midday made a white blur, but the hills between were blue, and the valley floor, so sharply below them, was golden pink, from the sand.

"When did they go away?"

"They think about seven hundred years ago. Nobody knows how or why. There is a palace up on the next level where things were

found that told of occupancy right up to the moment of abandon-
ment, evidently."

"What things?"

"Oh, furniture, pots, dishes, toys, and even the exposed body of
a dead man. His skeleton was found surrounded by little bits of life,
like a clay kettle, a bone awl, and some fabrics. Things of that sort."

She looked up at the upper cliff.

He nodded, and led to the weathered wooden ladder that leaned
against the next ledge. He told her not to look down, and asked if he
should go first. She nodded. He started up. At the ledge, he leaned
down and helped her up, and now they were on a ledge which was in
effect a one-sided street. Hundreds of rooms looked out over the valley. They were cunningly carved out of the sandstone itself, or as cunningly built into the natural contours of the cliff. Their security, their
wisdom, their shelled design for human life, were profoundly moving.

"It is the most extraordinary place I ever saw.—The most extraordinary *feeling* I ever had…" she said.

"I know. You cannot put your finger on it. It asks such an eternal question. It is a question we can answer in the heart, but never
in words."

"There must've been hundreds of people."

"Oh, yes. Easily. Maybe thousands."

She shook her head.

"I feel almost *unwanted* here. Don't you know what I mean? As
if *they* would not want anyone here?"

He laughed.

"They were peaceful people. I think. One school of thought
says they lived up here because they were afraid of roving warriors
down in the valley. Another tries to suggest that these people were
themselves warriors, who sallied down from this fortress, robbed
and killed, and came back to security here. I don't think either of
these is enough the truth."

"What is?"

"Can you climb again?"

She nodded.

They went to another upward ladder, and scaled a long blank face of stone, until they came to a u-shaped landing at the ladder's top. Here they found a trail worn smooth in the rock, curving out of sight like a slow spiral stairway, which brought them around a tower of boulders until they were on the very top of the valley wall, on a high mesa where long silvery grass grew, stretching away to the west in the blinding white sunlight like shimmering water.

Another city stood there, built up from the ground of adobe and stone. It was in ruins. No roofs were left, hardly a whole wall. It was like a comb of honey, cut and emptied and dried brown by the sun.

"Now look all around," said Peter. "Imagine morning up here."

Facing the east was a long redoubt of grass-grown earth. It curved like a half-moon. It was a sort of ramp, or walk, and it was the easternmost thing of the mesa city.

"Good people came there in the first hour of daylight to make their devotions and learn the day. I think they lived here not because they were scared or were bandits, but because this is a noble place for a city, at one with the sky, the plain and the river.—Doesn't that sound as plausible as anything to you?"

"Yes, of course.—It is a heavenly spot.—Somehow, I am more comfortable with these ruined houses on top than I am down below, where the walls are perfect, and the doors, and windows, and stone benches, and where it simply seems like the noon hour, and everybody will be back at one.—You know?"

"Yes, sure. Any kind of a mummy is disturbing. That is a mummified city down there.—Man has never been satisfied with physical attempts at eternity, or survival. We know more about it with our souls, which never need more proof of anything than their own conviction.—But it is so easy to look at the cliff, and see them all again, under the sun."

"Were they happy?"

He smiled fondly into her eyes.

"Yes, I think so. The men had much work to do. Look at that much rock to be carved. And the farms up here on the meadow.

And the women—this is a country of the man. Remember? The sun, there, he was the begetter. You asked a woman's question, didn't you."

"I only hoped they were happy.—Shouldn't we start down?"

He looked at her searchingly.

"You don't much like it here, do you:"

She shook her head. She didn't know what was responsible, the climb, the poignant emptiness of the city, or the solitude with him, but she was shaken. Her face was white, in the shadow of the broad-brimmed hat she wore.

"I don't think I like Indians," she said, trying to sound light-hearted. But it sounded petulant, and she was sorry to have said it. He shrugged, and led her back to the ladder.

"Even dead and vanished Indians," he murmured. She saw that he was nettled at the failure of his expedition. They went down the ladder to the next level, where all the houses stood throwing back the heat of the sun.

"Please," she said, "I'm sorry, if I seem so miserable about every-thing.—I am just very much moved by this whole place."

"Of course. I know.—Shall we rest a moment?"

They leaned and sat on some large boulders by the foot of the ladder, and gazed out over the valley. The blood was thudding in their ears. The littlest exertion at this altitude was noticeable.

He longed to speak to her with his arms.

In the silence, they rested. The heat! The clarity! The empty rooms! thought Molly, closing her eyes.

3

And then suddenly, at their level, and near to them, a brown and white bird flew past, the only thing alive which they'd seen. Molly didn't see it, but Peter watched it. It brought the sky to earth, and the valley floor right up to them. As it passed, the bird called sud-denly out. The sound was like a flash of lightning made hearable. Terribly loud, it echoed and struck from the cliff over the silent valley. Molly looked, and the bird cried again, farther down the cliff, and she felt her heart turn over within her.

How could a single bird so fill the deathly city that its cry sounded from end to end of the riddled cliff?

It was like something out of time, that cry and passage, a shearing scream of abstract melody, and it pierced them. It seemed to tell of people gone, and of life surviving.

"It unselfs me!" said Molly. "That poor, amazing bird!—In this silence and heat and emptiness!"

Peter nodded. He too was reached by the bird's cry, a spirit's whistle in the windowed street.

His hand was trembling as he put it forth to her. The bird's cry echoed in their ears. He bent down slightly, looking into her shadowed face, and he smiled sweetly and shook his head a trifle, as if to deplore for them both what he would do. He kissed her enfoldingly.

She was lost, and he was too. They shut out the dazzling day, the silence, the solitude, in each other.

Overhead, flying back from the far end of the cliff, the bird returned. His piercing cry echoed again, and they blinded themselves to it, shutting their eyes and hungering and easing through their kisses, which said no, and again no, no, to the dry caves of death above them in the cliff wall.

XXVI · MARTHA AND NOONIE

I

Martha knew little enough with her head about what had taken her heart whole. Ever since the night on the mesa, she had been full of a bewildered, sweet guilt that turned her cheeks pink whenever she remembered it. Heaven only knew! if they hadn't left when they did! what might! How can I tell anyone what it is like? And why do I feel that I must tell someone? And who is pure enough, who *knows enough*, to listen to me without smiling, or being sickened at what I *feel*, not at what I have *done*, for I have "done" nothing…?

How ashamed I am for washing out the taste of his kiss the first time he kissed me!

Is it the very same thing he gives me that I give him?

Does he think of me like this all the rest of the time as I do think of him?

What if: but it is ridiculous, I know: yes, but *what* if I had his baby, *now*?

What do women talk about when they are together? Has it ever happened? Does anybody know in her heart if a baby ever came to life from just *loving*? The way *we* love? *Enough* love—this would give life to a babe, without sin. For people do talk about sin. Do I know for the first time what miraculous beauty lay at the root of the birth of the Infant Jesus?

I pray: I do not mean to blaspheme to compare myself with the Virgin Mary. I pray and I argue that all love *starts* as purely as Hers. This is what it means, oh surely, this is what it means!

Nobody who looked at Martha in such moments could fail to have a pang for her possession by life; her eyes were so full of light, her skin so fresh, her breath so deeply drawn and so rueful, somehow, with what bothered her. But for many whom this aspect delighted, without their knowing quite why, there were others whom it distressed.

2

In the afternoon of the same day when Peter took Molly to the empty city in the cliff, Martha went to see Mrs. Rush, at an hour when she was pretty sure the Doctor was out. She knew that Donald was with Wayne, somewhere, they had gone on their bicycles. In her exquisite confusions, Martha was thinking that Mrs. Rush always looked so gentle, and smiled so kindly upon everyone and everything, that she wanted to—what did she mean?—sort of to *test* her love for Bun on somebody else, and perhaps see how it would strike an older woman. After all, she was going to spend the rest of her life with him, wasn't she. How proud she would be to hear someone say that it was a most suitable plan. Martha couldn't tell herself clearly why she didn't want to say anything to her mother Willa. But the whirr and the clatter, the worry and the looking at the problem from every angle that would ensue, she simply could not face.

But she did long to share her news, and see it sanctioned by what must follow: exclamations, questions; promises; perhaps a trifle of envy that would be flattering, and then some tender advice? It would be like seeing her love in a mirror, from another angle, and seeing it as if she were somebody else, and knowing what they would think.

Noonie had just come home in her car. She was still wearing her street clothes, and the little foray into town she had made gave her excitement and a sense of achievement. She wore a hat with a veil. She had brushed her hair very particularly and her little head looked smart. Her eyes had a dimmish look that was vague and appealing. Her suit was neatly made. Her white gloves were crisp and clean. She had been reluctant to get out of these clothes, and caught glimpses of herself in the hall mirrors with satisfaction. If people saw her as she really looked, that day, she mused, then she must have made a charming impression. Her thought leaped up as if to say to her that every day of life brought new hope with it; what if she had been, for so long, so tired, so listless, so unresponsive to the thing she wanted most, and that was her husband's love? She wished now that she had gone to call on him at his office; but she realized too that with patients waiting to see him, he would never have been able to greet her intimately.

When Martha rang the bell, and was taken by Cora into the green velvet and white enameled sitting room, where the pianola was, Mrs. Rush was delighted. She decided to come downstairs in her hat, veil, and gloves, and receive this caller with what would surely be described as charming formality.

When she saw that it was just that little Shoemaker girl, Wayne's sister, but so grown, really, she laughed at herself, and began to take off her gloves, her veil and her hat, and explained that she had just this minute come in from shopping.

"I think it's very cunning of you to come see me," she added. "—We do so love Wayne in this house..."

"He is a darling, and of course Donnie is an absolute member of the *family* with us, Mrs. Rush."

"My, you look sweet, Martha, you are so-so grown-up, suddenly, it seems ages since I've seen you."

At that Martha blushed.

"I know it, I go to school, every day, of course, I am working really very hard."

"Oh, I didn't mean to reproach you.—You've become so pretty! That's all I meant."

Noonie stared at her. She could feel herself growing tired, a creeping sense of heaviness in her own limbs that she knew so well, and dreaded almost daily. What was in the girl? Why did she blaze with such beauty? Her eyes melting at their own messages? Her lips like petals, her body poised as if unable to take an ungraceful shape? Why had she come? In the face of any such likeness of life, how heavy and empty anybody else seemed, anybody like herself, Noonie thought miserably. Had she herself ever looked like that? Surely all girls didn't look like that. Only those to whom something wonderful was happening. What was happening to Martha?

"Mrs. Rush, you'll have to forgive me, I am really an awful fool, but I—"

"Oh, no *I* am," interrupted Noonie in an unbearable burlesque of her own misery at feeling so poorly in the face of such vitality as the child's.

"Mrs. Rush, honestly, I don't know why I wanted to talk to you, but I had to, and my poor darling Mumma works so hard and is away all day, I couldn't ever get her to listen…"

"Your Mother is—Doctor Rush and I both admire her ever so much, you and Wayne must be very proud of her!"

Her eyes looked teary.

"We do, how can we ever show her—but—but I never know *what* she'll think…"

"About what? You'll make me nervous, if you beat around the bush much more."

Martha looked at her with pleading.

"I hope you won't mind, I really have no right to talk to you, but Donald and Wayne are so close, and I always think of you and the Doctor as *part* of us, Mrs. Rush, I am simply terribly in love!"

She showed all the polite signs of regret at making such an intimate confession and possibly embarrassing someone; but it was only a show; and behind her words was such a total sense of, yes, glory, that to Noonie, it sounded boastful.

There was a silence for a moment. Then Noonie with a great effort said,

"How charming, how happy for you, who is it, anybody I know?"

"Yes, at least, Doctor knows his father, it is Richmond Summerfield."

"Oh.—Yes, of course.—Yes, I remember him, but he's so *young*, Martha."

"I know. Can't help."

"I know.—But you're both just *school* children, my dear. Does Mother know? Shouldn't she?"

But Noonie needed no stormy proofs that it mattered none at all if they were just school children. She could see how Martha was wholly given and taken in love. Her heart sank. She was full of pity for the young people, sorry for what would come to them, and miserable over herself. When had *she* ever been so consumed by anything outside herself? How could *she* ever hope to feel herself again in the great pull of life toward creation, as these infants were? Well enough she knew why Martha would have to tell *someone*. She was touched that Martha had come to her; but it plunged her into the deepest sorrow for her own frailty, her own division from the most thoughtless and profound experience of everyone else. She came to Martha and embraced her, and Martha had the curious idea, with revulsion barely concealed in her movements, that Mrs. Rush was feebly appealing to *her* for—for something, instead of the other way round.

"I hope you will be very happy, then, Martha." She returned to her chair.

"Yes, we will, of course we can't be married for simply ages, yet, he has to go on to medical school, and so on.—Sometimes—maybe you have never been *uncertain* of anything, Mrs. Rush? It is a terrible feeling!"

How bitterly Noonie felt those words. When had she ever been certain of anything? She wished this exquisite girl would go away and leave her to her own ashen self-awareness. She had a sense of crisis gathering in her breast. She said to herself dimly that she was looking straight at the thing she had lost in her own life, through nobody's fault, and she spoke with utmost effort to Martha.

"Uncertain? What about: what do you mean?"

"We have made love, oh, *terribly*, Mrs. Rush, I am simply crazy with love when we are together, and I sometimes hardly can tear myself away from him before we—but I know, I know," she added, at the alarming expression on the older woman's face.

Martha was anguished with modesty and foolishness, and she sounded almost patronizing with her next remarks.

"I have thought it all over, we might get married right away— I've been looking around, in the shops, and there's a china pattern down at Rosenwald's which I like. And then for silver, I've selected that Dickenson 'Regent,' you know, it is so severe, with just that primrose pattern at the top?—But I suppose we *can't*, for ages. Of course, I'll leave everything to Richmond, I always feel that family decisions must be made by the husband, don't you? Marriage always seems to me a sacred trust, I don't believe enough people remember that, do you, Mrs. Rush? It has to be a partnership, I have always said that, it has many problems to iron out *together*, and we believe in talking things *through*."

Then she looked at Noonie, and blushed at how her words had sounded, but she shrugged energetically, as if to say that in terms of what was in her heart, she didn't care how she appeared to anyone else.

Noonie could not laugh at the child. Martha's glow and boundless depth of the commonest possession in the world shone through even the bumptious prattle she indulged in. In the girl's preoccupation with all the hardware and the platitudes of marriage there was a tender sort of betrayal of the world of desire, and dream, and the mundane prices of love.

"You are such a goose, Martha dear," said Noonie, standing up and taking her by the hands, and clasping her in her arms. Martha hugged her and shook her head.

"I know it, but somebody had to tell me so, or I would've died," she said, meaning she wanted to live beyond anybody's power to say.

"Now kiss me and go along and be as sweet with your Richmond as he wants you to be, and if he is as fine a youngster as I am sure he is, you are both safe."

"Oh: Mrs. Rush:" said Martha, "you've been darling to me.— Don't you ever tell anybody what a really big damned fool I am!"

"Hush, such words."

"You look tired, I hope I didn't tire you out," said Martha, with solicitude which wounded the older woman inexpressibly. "I'll run along now."

She kissed Noonie swiftly on the cheek again, and left, seeing nothing of what she left behind her.

3

With her hands on her cheeks, Noonie went upstairs to her bedroom. She found a little bottle of tablets in the lilac-scented handkerchief drawer of her dressing table, and went to her bed, rolling a little mound of the tablets out into her trembling palm. She put them into her mouth and tried to swallow, but had to take some water from the Thermos carafe on the bed table first. Then with tears streaming down her face and making no further sound, she lay down to die.

XXVII · THE RETURN OF NOONIE

I

Once across the river again, and in the cool if meager shadow of the piñon trees, Peter and Molly felt that they had come back to their own time and place. They had the cool sweetness of the pine boughs in their feelings. Their spirits were almost hilarious, and they talked like children, of anything that entered their heads. He thought he had never seen her look happy before. He thought he saw why she paid so much attention to the idea of being happy. They agreed that they both knew this was coming, sooner or later, from the first day they'd met. They reminded each other of the various ways they'd used to conceal from each other what they'd felt all along.

He had a picnic lunch in the car, packed for him by the Harvey House dining room. They ate it there among the scrubby trees.

One half of him spoke with caution, in his thought, and said that he was now stripped of everything he knew and had put on with his years. He felt like a boy again, and even at the moment, could smile at how often he'd heard other men say that, and of the joke it made, when you saw their jowls, their pendulous bellies, the blur of leg where once had been a hard line of thigh like a curved blade. He said to himself that he must not be a fool. But he knew he was ready to be, if that meant what he felt now, with her. She was voracious and exquisite. Her animation was like the most perfect extension of good manners. He thought her pretty before, but now she seemed grace itself. He believed he had only half known her till now. She took his thought from him, and said,

"I feel truly myself for the first time in years.—Not that it has any originality, most truths are maddening about that, they're so *same*, as we used to say when I was a child, but I do really think a woman without love is only half herself. The trouble is, sometimes, fitting it in where it belongs in—in the *scheme*."

"Scheme? What scheme."

"Why, the scheme of how things *are*. That's all that has ever given anybody any trouble about love.—I'd like to call my next book that. *Trouble About Love*, by Mary Carmichael. Adam and Blaine, New York and London.—Darling, what'll we *do*! We can never talk shop together."

"You *mean* this scheme thing, don't you."

"Of course I do.—What are *we* going to do, for instance?"

The shadow of a big cloud often came over the open land and made an island of dark blue, drifting on the serene face of the plain. It brought cool, too, and a somehow different day. Something like that happened across their faces now. He shook his head at her, as if he had no answer, but this one, and leaned to her and kissed her again.

She went into nothing in his arms, as if she had turned into fire, or water, another element. And when that happened, he became firmer being than ever, power in flesh.

Presently, he looked at her again, and shook his head, meaning that she was right.

"You know something?"

"No."

"Well, when this can happen to us, to me, grown-up, and full of beliefs about the way to *be*, and so on, then how in the world can young people, even little boys, like my son and his confederate the Shoemaker boy, how can *they* know what to do?"

"When?"

"When they want to raise hell."

"Are we raising hell?"

"That's what would be *said*, you know."

"D'you mind?" she said, looking cool.

"Yes."

"For whose sake?"

"All ours."

"I know."

"Just the same:" he said, but stopped.

"Yes?"

He ground his jaw a trifle, smiling at her, with almost a comic tenderness, and she laughed in a little gasp.

"That look!—You look like one of those painted fauns, or satyrs, if you ever look at me that way in front of anyone else, my reputation won't be worth a shred.—If you weren't so sweet at the same time, I'd say you were leering."

"I am leering."

"—'Said he, meaningfully.'"

He nodded.

"Well, you asked what were we going to do, and I wish I knew.—I know what I'd *like*."

"What?"

"We'll get in the car and start back. I'll tell you as we go."

They gathered their things.

"Do you notice all sorts of things about me?" asked Molly. "Because I do, about you."

She sounded so like a complacent little girl, laying down "tactfully" the rules of a new game that he burst out laughing and told her just that.

She sobered for a second, and said,

"You'll know pretty soon about me that I'm an awful lot a child, still, and one thing about it, is, I suppose it is what *makes* my work. I mean, to see things like a child, and think about them as a woman would.—I have a frightful temper, too, darling, the awful kind that doesn't throw things, but smolders and plans campaigns of hurtful things to say, and lets them out one sting at a time, all in a cloud of perfect composure. That's why I look so ridiculously young at times. —You look out. A passionate child inside a woman is *something*."

"You sound like Carmen."

"What do you know about Carmen?" she asked in surprise.

"I used to go to the opera in New York years ago when I was an intern. One of the other fellows was a brother of one of the singers, and he had tickets now and then. I heard *Carmen*. I loved it."

They crossed the plain again in the car. The afternoon was hotter than midday, and full of the herblike scent of the baking desert.

Presently she asked him what he was going to say.

"You always answer questions five remarks later, don't you," she said.

"Do I?—I hope it doesn't sound shrewd. I don't like shrewdness."

He drove silently a little while. Did he want to say it? He thought about it for a mile or two, and then to his own helpless amazement, he said,

"I wish we might go off to California together.—California is the Nirvana of everybody else in this country."

She was silent. He looked at her.

"Would *you*?" he asked, looking at the road again.

"You mean, simply run away? for a while? or forever? In due time?—All *that*."

Again he was astonished and pained, when he said,

"Forever. Another life."

She took a deep breath.

"Yes. But I probably think it is harder to do than you do.—I probably want it more, and see the troubles more than you do."

"I doubt that. It—a lot of sorry suffering would be involved."

"But there would be so much else!" she said, perversely, thinking of the way her heart tumbled with excitement when she saw his car coming, or heard anyone mention his name.

"This is an *enchanted* day," she said. "I will tell you how we shall be, whenever everything is arranged. No, not *arranged*, that is like an undertaker's word. I mean, when we have bolted and run."

All through her gaiety, the comedy she made out of feelings so true and yet so chanceful that she seemed hardly able yet to grant them their future, he was full of revolt. He asked himself why he should not seize the joy which was within his grasp. Betrayal? Well, but if people knew: and yet a shred of light somewhere in him shone clear, and meant that every betrayal ultimately would come back to himself; it would be himself he betrayed most of all in betraying anyone else. He frowned such ideas down. He wiped out all the years of his manhood with delight in the impatient longings alive in him now. He kept saying to himself that if it were someone else, a commonplace creature, a dull, promiscuous girl from God knew what kind of life, all his qualms might have power. But not with Molly. She was truly delicate, passionate beyond her frailty.

As the miles went by in the blazing dust of the afternoon, and they crossed the sand again, and saw the river vein of green in the glaring desert, and the mountains take shape and change and elongate and veer, like grand squadrons on a horizon of sea, he hardly listened to Molly, but sought and found what he called his formula. He said to himself that Noonie certainly wasn't happy *now*. It was likely that "the other way" she would probably not be happy either, but probably not much unhappier, if at all. Perhaps she could go home, back to Rochester, and find her old life again. She had plenty of money from her father's estate. Wouldn't it be a relief, anyway, to have something settled, one way or the other?

He searched all such notions for the frame which would justify the surge of sweetness he felt; the breath of desire he breathed.

Molly was at ease when he was silent. Once or twice she glanced away from him, looking at the glare of the land. She felt that rather gulpy fullness in the heart which people have at a stroke of preposterous good luck. Things will work out, she said to herself. They've got to, if this much is true.

"We shall become a legend in town," she said. He smiled, and she didn't really need him to listen closely, but let him alone with his thoughts, while she went on with her parody. "Of course everybody knows everybody else, and we'll hardly be gone to California until the telephones begin. I think like this: I'll go back to Kansas City in the most public of all possible departures, and then take the next train back to the Coast, and when I get to town here, you will get on the same train, to attend a medical consultation in Los Angeles, and I shall sit in a drawing room with the shades drawn and the fan going. As you stagger by my door laden with luggage, the train will start, and you will stumble having lost your balance, and fall against my door. The door will fly open, and you will lurch into my drawing room, and out of surprise, you will give such a start that you will fall upon the seat opposite me, and your shoulder will brush the window shade, which will fly up, exposing us to the gaze of three professional gossips who are paid by the railroad to watch the California Limited go through every day. They will gasp and say, Isn't that that attractive Doctor Rush, in the private compartment with that Foster woman? Yes, it is he, this can mean only one thing. And as the train pulls westward, word is already abroad in the streets.—Do you wish to hear what comes next?—Well, the Associated Press inquires where I am. My publisher denies everything. Mr. Hearst's Sunday scandal-sheet (I have met Mr. Hearst, who thought I was a picture actress, which enchanted me), will have a full page about it, with a pen drawing of me showing my blonde hair in wavy lines, and an old photograph of William Farnum, with a mustache added, which will be you, saying you were the stroke of the Cornell crew. The point of the story (designed to please Mr. Hearst) will be that you have found a new cure for old age, and that my new novel will tell about it, and that the cure was what undermined your family life, and what we went away *about*.

"—Then, in California, we will be asked to go into the movies, having become national figures as a result of all the unsavory publicity, and both of us being very natty looking. I will be tempted to accept, but you will never understand why, and the Los Angeles papers will say that while you and Douglas Fairbanks have left together for an unknown destination, I am the guest of Miss Pickford who is trying to reach you by long distance to patch up the quarrel. Miss Pickford will succeed, especially since you and Mr. Fairbanks have only been out on the golf links for a quiet game.

"Finally, I decide that a small brownstone house in San Francisco near the Pacific Union Club will be suitable, and we go there to live, where we have rather 'fast' parties on Saturday evenings, and all the 'Bohemian set' will come, and I will appear to be both tragic, and deliriously happy, as befits a notorious woman of great talent, in whom many things can be pardoned…"

But such nonsense was only another delicacy on her part, for she could not really weigh her happiness yet, in terms of decisions; and wished to leave them for him to make. The teasing sort of irony in her novelette of their future was almost like a guard, should it turn out that she needed one.

He drove into town and before they came to her house, he laid his hand upon hers, resting it in affirmation on today's happenings. She got out of the car in great content.

2

It was not quite six o'clock that evening when Peter came home and went upstairs, wondering what he would say. In the big front bed-room, he found Noonie, as he thought, taking a nap. She was lying on her bed. On her face was a smile of such dazzling sweetness that he was spellbound by it for a moment. However long had it been since she had looked like that! He remembered it well. His heart came up into his mouth, and he shook his head for the difference in her. But in a second, her breathing alarmed him, and he bent over her. Then he saw the bottle on the glass table by the bed, and knew what she had done. Then he had a rise of rage in him that anybody should throw life away, and he set to work to recover her.

With the first hint of success, his heart turned over, and was weak with gratitude. He made her sit up, and shaking her back to awareness, he kept saying aloud to her, "Poor Noonie, poor Noonie."

Her face looked pathetically young, and flushed, and the first moment she opened her eyes, he felt a little unearthly about it. He was looking through her eyes at the return to earth, of one who had tried to leave it behind forever. He could not see the images in the pool of her unconsciousness, but she had made that journey toward Lethe, and had looked upon the face of her fear. She saw again while dreaming toward death what had happened one day, years back, when she was a child at home. Her brother Roderick, that tall, dark-haired, black-eyed governor of her childhood, whom she had adored, said to her one day in the garden of the house in Rochester when they were playing a favorite game of making rival kingdoms out of the flower beds, and conducting wars between them,

"How little you know."

"I do too."

"No, you really do not understand anything."

"What, for instance?"

"You only *think* you love us all, here, at home."

"I do too! I love all of you!" and she had begun to cry.

"No, you will forget us all some day."

"I will not! I never, never will!"

"Yes, you will go far away, leave us all, marry, and have children, and we'll never see you any more!"

"No, no, no, I'll never!" she had cried, storming and weeping, imploring him to "Take it back." But he was obdurate, he condemned her to a future faithless to this childhood hour, and it was more than she could bear. She cried as if her heart would break, and as if he had cast her off, with his smiling clever face, his authority, his piercing black and white eyes, his whim of elegance so impressive to an adoring younger sister. She begged him to say that she would be forever faithful and secure at home, and he smiled and shook his head, and said,

"Well, after all, that's life."

But she was so hideously distressed, her suffering was so appalling, that he had created more of a sensation than he had bargained for. At last, touched by her protests of love for her father and mother and himself, and her vows of eternal devotion, he sighed, and said that perhaps he was wrong, and she really meant what she said. He smiled, and the garden seemed a fair world again, with its high screen of trees, and the flower beds like continents in a green sea of lawn, and like a gracious monarch granting the most binding of favors, he extended his hand to her, and permitted her to kiss it respectfully. It was many minutes before her sobs retreated entirely, but she came back to content at last, and had she only known it, had bought the present at the expense of much of her future.

This scene was so vivid, so enchanting, to Noonie, that afternoon years later, that she was smiling at it when she was discovered by Peter. He was bringing her back, he was arousing her, and it was like the movements of waves, like coming back from a drowning lake, and she saw again the wreck of the yacht *Affinity*, and the terror, and the faithfulness, of how she had saved her brother Roderick from the black water that night on the lake. She saw again the glow of the white sail fallen on the water, and barely showing pale in the starlight. She prayed again the words she had said that night, to ask God for strength to save Roderick until Peter should return with help. It had been so pitiful and so earnest that it had bound her like a vow of fidelity. She smiled exquisitely at the safety they had all found at last, during that night.

Peter slapped her to restore her. It was a stimulant of pain. She yielded to it, and she began to come back to consciousness, and with the other memories there now merged one of childbirth, and when the three memories had all come together their fears were seen lingering on the edge of daylight, as she awoke. When her eyes first saw Peter now, they looked back at life in perfect serenity.

He thought it was because she did not yet realize "where she was."

But it was the look of someone exorcised of terrors confronted and banished.

Still smiling, she wept for shame and gratitude, at peace with him. He looked upon himself bitterly, and stroked her hair, and stayed by her.

XXVIII · FAREWELL TO MOLLY

I

None of this was ever known around.

Like many mortal decisions, those in this case were made in private, with the persons involved looking the truth in the eye, alone, and, in terms of their natures, admitting its power. Romance would have dictated neater solutions, grander fulfillments of the moment; but given how things were, what prevailed was the formal outline of "morality," which was an unfashionable term, but which carried a timeless authority.

2

Peter telephoned Molly and said he wanted to see her alone as soon as she could manage it. She said to come the next afternoon about three. Miss Bridges would be out with Brisky, the spaniel, and she herself would be supposed to be taking her siesta, to which she always retired with a column of books and a lap-desk for the writing of notes. She wrote dozens of notes a week, five- and six-line greetings to people all over the world. It was one of her pet vanities to keep in touch with everyone, and she enjoyed it when everyone asked plaintively how she managed to find time to do so many things.

He went about his work as usual the day after the awful discovery at home, but he had waves of remembrance now and then during his busy hours, and he would ask himself how could he ever have thought that anything else would ever have done, than what he had been so powerfully shown was his duty? However much it may have lacked freedom and glamour? Nobody suspected what he was thinking about, or that there was within him a recognition of the depths of his own fault. How long he had hoped that Noonie could be spared a crisis; how certain he had been that it was coming; how much, now that it had happened, he himself had learned from it!

In the afternoon, at three, he drove up to the big log house, and was met by Molly. She was cool looking and exquisite. The awnings were down outside. The big room was dark. She was so glad to see him that he began to frown, and barely took her hand. She saw at once that nothing was as they had left it between them yesterday. She moved away from him and lighted a cigarette, and sat down opposite him by the cold fireplace. He saw her bring her head up and regard him with a sober little face. The childlike sweetness in her eyes, at seeing him a moment ago, was gone. She was expressionless; and when she was like that, there were little signs of strain, of—of *experience*, that showed about her eyes and her mouth. She was still very pretty; but it was a sceptical prettiness, that had looked on so many things in rueful discovery, that she seemed like another person.

She was dying to ask him what the trouble was. But she so dreaded to hear what she saw in his face that she stayed silent, and held her cigarette up before her and watched him. He was burned darker by the day's outing yesterday, and he was scowling. He licked his lips, and kept looking into the charred cold fireplace. It was only a moment or two, but he looked for that time like a youth, appalled

by the world. Then he lifted his head and looked at her, and his eyes
were so full of compassion for things beyond them both that she
felt the breath forced out of her breast as if his hand had pressed her
over the heart, and she said at last,

"Peter: what is it:"

and he told her what he had come upon at home last evening. She
listened to him quietly but her heart turned cold. She felt abomina-
bly chastened by the terrible news he had, and she saw immediately
what it meant for the two of them. Not until now had her feelings of all this time seemed anything but blessed. Now they seemed
mean, and vulgar, and cheapened; and she could tell herself even
while she listened to him that this violent revulsion of her heart was
simply proof of how deeply she'd longed for what she had found.
What a coward desire was, how it shriveled up and vanished, when
other claims opposed it tragically! When he finished his little history, which he made as matter of fact as possible, she saw in his eyes
the loving look she had come to know in him, and she also saw that
he had made his decision, and that it was final.

She wanted to go to him and shake his shoulders, and say to
him that everything was just as real as it ever was, time would help,
there were always ways to heal wounds, nothing could change what
they had discovered under the time-silenced city of the day before.

But she saw that for everything she could say, and believe, he
had something that was even truer for him. And so she held her
tongue, and looked at him until he looked away again. She began to
cry in silence. As if she were a creature in one of her own stories, she
saw herself stop the crying with a handkerchief and a hold of her
breath, so that when he looked around again, he wouldn't have to
face the added difficulty of a weepy female. Her mind heated with
bitter comedy when she saw herself rapidly review a series of codes
which would be useful, and select the one that became her most at
"a time like this," and she smartened her shoulders, and assumed a
wistful half-smile, and she knew she was pretty that way, and she
believed that this might trouble him, but it was the least she owed
herself until she could be alone. She got up and went over to him,

and said, aching with insincerity,

"There is only one thing for you to do, and that is, to stay home.—And only one thing for me, and that is, to go away. I am so sorry, dearest Peter."

He jumped up. His awkwardness, no, his brutality, almost, she thought, was a cleansing thing. He had no repertoire of emotional notes to strike, as she had. He was awry and disordered and he expressed it in every movement and every word. He was rough and miserable. He put his hands on her shoulders and leaned to her and kissed her hardly, and her heart sank. It was so unlike a last farewell of storied lovers, so little declaration, so little expressed nobility, that she felt the poor truth of everything all over again.

"Yes, yes," he said, "Molly, I have been in torture all night and all day.—You see that. This is where I must stay with everything. After *now*, I must. I don't know how much she knew, or if she knew anything. But nothing like that is ever any sole person's responsibility or job. We're going to stay with it. I had to tell you as soon as I could. You see it. I knew you would see it. I'll never forget—"

"Oh, shut up!" she said, losing her exterior. She dropped her face into her hands, and she sobbed, and he saw her true self come before him, and it was somehow a relief, after the poised creature he had seen here today. It was just as bad as he had expected it to be. But he said to himself bitterly that he had earned this, too, just as much as all the rest of it, the delight, the promises, the prophecies.

She clutched him with her hand, and then with her other hand on her sobbing mouth, she let him go, and went out of the room.

He reached to the silver urn on the table and took a cigarette, lighted it, and went out to his car and drove to the hospital, saying to himself that it couldn't be worse, and that nothing of it must appear to anyone else, who might need him for help or comfort in any way.

He knew he would never see her again.

Not even then could he hate the order of the world, which had cost him so much. He followed Molly in his thoughts as he drove, and if to have a heart full of demands for the safety of someone is to pray, then he prayed for her as he rounded the gravel driveway of the hospital and came up to the white-pillared entrance out in back where the staff always entered. He rode upstairs in the automatic elevator to the fourth floor. Walking down the corridor to the operating room at the end, he passed the chapel. The doors were open. He stopped and looked in. Four nuns were kneeling far from one another. Their backs were to him, as they faced the altar anonymously. It was an image of prayer in the abstract. He felt his heart thump at their certainty that man's lot could be alleviated and understood through their faith in the power of prayer.

"Yes," he said to himself, going on down the hall. He meant a great deal by it.

3

He was surprised, a few days later, to bump into Judith Bridges down at the railroad tracks, where he was seeing a favorite patient off to the East. The patient had recovered from tuberculosis, and was heading home to try a few months of his old life, to see if he could stand it. After the train left, Peter dawdled for a few minutes, watching the elegance of the observation car diminish into the desert perspective. Miss Bridges came up behind him, and said,

"That's us, tomorrow, but going the other way."

"Oh: hello: to California?"

"Yes. I thought you probably knew."

"No.—I haven't seen Molly."

"Yes," said Miss Bridges, looking at him with perfect frankness, and much interested in what she might see in his face, "we feel we have exhausted this environment. I've just been getting tickets and things. It would be difficult to stay, now.—You know what I mean. She told me all about it."

"Oh."

"Good Lord, don't look at me like that, I'm her oldest friend in the world, and anyway there'll be a book about it some day, there's no use fooling anybody.—I needn't beat around the bush. I'm glad it all busted up in time."

"Look here, Miss Bridges, I—"

"Don't run off, yet, Peter. You hate me for meddling like this. But what *I* think about it is just as much part of the truth of the situation as what anybody *else* thinks, who *knows*. And *I* think it's a damned good thing."

"You're a strange sort of friend."

"I adore Molly, and she's practically saved me from a bad crack-up after the War. But that doesn't mean I can't *see* her."

"See her?"

"She's Lady George Gordon Noel Byron."

"What does that mean?"

"She's an artist first of all. And anybody like you could never be second-of-all to anyone. And you would've had to try."

He looked cross and outraged, and she insisted on her point by nodding.

"Yes, she was. She *is*.—*That's* what she's married to, and just how good or how bad she is at it, time will tell. I think she's pretty important, in at least three books, anyway. But once it got her, the power of the word, it kept her. And everything tends to nourish that, as if she were a pretty blonde lady spider with cornflower-blue eyes.—That's what went wrong with her first marriage. Dick Foster never really got to know her, and nobody else ever could, *that way*. So he, being a weak character, got sorry for himself in a bottle of whisky, which was the end of him, finally.—But it'd be ridiculous to pretend that anything could ever come of it if she tried it again.— Poor darling, she keeps *thinking* and *hoping*, herself.—She doesn't know all this about *herself*."

"But you do, eh, is that it?"

Miss Bridges leaned down to stroke Brisky, the pale-yellow spaniel who was panting in her shadow.

"I certainly do.—Can't you *allow* it in her, Peter? Or did you see her as anything at all but a darling little blonde with twirling blue eyes?—I sometimes think no man ever saw a woman as a live human being, as full of holes and flaws as himself. If any man ever did, and admitted it, and loved even the flaws, what a lover he would be!"

He looked down at her, with a frowning smile. You busy, hard, intellectual virgin you, he thought, even if you've slept with a hundred people, you're still virginal, because you've never yielded up your self-image, have you. But he didn't say anything, and as she stood up, she held out her hand, and gave him a hearty handclasp, and he then believed that she meant to wish him well, almost hungrily, and he had an echo of sense in what she'd been saying, when he saw how sincere she was. He watched her stride off up the brick platform with the brushy dog frolicking along at her heels. He guessed she said all that sort of thing with difficulty, but out of a conscience born of much trouble in her own life.

Then came a confirmation from Molly herself. It was a letter, written to him from town the night before she took the train westward. Without salutation, the letter read:

> I still have a few of your books which Judy is going to mail back to you, to your office address. I have much enjoyed them. It touches me to know how much they mean to you. It is one of the things I feel I really and truly know about you, the actual aliveness in your thoughts, of all this country, and your hunger for what it used to be like here. I have long since concluded that you really do find things in the life of the past which help to illuminate for you how people are today, and I dimly feel that you've learned more from such reflection than I ever could. It saddens me for myself; but it gladdens me for you.
>
> Whatever will remain of what you now think about me?
>
> But that is a question which it is unfair to ask you. As for me, I am humiliated, now, and in time, I may be grateful. What you see by my writing here is how my habits are forever formed, and whatever happens to me is material to be analysed and stricken off into images. If the world ever knew all this, they would say that I have been

saved from a folly by your goodness. How cruel goodness sometimes is!

If I close my eyes, I can see again that terrible sun-lighted cliff of empty houses, and I can hear again the scream of that single bird, which struck some strange kind of life from our intentions. Were you moved by this? I never felt that you were moved by it in just the way I was. I have none of the mystic in me, ordinarily, but I must admit that on that day, I felt all those vanished lives all about. Pity, pity! How much of it is love?

I have been hurt, but that is of no consequence. I pray that you have not been. I love you. I cannot worry about you. There is the most immovable strength in you. I could see that when you came to tell me good-bye. I was jealous of it. You wouldn't really like me, at my utmost. I hope you can admire me, and so I shall say that I hope your troubles will truly be over, and that health and peace will come back to you all. Perhaps you yourself can be the source of that for those you love; for that you do love them is what your faithfulness finally means, doesn't it? I think it does, and I hope it is so. I can bow my head to that with real humility.

We leave tomorrow.

As Lady Caroline scribbled to Byron, "Remember me!" She was ardent and addled, and I am behaving very coolly. But oh how I mean it. Good-bye.

Mary

When he was done reading it, his cheeks were hot with a flush that rose to darken his whole head. He tore the letter into tiny pieces and snowed them into the wastebasket by his office desk. His heart was beating rapidly. The faint flavor of irony in her letter troubled him almost more than the frankness of its feeling. Oh my, oh my, he thought, recognizing that this was just one of those things you have to wait for to be over.

BOOK IV

The Earth's Heart Beating

XXIX · GROWING UP

I

Wayne came home a few days later at suppertime and told Martha that Mrs. Rush was very ill. Donald hadn't been allowed to see her for several days. She was going to be all right; she was terribly weak, they said, and Doctor Rush was pretty worried. Don didn't know what the trouble was. But he wrote her little notes and sent them in, and the nurse brought back the answers. It was something sudden, one day she had been perfectly well, and the next, bang, sick as a dog.

Martha was getting supper for the two of them. She paid small attention to his gossip. She was curiously interested in looking at him. It was too bad about Mrs. Rush, she had looked so pretty that day, perhaps she had taken ill that same night. You never knew, did you. Anyway, it was Wayne she was regarding with a new sense of his person.

He is simply amazing, he has changed overnight, too, isn't it strange how I never saw it coming? Or is it me; do I see everything differently, even my young brother? He is ranging out, taller, he has that hair like a field of long yellow grass, it trembles as if it had a wind playing in it gently, all the time. I used to pull his hair when we were both younger and he would not let me alone. I had to do *something*, he was a fiend, maybe he still is, it doesn't show anymore.

He looks as if he knew a lot, now.

I'll bet he doesn't.

But why should he look so?

I always used to think he was a cute little boy, with his dark lashes and pale hair, and I used to pretend to everybody else that he was an angel, but that was to hide what a devil he was, and just because he was my brother.

But he isn't cute any more.

Sometimes he looks very sad, like a puppy dog that is hungry, and doesn't know where to turn for something to eat.

And sometimes he looks powerful.

Look at him curled up in the chair there with the evening paper, staring at the page as if it were resisting him. His face is brown from the sun, and his arms are more than long nervous bones now, and his legs are shapely. Does he know it?

What has happened to him without our seeing?

But I am a fool.

It is just that I never knew before what growing up meant. I never knew that you grew toward everything all at the same time. I thought you just grew bigger and stayed the same little girl you always were and that eventually you seemed to be grown-up and could never remember anything about children.

She was setting the table.

They hadn't needed the *Spirito Santo*'s fire for some time, and Wayne stared at it critically. In summer, the base burner was something yet again. They kept flowers on it, and yarn waiting to be wound into balls, and the mother's purse often hung on the knob of the handle of the poop-deck door with its mica panes. The stove was the central object in the room, and they often propped notes for each other up on its top when there was no fire in its deep belly.

"What?" said Martha, in the family habit to share in the other's thoughts.

"Nothing.—The *Spirito Santo*."

"Oh. What about it?—I always said it has such *personality*, don't you think so?"

He made his face severe and weighed her statement so long that she turned to look at him, which was what he wanted.

"I do not," he replied finally. "If it has anything, I would agree to say that it had *stovality*."

She felt obliged to lift her eyebrows at this preciousness, but she was touched by pride in his ruthless intelligence. She felt dimly how he really saw the *Spirito Santo*, its short powerful little legs, its bulging shell like dull old black silk, the glistening window with the light of opals in its tiny panes, the royal headdress of the nickel urn on top with the florid handles, and the smoke pipe, rising so powerfully to the roof. It was not too much to say that Wayne's whole life would be educated and affected by pangs of comfort and well-being related to the old stove.

He suddenly wrenched himself out of his chair, went to his room, rummaged in a box he kept under his cot, and came back with a piece of red tissue paper which he had saved off a Christmas package. He next went out to his bicycle under the great tree in the back yard and detached his dry-cell flashlight from the handlebars. He returned to the house and opening the main door of the *Spirito Santo* he set the flashlight on the cold grate which smelled so sweet of cold ashes, and slid the switch turning on the miniature electric bulb behind the flashlight lens. Over this he then laid the red tissue paper, and closed the mica'd door, and backed away to see the effect.

Martha watched him.

He paid no attention to her until he decided to remove the things inside. When this was done, he acknowledged her witness by saying, "Just something to try."

He put his things away and settled down again in the big chair with the evening paper.

2

Yes, she thought, he too.

She began to blush and turned away to hide it in case he looked up suddenly.

He'll be like Bun someday, doing to some other girl what Bun does to me, *that little male*, and nobody else'll ever know what he'll feel. Of course, I am the happiest creature in the world; but will *he be*? Can I save him, in any way? I should hate for him to be hurt. He should be so careful! I wonder if I could talk to him.

But this idea was ridiculous when she glanced back at him. He was so secure, so complete in his own person, so cool in his attitude, the way he kept his eyebrows up and his mouth pursed in a silent whistling, that she realized how far apart they were, and ever would be.

She called him to come to supper, and he came, a miniature lord, and sat down, and cocked his eye at her, and asked her if she'd had a busy day, without really being concerned for the answer. She could've laughed outright with joy at his imposture that was yet more of a prediction; and could not resist leaning over and chubbing his cheek, as they used to call it in the family, taking his smooth cheek in her thumb and finger and giving it a pinch and a shake. He flared, and sparred her hand away, and all but hissfully spat at her. His wheat field of hair swept back and forth over his tall smooth bony forehead.

He instructed her coldly to be her age, and keep her cute little tricks for her boy friend, and when he saw how this had scratched her, he inquired with an elegant burlesque of charm, whether she hadn't better get wise to herself? and cease from robbing the cradle?

He was the first worldly rub which her passion met up with.

They ate their supper in silence.

Of the two, he was already the stronger, and they both knew it.

3

After supper, Wayne went off on his wheel to meet Donald, and Martha did the dishes, and then met Bun later on. When he asked her why she was so silent, she tried to tell him about Wayne; but had no way to make him, and herself, see clearly her discovery that life reposed for donation in all creatures, even in her little brother Wayne.

That year an airplane came to Albuquerque to stay. A barn-storming pilot had put up a shack of a hangar out on the mesa, and took people up for rides, at three dollars for ten minutes.

"I went up this afternoon," said Bun, sensibly getting her off her funny ideas, which sounded almost as if she was *sorry* for everything.

"You didn't."

"I certainly did. It was wonderful."

"I'd've been scared to death, if I'd known."

"—Why I didn't tell you. But what you can see! Next time I get three dollars, you're going up with my compliments."

"Oh never!"

"Sure, you'll love it."

"What can you see?"

"To hell and gone.—The mountains look entirely different. The river never starts and never ends, it's all the way you can look, north and south. The funniest thing is the *green*."

"How do you mean?"

"Well, there's this straggling path of green by the river, and that's all. You think here, in town, on the ground, you think the trees go on just because you're among them all the time. Even if you drive up to the mesa, you don't really feel the trees stop, they're right back there, in town, heck, you can go back. But from the air, you see the other part, the plains, the desert, it's all like rock, full of light.—And the houses, at first you can't tell which is the house and which is the shadow. They both look flat."

"Flat?"

"Yes. It's wonderful.—We looped the loop."

"No, oh Bunny, how could you take such a risk, think of *me*..."

He squirmed a little, because if there was anything about love he didn't quite care for, it was how they always tied everything up to *themselves*, everything a man did, whether he did it for himself pure and simple made no difference. But that was a small enough disadvantage, and he thought the wise way to handle it was to ignore it kindly.

"There's nothing to the loop. It is a tail spin you want to look out for.—I was deaf for twenty minutes when we got down, too. Open cockpit. The motor sprayed a little oil, not enough to mean anything. I got some on my shirt."

She was jealous.

Would she always be discovering things in him that derived not from her, but from other things he liked, and had to do?

The difference was, she loved herself through him, and he loved the world through her.

Later on, under a tree in shadow around the corner from the library building, and in between the passing of cars with their sweeps of light, they resolved that difference for a little time of kisses.

XXX · HIGH FEELINGS FROM LONG AGO

I

As soon as he could find time, Peter went out to Old Town to see Don Hilario Ascarete. It was another Sunday morning, there was nothing to do at the office, and things were quiet at the hospital. He found the old man moving along the ditch that ran past the adobe house of the Ascaretes, and out through the alfalfa field in back. Don Hilario made every step as though it were a separate event, to be considered, decided upon, and taken. The water idling down the ditch moved ever so much faster than the old man. Peter marveled that he was living every time he saw him. He ate hardly anything at all, they said, in his family. And as for sleeping, if anybody ever looked in upon him at night, he was always awake. He was up before anybody else in the morning. Some days he could hardly move, though he never seemed to be in pain from anything. He would doze all day, but if anything "went on," they would find that he was aware of whatever it was. Some of the younger great-grandchildren said he gave them the creeps, and coldly wished he would stay out of the way, or die, or something, because he upset them with his knowing indifference to what seemed of the utmost importance to them. He was an uneasy reminder of large, simple, eternal things, in the midst of the selfish excitements of their young world.

Peter came up to him, and walked around to face the old man, and greeted him in the special cordialities of Spanish.

Don Hilario stood with his mouth open, regarding him, nodding, leaning on his apple bough, and though the sunshine was bright, staring at Peter's face with unblinking eyes, a long moment, before he answered.

"Yes, yes, yes, good morning, my young doctor friend. You've been a long time coming. Shall we retire to the patio and sit down? I have much to tell you."

"About the old house?"

Again Don Hilario looked keenly at Peter, and appeared to be reading him with attention and ease.

"Well, the house, and possibly about many other things.—We'll go back along the ditch. Today is the first day our ditch has run this year. Look at it."

The water was muddy and lazy, and smelled rich and sweet. They made an infinitely slow progress along the bank, to the L of the house where Don Hilario liked to sit, and which he referred to as the patio. Peter studied him as they went. The old man was tiny and frail. Peter supposed he hadn't been bathed in years and years. He was neither dirty nor clean. He was like a patch of ground, baked by the sun, and dried by years, and clothed in his own element. Presently they were sitting by the wall, feeling the heat through their backs.

"Everybody has gone to Mass," said the old man. "I would go, but it takes them too much time to get me ready, and into the car, and off to the Plaza. I walk over there by myself now and then, when the Church is empty, and at such times, I explain everything."

"To the priest?"

Don Hilario made his silent laugh, that rounding of his open mouth.

"No. To Our Father in Heaven."

"Oh."

Peter was delighted at a man who was on explaining terms with God.

"Well," said Don Hilario, looking at him, "everything is not always as simple as that, is it."

"No.—What do you mean?"

"Nothing. You are like my grandchildren, when I know too much. They shy away like a horse that does not want to be caught."

Peter had the feeling that simply by looking at him, old Don Hilario could read the depths of his heart, and see its trouble, its suffering, and the faithless impulses it had held. He began to blush like a schoolboy. What curious perception lived in the aged! he thought, leaning down to pick up a pebble to hide his confusion.

Don Hilario said,

"The worst pride is that which considers itself above trouble, and it always falls the farthest."

Peter looked at him and burst out laughing.

"You old devil," he cried fondly, "what are you getting at?"

A ghost of coquetry, of slyness, appeared in the old face, as Don Hilario replied with a marionette's surprise,

"Nothing, why, nothing at all, except the things I have to tell you about the house down the street which you asked me about.— Why. What else is there to get at? Have I touched you?"

This was an elaborate courtesy. Peter knew that somehow the old man had seen in his face or felt in his presence the echoes of the last weeks of what he had been through. But he replied,

"No, what else could there possibly be. Well. Tell about the house."

"Well, I thought and remembered, and I thought and remembered."

He shook his head as if in wonder and compassion for what people had suffered in their far lost energy of life. Then he went on to say that the house down there on the corner, where the Sanchez family had that grocery store, was once the property and the establishment of "La Voz," as she was called, though more properly known as Doña Catalina Anonciación de Gutierrez, the celebrated female gambler and singer, who had also made a fortune out of professional love.

Don Hilario said he had seen her as a very small boy. Everything he knew about her, and which had taken some time to recall in its proper relation and order, as befitted a legally trained mind, he had remembered from other people's accounts, and what a stir of gossip there once had been.

"High feelings from long ago," he said, with a sort of dusty humor in his dim voice. But he looked at Peter, to show that he meant to be more than funny.

2

When Don Hilario was a young man, the house had already long been built, and now that he was an old man, it was still standing, though it had changed hands and become respectable, since now what was left of it was a combination grocery store and dwelling for the family named Sanchez.

It was on a narrow street leading away from the Plaza toward the north. The Church of San Felipe de Neri was only a few yards away, with its twin white towers that had white-shuttered belfries and black wrought-iron crosses. The cloister and garden of the priests was on the far side of the church. Doña Catalina's house was on the near side, and of course, rather more removed, but still in a curious juxtaposition to the house of good. People remarked it always, meaning to be sly or horrified, according to their temperaments. The house of Doña Catalina was a celebrated brothel and gambling place.

It ran for a hundred feet along the road, where the walls were always well plastered, and turned the corner by the irrigation ditch, and made an L for one half of the patio. The base of the L was sixty feet long, and was met at right angles by a high wall which wavered in its course to enclose several big trees. The fourth side of the patio was a long outdoor sitting place, a *portal*, where in the evenings you could see the watermelon pink of the sunset mountains, and drink your wine, and smoke your cigarette at ease. There was a well in the middle, plastered and tiled in bright colors. Doña Catalina kept a flock of parrots, and their lively conversation, which scandalized passers-by and educated small boys who listened outside the forbidden walls, made a wicked kind of music in the still clear air.

There was a heavy lawn in the patio. The interior of the house was whitewashed, and the walls in daytime reflected a green light. At night, the shutters were fastened to, and no light escaped, or eye looked in. The shutters were supposed to be armored, because Doña Catalina made more money than anybody in Albuquerque, and was subject to banditry. However, she had been molested only once, by a repentant young *rico* who had thrown away all his money gambling and had drunkenly returned one night with three companions, all masked, and had tried to break in and commit robbery. The loyal patrons of Doña Catalina had resisted the assault bravely.

The proprietress herself had come from El Paso at the age of thirty, already a woman of authority and charm. She was wealthy from a career in Mexico City, where she had been a theater singer, and mistress to a high government official. When he was overturned by a moderate revolution, she had left both his protection (which had simply ceased to exist) and the theater (where she felt the work was too hard for meager returns). But he had taught her to gamble, and she announced on arrival in Albuquerque that she intended to run a gambling palace, and invited all the gentlemen from the garrison, the ranches, and the town itself, to inspect her house at a grand opening.

She was an exciting addition to the life of the shady river town, almost a hundred years ago.

She was far from beautiful. Don Hilario said her face was really almost that of a toad, with bulging eyes, and a flat nose, and a wide mouth. But he said she was clever, her eyes were always dancing (he showed how with his own old blinkers) and she painted her face which gave her, he said, a very "imported" look, and fascinated everybody. She was a little bit of a thing, lively as a wasp, and nothing could put her down. She often slapped the face of a drunken patron who was angry and troublesome at losing all his money at the tables. The priests thundered execrations at her from the pulpit, and she was always there at Mass when they did so, with her black *rebozo* modestly pulled over her face, and sometimes she seemed to nod in agreement with what the scathing sermon was saying about her kind of woman.

Out of church, she was generous and friendly with the priests, sent them fine foods across the Plaza, and curtsied and crossed herself when she met them in open air; and they bowed to her, blessing her and thanking her for the offerings she made, and in general recognizing her humanity without condoning her expression of its failures. When asked why they didn't simply take their Franciscan cords and whip her out of town, they replied that the chances of sin resided in us all; let us all conquer them within ourselves. They knew that to persecute Doña Catalina would not ultimately solve anything.

Life was so lived then that the women were resigned to what befell them.

The men though made a sort of club out of Doña Catalina's establishment. In time, it was recognized as a legitimate social feature of the old town, and there were many men who went there simply for companionship with each other, to gamble, to gossip, to drink, to make brown-paper cigarettes and talk.

When a boy began to talk like a raven, and pull at his lip with fingers that believed they had found a mustache starting, and pass in and out of alternate clouds of modesty and desire, it was the commonest thing in the world for his father to bring him one evening to Doña Catalina's, introduce him to her with an air of ceremony and occasion, and yield him over for initiation. A personable boy would cause a great commotion, be exclaimed over, petted, praised, and in general embarrassed out of his wits by the approval of Doña Catalina's women. And of course there were men in numbers who came as regular patrons to the row of small rooms that flanked the *acequia* at the far end of the patio. Each of the rooms was named after a different flower, and was plastered and frescoed and furnished to suggest its quality. The lady occupant was known by the name of her particular room.

This was all about the time the American occupation happened.

Don Hilario had been a boy then, but as he grew up, he came to know the tradition of Doña Catalina's and was able to report details he may not actually have observed himself.

None of the respectable women ever spoke to Doña Catalina. When they would go to the markets or the bazaars or hurry to inspect the contents of a wagon just arrived from Mexico City, the respectable women couldn't help bumping into her, for she was an ardent shopper too, and had more money to buy the first luxuries with.

The house had splendor, in terms of the taste and the difficulties of the time. The main social room was fifty feet long, with heavy beams crossing the ceiling, and immensely deep window niches curtained with olive-green velvet and shuttered with iron. The furniture looked religious, with carved crosses and enormous silver candlesticks with what looked like fists of silver knotted in decoration in frequent stages of their upward way. There were heavy paintings of ladies and gentlemen nobody ever recognized. But Doña Catalina enjoyed traditions above all else, and gave herself dynastic airs and satisfactions with her pictures. There were benches that resembled choir stalls along the walls, and decorum was encouraged, and even rendered inevitable by the uncomfortable magnificence of the furnishings of this main room. Here concerts were held, and the Señora herself was sometimes induced to sing, which she did in an inexpressibly bright and unmusical voice which reminded everybody of one of her own parrots. But when she sang, the eye, if not the ear, was moved, for her animation surpassed anything they had ever seen in Albuquerque. She was full of references to the cosmopolitan world of Mexico City, and its own faint echoes of the great world of Europe. In a society as remote as that of the old river *villa* in the mid-nineteenth century, this was more important than might at first seem plausible.

The gambling went on in rather smaller rooms, opening off the main *sala*. There were richly shadowed, candlelighted groups around the heavy tables, and little sacks of silver on the board, and gold pieces like autumn leaves piled up, and a general air of insincere good manners behind which greed flickered like fire through a grate. The gambling rooms were as plain as a barracks.

Beyond that were the living rooms of Doña Catalina and her staff; and they were as casual as you please, disordered, capricious and without the rigidly maintained style of the rest of the house. The kitchen was an enormous room with an open range and a huge copper hood that led to a hole in the roof.

Nobody was fooled, of course, by the accents of grandeur and propriety that were to be seen in various qualities of the house. It was just as wicked as such a place could be. There were no vices that were not enthroned there, and plenty of lost souls could be seen failing to find themselves in Doña Catalina's care. She had a great capacity for sympathy, and in her etchy voice she used to make little scenes of pity and concern over her most drunken or vicious customers.

But in herself she was a scrupulous and remote woman. She never took a lover, from among her friends in town. She made an edifice of her personal virtue, and it really seemed to be a citadel in which her spirit could lurk, as if in remote purity, to supervise the sins of others, of which she was innocent herself. This gave her an authority which infuriated others at times, such as her employees, and to them she would show a side of her nature rarely displayed to the town; a fantastically sardonic and icy face, uttering the most cutting of execrations, reciting the depraved accomplishments of the miserable inmates to their faces, and whipping them back to submission at last, weeping and conscience-torn.

All told, she was a successful and interesting figure for several years. She had amassed a fortune, nobody knew how much, but she kept buying jewels and furniture and dresses and silver services and sending sums to the church and having painted carriages brought from Mexico and pictures from Italy until everyone assumed that her wealth was far greater than it actually was. She had reached an age when she would make a whole evening of mellow comedy out of picturing in words the time when she would leave the active life, retire, buy a place "in the country" (what a citified expression! this whole town was practically "in the country") and by a few adroit gestures, win her way into respectable society and become a great agent for style and goodness in Albuquerque itself.

3

But before this could happen, the United States Army marched down the river from Santa Fe under command of General Kearny in 1846. It was a cavalry force, and it had peacefully annexed the whole territory of New Mexico, proclaiming amnesty and bringing a beginning of civil stability to the little towns and pueblos. There had been trading parties through here before, and legendary trappers who one by one as single human beings conquered the wilderness of mountain and prairie. But there had never before been so many Americans anywhere in New Mexico at one time. These troops were the most exciting thing to happen in generations; in fact, since the extraordinary visit of the Bishop of Durango and his suite in huge carriages with leather curtains in the previous century. The province was overwhelmed with the importance of the expedition, and very shortly after that, enchanted with its conduct. Troops were going on to the West coast of the continent if they could get through. What was this: a printing press which they had brought along? There had never been such a thing here before, the American General's proclamations were set up and printed right here, and handed around before the ink was dry. Society had more to do than it could manage. There were balls, and suppers, and reviews, drills in the Plaza, and during the few days while the Army halted in Albuquerque, the house of Doña Catalina was "like a blacksmith shop" (according to what she was said to have said), ringing with bottles and glasses, and the sound of coins on the tables.

The local gentlemen took the visiting officers to Doña Catalina's as to a club. No other establishment in the town had the resources, the richness, the profusion of foods, of drinks, of simple room, space itself, to entertain the Americans in, and enough women.

To explain what then transpired, Don Hilario reminded Peter

how the women of the Latin race sometimes reacted to the *gringos*.
A heat came on them suddenly, he said, when they saw blue eyes, or
yellow hair, or pink skin, and only the most rigidly instructed girls
preserved their ordinary reserve during the American Army's occupation. The soldiers were on the average much bigger than the men
of New Mexico. They had laughing humors and in comparison with
the dark-skinned New Mexicans, they seemed very open-faced and
innocent. They were, in brief, like a lot of huge boys. Mexican men
matured early, and there was little difference between a boy of eighteen and a man of thirty. But these Americans had pink color showing under their tan, and they played like big puppies all the time.
They seemed never to be serious. They bought like princes, and had
the most refreshing manners, without guile, which the women expected in their own men, and without ceremony, which generations
of Latin tradition had made habitual in the New Mexicans. They
were gay without getting drunk, and as conquerors, they were more
like guests at a party, charmed with the arrangements, wide-eyed at
the social novelties they beheld, and certain that everyone was as
nice as could be.

There was an officer named Captain Henry Houghton Somers
in command of one of the troops. He was a well-bred young man
of thirty from the little town of Batavia, New York, and had been in
the Army for twelve years. He was able to remember echoes of the
War on the Great Lakes, and the triumphs of Commodore Perry.
He believed that service in the armed forces of his country was
the most honorable of professions. His wife and two babies lived
in Batavia. He wrote to them last from Saint Louis, but a package of mail was going back from Albuquerque, and he was getting
a bundle of pages ready for the bag all during his visit here. He
was over six feet tall, he had hair the color of autumn corn shucks,
and long sideburns, and his head was richly framed by the high
gates of his full-dress collar with all the gold lace on it. His eyes
were blue. He hardly ever sat down, but had a way of lounging in
muscular ease against the furniture or the walls or a doorway. He
smiled frequently, and tried earnestly to speak Spanish. He was like

the biggest and most awkward and most willing pupil in a class of schoolboys who pretended he might be stupid out of some kind of good manners, because he was really very smart. The new country and the strange people he was seeing stimulated him highly.

What was a sparkle of interest and intelligent appraisal in his fond eyes looked like something else to Doña Catalina.

Turning false to all her shrewd principles of professional detachment, she fell publicly in love with him, which is to say, her infatuation racked her and betrayed her to everyone.

He went to her house as a matter of course, with all the other soldiers, and met and talked with the local gentlemen. He would take a drink, and ring a coin or two on the table in the inner room, and bow charmingly to the ladies of the flowery rooms when they made their formal gestures of blandishment for his benefit. He was made to realize that an extraordinary honor was paid him when Doña Catalina herself took his arm for a whole evening, and went with him through the rooms, and sat with him in one of the misplaced choir stalls, and explained all her extravagant treasures to him. She even drank with him, which she had never been known to do before with a visitor. She wore every one of her jewels one time when she expected he would be in attendance. She powdered her face to a dazzling white and painted her mouth with red paste, and dug fascinating caverns of shadow about her eyes with black paint so that there would be flashes and sparks riding on her glance. She used a fan with theatrical archness. She smoked and blew the smoke over his face and hid her mouth with her silver lace mantilla. She said her heart was a girl, and that was all that mattered. Captain Somers was gay and cordial; he would laugh uproariously as if this was the heartiest joke on earth. He escaped her by his simple enthusiasm, you might say. Everything delighted him, equally.

The inhabitants and visitors watched the desperate romance being played before them by Doña Catalina during the stay of the American soldiers.

Another evening she would appear in a new role, her face uncolored, her eyes subdued, a black mantilla over her head, her gown

of black, black lace mitts on her hands, no jewels, but an onyx crucifix hanging on her lace-covered bosom. The Captain spent the
evening admiring the crucifix.

4

With her heart sinking as the day approached for the Army to march
west, Doña Catalina decided to give a party for the officers at which
all her gifts would be most flatteringly and convincingly displayed.
She commanded extra musicians in from Atrisco, Bernalillo, and even
a harpist from Santa Fe. She had the main *sala* cleared for dancing.
Supper was laid in the patio on newly built tables. It was midsummer.
The moon was like a lantern among the tops of the immense cottonwood trees. The fragrance of the river mud and the faint bitter smell
of the cottonwood leaves and the drift of cicada music out of doors
and the bump and pulse of the orchestra in the big house, guitars of
all sizes, the harp, four violins, and a zither, and a hint of summer off
the mesa in the grand drift of cool air…it was such a night as they
would always remember of Albuquerque. The officers were in full
dress with swords and white gloves. Doña Catalina and her court
were in spreading skirts of silk and satin over which their long man-
tillas cascaded to the floor in back. For fields away, the people outside
could hear the bass guitars gulping the music like bullfrogs, and see
the lights reflecting upward on the big trees that stood within and
atop the house. They could hear the laughing and the singing. The
soldiers sang a chorus, a bawdy song in English, and smashed one
of the improvised tables by banging on it so strenuously in rhythm.
Outside the house a whole string of horses waited for their masters.
Mexican servants and Army orderlies waited too, and they felt giddy
under the moonlight, just listening to the party within.

    Doña Catalina gave a toast to the visitors, calling in it for a
drink and a kiss, and since every man had a girl on his arm, and
some of them two, they drank, and kissed their girls. Captain
Somers was the guardian of Doña Catalina herself, and at the end
of her toast, she turned up her vivid, ugly face and he kissed her
out of sheer good manners. When he heard the high cheer go up

from everybody else, he realized that they were being watched. He blushed like a student and bent over and shook hands heartily with the proprietress, strode out to the front hall holding his great sabre off the floor, went out, called his man, and rode off to the encampment which was glowing with white tents in the moonlight and the remains of the cook's fire in a field north of the Plaza. Once there in his tent, he wrote for a few minutes, the sentry could see his shadow on the tent, and then went to bed.

The party was ruined.

Doña Catalina was in a rage at everyone for commenting so openly upon her love, which had driven him off. And that he had gone, "just-like-that," was an insult to her. She hated him as much as she loved him, both at the same time. She drove her guests away, retired to her cluttered bedroom, and raged all night. By morning, her sense of injury was full-grown. She sent for a friend who had often patronized her place, and said he must do her the favor of challenging Captain Somers to avenge the insult.

The second chosen by Doña Catalina's champion waited upon Captain Henry Houghton Somers the next morning after the party, and was received with a perfectly charming burst of unaffected laughter. It was inconceivable to the happily married officer that he should risk his future in a ridiculous brawl thousands of miles from home, here in this outlandish river town, and all because of a clever but miserable woman who kept a bawdy house. He assured the second that he failed to see that any insult had attended his departure from the party the night before. He was tired, he had returned to add a few pages to his letter which was going to his wife by the next bag, and he begged the Señor to understand that the valor of arms were better reserved for a serious need, such as the United States cavalry might well encounter when they marched tomorrow for the Indian country to the west.

It was an unheard-of refusal.

The second returned to his principal, who flew in fury to Doña Catalina, who in her turn thought she would die of the rage and misery in her breast. To be repudiated *this* way also was too much.

By evening, the whole town knew what was up, and there were factions, mainly three, divided between those who believed in respectability and considered the Captain right; those who sided with Doña Catalina out of sympathy; and those who—entertaining no views as to the merits of the complaint—still considered honor an abstraction whose formalities must always be observed, and thus felt the Captain should accept the challenge. But it took the energy and originality of Doña Catalina herself to focus all the conflicts of opinion with one supreme act. She dressed herself like a rich widow, sent for her carriage, drove to the headquarters of the American General, and demanded an interview.

General Stephen Watts Kearny was a model of tact in his dealing with the inhabitants of the province he had taken for his government.

He had met the lady before, and now caused her to be brought into his office.

He treated her with much courtesy, and listened to her florid complaints with composure. She claimed that the only thing that mattered to her *now* was that Captain Somers had refused the challenge of her protector. This was an intolerable affront. She demanded of the commanding General that he *order* Captain Somers to accept the challenge, and by fighting for his own honor, *prove that she had some, too.* Otherwise he was a coward and not fit to be an officer in any army, much less that of the United States. There was still time for the duel, the troops were not leaving till morning. It could be fought by firelight in the field beyond her own patio. She would have her personal physician there, and the Army surgeon could attend also. She would be content with a superficial wound. She had never in her life been so humiliated, and only considerations of the highest propriety made her come, this way, to humble herself before the friendly and talented General of the United States forces.

He watched her with great interest as he listened to her passionate demands, in which vanity vied with desire.

She was impressive though anything but handsome. Her eyes smoked and flared with the inner lights of her emotion. Her bosom, which was pretty, became a dramatic organ in its own right. She wrung her hands and her jewels danced in the air.

But the issue was plain to them both, a ruinously commanding issue. It was good sense against fantastic frustration; respectability against outlawry, really, the moment at last when Doña Catalina challenged the other world in its own terms. She knew she could not afford to be beaten.

The General let her rave, and when she was breathless and silent, he took her hand and pressed it ardently, like a grand-uncle. He said that if Captain Somers accepted the challenge, he would be dismissed from the Army. There was a very strict code about such matters, in *gringo* life; just as strict in its way as the dueling code was among the Latins. He would have to admit that many duels were fought unofficially, and all of them were deplorable. But this case was now a matter of official record, alas, *through her own statement of it to the Commanding General*; and he might actually have to consider *placing a guard* upon Captain Somers until the departure of the troops, to insure that he *did not weaken*, and enter upon the engagement at arms *after all*. Somers was one of his best officers, he said; let nobody think him a coward for returning the challenge. It simply would not do, that was all.

But if she desired, he would send for Captain Somers, to afford him the opportunity of making an apology.

She sprang to her feet. Her silks whistled as she whirled to the door in a fury, and in a fire of Spanish invective of which, everyone agreed, she was a formidable mistress, she burned the General's ears, and left him.

The town was waiting for the duel.

Nothing happened.

The encampment went to sleep, with all preparations completed for the morning's march.

Doña Catalina's house was dark for the first night in years.

5

The bugles called the soldiers in the morning. The town awoke with them. An August morning, with white sunlight rising over the mountains. The troops were going to march on the river road as far south as Socorro, and then turn west. The New Mexicans turned out to see the assembly. In the preparations, they could see Captain Somers moving about his duties like everybody else. He seemed earnest, at ease and in fine humor. It was a little after eight when the troops mounted. The wagons were drawn up in formation. The guidons fluttered in the air. There was that pause, waiting for the General, when everything was ready but himself in his own saddle. But at last he came out of the house where he had held his headquarters, and this was the signal for the bells of the Church of San Felipe de Neri to start ringing. They clamored and tangled their stinging sweet discords in the white-shuttered belfries.

General Kearny nodded to his adjutant, who turned in his saddle and saluted the commanding officer of the first squadron, who raised his arm, and signaled *At a walk, forward march.*

The General let them ride for a few paces at attention; then another command was passed "through channels" and the men were at ease. They waved, they called out, and traded the last, most insincere and charming of promises with the people, largely the women, of Albuquerque. Going under the big cottonwood trees, they were showered with coins of sunlight through the leaves.

In a little while, the dust was down on the road again. The saddle creaking was part of the morning farther down the river. The hot day was under way in Albuquerque. Shutters were closed against the heat. After the troops forded the river, they went up that little rise on the other side, and then down again, and were out of sight.

But the quiet of summer in the dirt plaza was hardly drowsing again when the door of Doña Catalina's house flew open, and she came out to meet her carriage which came richly braking its own speed around the patio corner. There were four little mules in the harness, trotting rapidly. She entered the coach which had its leather curtains closed, and set off to overtake the Army. She forded the river, came up the rise on the other side, and looked her last on the little town where she had been so successful for so many years.

But she would never have been so, if she had not had a most realistic stripe in her character.

She now summoned it to her final aid.

A carriage alone can travel much faster than a body of troops.

Overtaking the Army on the road to Socorro, Doña Catalina's carriage jingled and rang. The driver and the servant on the box cried out for passage. The troops closed in to the edge of the road. With its painted and paneled body rocking on its leather springs, and its leather curtains flapping in the speed, it carried Doña Catalina rapidly and disdainfully past the slow-trotting soldiers on the road to the south, in a cloud of white dust that rose like the breath of summer in the wilderness, and settled back again in country silence.

If they expected to find her at Socorro when they got there late the third day, the soldiers were wrong. She had gone through on the way to El Paso, they heard, and that was the last of her in these parts.

A few months later her grand furnishings were packed and shipped to her in the city of Chihuahua, where later travelers saw her queening it over local society and getting richer by the minute.

6

"Yes," said Peter, "I've read about her life in Chihuahua City. I've got a book by a man who went down there in the fifties, and saw her. He was pretty hard in his opinion of her."

He remembered Molly as she read aloud to him the description of "La Voz" by Elias Gray, in *The Western Attorney*. Had there been a prophetic irony in the act? He remembered her voice, its cool, cultivated sound, along with which there always sounded an involuntary catch of breath now and then. He wondered how long such details would have the power to turn his heart over.

"No," said Don Hilario, "it is not necessary to be hard in one's opinion of Doña Catalina. She was simply one of those women, and I have seen many of them in my day, one of those women who think love is an end in itself, and can be bought and sold, without paying for it with life. That is what children think, too, isn't it?"

He looked at Peter again, as if from across the grave.

Peter stood up. He knew he was no match for the old man in a duel of proverbs or epigrams. Don Hilario had the facility of his race at polishing off a situation with proper saws.

"Would you like to read the book I mentioned?"

"I haven't read a book for twenty-five years, since I retired from the Supreme Court of New Mexico. Sometimes I sit and hold one, because I like the shape of a book. All my books were sold when I moved here. I had one of the finest libraries in the Territory of New Mexico, and I could quote more law in Spanish and Voltaire in French and Gibbon in English than anybody in these parts. Sometime I will tell you about my trip to Paris, and the time I met Count Cavour in Rome, and discussed the freedom of Italy with him."

"I'd love to hear it."

"You will have to give me time to remember it."

"Indeed I will, and thank you very much.—Perhaps I might just listen to you now, before I go."

He meant that he would use his stethoscope on the old man's heart. Don Hilario shut his eyes and appeared to remove himself from any part in the examination. Peter listened to the heartbeats. Widely spaced, they were remote and delicate, and made him think of steps walking deliberately along which one day, and not very far off, would simply cease walking as if to end a journey in good order. He straightened up and nodded, and Don Hilario nodded back, with his round silent laugh, as if to say that such witchcraft was nonsensical, an unnecessary refinement, at his time of life.

He accompanied Peter to the front of the house. Down the lane they could see the Sanchez grocery store on the Plaza corner. It was stuccoed gray, and the plaster had caked off here and there. There was no sign of the old patio. The ditch still went by the rear of the place, but was now fenced off by a neighbor. The huge cottonwood trees Don Hilario remembered of the old patio were gone. He said you could see a stump of one of them left, and when Peter passed it a few moments later, sure enough, there it was, covered with a vine of sky-blue morning glories. At the corner, he saw the windows of the Sanchez grocery store, full of cardboard cigarette displays and merchandise and spider webs. There was only one detail left which might recall the house of a hundred years ago, and this was the style of the windows, and of one door, down on the alley side of the house. The face of the house wavered and sagged, betraying the neglect of a century. But in it were set that doorway, and those windows, deep and severe, with classical pediments of carved wood, long softened by repeated paintings, and as grand in their dilapidation as they must have been in their heyday; for their design was pure to start with, and always would be.

XXXI · BUSINESS: A SKIRMISH

I

Just before the Harvey House dining-room doors closed for "late," Willa saw the man come in for breakfast, treading heavily on the sunlit floor of the restaurant. He was enormously fat, and walked with his weight poised so that he leaned a little backwards. He was spanked for the morning, with powdery pink jowls, cheeks that dew-lapped over one another in tingling splendor. Beautifully groomed, too, a fat man who cherished every inch of his great surface. His eyes were still liquid and blurred from sleep; but so enclosed by the flesh which he put forth that they seemed remote little vials of intelligent blue, lost in that Chinese profusion of curved surface. His movements had something of that spacious and impressive quality to be found in a larger reproduction of something ordinarily familiar on a modest scale. He was captain of an incidental majesty, and moved to his table like the essential half, the completive force, of any whole.

When he sat down, he opened wide his legs, so that his southern hemisphere could depend in space. He set his left hand elegantly tented with spread fingers on his serge thigh, and gazed upon the menu. There was a very special melon announced. He conversed about its promise with Willa and she gave it a fine character. He ordered it.

In the little pause, he looked around, and yearned for newspapers on a near-by table, but let them lie. His neck rolled like a rubber bag full of water over his tight and beautifully pressed collar. His hair was brushed shining flat on his Roman pate.

Then Willa started across the room with the melon, and he watched her.

He watched the melon coming toward him, the cool succulent, taste-thrilling sight of it, that pale sparkling heart of fruit, with the chilled lime lying on it to be squeezed. He settled a little nearer the table, and his great pink head moved to follow her as she curved around him to set his fruit down.

And now the morning became spangled and tingling with delight.

He sat so close to the table that he had to look straight down his rolling cheeks to see his plate. This would have buried his little avid eyes in their sacs if he had not raised his eyebrows to stretch his upper lids open so that he had drawn mandarin folds of skin there. His mouth worked slightly open, and appeared to pretaste what he readied.

His whole immense bulking body was intimate and tender with anticipated pleasure. His clean, packed fingers turned the melon and sparkled the lime juice on its every facet, and his lips worked, his cheeks shrunk with tart excitement away from his lips, and his hands were delicate, so fond, in their touch. His tongue was the agent of his hope and want. The taste buds electrified him with the messages he liked best of all in this world to receive. He moved in little pressures against the table, toward his dear melon, that cold and glorious experience at the start of day.

He had the confidence of the blessed. If after all this it were not a good melon! But he salted it, and the sparkle of the salt and the fragrance it induced from the melon meat could mean only one thing. He set the plate a trifle away, then, the better to see, and like a pianist serene with arrogant technique let his right paw fall to the silverware where it ever so lightly and surely took up the large spoon.

He moistened his lips.

He opened his mouth, while he spooned out a large and inspiring morsel of the melon, and because his bosom was so vast, his arm had to travel not across it but around it, and the elegance of this arc was like a consummation.

The delicious, dripping moment arrived, and he expressed appreciation in every fine and happy pound of his being.

He took the bite in his mouth, and from his little eyes so genial and so fattened over, there came a tiny stream of appreciation, the fat man's ichor, his thanks for this Thy bounty, and his right thigh trotted ever so slightly on the edge of the chair seat, and the spoon descended for yet another and another scoop of chilled fibrous fruit.

When he had filled his cheeks several times with the luscious grainy meat, so that he was assuaged for a moment, he took a deep breath and turned his attention to Willa, believing that he was doing so without her noticing. He wanted to size her up. Clever thing to do, come here for breakfast first, get 'n impression, make plan, not enough men in bizness took trouble, look ahead, find out class of client got deal with, that was all. He was almost panged by the "pushover" before him. She was little, and gray, and pathetically eager, he felt. A word from whom? from a majestically dissatisfied patron of this dining room, and what? What: out she goes. Power. Big man, Treadwell. Everybody said Treadwell was a shrewd bizness head. Otis L. Treadwell. Name's on m'card, here, in m'inside pocket—and conversely, a kind word, flattery, and likely the deal was done.

Willa saw him, all right. A salesman type. She knew enough about them. No more morals than an alley cat. *Look out*, she always said, look out for a man who spends so much time on *how he looks*, fat or lean, don't matter, all they want is feed theirself, at somebody else's expense.

She served his breakfast silently and neatly, and when he strode away with the gentle ponderousness of his weight, his arms swinging out from his body because they couldn't hang down, she snipped her nose in the air with her opinion of him, but said again that the public was made up of all kinds, never forget that, she was before the public, and she always felt almost more like an actress than a waitress when she remembered that; a charming dare.

2

That same day, Willa was sitting down for a moment, just a *moment*, for a glance at the morning paper (it was the middle of the afternoon, at that) (first moment she'd had all day) (who could begrudge her?) when Margaret, the headwaitress, came to the pantry and said there was a man out in the dining room who wanted to see her. It was a chilling announcement, as Margaret made it, bringing Willa all the little rises of worry that a life of expectations instead of achievements could make. She got up and started through the swinging doors, and paused a second behind the leather screen to shut her eyes and squeeze her fingers in a prayer. Then she went down the long room with her quick steps and a birdlike alertness in the set of her little head. There *was* a man waiting, by the far doors. He had a heavy, red face and was holding his hat and a cigar. She began to feel easier as soon as she saw him; for he seemed to be making various small attitudes of ingratiation, such as a policeman, or an undertaker, or any bearer of threat or bad news would never make. Then she saw that it was the fat man of this morning's breakfast. She added dignity to her carriage.

As soon as she came within range, so to speak, they commenced instinctively a little ritual of approach and parry; almost a miniature social ballet, in which he advanced and retreated, with male waggery, florid, confident and artfully chaste; while she impersonated a grand lady, choosing to miss his suggestive flattery which she had seen so often from men of his type, who made a male-female pattern out of the idlest contact, such as that between a waitress and her gentleman customer. She nodded grandly to him, and indicated that he might sit, in a dining-room chair, while she stood to hear him. He begged her to be seated, sweeping his fat red hand with its nugget of a ring toward the chair for her, herself. They ended by both standing. She privately guessed that he was a heavy drinker, and worse, and she was cautious because he seemed so cordial.

"This's Mrs. Shoemaker, I believe?"

She bowed.

"I am Mr. Treadwell, representing the Diamond Realty Company.—I have a card here," he added, fumbling in a shiny wallet and selecting a fairly clean card from a little sheaf under one of the leather flaps. He gave it to her as if in his fat, sober gesture there lay a sacred donation of his person; his quality; asking it to be honored as he would be honored. The scrap of soiled paper was full of dear excellence to him.

"Thank you."

She looked at it and bent it with gentility against her thumb nail, waiting for him to proceed. Neither of them referred in any way to their encounter of the morning, the patron-waitress relation.

What on earth could he want.

He seems to *want* something, it sticks out all over him. I've seen *him* before. Well, he'll get nowhere *making himself* at me. I have no time for his type.

"Mrs. Shoemaker, I believe you own some property out on the mesa?—A former chicken ranch, I believe?"

That riddled her with apprehensions.

Swindle/tax foreclosure/my babies/last thing own.

"Yes, I do."

"Mrs. Shoemaker? Would you be i'rested in selling?"

"Oh."

He entered upon his still-dance of ingratiation again, his fat elbows up, his head forward, his knees springing ever so slightly.

"I represent a party who is prepared to pay well for your land. Like to say he is making a very-very generous offer.—Had you any thought of selling?"

She looked at his card again to prove that she was no fool, and could be as shrewd as the next one, and was not one to be swept off her feet by the first red-faced, barbered and powdered fat man that came along. He relished the details of the transaction. He glanced with his wet-shining eyes at the cigar wreck in his hand, and asked if he might smoke? She nodded, and, somehow making it seem a tribute to her presence, he put down the cold butt on an ash tray, and drew out an entirely fresh cigar, which he clipped, rolled, licked, and lighted without once removing his white-lashed eyes from her face.

Her heart was beating so that she felt it.

It may be m'chance, she said to herself, the two buildings on the place should be worth so-much, and the road, we helped make that road, there, fifteen years ago, there's that fence, and the land itself, and the chicken house is a *model* chicken house, the glass alone is worth a small fortune, I'll sell, and *we'll go*. I'll have Martha's clothes all done over before we go, she'll be the prettiest thing to hit Albion in years, since *I* left it, for that matter, and Wayne'll be in seventh heaven with the train, it'll *take* two and a half days, I'm not getting any younger, *why not?*

"I *have* thought of it, off and on," she said, lifting her head. But he saw her hands going, the card trembling. Her hands were little gathers of bone and vein; hardly any flesh on them at all; he "spat" mentally at how easy it was going to be, if he just remained genteel, because he felt sure that his subtle fleshy hints of flirtation were what fetched the poor little thing right off.

He took a deep breath and it made him wheeze, and he coughed, and the cough turned into a laugh, an explosion of great sociability in the huge empty dining room. He was like a bullfrog enchanted at good fortune, and when he got his voice back, suggested that they just get in his car, out front, and run up to the mesa, and look at the property, while he relayed the offer he was privileged to make as agent.

"I believe I can arrange to get off for half an hour," she said, and went to ask Margaret. If Margaret refused permission, then: then she would *resign*. This was a matter of business. Fortunately, Margaret understood that, but wished to know what it was about. When she heard that it was about some property, she was briefly haggard at the really impressive note of this.

3

All the way up the hill, Mr. Treadwell made conversation. It was all calculated to arouse sympathy and pity for him, so that *she* would feel almost responsible for *his* welfare at the moment of closing the deal. He said that she was very lucky to have such a nice piece of property, and he only wished he could be sure of leaving anything as suitable to *Miz* Treadwell. Or at least: he *would've*, except that lately things didn't seem quite the same between Miz Treadwell and himself. He naturally had to be away a good deal on business, and last time he'd come back, she's gone. Slick's a whistle, gone to Abilene, where *her* mother lived, and the old lady was *sure* a hellcat, if she would pardon him. Lonely? Nothing's lonely's a house where the *lady's* away. Like to say it was an attractive house, too. One letter since she'd gone, not a word about returning, not *mad*, mind, not *final*, or anything, just up and lit out, and he guessed she wanted him to get in the car and come after her, and bring her back, had had to do it before, and guessed go' have to do it again. He sighed, and pressed his lips together around his cigar, and glanced elaborately out of the car as if to conceal feelings which struggled to betray themselves.

Willa hardly heard him. She was calculating the future in exact terms. They'd have enough money (she was sure) to go to the Hotel, and stay there as long as the Albion visit lasted. They'd take a suite with a living room, and keep it full of fresh flowers, and Martha could meet her little friends there, and all the *old* friends could come in, what good times they would have remembering everything together, and bridging the gap of years that had lasted as long as— as it took to rear a lovely daughter like that one, there. Dennison Yeager probably would have a car of his own by now. Summer in Albion was terribly warm, but oh! so sweet with the smell of the green hills and the vines and the roses that grew almost in tufts, they were so thick. Those country roads would be just the same, long tunnels of shadow in the starlight, and if it was hot in the evening after dinner, there would be drives. And a whole summer of it, there would be parties at the Yeagers' place, the paper said they were rebuilding already, the old burned brick farmhouse had been torn down, and Grace was putting up a Norman-French château-type of new house, according to the *Recorder*, out of Indiana limestone and asbestos shingles. It sounded wonderful. Martha would take her place easily among such surroundings. Perhaps Lawrence wasn't yet too old to play with Wayne. Somehow a bicycle for Wayne would have to be managed so he could get around, too. Wayne would see where his father had come from, that white clapboard farmhouse which had long ago been sold to the Mastersons, but still, if she went with him, and pointed it all out, as she remembered it, and took him by the Kalamazoo River and showed him the dam where they used to have picnics, and then that pool where the fireflies were really *reflected*, because they flew so low and the water was so still, why, then, he would see *what-she-meant*, and about his father, who had started out there, even if he didn't end up there, and it was *home*, and that was probably what she meant, by *all this*, anyway.

Grace Yeager was always clever. She could look right through me.

She always thought I wanted to get Martin, and she got him instead, and of course she is the rich lady of the town, and I don't think she ever loved Martin as much as she loved his horses and rigs and the old brick house, it burned down, didn't it, she used to take on so over the *antiques* in it, and she never *heard* of an antique until she became Mrs. Martin Yeager.

They have those boys.

And I always thought: and now Martha and that Bunny: and *Sacred Heart of Jesus, have it not too late already*, think of it, if Martha married Dennison Yeager, he is twenty-one this year, 'll be out of college in June, I saw his picture in the *Recorder*, blond, Grace's eyes, sweet-looking boy, and with Martha's honey-look, what a couple they would make, and all that money, say what you like, money counts, *I know*, when has Grace Yeager ever worked on her feet all day, running trays in and out of this dining room and pantry, how I hate the smell of wet drain boards, it is the only *clean* smell I hate.

Or if not Dennison, then the younger one, Lawrence, they say he's rather fat, but he'd be good-natured, and Grace's spoiled him, she always was a fool, still, a Yeager, Martha would go home and assume her *rightful position*, after all, we left when I was just a girl myself, but I couldn't even take her home to *visit* if:

She had no idea her longing to get back was really as profound as it was until the chance to go really seemed to have arrived. She had a misty shine in her eyes, and Mr. Treadwell thought it was in tribute to his virtuosity. His own eyes flooded in sympathy with hers.

They came to the ranch lane, and turned off the highway. She leaned forward, and saw it before he did. Years since she had come up here. Was that all it amounted to? She must conceal what she felt. How far did twenty-five acres stretch? But the buildings're bigger than that, they always have been, she thought in panic.

I do want Martha to marry "East," she thought as they drove up, Wayne and I'll return here, that won't matter, but I'd love to have a daughter in the East, it is where *I* was born, and raised, and fell in love, and married. She was holding dearly to her own past by these wishes, with small regard for Martha's.

"Here we are," declared Mr. Treadwell. He flourished her out of the front seat of his car, and they stood, looking around. The afternoon light was sweeping in long rays from over the river, and the whole mesa was golden. The mountains were cast with a pale silvery light over their rocky gray.

"Now you may wonder," he said, "why anybody should want to buy this property, Mrs. Shoemaker."

"Indeed I don't, it's a very fine piece!"

"Oh, no, I didn't mean *that*, I assure you, a very fine piece, for what it *is*, if you know what I mean. No, but the point is, like to say my client is a fair-minded man, and willing to go the limit. Point is, he has just bought all the adjoining property from the former owners, and lacks this piece here to complete his section. Like to say he feels he'd like to complete his section, and so wishes to buy your property. Not that he needs it. Run all the stock he wants on what he's already got, for that matter.—Now your fence runs—"

He pointed over the land, but she was again not paying any attention to him. She had found the ruined front of the chicken house.

She exclaimed, and searched for a single whole pane in the framed front, and found none. She bent down and gingerly touched the glass dust on the ground. The place was wrecked. It would destroy the price. She was sick with rage and couldn't say a word. Her plans—which always turned into realities for her—crumbled in ruins. Mr. Treadwell tried to get her to stand up again. He couldn't understand why she was so concerned.

He said that as a matter of fact, his client was going to clear away the little buildings right off, anyway, when he got possession. The buildings had never entered into the consideration, one way or the other, he said. All *he* wanted to do was to straighten out the fences, and close the sandy road that led in from the highway, and keep everybody out from then on.

But Willa was honestly outraged at the destruction of what she had always thought of as tangible assets. She said she wished she could get her hands on whoever did a thing like that. He answered that why look, there're car tracks all around, he said lots of people must use the place, and come on out here, and *park*, the wonder is the whole walls ain't down and hauled off.

She searched the ground miserably for answers to her indignation.

In a moment she found one.

There was a scatter of empty copper cartridge cases for a .22 rifle, hundreds of them. Somebody had shot the glass to bits.

"Well," said Mr. Treadwell, "now that we've looked it over, you'll see that my client is making a very fine offer. Like to say you won't do better anywhere else."

Willa could always do it when she had to, she reminded herself. She looked right at him, and her small sober face dared him to cheat her.

"Well?"

He proposed paying her five hundred dollars for the whole

property, but his white-lashed look was indirect, and she attacked him like a furious martin. She said they'd put thousands into the place, and she'd paid taxes on it for years, he could look up the assessor's record and see what the county thought it was worth, and everybody knew the tax assessments were half or less of the actual *business* value, and she said she never would've come up here with him if she'd even thought he was going to make such a ridiculous proposal. If that was all there was to it, she would turn around and *walk* back to the Harvey House, before she'd deal with him on any such terms.

Her disappointment lived in images, not dollars. They couldn't *go*, on five hundred dollars, the three of them, not the *way* she intended for them to go. She was in a passion of fear and loss. The future was gone. She started back to the car, too addled by misery to recognize in Mr. Treadwell the idiomatic dodges of trading. He was appalled at her reaction. He had orders to buy the place, and a top limit of two thousand had been placed on it, that was all, whatever he could get it down to, why he could "sidetrack" the difference between the actual sale price and the limit which his client was willing to go, that was all, probably it was better judgment to say it'd gone for eighteen hundred, good-by to the other two hundred, too bad, but better to be safe, and not be greedy, that was all, the papers could be fixed, and anybody else'd be's shrewd as that, given the chance, that was all.

He started after her, taking the air with each hand before him in an energetic heave, being so fat and wanting to be in motion so quickly. He patted her shoulder, and said he hated to see a lady so upset, and after all, there was such a thing as an opener, that was all, and he'd like to say he was ready to hear her asking price, the thing wasn't settled, yet, anyway.

It was with a deeply fleshed sense of exasperation and shame that he ended by agreeing to pay her twelve hundred and fifty dollars for the property as it stood. She was either an outrageous fool, or else the meanest little woman he'd met in a long, long time. Without seeming to make an effort, or resorting to any of the dodges he was used to handling in business deals with men, she had taken him for something of a ride, and he seemed to've been *watching* himself going down the chute, without knowing how to stop it. She was so bent on *something*.

He was a huge and sore man, baffled once again by what a woman *had*, there was simply no dealing with them, if one of them ever made up her mind she wanted something a man could get her, then God help the poor son of a bitch, was all *he* could say, wow!

The papers were in order, and the next day, he mailed her a cashier's check for the full amount.

4

Like to burst she was so happy, she said to herself, when she reached home at night with Mr. Treadwell's check in her purse. The house was still. She listened holding her breath to "see" if the children were in. She always did this, and rarely was able to detect her answer without actually going to look. As she was about to cross the tiny front room to look out on the sleeping porch, she saw a square of paper, an envelope, leaning on the top of the *Spirito Santo*. On it was written "Mother" in Wayne's writing, in pencil, heavily pressed into the paper, and made largely, as he always wrote, with a certain strength to the formation of the letters, as if he were building a fence out of the words he made.

Now what/good Lord/let me see, she fluttered, taking it up and scratching the envelope open. Inside was a sheet of paper from his school notebook, ruled in blue. She could read it without her glasses.

> Dear Mother,
>
> I am not worthy to be your son. I have worried for weeks and I cannot any longer defer my statement that I must make to you. This is my statement. I went to the ranch that Saturday with D. and broke all the glass in the chicken house shooting at it with D.'s new birthday twenty-2 rifle. We used the boxes of twenty-2 bullets I got him for his birthday. Ever since it happened I have

suffered the tortures of the damned and now it will be hard for you to forgive me. But I will earn the money somehow to give back to you. All I ask is that you only give me the chance, after the ruin I have inflicted. I did not stop to think. I promise you hereafter I will always stop to think. After the way you work and slave all day long for us, I feel awful. I could not desist from telling you any longer. No matter what you will think of me, I am

Your loving son,
Wayne Shoemaker

P.S. Of course I have been to Confession about this. *W. S.*

Rascal/darling/precious boy/how could he/what a nicely written letter/where does he get such words/that's *right* the cartridges!

She listened for him, now, and tiptoed to the porch. Her heart beat longingly. Wait till he heard *her* news! He was asleep. She was a trifle disappointed. But what could make her feel more reassured about him, more secure in what she had given him (of herself, her hope, her goodness) than that letter? She went to the icebox and found an apple, cold and hard, and went back and laid it on the wide mattress next to his pillow. If he awoke and found it, he would know right off who had put it there. Here: she slipped his envelope under it so he'd know she'd read it. She wouldn't be surprised if they neither of them ever mentioned the thing again. But she held on to his letter, and would keep it forever among her few treasures.

XXXII · PETER'S OWN EARLY WEST

I

Noonie thought for many days about something she wanted to say to Peter. But she didn't want to risk in words the hope she now knew. She felt obscurely that if she spoke it aloud, it might disappear. What she meant was that now that she could *see* that she had been ill, she could get well again. What had happened to her? She had been delivered from a spell. It was like something out of untold time, the stories of folk experience and need in the common heart, a parable of the lover who broke through an enchantment, and saved, freed, the beloved.

What was character but the world's own material of magic?

2

Peter had to admit to himself that it had not surprised him; though he had kept on hoping that Noonie in some way might never have to face the tragic issues of her own weakness. The days after his discovery of her at the brink of dying were oddly peaceful for them both. He had a nurse with her all day, and so felt safe to leave her for his work. He saw Noonie growing more relaxed and he began to wonder if he saw something in her eyes that had not been there for years. But he was patient, and he had also a tactful allowance for the secrets that gave trouble to other people; even to his wife. And so it was not until she was recovering from the shock of the terrible afternoon that what he hoped in his heart could be risked in words between them.

One night in the darkness he said to her, "When you've nearly lost something, it becomes perfectly clear how much you want to keep it."

She was suddenly terrified.

She clutched his arm and he could feel her trembling. Now she saw what she had tried to die out of.

"What is it, Noon?"

She could barely speak. Her tongue clove to her mouth, and she had to free it desperately. Waves and floods of feeling poured through her. She was taken and trundled by such feeling as she had not known for years. It was like waking up from a paralysis. She had never thought she would ever feel anything again. She was borne upon a wave of belief and realization, and it flowed to her from him.

If there was a moment upon which they could later have fixed for the return of her health, this was it. She began to weep, but it was not with pity for herself; it was with gratitude for being again alive to the reach that came to her from her husband, the vessel of duty and debt in life.

He knew the relief that followed the delivery of a patient from a state of shock. He saw it happen to her that night. But that it should come in response to something he had said to her, the thing he had shown her, was in its way quite as curative for him as for her. Whatever had developed those years of increasing remoteness in her, pity, apathy and doubt, he could never determine; but he believed now that it didn't matter; for this was a strong tide beginning to flow in the other direction. It gave him passion; and this he gave to her, too. They felt that they were solving not only this moment but also an unsaid, unsayable, problem out of the past.

He thought much, alone in wakefulness long after she had gone to sleep.

After all, it was pretty desperate, wasn't it. This is the only direction in which things *could* turn, there wasn't any more room to travel in the other direction, was there.

Even now; what a narrow escape; if I hadn't just happened to feel it was the right time to say anything to her tonight—but it was right. Lord! Lord! Lord! I hope it does keep up, I hope I am right in what I *feel* about it.

It must be a lock, locking us together, so that when there are any other threats, the aftermath of despair which is now so sweet will not fall away as suddenly as it came up.

So for days there was one half of him that was almost judicial in a terrible, impersonal way. He knew what might happen most clearly, if Noonie's almost-fate threatened her again. He was on the watch for it, like a captain at sea, riding the unknown forces which may produce the known disaster all over again. And he was ready for it if it should come; fighting against it with all his power, which was revealed prosaically in the response they were able to make to each other in daily trivialities. If they both held on long enough,

almost like children holding their breaths for fear something wonderful would vanish as soon as they *let* go, then: then maybe in peace
they could keep each other all the rest of their lives. What would
finally tell them? Something would tell them. Health, if nothing
else, would tell them. He felt *yes* about it. *Yes* he would save Noonie.
Yes things could be found out in time. *Yes* a man has powers to
use. What else was his life dedicated to, after all? What else had it
shown him?

3

No one had a really true picture of himself. Peter didn't know just
how inevitably like himself he had acted in renouncing the future
that had tempted him. He thought a lot about what might have
brought Noonie to the edge of the abyss, and he said he wished it
was possible to put your finger on the one moment, long ago, the
series of moments, which had precipitated a consequent chain of
weaknesses. If you could do that, how easy it would be to understand, to help!

This suggested the obverse of the situation to him. He suddenly
recalled an episode of his own youth when, if he had turned another
way, and yielded to something that he was scared of, he too might
have carried the obscure scars of it all his life. Pictures from his
boyhood came back to him with a sort of simple clarity, and he saw
again one of the things in his whole life that he could put his finger
on and know as an achievement.

4

He went up to Colorado during the summer twenty-eight years ago,
when he was fifteen, to visit his cousin Jack Winterhood. He didn't
know Jack very well, but Jack's mother was the sister of Peter's father.
She was a widow who taught the rural district school in the country
of the South Fork of the Rio Grande. She had a large schoolhouse
built of logs stained brown, and it seemed to Peter then the only
desirable school he ever saw. He stayed with her and her son, who
was a year older than himself, in their white-painted farmhouse, set

in the greenest field he could remember. The big river ran past their place two hundred yards away.

What a river! It came rushing grandly down through the open tunnel of rock, and the water was the color of smoke-colored obsidian, but perfectly clear: the color of daylight reflected in a dark mirror. He used to lie for hours and watch the water go by, swept in thought by the mystery of its movement, and the eternity of its source from the mountain groins in the rocky peaks that lay back against the northern sky.

One branch of the river came from the west and the north. The other came off Wolf Creek Pass to the south. Where they came together, going mightily out toward the plains, there was a point of land that narrowed as the division between the streams until it was gone. But off the tip of this point there was an island, it lay in a tangle of willows and cottonwoods and it seemed to be removed from all the life around it as completely as if it were another world. It was a long spit of land, not very wide across. The river was deep and full of silvery rapids on both sides of it, and below. But above it, by a curious roil in the meeting of the two mountain flows, there was a deep black pool which turned slowly and mysteriously like a magic lake, lapping delicately at the island's upper end, as if independent of the powerful quick river forks that met so urgently at the island's other end.

Cousin Jack Winterhood was a calm active boy with brown eyes and a pale freckled face, and short-cut brown hair. He had flecks of yellow light in his eyes, and when he was thinking something over, he would simply regard Peter, and those flecks would seem to kindle with deliberation and justice, and when he decided what he thought, or would do, he spoke crisply and Peter could never do other than his will, for it seemed to have been so inevitably arrived at. Peter was at the age when it was instructive to imitate someone, and it was his cousin Jack whom he most wished to resemble, though oddly enough, he made Peter see virtues in his father which even he had never before recognized, the rancher in New Mexico. Jack admired Mr. Rush very much, whom he used to see passing through on the D. & R. G. railroad on his way to buy cattle in Western Colorado.

This railroad ran through that valley, along the river course, in and out of canyons. It fed the gold and silver mining camps up in the mountains to the west, and it hauled cows back to the plains and connected at junctions for reshipping on broad gauge railroads to the markets of Texas and Kansas. One of the main delights of that summer was to play along the right of way where the miniature engines and cars went trolling by. In that green canyon country, where bare rock looked so silvery in the sunshine, it was music to hear the whistles of the D. & R. G. engines come beating ahead against the Rocky Mountains and to hold your breath and listen again for the echo that would follow sometimes when the wind was right, and to hear mixed with the whistle the sound of the river slipping fast, fast, through the green and clear-cut channel, with the hushing sound of silk.

The station was painted ocher yellow with a dark-red shingled roof. It stood in a miniature park of grass and flower beds filled with cannas that drank the sunshine and turned scarlet among the coal-black shadows of the station house. Jack introduced Peter to the agent's son, a boy their own age named Ted Barksdale. Ted regarded Peter as a native of another country when he heard he came from New Mexico. He thought Peter should speak nothing but Spanish and ride a burro and eat chili peppers. When Peter protested that he was an American just like him, and that New Mexico was only a hundred miles away, Ted would laugh and say that he would understand him if he'd say it in Spanish.

Ted and Jack were in a sort of implicit league against Peter as the outlander in their land. It was a humorous attitude, and merely a convention of hazing the newcomer, and if Peter had had another stranger along, to back him up, or if he had been older, their superiority would have disappeared.

It was in vain that Peter poked fun at Ted Barksdale for having to spend time on some days working at the canna beds or cutting the lawn at the freight house, when the other two could be off fishing in the meadows below the house where the grass ran right down to the great river. Nothing ever upset Ted. He was the best hunter of his age anywhere around there, Jack said. He said Ted could go out in the winter with his father's rifle, when the snow was high up along the trunks of the pines, and disappear for two or three days at a time, alone. He always came back safely and with game, as much as he could carry, and caches made of what he couldn't carry, to which he and his father would return to collect what he had shot...turkey, deer, mountain cat, and once even a bear. Ted was the cleanest-looking human being Peter ever saw. It was a quality of his skin, which was smooth and the color of the softest brown buckskin, only with a warm rose in it somewhere. His eyes were pale blue and below them were rolls of flesh in a perpetual expression of merriment. His hair was buckskin colored too, but on the yellow side. He seemed all of a piece in his coloring. And he was this too in his character. Peter decided that he was near to what an Indian of the great prairie days must have been like. A fellow of the animals and the plains and the weather, cleaned by them within and without.

5

Peter was only there two weeks that summer, with his aunt Winterhood and those two friends. Ted got his father to let all three of them ride up to Creede on a freight train one time, and they faithfully stayed in the caboose because that was their agreement. Every time the train crossed the river they could feel the trestle trembling with not only the weight of the cars but the black hurry of the river itself. They all felt bigger than usual in the tiny caboose of the narrow gauge. They sat and listened to Tode Chedester the brakeman, who was the most evil-mouthed man Peter ever heard. He told them stories and rhymes and vicious chronicles, all with a hesitant zest which was deceptively modest. It was just the manner to make them think they were hearing about "life." He went on until Mr. Richards, the freight conductor, came into the caboose. The conductor was a family man who carried around in his pocket a volume of

the sermons of Henry Ward Beecher, in which he marked passages
that struck his stern fancy. He read this one aloud to them:

"By fire, by anvil-strokes, by the hammer that breaks the flinty
rock, God played miner, and blasted you out of the rock, and then
He played stamper, and crushed you, and then He played smelter
and smelted you, and now you are gold, free from the rock, by the
grace of God's severity to you."

In this sentence, the conductor found himself.

Peter's aunt often made them packages of food and sent them
off for a day's tramp, following the river. One day they climbed so
far that they caught sight of the falls of Wolf Creek Pass long before
the wagon road showed it to them.

Cousin Jack was planning to be a lawyer, and to live in Denver,
which was grander in his dreams than London or Paris or New
York. He used to ask the other boys if there was any capitol dome
in any of *those* cities covered with genuine gold? It was hard to understand now how much the sound of the name Denver could bring
alive in the West of Peter's boyhood, but he remembered how Jack
Winterhood sounded when he used to speak it. Jack was a worldly
boy even then, in a sense that Peter never thought of being, and that
Ted Barksdale never even heard of.

6

One day Peter asked Jack about the island at the confluence of the
two rivers that ran together like liquid obsidian. (It was this Peter
recalled with the piece of obsidian on his desk upstairs in his room
at home. He loved to pick it up and look into it against the light,
and see again the heavy stunning flow of the river.)

"There's nothing on it."

"Have you ever been on it?"

"Lots of times."

"Has Ted?"

"Sure. He took me the first time."

"Is it hard to get there?"

"It's hard or easy, depending."

"How do you mean?"

Jack explained.

You could go to the west end of the island and swim across the backwater there, which was no trick at all. You had to cross the South Fork of the river to do it, and the most convenient way was to walk over the railroad trestle on the open ties, with the water running beneath.

That was the easy way, if the longest.

"What is the other way?"

"The other way is to go about a mile and a half west along the main river past our house, and when you get opposite *this* end of the island, why, to try and swim it, there. Do you remember how it looks there?"

"Yes," said Peter, coming to mind of the willow-laced banks and the fall of the meadow to a pebbly shelf of shallows where the trout played in and out of rays of sunlight on the polished stones. He thought of the freshest and thickest of green and the clearest and coldest of water, and a few yards from the near bank, the plumy rise and boil of the river where its doubled stream hit the drowned sierras of the rapids. It was deep there, where the river went free; where it was impeded by the stone, there was a clash of force and firmness. Outstream, the water even seemed to run more swiftly than here by the near bank. Looking up the river Peter could see the endless lifts of the current coming toward him. How often he gazed and marveled at the anonymous power in the river's flow. How thoughtless it turned him, and how river-taken he had been in his desires. With that strength and certainty, he would so obediently move in his course, too, if he could…

"I remember how it looks there," he told his cousin Jack Winterhood. "Have you ever swum it? Has Ted Barksdale?"

"You can't get to the island unless you swim."

"Yes, but did you ever swim the rapids at the east end?"

"We always went by the west end."

"Where the pool is?"

"Yes, by the pool."

"Has anybody ever gone the east way?"

Jack gazed at Peter with his lawyer look, keen and yet absent-seeming, the yellow pips of light in his eyes dancing with thought. His nickname was "Judge," even as a boy.

"Well, not exactly. There was a fellow here named Hound-dog Cooley who tried it."

"Did he make it?"

"Nope."

"Why? Did he turn back?"

"Nope."

"Well, *what* did he:"

"We fished him dead out of the Rio Grande eleven miles farther down the next morning. He was cut up pretty bad. Lot of rocks in that water."

"Oh."

"It can be done, though, I believe. Hound-dog was drunk and he took it on a dare."

"Oh."

"I've always meant to try it. I'll tell Ted you want to try swimming the east way to the island."

"I didn't exactly say that."

"You sounded pretty interested."

The simplest thing is often the hardest for a boy to say. His cousin Jack Winterhood had it in his mind, at first out of orneriness, and then out of conviction, that Peter was dying to swim the Rio Grande at the confluence there, and the next time they were together with Ted, he said,

"The Mexican wants to go to the island by the east way."

"You don't say," exclaimed Ted. "Has he ever so much as glanced at it?"

"I have, of course I have," Peter said, "but I never said I actually wanted to swim it. I just wanted to see what was on the island."

"Why don't we?" asked Ted, with a rise of his brow.

"Well, we've meant to, often enough, haven't we," said Jack. "All right. Since my cousin from Mexico really wants to," he added, "I feel it only meet and fitting that we do our best to entertain him. I believe we ought to go tomorrow and swim the east way, and spend the afternoon on the island. There'll be nobody around to bother us. We can leave a note under a stone, and then of course on returning we can always pick up our own note, and tear it up and nobody'll ever have to bother with it."

"A note?" Peter asked, but he knew Jack meant that in case they never came back, somebody would find the note and discover what they had tried and at what they had failed.

He couldn't tell whether they were nervous about it, and he searched their faces. So far as he could see, they were unconcerned.

Later that same day Jack was hunched down in a book in the front room of the Winterhood house, and Peter said to his aunt that he thought he would go for a walk by himself. She looked at him and asked if anything was troubling him, and in her eyes he saw his father's look, whose sister she was. He had a lump in his throat, but he assured her that everything was fine, and that he was having the best summer of his life, visiting her and Jack and Ted Barksdale this way.

He went out and drifted to the river. He watched the willow shadows creep across the glassy flow as the sun fell, and when it was chilling to dusk, he came to the point on this bank opposite the east way to the island. How black the rapids were. What white ruffles they made. How stony the roar of the waters when he held his breath and turned his head to listen. A mocking bird was somewhere about, and his powerful pipe was doubled and made into song by the echo off the river. The hazard they were committed to for the following day seemed to Peter unbearable. He stared at the shining depth as it hurried past. Evening arose in misty breaths off the island opposite. He thought of his home in New Mexico, and the plains, where the sky was yellow at sundown, and the mountains were distant and rosy, and the river—the very same river as this one—was an idle, shallow, warm muddy stream going lazily past the town of Albuquerque. Here he was surrounded by the rocky dark of mountain and canyon. We will never make it, he thought. I must persuade them that it cannot be done. Remember Hound-dog

Cooley, I will say, and what happened to him, how would you like to be found eleven miles downstream gashed by the rocks?

Late that night he awoke and lay hearing the river. If he lay on one ear it could seem as if the sound of the river was inside his head. But if he rolled over on his back and looked up into the dark, he could hear it plainly and actually, and it sounded dark and cold. Jack and he slept on the back porch of the white house. Jack's cot was across the doorway from Peter's. He didn't stir. Peter wished that he owned a legal mind. He was sure he knew what Hound-dog Cooley looked like, and the only thing that permitted him to go to sleep again was that he vowed he would speak to Jack the first thing when they woke up.

7

Yet all the next morning he could not. They were going to meet before noon, take a lunch from Mrs. Winterhood, and their swimming trunks, and set forth. Ted was in high spirits, and Jack was solemn, as befitted one who would enter wholly but not lightly into a pact with death. Peter thought that they were deliberately not looking at him, and he believed that he must have showed his misery.

It was a bright summer day. The air in those mountains was like a mirror for the sun, so clear, so golden. They walked the same way Peter had gone the evening before.

About noon they were there, and Jack said they would eat their lunch first, then lie down for forty-five minutes to take a nap and digest their food, and then they would try it.

Still Peter could not say anything. He ate his sandwiches and beat his mind wondering why he could not bring forth the anguished protests, the certainty of folly, that he had within him. They seemed sure of themselves, and talked of this and of that, and for the first time he heard Ted's ambition: somehow to get passes on all the railroads leading to the Northwest, and to ride on these passes until he found himself in the Canadian Rockies. Once there, he would hunt the biggest game in North America, and explore the most echoing wilds. He believed that a man could spend years in such a grand wilderness without beginning to exhaust all that it held in the way of challenge and reward. When he talked about it, his stone-blue eyes flashed and glittered. He scaled mountains and glaciers in his mind, and lovingly brought down the most dangerous of animals. Peter's heart ached because he knew that Ted would be drowned long before he could find another frontier.

Jack asked Ted if he never wanted to go to college, and learn something.

Ted replied that he knew enough to last him all his life, right now, for what he wanted to do.

Jack laughed and said he had a life-sized picture of anyone getting rich by concentrating his mind on new ways to get off to some forest or other.

Ted said he didn't want to be rich, especially, once he had all the railroad passes he could gather. He said it was much better to ride on passes, even if you could afford to buy all the tickets you wanted. Passes were harder to get.

They kindly turned to Peter and asked what he wanted to do, and he replied that he was supposed to be a rancher, for his Dad's sake, but that he really wanted to be a doctor. Jack nodded with approval, and said that some of the biggest men in the medical profession made as high as twenty thousand dollars a year, and were pretty important men in their communities. The hauling river tore itself in long sliding shreds not a hundred feet from where they sat munching and talking. Jack Winterhood had the look of someone who knows exactly how things are, and when you know that, Peter felt, then you could not help getting what you wanted out of life, in the way of material returns. Peter suddenly loved his cousin for his serene unawareness of his destiny.

Jack now said they must all lie down, for they would need all their strength for the coming struggle. Peter asked what they would do with their clothes. Jack said they would leave them here in the willows with a couple of stones on them, where they could find them when they returned. As he lay down he took out an envelope from his pocket and handed it to Ted, and nodded him to read the

page within it. Ted glanced at the paper, and with perfect indifference returned it to Jack. Peter could imagine what it said. The sunshine cleaved the broken river with swords.

They lay down to their naps.

Once during that awful restfulness, Ted drowsily asked Jack if
he thought their things would still be on the island from the last
time they'd gone there—over the west pool, of course. Jack replied
that he imagined so. A few minutes later, with sudden energy, Jack
raised his head and said,

"You can *swim*, can't you, Pete?"

Peter said he could.

Jack sighed with elaborate relaxation, and went back to his nap.

Peter was so tired from anxiety and from choking on his own
words that he fell asleep. The next thing he knew, Jack and Ted
shook him, and danced off down the narrow shelf of sand and peb-
bles to the water's edge, calling to him to hurry and come on. It was
time to start.

They had put their clothes under the flat stones back of the willows a little bit up the bank. He put his there too, and saw the envelope, the "note," on which Jack had written "To Friends of Judge
Winterhood, Ted Barksdale and Peter Rush, July 27, 1892." He was
suddenly overwhelmed with gratitude and pity for being included
with their names on this mortuary document. But they were calling him, standing in the sunshine and shivering by the river's edge.
The light hit their cheeks, their shoulders, their flanks with dazzling
brightness, and blazed without color as if on metal. He ran to join
them.

Like man in his ultimate contests with Nature, they were naked
and without weapons as they waded into the Rio Grande.

The water was icy cold. The boys skirled at the touch of it, and
waded upstream gingerly until they were opposite the deepest and
yet most powerful channel. Jack's purpose was to launch into the
current and fight diagonally across it, until by perfect timing they
would be deposited on the very last tip of the island, and of safety.

There was still time; but Peter could say nothing.

The river flashed in their ears and eyes.

Jack began to run with the clumsy gait of tugging water. It was like gathering himself for the final plunge. The sun was hot on their backs. The island had a thick screen of willows and scrub cotton-woods facing them. Beyond that lay what they were seeking. Peter didn't know what it was. He caught his breath when Jack plunged, and then Ted, into the black glassy run of the current. They swam powerfully and with valor, and were taken away it seemed so fast that he thought they were lost from the very first. In obedience to something they left in the air, in his mind, behind them, Peter came to the same place and plunged in, and he too was lost, for the bearing motion of the river swept everything else out of him. He beat with his arms and kicked and hugely drank in air when he could, and felt the mindless flow of the water; of the earth; of Nature, and it seemed to him the very essence of death.

"No!" something cried in him.

But there were two ways to make that answer.

He turned and buried his head in the current, and given might by the fear in his breast, he kicked and beat his way back to the shallows behind him, and sobbed with the water in his mouth, and felt fiery with determination even in that icy race, and sure enough, in a few minutes he was back and safe and hanging on all fours like an exhausted dog over the little stones and the idle back eddies of the river at the shore he had started from.

For a time he could not do anything but hunger for breath, and try to hold his joints together against the weakness of fear and relief. The river roared in his ears, and he shook his head. And then he thought he heard something, a shout, above the river sound that filled the whole day.

He turned around sickened with what he must see, and at what he saw, his heart sank, but not the way he had expected it to.

On the edge of the island, dancing in front of the rustling green, were Jack and Ted, yelping like Indians, and motioning him to come, why did he not come, what was he doing there, look where they were! Come on!

"Come on!" they shouted, and swept the water from their bodies with their palms.

It took them a few minutes to realize that he was afraid.

When they knew that, they produced themselves as triumphant proofs that the east way could be swum. Come on! We can't wait here all day!

He nodded and shook his head.

He had tried it, they knew that, why did they keep making him have to try it again?

They were laughing and playing in the highest of spirits. They had earned the right to play. They boxed together and danced apart, and turned to Peter and exhorted. He could hear hardly a word. But he knew everything they were saying and meaning. Come on! We'll help you, see? They crouched down at the island's edge and held out their hands to show how they would grasp his when he came to them. Jack shook hands with himself at him in the air. Ted put his hands together pantomiming the act of swimming and gravely indicated that that was how it was done. Jack trotted up the island and motioned Peter to parallel him on the other bank, and when he stopped, Peter stopped, and there, he showed, was where he should start again. It would be just the right angle to bring him to the island's lower tip. Go on! he waved, start now, and I'll run down to the tip, and meet you!

Peter was shaken with the most crippling of agues. It was one within. He wrung his hands and said no with his whole body. Two were strong and successful, and one was afraid.

They finally looked at each other, shrugged, and shook hands, as if in witness. Then, their bodies, dripping with sunlight, broke against the willow screen on the island, fought the green fantasy of the boughs for a moment, and were gone into the interior. They had done all they could. Peter was alone with the river.

8

Then he knew that he must join them. He must be of them. To belong was the strongest of all forces at times. That was why Peter couldn't speak last night, or this morning, when the folly of the scheme seemed to him so final.

He had his breath back now, and his doubt was gone, and instead of fear of something that might happen, he had a perfect certainty that he would go out into the river, and that he would drown, but that they would know later that he had tried to fulfill what they had all agreed upon; and this seemed to him the most powerful reason on earth for going.

It was worse, alone.

He cheated a moment or two longer, catching the cold water and splashing it over his breast. But that couldn't go on very long, he could think of no excuses. He went out again, and fell on his belly and began to fight.

He didn't know whether his hunger was going to be greater than the river's.

He tried to swim with long, powerful strokes. He tried to remember to be intelligent about not holding his breath, but to drink deeply of the air when he could, and expel it as deliberately. The first time he looked up toward his goal, it seemed like a vision drowned, all wavery and slowly moving. But he knew in a moment that a wind was bearing against the willow screen on the island, and he saw sharply that he was going downstream past it. No, he said, and squeezed his eyes shut, and rolled from side to side in the current, as if to bore his way through it like an auger.

It could not take forever, he knew, until the results would be clear.

But when he saw himself more than halfway across, and the island still tapering a little way below him, the conviction turned around, and he shouted in his heart that he could make it, and that he must make it, now, and that if he stroked and kicked twice as hard he would not feel so cold, the warmth would come back, and warm him in his small displacement of the river. Come on! they had cried, over and over. He dug a tunnel with his buried head and beat the slipping, pulling water, and his breast felt like breaking open, like the bottom of a wooden ship whose ribs are beating upon rocks while the waves drove after life within.

His breast was stabbed with pain, and he coughed for air, and shook, and looked up, and was himself like the ship on the rocks, lying on a jagged stone, and he could stand up, and wade the rest of it, to the wild grass that lay like the shadow of the willows along the island edge. In his breast there was a deep cut from the rock and the blood was washing down. He touched it with his fingers and in some ceremony forgotten and remembered from what primal impulse, he put his bloody fingers to his tongue, and tasted the cost and the proof of triumph. Dear river, I have beaten you, and I love you, he said in his blood.

He washed off the blood, and recovered from his gasping. How eager he was to find the others! And yet he was not ready to go and look. He fell down on his back and lay cruciform, gasping his way back to ease. He wanted to be alone for just a moment longer, to appreciate what he had done. He stared at the golden-blue sky and what he felt was thanksgiving not that he was alive but that he had dared to die.

9

The island was very narrow, a sandy spit made by the river itself, in which the young trees would stand only until the next year of flood. He was suddenly recovered and eager to find the others. It would not take very long to search the island. He leaped up and began to arm his way through the tender thickets of willow branch which cut the sunshine into showers of gold light.

The island was boat-shaped.

He tried to walk as well as he could down the center. The sand was white and deep and hot under foot. He started a bird or two. He turned his head to listen. Everything was washed out of silence by the slide of the river on each side of the island. So he did not hear them and they did not hear him when he came upon them, at what would be amidships of the island.

Jack and Ted were sitting on the sand, playing blackjack with a withered old deck of cards. They were smoking cigars, and the smoke was pale blue in the sunlight. They had the air of being perfectly at home, sure of seclusion, like members of a club. Half buried in the sand to keep it standing upright was a pint bottle partly full of whisky. For poker chips they had piles of tin disks used with nails to tack tar paper over pine boarding. They had a perfectly settled look, as if their present comforts and refreshments were the most natural thing in the world in that small wilderness. Peter was shy for a second about intruding; they seemed to have forgotten his existence, but he then thought, Why shouldn't they have forgotten my existence? and this was enough to make him sail forward out of the thicket with a yell, and sit down before them.

They jumped up, and yelled back. Their delight was great and genuine. They slapped their legs and capered, and tugged at his hands and pulled him up, and shook hands with him over and over. They asked about his wounded breast. They took him back among them. He belonged again. They began to fall all over themselves telling him about "their" island, and how often they came, and what they had, see: the wooden box which they kept buried when they were not here, but which they could always find, it contained their things, their cigars, matches, the playing cards, the whisky (come: he had to have a pull at the bottle:) the tin poker chips, a rather sandy hank of licorice, some reading matter, and an old leather case made like a cylinder.

They gave him a cigar and lighted it, and they all sat down again. They taught him to play blackjack, generously handing him a lavish pile of tin chips. He won for a little while, which seemed to delight them all over again. There seemed to be nothing of theirs of which he had not rightfully now earned his due. When they were tired of playing poker, Ted said to Jack, that since Peter belonged on the island now,

"How about the telescope? Why don't we show that to him?"

Out of the box, they got the old leather case and unstrapped the cuplike top, and drew out an old brass telescope tipped with rusty black leather. Peter's eyes swam and his mouth watered at the sight of such a treasure. It was evidently the choicest thing they owned, too, and they handled it lovingly, passing it back and forth.

"Sometimes we spend whole Saturdays here on the island," said Jack, "looking through this glass at everything around here. Try it."

He handed it over. Peter went to the edge of the island and they followed. He put the glass between the branches and looked out over the fields across the river. What a world bloomed alive in the silver-gray light of the lens, a curious and beautiful halo of blue and yellow around all objects. The signal arms by the railroad embankment which unaided he could barely see as a pole standing against the distant bank of green hill was, through the glass, a brightly painted toy set near enough to touch. They let him sweep up and down the valley with the glass, smiling at his exclamations. But at last Ted took it away from him and said that was fun, and all that, but what was really interesting was to set the glass on a spot—any given spot—and lie down on your belly and watch. Just watch. Any spot. He'd bet ten dollars if you watched long enough that something very interesting would come to pass right there, no matter where you plopped your eye. He said that was the way they used the glass. It was a serious scientific instrument and should be respected as such.

They settled down with the glass. They made a carriage for it out of heaped sand. Jack trained the lens on a miniature bay in the opposite bank of the river...the side they had come from. Leaves hung over it, and shallow water idly backed up into it. Shadows on the grassy bank made it look cool and damp and remote. You could barely notice the little bay with your naked eye. In the glass it was like another country made visible.

Nothing moved in vision.

"Just leave it there and keep looking. Chances are you'll catch something," said Ted.

Jack yawned. But he had good manners, and he knew that the telescope experiment wouldn't be as much fun if he went to sleep and could not be reached with reports if something interesting did come into the lens. So he sat hugging his knees and chewing his cigar, and seemed to be thinking, as Ted Barksdale never seemed to do.

10

After a while, Jack said,

"Do you remember the way Tode talked that day we all rode up to Creede in the caboose?"

Ted nodded.

"Well," said Jack, "I have decided that if I ever hear him talking like that again, I will stop his mouth."

This was a striking promise. Peter turned away from the glass, and stared at his cousin. Jack was frowning splendidly, his eyes with their yellow flecks flashed with sober spirit. Ted looked happy, like a fawn-colored puppy, lean and big pawed.

"Why, Judge? I thought you were enjoying all the dirty stories as much as we were," said Ted.

"I was," said Jack. "I laughed as loud as the rest of you."

"He sure could tell'm," Peter said. Tode was able to suspect and seek out and touch the most secret susceptibilities of other men. Though he would seem to be telling his depraved histories in a sort of musing comfort, as if for his pleasure alone, his little eyes in his scrubbily bearded face had looked sideways at the boys in sly estimate time and again. Until he saw them het up by his talk, he was not successful.

"Yes," said Jack sternly, "I suppose I would laugh as loud as anybody if he started some time again; but I think now that I would have to tell him to shut up."

"Why?" asked Ted lazily, rolling over on the sand.

Jack hesitated, looking around with his light-kindled eyes. His face was always pale, with faint golden freckles. His body was as white. He never tanned under the sun. He was muscular and spare.

"Well," he said at last, "it wasn't only that Mr. Richards came in and began spouting sermons to us. Though of course that was proper. I just have decided that it is within our power to choose our characters. I just don't think Tode is a very admirable individual. I don't think he would do as my Mexican cousin just did, just to prove to himself that he could do it."

Ted looked at Peter with the impersonal eyes of a forest animal, a deer, perhaps.

"And besides," said Jack, "I like the kind of talk that Mr. Richards can do better than Tode's. I am going to study law, and when I stand up, and open my mouth, you will be stunned at the magnificent things that will roll out."

He got to his feet.

"Did you ever read the Webster-Hayne debate?" he asked.

Ted Barksdale laughed.

"You needn't laugh. We have a set of books at home of the best speeches of all time, and I have been reading them. Yesterday afternoon I memorized something. Listen."

He turned and walked a few steps off, and then faced the other two boys in an attitude, and began to declaim in a loud voice, but with great deliberateness,

"But, sir, the coalition! The coalition! Aye, 'the murdered coalition'! The gentleman asks if I were led or frightened into this debate by the specter of the coalition—'Was it the ghost of the murdered coalition,' he exclaims, 'which haunted the Member from Massachusetts, and which like the ghost of Banquo, would never down'?"

Jack's voice rolled sarcastically forth, and he scowled, revealing his belief that great oratory and anger were indivisible. These words of Daniel Webster were like meat and drink to him then.

Ted and Peter sat up, and stared.

It was such a scene as one boy could make for other boys only if they were removed for the moment from the world; where no value persisted to embarrass them but their own; where intimacy was a matter of being together in a fellowship of hazard and idleness. He tried his powers and the other two were enthralled. Denver! How could Denver one day fail to bow before him, with its pure-gold dome, the famous men and women posed by the iron balconies of the ten-story court of the new Brown Palace Hotel, the cavernous mirrors of the old Windsor Hotel, the superb teams pulling flashing carriages down the mud-and-cobble streets!

"'The murdered coalition!' Sir, this charge of a coalition, in reference to the late administration, is not original with the honorable

Member. It did not spring up in the Senate. Whether as a fact, or as an argument, or as an embellishment, it is all borrowed. He adopts it, indeed, from a very low origin and a still lower present condition." Jack showed, with his hand, as well as with his growling voice, how low. "It is one of the thousand calumnies with which the press teemed during an excited political canvass. It was a charge of which there was not only no proof or probability, but which was, in itself, wholly impossible to be true. No man of common information ever believed a syllable of it. Yet it was—"

Here he forgot. He held his command with lifted arm, while his eyes roved back and forth, searching for what came next. He snapped his fingers for it to come to him out of the void. But not wasting too much time on a mere lapse, he shook his head impatiently, and returned to what he believed the character of Webster to have been like, and jumped ahead to his tremendous conclusion, speaking slowly and with a fine-grained irony that held them transfixed.

"—It is the very cast-off slough of a polluted and shameless press. Incapable of further mischief, it lies in the sewer, lifeless and despised. It is not now, sir" (he glanced at the imaginary president of the Senate, a lightning dart) "in the power of the honorable Member to give it dignity or decency by attempting to elevate it, or introduce it into the Senate. He cannot change it from what it is, an object of general disgust and scor-r-n. On the contrary, the contact, if he choose to touch it, is more likely to drag him down, down, to the place where it lies itself."

Ted and Peter were spellbound when Jack finished, and could only look at him with open mouths. He rubbed his short-cut hair and in his modest, everyday voice, he tactfully brought them back to the present. He said,

"I just don't think I have room in myself to entertain *both* Tode and Daniel Webster in my studies."

Ted was too excited by the performance to sit still. He got up and ran off a way, yelling and slapping his hips, bounding like a dog. It was, in its way, a real tribute to an eloquent communication. Jack laughed in delight at him.

"I can't make hide nor hair out of what you recited," said Ted when he settled down again, "but it certainly was pretty the way you did it, Judge.—What about our books, in the box, over there?"

"That *is* true," said Jack. "I had forgotten them."

"What books?" Peter asked.

"Just some dirty books we've got.—You haven't looked in that glass for a long time. You might be missing something."

11

Peter turned back and set his eye, and called out at what he saw. In the field of the telescope, a round picture cut forward out of another world, he saw a big striped snake trying to swallow a fat frog. The snake had the frog's left leg in his gullet, and was struggling to enwrap the other one. The frog was struggling slowly. Slowly the snake was working. The mortal combat went on with slow intensity and the blades of grass in which they moved showed up clear and bright and stiff in the lens. It was immensely exciting, and Peter told them about it, and they came and looked, and they all hated the snake. They pulled for the frog, watching the sun-fixed struggle as helpless partisans.

"You should have watched," shouted Jack, "maybe we could have thrown stones and scared him off if we'd seen it start!"

The lens was so faithful and so powerful that they could see the snake's eyes like drops of dew, black with a pin of light in them. As he worked and swallowed, his eyes would roll from sight and then as he relaxed they would show again. The frog's eyes seemed to look nowhere and everywhere. The snake coiled himself elegantly about the frog's body to reduce it if he could into a palatable shape. The river ruffled past in the miniature bay, and at one point in his sliding of efforts, the snake's tail wove in and out of the laplets of water behind them. Now the battle seemed halted. They rested a moment, perfectly still, locked in their parable of life and death. Peter could not take his eye off them, and the others let him keep the glass.

"What was that!" he cried suddenly.

"Where?"

"Something came across the glass, a shadow.—There it is again!"

Jack looked along the telescope as if to see with his own eye what Peter was seeing in the brass tube. But it was Ted who saw it first.

"Look up!" he whispered loudly. "It is a hawk, he's sailing around to make a dive. You must have seen his shadow when he came down before."

They looked up and there in the white sunlight was the superb bird. He was sailing down in a narrowing ring and Peter had seen his shadow waft over the tiny meadow where the snake strove and the frog strove so silently.

"Watch!" said Ted. Even before the hawk dropped, he knew when it would; many the hawk he had had in his days outdoors.

"Use the glass!" whispered Jack to Peter.

Peter looked.

The clash of claw and beak and feather was tremendous in the lens—the black beating shadow with the golden flecks of feather, the white breast, the green whip of the snake. He saw the sharp elegant talons make their clutch, and the cloudy wings batter the ground for a second before the heavy rise into the sky. The hawk's scowl in the powerful head flashed once into vision. The snake curled and relaxed, curled and relaxed, but was taken away, and the frog fell free on the grass and remained panting. Its white throat vibrated like a little drum.

He moved away from the glass and told them to look.

The hawk climbed and climbed.

Jack used the glass on the frog, and said,

"He's trying if he can move.—There he went. He jumped into the water. I'll bet he's glad!"

So were they.

Ted was true to himself when he said,

"Golly, I wish I'd had my rifle with me, I'd sure potted that hawk on his way up.—I could do it easy from this distance."

Jack was too, when he said,

"Well, that is the law of wild creatures. They take what they are. But we may say for ourselves what we shall be."

He went over to the box.

"What're you doing?" asked Ted.

Jack nodded but did not answer. He picked up the gray-looking paper books in the box, and with exaggerated ceremoniousness, he carried them to the edge of the island and threw them into the river. They floated rapidly off downstream.

Ted shrugged.

"Well, I had read them all, anyway," he said.

"Let's all have another drink," said Jack.

There wasn't much whisky in the pint bottle. They passed it around. They all choked on it, and swallowed it, and felt important and secure in their island league.

12

The sun was going over. Dusk came early even in summer because the mountains over there were so high and met the sun so soon in its decline. They sat around and talked a while longer, and Jack advised them to memorize a passage every day from the debate between Webster and Hayne. Ted said he believed they all ought to practice marksmanship at least once a week; said it was the one thing a man could rely on for himself. Peter wanted to contribute to this symposium, and could only offer his belief that the first thing a fellow ought to learn was how to swim, because you never knew when it would come in handy.

They showed him how things were stowed away in the box, and how the box was fastened, and how the box was buried. They told him that he was now privileged to come here and use the box at any time. They said they had built the box, using Mr. Barksdale's tools at the freight house.

It was turning chill with the lessening light. The water already looked dark, like shining mineral, and Jack said, when they were ready, that they would go back by the west pool, where there was hardly any current to speak of.

"We have earned the easy way," he stated, like a judge handing down a decision.

They ran through the little trees to the other end of the island.

The sky was still white, but the ground was bluing with shadow. The pool was black and calm, its surface turning majestically in a slow wide wheel. They dived in and crashed across to the other bank and climbed up on a cool green field.

That was where the river made a Y, and they had landed across the right arm, and still had to cross the leftmost arm of the Y, to reach their clothes, and be on the home side of the river forks. It was now twilight, and no life stirred. The fields were quiet. They skulked along the edge of the bank. A few hundred yards off was the D. & R. G. trestle. They were going to walk across that to the other side. Just before they reached it, they heard an engine whistle. It came from behind them, up the canyon. They might not be able to beat it across. They crouched below the cindery embankment and waited till it came. It was a combination freight and passenger train, and it was on them before they knew it, trembling the earth as it went by above, clouding them with steam, and adding to the fall of night with its heavy soft coal smoke. It sailed on the slow grand curve the tracks made approaching South Fork. The boys stood up when it had passed, and saw the red and green caboose lights drifting evenly through the dusky distance.

Peter thought of Tode and the freight conductor within, and of their two wills.

They hopped on the ties across the trestle, came down to the branchy cover of the other bank, following it to their flat stones. Jack said "H'm," when he lifted the stone and found the envelope he had left there. With a kindly sort of indulgence of themselves as they had been a few hours ago, he tore it up, and they dressed.

They started back toward the houses across the fields.

There were a few lights showing.

They suddenly felt hungry and cold and were ready to go separate ways.

When they reached the freight house where there was no trace of the important little train that had just passed through, they paused and said good-by to Ted Barksdale.

"Well, Judge, one thing more," said Ted to Jack. He said that there would be no further point in speaking of Peter as a Mexican, since he was no longer a foreigner. They shook hands on that point.

XXXIII · "HUSH!"

I

During his office hours one day Peter had a telephone call from Old Town. Don Hilario Ascarete had died an hour or two ago, and the family intended to hold open house that evening, if he would care to come. Everyone knew how much the old man liked his young doctor friend. The funeral would be tomorrow. After lunch, Don Hilario had retired for his usual siesta and when Catherine, the sixteen-year-old great-granddaughter, had gone in to say a word to him on her return from school, she had found him "gone." Everyone couldn't be there tonight, of course, you couldn't assemble such a huge family just-like-that, but there would be plenty of them, and if the Doctor would come, it would gratify everyone immensely.

After nine that evening, he drove out to the party. The doors and windows were all open. Orange-colored light spilled out on the cleanly swept yard. The air was full of bittersweetness from the rustling cottonwoods. The fields out that way were cool the minute the sun was gone beyond the river. There were cars parked for a block and a half. In the Plaza, light streamed forth from the open doors of the church, where preparations were being made for tomorrow's funeral. Peter could hear loud talking and laughter floating in the air as he came down the street on foot, having left his car in the Plaza. He could see candles burning in the front room, beyond the animated heads of the crowd. The whole house seemed to be full of people. They were laughing, eating, drinking, without boisterousness, but with good cheer. He came into the front room, and when he was recognized, a gay clamor arose to greet him. Way was made for him, he was received with respect, and taken at once to gaze upon the bier.

Don Hilario lay in an open coffin, dressed in an ancient suit of evening clothes which was far too large for him. But it was of stiff, rich material, and its faded grandeur covered him with almost hilarious distinction. His face was tiny, and his mouth was suddenly prominent, for the cheeks had fallen in and left the lips protruding. It was as if he were uttering an eternal "Hush!", but not chidingly, rather in a polite invitation to listen, and hear what went on behind the clamor of the world. In his expression lingered some odd ghost of his lifetime's humor and resignation. Peter never expected to feel so moved as he stood there looking down at the ancient body in the midst of the social noise of the room. He supposed he was the only man in the room who had any actual notion of the scope of the old man's experience, and he smiled ruefully at the thought that now he would never hear about the interview with Count Cavour, and the freedom of Italy.

Presently he turned around, and was spoken to in turn by each member of the surviving family, and he saw that many of them were proud of their ancestor, and that the very size and bounty of the party they were giving was proof of the importance he held in their family tradition. They were proud too of the worldly aspects of their kin, and all the Ascaretes who were, or were married to, figures in politics and the professions were introduced by title, Judge This, Professor That, Assistant-County-Superintendent of Schools So-and-So, the Reverend Father Et Cetera. This house belonged to one of the poorest of the clan, with whom the old man had elected to live out his days. Now it housed enough dignity and propriety to make anyone at all feel welcome, to pay homage to the little old man who had suddenly, after twenty-five years of retirement, assumed the most final of importances.

2

All evening the cars rolled up, visitors came and went, toasts were drunk, little eulogies were delivered. Someone had to stay up all night with the corpse anyway. It was such a beautiful night outdoors. The moon was nearly full. The young people drifted outside, and walked along the ditches where the moonlight shimmered upside down.

The women gathered in groups, some in the bedrooms, some in the front room, some in the kitchen, and exchanged news. Some of the political cousins went off in a corner and accomplished several things toward the fall elections. A handful of children, unimaginably remote in their relationship to the figure in the coffin, played out in the alley, and presently began to shriek with fury and attack each other with mud and stones, making a scandal of the moonlight night. A cow was tethered out in back in the alfalfa field, and often she lifted her heavy head and groaned through the cool air in response to the disturbing activity of the house. The mocking birds stayed up, too, and whistled and mimicked across the low roofs of Old Town. The smell of the slow, muddy river came across now and then, the smell of wet earth, and it was like a pleasant shiver in the other elements of the scene.

Lying there in the middle of all this, old Don Hilario was finally ignored by the gathering.

Peter said good-by to them all and drove home through the ravishing night, in which the very qualities of the moonlight, the song of the mocking birds, the scent of the cool river, seemed to be interchanged, so that you could not say whether the moonlight made such silvery sound, or the river gave such sweet glow, or the mocking birds brought the river airs with them. He thought the old man was like a cottonwood tree, at the end, with the gray of its bark on his skin, in a very harmony with the earthen, grass-sprung, river-turned place of his life; arrived at death as if at a completion, rather than at an interruption. "That's what I mean," Peter said to himself.

XXXIV · THE FAREWELL

I

Willa's joy was the most tragic thing in life to her daughter Martha. There was no resisting so powerful and innocent a force as her mother's delight in the dream that was coming true, bag and baggage, off to Albion for the summer, to show everybody back there who's who and what's what, you could just bet your bottom dollar!

Martha's first intention was to refuse flatly to go along on the trip. It was as if her love were a creature living independently inside her, which flared into savage defense of itself when threatened from without. She was sick with the impact of the news; she felt hollow, her head ached with an insistent banging pain, and all she wanted at first was to be alone somewhere so she could sob extravagantly without anyone around to hear her and ask her what was the matter.

Never before had the whole little family's life-long dream of going "home" seemed a menace to her. Her mother was so confident of everybody's delight in the news of how at last they could go, that she never watched how Martha would take it; and with great control, Martha managed to exclaim, and give Willa a hurried hug as if she were too delighted to say more. But the minute she was able to, she left the house, and walked toward the country at the end of the street, leaving Willa busy with lists at the table in the front room.

How could she tell Bun?

Would he regard her as a traitor to their passion, if she ran off from it now?

She knew well enough what the plans were in the back of Willa's head.

School was out. Wayne was free to leave town now. The business college closed about the same time, and she had completed her course, and could get any job she liked, if the college was to be believed. She made a dozen schemes a day, and they consisted largely of variations on the plan that she would get a job and work, here at home, until Bun was through all his "premedical," and then, and then, they would get married, and with all the money she would have saved, they would be able to keep a little apartment while he interned in some big hospital somewhere. If the hospital had rules against interns marrying, then she would pretend to be his girl friend, and they would go on having "dates."

How easily she could slide into such visions of the future! How impossible, when she was so happy, to remember the dismal facts that had to be faced, and sooner every day!

What lay in store for her?

She was to be taken back to Albion and thrown at the head of that boy she had never seen, Dennison Yeager. He was a rich boy. She *hated* rich boys. He would be a stuck-up prissy boy with his own automobile, and probably treated all girls as if they would fall down and *worship* him the minute he smiled at them. She wished she had a million dollars so she could *buy* the Yeagers out of their house and home, and then disdainfully turn the place over to—to a cat and *dog* hospital or something worthy. Nobody on earth, no one's cheek, or hand, or voice, or blue eye, or combed hair, or shoulder blade under coat, or dancing confidence, or musing grin, or cool ears, or beliefs, could ever possibly mean what these things of Bun's meant to her. Nobody ever loved anybody as hard as she did him. If it would *help* any, in any *way*, she would go and die, like Juliet, more sorrowful, and prettier than ever. She sat down on a bank of sand grass, and hugged herself and wept.

One thing she knew. She would have to go. You can't wreck the twenty-year hope of anybody else, for *any* reason. She hated her mother, she now believed; but she couldn't make anybody as unhappy as her refusal to go would make her mother. Besides, to be honest, her mother still had the more power and strength of the two: Willa would grow hoarse, and seem thinner than ever, and command her to stop being a silly, and get ready, 'cause she was *going*. That was the truth of the matter.

But beside that, if Martha knew she had to go, in her heart which served as a temple to the solemnity and purity of her feeling, she vowed that she would let nothing turn her from the love of her life, and that Dennison Yeager or no Dennison Yeager, she would come back in the fall. Her heart beat even now at the picture of how they would meet again after being separated so long…

But how should they say good-by?

2

For the next several times she saw him, she was afraid to tell him what was ahead for them both. He was as animated, as gentle, as amusing as ever. Now he was excited by something that made her jealous. In the store the other day, who should come in but Doctor Peter Rush himself, to get a prescription filled to carry in his medicine case. Bun took the written application to the pharmacist in the back room, behind the swinging doors, and then came back to talk to the Doctor. The Doctor asked him what he was going to do all summer. He said he was not sure, he supposed he would work in the drugstore, though some fellows were going fishing in August up the Pecos, and he might go too. The Doctor said that was fun. He added that what he really meant to know was whether Bun really was going on to study medicine eventually. He said sure, he always meant to. Doctor Rush said that was the spirit, and asked him if he'd like to watch an operation occasionally? Now and then there would be cases from which a youngster could get something, by watching. It used to be a good system, when an old doctor would take an apprentice, and teach him through association and example. Not that anything should ever take the place of a good schooling and first-rate interning. How about it? Well, Bun was so surprised he could barely answer, but he made the Doctor understand that nothing would delight him more, than to actually see an operation, and get the *feeling* of it so early in his career.

So Doctor Rush said he'd call him up sometime, and they'd "see." This was all Bun could talk of.

While her heart was cracking and washing away and floating down the *river*, he was alternately telling her about how it would be, and staring silently and smilingly ahead of him at the future.

He never even noticed that something was *wrong* with her.

She began to think he was making her as unhappy as Willa was. Everything was wrong.

She dreaded quarreling with him. She knew that if she didn't tell him soon, his innocent failure to console her would make her do something or say something she would be sorry for.

Their evening dates were curiously settled, as if they were married. She wondered why they didn't go ahead, *and* marry, and then the fact that this seriously should occur to her made her miserable at how *sane* the world was, and how impossible it would be to be married now, with college ahead of him, and medical school, too, and the interning years.

3

Finally, she wrote him a letter, explaining what was ahead for them. She mailed it so he would get it the day before they were leaving. That night would be their last. In all honesty the tears rolled up into her eyes and fell down on the letter. She dratted it, and said she would have to copy it over now, because the ink ran. But a second wave of justice overwhelmed her, and she said, Why not, why shouldn't he *see* what it's doing to me? He will know I am crying, as I write to him, I *want* him to know, I don't *care* if this looks like an old movie with Viola Dana in it… She mailed it as it was. Now when they met, as usual, after supper, he would already know what was about to befall them, which she had actually been afraid to tell him for the past days.

And sure enough, when he got to the library, and found her waiting in the vestibule, where it was fairly dark, he took her arm, and said,

"Hey, *what's* this:"

He sounded half-furious at having his life upset that way, and instead of bursting into tears, as she fully expected to, she felt herself *freeze* with dignity and self-possession.

Love.

You simply never knew.

"You know perfectly well, I wrote you all about it."

"Why'n't you tell me?"

"How can you *speak* to me that way, especially now!"

"What way, I'm not speaking to you in a *way!*"

"You are too, you sound so-so critical!"

"Oh, *bilgewater*, you don't—"

"Don't you say *oh bilgewater* to me, Richmond Summerfield!"

"I'm sorry; but this goofy idea you wrote me about, about going on a *trip*—"

"I daresay if my poor backbreaking hard-working mother wants to take a little trip and have her family along, then I daresay she has a simple right to do it."

Her elevated social tone stung him and he entered upon the same irony.

"I daresay."

He was mocking her. She hated herself for defending the very thing that made her so unhappy. Why are we *doing* this? she wondered.

They were divided in silence, looking at each other. Then he melted her by blinking both eyes slowly at her, and sticking out his lower jaw in a calculating grin, a reminder of the expression he always assumed when he felt like loving. It raised them both out of the hostility of their meeting. He had made the overture with his eyes. She must respond. She licked her lips and said,

"Well, where'sh'we go?"

"I didn't get the car. I couldn't have it tonight.—Let's walk down to the river."

"All right.—Let's walk over the viaduct. Let's keep out of sight. *This is our last night.* Darling, I'll *die!*"

They crossed the main street and walked down in the darkness of South Edith Street, their arms locked together, their woes uniting them as closely as a moment before they had been widely apart.

She explained what had happened, to their family fortunes, and how it had always been her mother's desire to go back to Michigan someday and show everybody. They would be away all summer. But in September, she would return; and think of all the things they would have to tell each other!

He asked what was it like, back there in Michigan. She said she didn't know, couldn't remember a thing, she had been a baby when they left there to come here for her father's health. He sternly told her she'd better come back, he was speaking medically now, for her own good, and if her father had died of t.b., then she must take no risks of breaking down with the same thing.

He pointed out that the disease was not necessarily hereditary;

but the *tendency* to it was considered so. She shivered at his authority and charm, in discussing things as a youth which later on as a man he would be paid for saying to grateful patients.

The streets were dark. They turned the corner and saw the viaduct with its old lamps blooming in the night air over the railroad tracks, where a powdery glisten of drifting steam from below caught the light. They walked across, looking down at the tracks and the engines. There was a train standing by the Harvey House, headed East.

"Look!" she cried, grasping him and pointing.

He saw what she meant, she meant that tomorrow she herself would be on the same train, it was going East, and he would be left here. He would be a fixed point for her to come back to. He had the sensation of something wrapping his arched breast in tightening bands, and squeezing until he could hardly breathe. He seized her and kissed her with hunger.

Her mouth talked to him in devouring silence, even while her hands tried to hold him off, and when again they were desperately apart, she shook her head as if she had been hit, and said no, no, not here, this is too public, the cars going by now and then, and let them walk on. But she knew of pride and security. He wanted her that much. She loved him to the exact same degree. Time and distance would be trivial foes.

They walked out First Street, dark and dingy. They were deliciously startled now and then by dark creatures revealed in alleys by the sound of dim talking. The tall windows of the Santa Fe shops were so high and empty of everything but a sort of blue industrial light that they felt like lost children in another planet. It was a night of such darkness as happened between the shows of the moon, there, and even the high heavy cottonwoods were invisible along the streets, except where light spilled faintly forth from a nightlight in a store window, or gleamed in back of somebody's house in a yard where bootleg liquor could probably be bought.

It gave them anonymity to be wandering in this unsavory part of town. He knew well enough about the town's underworld from school rumor and boastful gossip. He would have welcomed a threat against her just because he could have defended her so mightily against anybody, the Joe Martinez gang, for instance.

They came around a half bend in the street, the pavement ended, and they saw a glow two blocks away, green tree, yellow doorway, and heard what: was it music? a nickel's worth of gaiety from an electric pianola?

"There's Borelli's, by the bridge," said Bun.

"Oh: I've heard of it. They say he is a bootlegger."

"Why, it's a saloon, and also a—I mean, you can just buy any drink you order there. He doesn't trouble to hide it, even."

"What else is his place?"

"*What* else, what do you mean?"

"You started to say it was something besides a saloon."

"No I didn't."

"Yes, you did."

"No, really, I just meant—"

"You were *going* to say it, don't you deny it!"

He wouldn't answer.

They were walking.

The bridge was ahead, they could just see its old iron basketry in the air, and hear the planks rumbling under a car coming this way.

They both knew they were skating perilously near to suggestions and words and ideas and guesses that lived under their words.

He wished she wouldn't talk like that, all around the point, and try to get him to say right at her what he was having a hard enough time with as it was.

She was wholly aware of her two selves, one acting serene and innocent, the other in a turmoil of longing.

They glanced into Borelli's doorway. It was a panel of light, with people sitting at the tables. The piano was raking its own entrails and the felted hammers could be seen through a glass pane wincing and striking under the impact of ghostly hands. The back yard and the vacant lot next door and the adobe house by the river edge were dark. They imagined they could hear the river. Their knees were weak. What was there about this place?

They went on up to the bridge and went out across nearly half-way and leaned on the rickety handrail.

4

After a while, he said,

"I guess this's where we have to say our good-byes, hon."

"Oh, I don't know," she said, but her voice was just simply lifted in half so she talked high and breathy.

"I won't have a chance to, at the train."

"I suppose not."

"I was sore, back there, at the library, when we met, just because I hated the idea of you going off."

"I know. I knew it all the time."

"You *did*?"

"Why, *sure*."

"You didn't sound like it…"

"Certainly."

They were clutching at any social pretenses to save them from the tides that were ready to run.

"O.K.—Just the same, I didn't mean to be cross."

"You're *never* cross, *darling*."

He swallowed.

"Don't *sound* like that!"

"Like what?" she asked, as if she were a little girl five years old.

"Oh God," he said in a whisper, hanging his head down and shaking it and staring at the shallow drift of the slow river which looked fathomless in the starlight.

She could not desist. She put her hand on the back of his neck.

"Like a Teddy bear," she said, feeling him there.

He bristled under her fingers, she felt it, the little hairs on his skull rose up.

They were pierced now by the frenzy that had gone around and around in him. Everything they felt told them formlessly of death and the passage of all fair things, and the very ingredient of beauty itself which was mortal.

They heard the clank of indulgence from Borelli's piano across the river water, and they smelled the bitter flavor of the cottonwood trees which the night air bore.

There lived a suggestion in the very atmosphere. It was no accident, nor even a decision, but a fatal pursuit in his half-dream-mind that had led them there together.

He turned upon her, and she said,

"Tomorrow night I'll be gone,"

and he groaned and hurried her to him in a misdirected kiss that hurt them both. But they modulated themselves and flowed into each other through their embrace.

Presently in a voice like the night itself he whispered to her and ground his jaw upon her cheek, and told her where they could go, down the embankment at the end of the bridge, and along the shore, all the boys used to play there, he knew every inch of the river, and there were little groves of saplings where no paths went, and it was a warm night, and the river flowed past, and the moon was under, and tomorrow and tomorrow and love and tonight and God oh God how I love you *sure* I've thought of everything before a million times and never forget and that is you and this is me and that is me and this is you, were you ever anything but sure yourself?

She turned up her lips and stopped his words and wouldn't budge otherwise.

Then long afterward, she tried to see his eyes in the darkness, and couldn't, really, but between them alive and waiting for an answer was simply the ? and the poetry that raged alive in their hearts must be delivered in flesh or fade away.

Of the two, he was, the man, the poet, delivered to the instant.

She set her hands to his face and accomplished that miracle which kept both his love and her inviolability.

She whispered to him that she was his for whatever he wanted of her, that was how she felt *now*; but she couldn't help thinking for just a tiny second of how they might feel later. She said this with a rueful sweetness that simply turned his heart over and he was a changed man. He groaned with tenderness, and everything urgent fell away in a chastened kind of strength that made him want to protect her forever.

Pretty soon, peaceful and dedicated, they came back off the bridge, and strolled with linked fingers across town toward her street.

5

Like a deep breath, that lifted her heart, and her head, a new notion sprang alive in Martha. She felt twenty years older, *at least*, and smiled privately at the so-recent storms of feeling that had troubled her. She now had once again, and more dearly than ever, proof of their love. Secure in that, should they not think, and feel, and do, for others?

"We must be very understanding, darling," she said to him gently, beginning a sober comedy of virtue.

"How do you mean?"

"We must not be selfish. I mean: after all, you know and I know what we mean to each other.—I think we should say to each other, when we part, Good-by, I love you with all my heart, now don't be lonely, but go and have a *good time*, until we come together again.—Don't you?"

"No. I don't."

"*Darling.*"

She hugged his arm.

"But what I really mean," she continued, "is about Mother. I mean: think what this means to her? I don't want to *go* any more than you *want* me to go. But if you knew how she's dreamed, and skimped, and planned why you'd see it as I do.—I understand Mother, of course, it'd be hard for you to see what I mean. But I mean: all that Mother wants, or has ever wanted, is something *real*.—I'm not like that."

"How d'you mean?"

"I'm such a fool."

"No you aren't."

"Yes I am, I'mean: I cry my eyes out over wanting something impossible.—I did, that is, until *you*."

"Until *me?*"

"Yes."

"Silly."

"Yes, but I'm not *afraid* to be silly now. I used to be so afraid to be silly or that I'd do something *ungracious*."

"You couldn't possibly. You're the most gracious person I've ever known."

"Oh, I *want* to be, for *you*..."

These exchanges seemed to them somehow profound and full of the future. They would have died laughing if they'd overheard another couple saying the same things. The power that held them gave them the gift of illusion, too, as well as that of desire.

"But Mumma—the wonderful thing about Mother is how she *makes* her dreams come true. I mean: don't you think that is a wonderful ability?"

"It's a miracle, if true."

"Of course it's true.—And you know why?"

"No."

"She never really wants *hard* for anything that isn't perfectly *possible*."

"Oh."

"No, it's more than just '*Oh*.' You don't *see*, darling.—It goes way back to her girlhood. She only wants to finish the story she began then, when she fell in love with my father, and married him. All she wants to do is go back home to Albion, and see it all again, and have all her old friends (I'll bet they're a bundle of *frights*) rave and moon over me and my little brother Waynie, and then come back here. That's all she has ever dreamed of. And now she's going to get it! I mean: it'll make her the happiest person on this *planet*.— She's going to buy me the most gorgeous clothes at Marshall Field's on the way through Chicago. She's been making lists for days. You won't know me when I come back. I'll be so *modish*."

"Do you suppose I could *talk* to your Mom at the train tomorrow night?"

"Talk to her? How:"

"About *us?*"

"Oh no. Oh *no.* It'd just upset her and I do think we must give her just this one perfect summer, don't you, darling, and then afterward, we can:"

He laughed.

"You mean afterward, we can raise as much hell as we feel obliged to, is that it?"

"I think you're mean to laugh.—And I wouldn't put it that way."

"But it's the truth, isn't it:"

"I suppose so."

"You're awfully clever, you must *think* all the time," he said in loving mockery.

"I do.—But you're *brilliant.* You have genius. You don't *have* to think. Things are just *there.*—Aren't they:"

"Oh, I don't know."

"*Aren't* they?" she insisted, defending him against his seemly modesty.

"I—I suppose so, after all."

"Sweet," she said, ever so proud of him.

"What does Wayne think about going?"

"I wish I knew! Sometimes I don't think that boy ever *does* think.—He always looks as if he were too superior to bother with a little thing like stopping and thinking."

"He's a funny kid."

"He's a darling, and don't you think anything else.—But sometimes I worry so over him."

"Worry? Why."

"Oh, he's getting so *big,* and you never know just how a boy is going to *mature, you* know what I mean."

"No I don't.—He's all right."

"I mean, in a few years, he'll be as old as *you* are, and then—"

"Then what:"

"—He'll get some *girl,* and God only knows what they'll—Richmond Summerfield, don't be so dense, all of a sudden, honestly, sometimes you can act just like a stone wall."

"Oh, I *see*. Well, more power to him."

"What do you *mean*?"

"*Now* who's a stone wall."

"I think you've got a horrid view of things."

"Just because it's your baby brother.—And what's more, I was just wishing him as much luck as *I* have got. That's all.—You mustn't *imagine* things, dear."

"Bunny, how darling of you.—You have as many facets as a rare jewel."

"Yaa."

"No, I mean it."

On the second proffer, he always accepted her tributes.

They walked in silence for a long time, resting in union through their fingers.

Then she added with a sigh, embracing life as she knew it,

"Momma is just true to her own heart, and I suppose that means, to everybody else's. It is the strongest thing in the world, you can't fight it. I'm resigned to everything, now, because I see it is right."

This was too much for him. He stopped and took her face in his palms and kissed her devoutly. How much! they thought, how much they drew from life through each other! Just being with each other! How much opened up, thing after thing, like the petals of a flower! What children they used to be, only a snap of the fingers ago!

She put her hands on his neck and held him there, under his ears, which were cool, as always, and said softly,

"Every night when I go to bed I will lie down facing the west, and every night when you go to bed, you lie down facing east, and we will fall asleep that way, darling, until we meet again."

They were drowned in inner music, the bare jazz of their period, and they heard it again and they beautified what it said; the pick-up orchestra that used to play for the dances for the high school crowd, sometimes at the Woman's Club, sometimes at Colombo Hall, a cornet, a piano, a saxophone, and the traps, of course;

an acrid combination, through which, nevertheless, they heard what was coming to them; and it sufficed.

XXXV · "INSCRUTABLE"

I

Summer was coming down the river.

It was the last chance Wayne and Donald had to go swimming before Wayne left for the East.

They had found a willowy room by the water's edge. The sunshine came in through the leafy lace like a school of little silver fish swimming in the warm blue. The boys were so silent that all sounds about them lived distinct. The very sound of the river seep glistening into the sandy bank could be heard, tiny, remote, like little lips meeting and parting. There was a hazy song of flying bugs in the air. Far, far down the way, it seemed, though it was hardly a mile, the boards of the Barelas bridge were trundled by cars and wagons crossing the river, and made an agreeable miniature thunder. The boys lay face down on the ground. Under him, each felt the earth's heart beating; how deep and personal it was, as if it beat only for him, and yet for all other lives too! Unimaginably far down and deep, and true, and supporting, that heartbeat went profoundly on. It felt as if the earth were shaken ever so slightly at each beat. Drowsily, thoughtfully, they felt it. Neither one reflected that it was his own heart that was thumping against the earth where they lay, and that it was they, not the earth, that shook with the beat. But whichever it was did not matter. They were upon their element, and contentedly were part of it.

2

But there were things to say, as well as to feel.

"I finally told my mother about the glass."

"What did she do?"

"Nothing, it is all right. But I had to tell her."

"Did you tell her I did it too?"

"I mentioned it."

"I thought you would."

"I am sure you feel as I do about it."

"Certainly."

"Have you said anything to your Dad?"

"No not *said* anything. But—but it is all *right*, anyhow."

"How do you mean?"

"I can't explain. But I think we understand each other now."

"That's good."

"I sometimes think it takes something funny to bring people together."

"What if you could always know what people would *do*!"

"I know, wouldn't that be wonderful."

"As it is, I believe you and I can conceal the slightest hint of what our intentions are from anybody else, don't you think so?"

"Yes. We are both absolutely inscrutable."

"If anything, I would say you were a little more inscrutable than I."

"Oh, I don't know."

"Yes, it is my blue eyes. People with blue eyes are never able to be as inscrutable as people with brown eyes. There's something about it."

"Well, maybe. But the ordinary person would never in the world regard you as any less inscrutable than I am. In fact, the fact is, *you* thought of being inscrutable first."

"Yes, that's so. I must say it has stood us in good stead, in school, for instance, and with Nick."

"He never knows what we are thinking."

"It's a good thing to be able to be. Any fool can *show* what he's thinking."

"Are you going to try it when you get East?"

"I imagine so. I will write you how it works out.—I don't really want to go, you know, all we could do here all summer, on the river, and the mesa, and everywhere. But my mother has no idea I *feel* that way."

"That was inscrutable."

"Utterly."

"I'll sure miss having you around. I think I'll put in my time till you get back, writing a novel. You can read it when you return."

"Why not let's write it together? I will send you ideas from Albion. Monsieur le Vicomte could be the leading character."

"All right. Think up things for him to do. I'll put them in."

"I'm hot again."

"Beat you."

They leaped up and crashed through the willows at the riverside and dived into the warm muddy stream, making a blinding explosion of water and sunlight when they hit it, summer's denizens.

XXXVI · THE TRAIN

1

At the station the next evening, Bun stayed out of sight, but she met him by the mailbox, and they were drawn in the face and excited and forlorn. All the nobility and resignation of the night before were gone. They kissed hurriedly and made what references they could to their understandings and pledges. Then he brought out something from his pocket, and handed it to her, and when she saw what it was, the mother he had betrayed for her, and what he had given of his symbolical past, Martha burst into tears and ran off from him and stood waiting for the train to go, while he watched her through the evening distance.

He had brought her the snapshot of himself taken by his aunt Susan on the front lawn, years ago, the day they had first given him the nickname of "Bunny."

2

Wayne and Donald stood looking up and down the tracks at the engines and cars. They had nothing to say. Presently Willa Shoemaker came hurrying from the baggage room where she had checked the family trunks. She was exhausted looking, and had bright spots of color flaring on her cheekbones. She was telling herself aloud the things that had been accomplished, which made their departure a safe and orderly one. "—water in the house turned off, gas company notified, my ferns taken down to Daingerfield's on the corner, to look after till I come back, oh yes, I nearly forgot—"

She turned and seized Donald Rush.

"You will remember, won't you, Donnie? About watering my petunias? Just tie that piece of gunnysack around the end of the hose, and let it run slowly, about an hour every other day? I'll just *die* if I come home and find them shriveled to a crisp!"

He promised.

He thought it was going to be a bore, with the Shoemakers away. Still he couldn't see why such a fuss was always kicked up when people saw people off, for now there came a hurry of female figures out of the Harvey House dining room, it was Margaret, the headwaitress, and some of her girls, come to say good-by to Willa. They were just in time. The engine bell began to roll, and the engine let off steam. It made a loud noise, but through it the high enchanted voice of Mrs. Shoemaker could be heard crying, "Good-by, good-by…"

XXXVII · MAIL FROM ALBION

I

Bun got a letter from Martha, written on the train, on the railroad stationery. He could imagine her sitting in the observation car and writing at the little desk with the pierced brass lamp, probably putting on the airs of one who did this five times a year, though it was her first trip since she had come West as a baby. Her writing was neat and clear. Even the lurches and impulses of the train couldn't make her page look like anything but a well-kept ledger. How remote she seemed, in this medium! But as he read, his heart kindled, and he warmed with longing.

The picture! Oh, my darling Bunny, the picture! I did
not expect such a parting gift from you. It is not much
as a parting gift according to the way other girls would
look at it, just a Kodak print. But to me it spoke volumes.
I shall always treasure it. I have looked at it six times
this morning, already. It is much more interesting than
the Godforsaken country we are passing through. Last
night I could not help crying as I fell asleep, just a little,
because the train kept going the way away from where
you are. But I must not let myself think of anything but
when I come back. Otherwise Mother's whole trip will
be spoiled. So I shall just act educated and attempt to
be pleasing, which will only be a pose, because how will
they know what is inside of my brain? Only I will know,
and you will know.

He had a postcard from Chicago, where they changed trains,
which said,

Nearly there. Gorgeous trip. We will do it together
some day.

Then for a week he heard nothing, and worried. On one of
those days he got possessed by something, he didn't know what,
which nearly drove him wild. He went to the post-office box five
times in that one day, and on finding nothing, even the last time,
after dark, he went around to the cement deck behind the post
office and knocked on the door, peering through the wired-glass
window, until a clerk came to see what he wanted. He blushed and
said he was sorry to make a bother, but could it be that a letter for
Richmond Summerfield, Box 446, might have fallen back on the
floor inside the wall of boxes? He was almost sure that there was
a letter, and yet he had not received it. If the clerk would look?
The clerk told him to wait, and stared at him a second out of tired
buglike eyes under a green eyeshade. It was a look that chilled the

young man's heart, for it seemed to say, from a point twice Bun's age, "What could possibly be that important? More important than my aching bones, which hurt the more with every step I take?" But he finally went to look, and Bun watched him across the big open room with its hanging lamps and their golden dusty cones of light in the dark air. The clerk came back and shook his head. Bun smiled energetically to hide his trouble, and went off with his head in a whirl. He couldn't imagine what was wrong. He hardly slept that night.

2

But when he awoke the next morning, it was in a sort of restored peace that was something like indifference; or so he thought, until he got to the store and found a letter for him which had been collected in the early mail at Box 446. At the sight of her careful and clever writing, a weight fell in his breast, as if he would never catch it, and he retired to the farthest corner of the stock room, among cardboard pyramids and wooden cases, and read her letter by the light of a window high up near the ceiling. Here he was uninterrupted, except once by Rollie, who seemed to be looking for something.

"Go, go, go," she wrote, sounding something like her mother Willa. "You must think me an awful pill for taking so long to tell you everything. But honestly, we have never been given a *moment. I never saw* such hospitable people in my life, though they say themselves that if a person's a stranger here they might just as well resign themselves to the cold shoulder. But when you *belong* here, why it is entirely different. You would never know Mamma. She looks ten years younger, we got the prettiest clothes in Chicago, you won't know me, and we are living here at this hotel, and I never would have believed it The way Mamma is somebody here. All her old freinds, the ones who are left, take her right in, you would think she is a girl again. I guess it must just be fine to come home that way, and find out that Willa Johnson is still very much loved by all who knew her. Mamma's family really were somebody around here, evidently. I can hardly remember Daddy, but we drove out and saw the house where he was born, it was sold some years back, but it is a lovely old white clapboard farm house, which is now a tea room and antique shop.

"But honestly, I'll never understand Momma. Here after all the talk and the planning and the breaking all our necks to *get* here, she says nothing is the same, and she worries about things back home, and the petunias at the house, and have I heard from you, she's suddenly gone crazy over you, and I'll never understand her as long as I live. She hasn't said so right out, but I honestly think that if either Waynie or I suggested it, she'd run for the first train home. Except that so many *affairs* have been arranged for her that she *couldn't* leave now. But you ought to hear her talk about her responsible position at home, with the Harvey System, and so on and so on. I simply *die* at her! She was telling everybody what a '*good*' boy you are, though not a Catholic, and the *best-looking thing*, she said. (Guess who else thinks so!) But Momma does have an air, and loves to spend money as if she never heard of it and as if it don't matter one way or the other if you have it or if you don't.

"Well, where to begin. There have been parties every single night. I never see Wayne at all any more. He has found himself a lot of little freinds." (He smiled fondly over her misspelling.) "We see a great deal of some dear old freinds of Mamma's, the Martin Yeagers, they all grew up together, and we take dinner there, or we drop in for tea, or we sit on the lawn in the evenings when it is so hot and watch the fireflies. They have three boys, the oldest one Dennison just graduated from college. He is really an old pill, but he is trying to be nice, and as I told Mamma, the least you can do is act appreciative, and I don't see anything wrong with making freinds easily, do you. Don't be jealous you have no cause. He is very good looking in a different sort of a way. Blond and brown-eyed, you see not a bit like my own dear blue-eyed Bunny, at all. (Jealous?) He has a Stutz Bearcat runabout and we all pile in I mean some of the younger crowd and go off swimming. You ought to see him in his straw hat, the first time I saw him in it I nearly burst out laughing right in his face and I never could even imagine you waering a thing as awful as that hat. He said everybody at Ann Arbor wore the same kind of a hat so I could kindly keep my *millinery opinions* to myself. I didn't even address a single remark to him after that until we got back for supper.

"The Yeagers live in a new house they have just moved into, after their old one burned to the ground. It is a stunning new Norman-French style country house, and all the old Yeager family heirlooms look lovely in the rooms. Mrs. Yeager has outstanding taste. Mr. Yeager jollies her and says there's no place in the house for poor old Pop, meaning himself. He is an awfully nice old man, and seems to have taken quite a shine to yours truly. He told me he was once madly in love with Mamma, and I nearly died laughing right in his face, until I saw that he meant it perfectly seriously.

"Well, what else. We're going to Detroit one day next week to go through the Ford factory, near there, Mr. Yeager has a freind" (he promised to teach her to spell that word) "who is high up in the company. Wayne can hardly wait. Why haven't I heard from you? Forgive me I will write more often now. Are you remembering to do what I promised we would both do, go to sleep every night facing toward each other? I have kept my vow faithfully. See that you do. Sometimes when I am with these other people and suddenly think of you I can hardly stand it, but what can you do."

He was vaguely disquieted by the letter, and read its final endearments with his heart in his mouth. He thought of his agony at the post office the night before, and he wondered if he was being foolish in resenting her activity, her new interests, the rich college boy she was tearing around the country with in a Stutz Bearcat. He had a wave of hot thought, it seemed to sweep over him, and turn him scarlet, and he rushed out the back door of the drugstore, and went down the street to the Western Union office. He wrote her a telegram:

"I LOVE YOU I LOVE YOU I LOVE YOU DARLING,"

making the even ten words, and not looking at the clerk, paid for it
and walked slowly back to the corner to go back to work. He wondered now that it was done whether she would think the telegram
both as passionate and as clever as he did. He felt deeply depressed.

3

Though he conducted himself as a relentlessly Christian young man,
Rollie Glovers was actually a pagan, adoring physical beauty with
a passion and an envy which the illiterate energies of his preachers
never aroused in him on Wednesday evenings, or Sunday mornings,
or during those week-long revivals which he attended in zealous
communion with other excited people.

He desired above everything else in the world to be strong and
shapely. He believed that as soon as his muscles bulged and his chest
expansion was increased to six inches, he would only have to look
at a girl with a meaningful glance to have her fall into his arms. He
hated Bun, and was elaborately courteous to him. He watched him
to see how he made such a grateful impression on people, mostly
girls and women who came into the store, and he knew Bun was
"soft on" Martha Shoemaker. He saw Bun read Martha's long letter,
and was tempted to sneak it out of Bun's jacket pocket and read it.
But he sternly told himself that this would never do. But the idea
aroused a passion of jealousy in him, and he wished there were some
way in the world for him to declare himself as Bun's rival, and then
simply "take her away" from him. But he supposed he had to content himself with his courses of self-improvement, first.

He exercised regularly and hunted through the morning papers
for columns on health to winnow of their self-improvement diets.
He sunbathed, and swam, and used the rowing machine downstairs
in the YMCA and never turned off his light to go to sleep until
lying on the floor he had raised and lowered himself ten times,
"keeping the legs stiff and the back well arched."

Then he would look into the mirror, and weigh himself, seeking
evidence of what he so truly desired.

He had come, lately, to an expression of his ideal which gave him such pleasure as he could afford. On the newsstand down the street in front of the pool hall, he got used to buying a magazine called *Body Harmony*, which came every month and contained articles on hopeful philosophy; advice as to exercise; many advertisements for physical culture systems which guaranteed to "make a man" of anybody who felt the need, and within ten days, at that; and best of all, a section of photographs, elegantly reproduced in a sort of powdery brown ink, showing "art poses" by amateurs of the cult of the body.

Many of these pictures were highly encouraging. Against board fences beyond which the despairing clutter of city alleys could be seen, they showed skinny youths standing in puny nakedness wearing loincloths that sagged about their hipbones. And then if you turned the page eagerly, there were other pictures of the same youths showing them six months later, displaying the fruits of their self-love in richly lighted poses made in photographers studios…impersonations of the Discobolus, the Doryphorus, the Dying Gaul, as well as improvised positions in which the young men fiercely yet softly grasped at their own wrists to make their biceps bulge, their breasts stand out, and their abdominal muscles turn into highlighted knots of strength.

To Rollie, these photographs of living bodies were the classics.

He longed for such splendor for himself.

He cut out the pictures and tipped them onto cardboards out of his laundered shirts, and tacked them to the wall until he had a gallery. Some of the figures, which looked as if they had been oiled before displaying themselves almost amorously before the lens of the photographer, wore loincloths of leopardskin, and stirred the darkest and most empowering of atavisms in Rollie as he looked at them. That was what it was to be strong! To do battle with a jungle cat and win his pelt for your own clothing! Or, barring that, to have the privilege of ordering a pair of such leopardskin trunks from the Hercules Physical Culture Studio, along with a set of bar bells, which could be paid for at the rate of a dollar-fifty-five a month until the bargain price was fulfilled.

He promised himself that someday he would have a pair of leopardskin trunks, even if he had to wear them in his bedroom, where nobody could see him.

So he contented himself with worrying about living cleanly, and taking wholesome exercise, and saving his God-given body for the girl who was waiting for him, sometime, somewhere; and doing all he could to improve it, like this fellow in the last issue of *Body Harmony*, on page 43—a picture decidedly worth cutting out and putting up:

> Herman Otto Janowski, 433 Pearl Street, Buffalo, N. Y., age twenty-two, who spends his spare time from his job as a linotype operator on the Buffalo *Volksfreund*, developing his superb physique, by doing bar bell work in the family backyard (Herman is unmarried—look out girls!) and meeting his friends three evenings a week for contests of strength in a neighborhood gymnasium. A fine example for those who believe their case is hopeless: just turn the page and see a month-by-month record of "Ski's" (as his friends call him) body development.

4

A few days later, Donald Rush received a letter from Wayne Shoemaker. It occupied three pages with a suggested synopsis for the novel to be written about Monsieur le Vicomte, which Don could use or not, as he chose. There were two postscripts. The first one said,

> P.S. This country would get on your nerves. It is too hot, too crowded, too wet and nobody does anything. What I really liked was the great city of Chicago, with its handsome hotels and museums and perfectly groomed men and expensively garbed women. I'll tell you all about it.

The second one:

P.S. 2. My sister Martha ran off and got married to
Dennison Yeager, a guy she met here, yesterday. (Married yesterday, not *met*. She's been sweet on him all
summer.) Everybody said it was love at first sight but I
do not believe in the being of any such thing. If you ask
me I think she did it out of spite for Mrs. Yeager who
did not favor the match but Mr. Yeager was all for it.
Mother don't know whether to laugh or cry. They drove
to Ann Arbor another town near here and got married
there. The next thing anybody knew was a telegram
from Toledo, Ohio. Boy oh boy. Quick work.

In the evening paper the same day, the town of Albuquerque read of the elopement. Many who read the account thought
it sounded rather like Willa herself, and concluded that she had
mailed it to the paper direct.

Friends of Mrs. Frederick Shoemaker who has lived
in this city for some years will learn with pleasure of
the marriage in Ann Arbor, Michigan, at the rectory
of St. Rose of Hungary's Church, on August 3, of her
daughter Martha Elizabeth, to Mr. Dennison Yeager,
of Albion, Michigan. Mrs. Shoemaker was an Albion
girl, and the Yeager family are old friends. The honey-
moon couple are motoring to Eastern points, including
Niagara Falls, and Atlantic City, and will return to
make their home in Albion. Mrs. Shoemaker and her
son Wayne, after completing their visit with friends in
Albion, will return to the city late this month, where she
is connected with the Fred Harvey system. Many affairs
are being given for Mrs. Shoemaker by old friends in
her girlhood home city.

It was this paragraph which told Bun the news. He found the
evening paper lying on the cash register counter, folded open at the

society page, with a ring of red pencil marking the item, and a large red question mark carefully written beside it. It was Rollie Glover's way of being in on something. Bun picked it up and read it during a lull of business in the store. He did not know he was being watched by Rollie, from behind a castle of Listerine bottles on the opposite counter. But he instinctively concealed his feelings, and folded the paper back together, and put it back on the counter and went off up the aisle whistling gently.

But his mouth was dry, and he wanted to go somewhere but he did not know anywhere in the whole city where he could be alone enough with his news. He stood in the doorway on Fourth Street, looking out at the hot summer evening as it settled like a fine cloud over the people, the store windows, the streets. Something like that settling happened over his spirit, and he did not think it could ever lift.

—Then even while she wrote to him that way, she no longer belonged to him? Still rehearsing the gestures of the love she had declared with him, there was another love alive within her, and gathering force that would at last prevail? Then she had just *practiced* on him, as it were? What about my own poor excellence: this very quality that *I am*, and which I wanted to give to her? What about that? Did it mean so little after all? Was it altogether a lie when I held her little face in my big hands and looked deeply into it? Is anything in the world as empty as my two hands now?

—And why couldn't she've told me herself, if this was the way it was going to have to be!

I'll never understand it.

The phone rang in the store. He ignored it because Rollie could answer it. But it rang and rang, and at last he had to go and answer it. He wrote down the order that came over the wire, politely thanked the customer, and hung up, bitter at the way things went on, even at a time like this. His own voice rang in his ears with saddening normality. And then he knew a wave of comfort in the distinction, the aristocracy of a grief that should be utterly private. It should be revealed to no one. If it was supposed to be a blow to his pride, as well as to his love, then let them see how many of them could make anything out of his reaction!

Rollie came back from delivering a package across the street. He had a pale and careful smile on his face, and he came up to Bun, and said,

"Sorry, Richmond, I really am."

"What about?"

"You don't have to be conventional with me.—I've seen the paper. I know what this will mean to you."

"I don't know what you're talking about."

"—I don't mean to intrude. But I have *known*, for weeks."

"Known? What?"

Rollie smiled patiently and lowered his eyes and a veil of *great understanding* went over his expression.

"Honestly, Richmond, you'd feel better if you'd just talk with someone—anyone, even *me*. You're going to be all right It's just hard to realize it *right now*."

"Why, I *am* all right."

Rollie closed his eyes delicately and said,

"Oh no, you're not.—She was everything to you, wasn't she?"

Bun put his hands in his pants pockets and tightened his fists there.

"Oh, now I think I see," he said. "You mean the Shoemaker gal?—Who just got married?—Why, just because I had a few dates with her, you thought—?"

Rollie sighed, and made a face of patient compassion, full of allowances for *how people felt at such moments*.

"Nuts," said Bun, and grinned at him, and frowned too, and was rewarded by a flick of doubt on Rollie's cream-colored face. "And I see now," he added, "who put a red ring and a question mark around the article in the paper! Well I'll be—Just a pal, aren't you, if that's what you thought, all along. Come here."

Bun took Rollie by the arm, and held him while he hooked Rollie's necktie with a finger and yanked it out over his tan starched linen jacket. He pulled the points of his neat collar up and left them sticking out. Lastly he brushed Rollie's shining, particular hair forward over his face. Then he patted him loftily on the head, and gave him a little push, having momentarily wrecked the most valuable thing in life to Rollie, which was neatness.

5

But if he won this petty skirmish, he still had the load of a defeat deep in his heart, and it stayed there for days, and actually got worse when he received a little package postmarked Atlantic City. It was a cardboard box, containing his grandfather's braided gold ring, and the same snapshot over which, he thought, so much war and love had been waged in their intimate terms. There was a little note scribbled and folded down into the box with these objects, but it told only one thing which they did not silently make plain.

> Dearest Bun, by now you must have heard, and all I can do is send these back, and hope with all my heart that you will continue to be my freind. I can never in the world explain what happened to me but all I can say is that it happened like lightning. I want you to know Dennison some day. You two would like each other. *I am so happy* and I hope you wish me well and can forgive me and count me always a devoted freind. I respect you more than ever now that things have turned out the way they have. If you ever come East, please know that we want our home to be yours.—Martha Yeager. (Mrs. Dennison)

He had the afternoon off, and he went strolling to the river. Maybe a swim would make him feel a little livelier. When he got there, through the sandy shore full of willows, he saw the river bed, so wide, so shallow, perfectly dry. The sun beat upon the dry sand and the pale cracked shells of mud, which blazed back at the sky. In August it was time for rains, but so far there were no signs of any, except the grand façades of cloud that hung in gold shadow on the remote horizon.

But he was alone, and that was a mercy, and he could still dimly obey a desire to tell his trouble to the river, if not in her waters, then on her great dry channel. He walked out on the sands into the light, and trudged among his sand-heavy thoughts down the river. When he got as far as he felt like going, he could double back to the river road, and pick up a ride with someone who was headed toward town.

The one thing that stuck in his craw the more he thought about it was the way she took the first opportunity that presented itself to sign her married name at him.

BOOK V

The Tributaries

XXXVIII · DR. MCGINNIS

I

In the main hall of Saint Joseph's hospital, Bun Summerfield waited alone. He was thinking of running away. It was shortly after two o'clock in the afternoon. The outdoor heat was muffled in this shining, dark corridor to an atmosphere in which clock-tick, the smell of polished woodwork, and a soft gasping sound far away that was made by a window curtain moving, got mixed up together. But before he could obey his racing heart, and turn and run down the steps to the street, one of the nuns appeared from a distant door and came toward him. Her glasses winked at him with unexpected hilarity, and when she stood before him, he saw that she was a little old woman quite capable of gaiety.

"Are you vaiting?" she asked.

"Where is Doctor Rush?"

"Ach, ja. He has gone upstairs to the o-per-ating room."

He licked his lips dryly.

"Where is that?"

"The elevator vill take you to the fourt' floor. And ven is the fourt' floor, turn to the left and go all the vay. You vill see."

"Thank you, Sister."

She was like a closed door behind him. He went to the elevator, got in, and pressed the button marked "4," and was conducted laboriously and slowly upward. He watched the bricks of the elevator shaft pass downward. He wondered if he was about to faint. He put out his hands and looked at them. They were not trembling. This did not reassure him. Perhaps he could tell Doctor Rush he had an errand to do for the store, but would be glad to see an operation some other time. The elevator stopped. He hesitated a moment, and then in rage at his panic, he hauled the heavy door aside and stepped out on the fourth floor. Far down the hall to his left he saw a partition of frosted glass, lighted goldenly from the other side. He saw two nurses pass across the hall from opposite doors, hurrying. He walked toward the end of the hall, and a sound in his own ears began to turn real and he heard steam hissing somewhere. There at last was an open door. He turned to it.

Doctor Rush was in the room, bare to his waist, scrubbing his hands and arms in a stream of running water over a deep stone basin.

"Hi, Bunny, I began to give you up. You'll have to hurry."

The Doctor saw an old image of fright in the boy's face, but he admired also the attempts at concealment which he saw there too. He believed it would be easier for Bun if he gave him little chance to say anything.

"Take off your shirt and use some of that soap. You have to scrub yourself raw.—Go ahead. Now. They've brought the patient up. I'm going to introduce you as a visiting doctor when we get you all hooded up and masked so your own mother wouldn't know you. I've had the orderly lay out a gown for you, gloves, everything. You might as well play the part right.—Scrub hard. You know why we do this, of course?"

Bun nodded.

His cheeks were dark red.

"It is a simple case of appendicitis, and I don't look for any trouble. We ought to be in there about twenty minutes."

The door to the operating room was behind them. Bun looked around. He could see vague golden shadows passing on golden frosted glass. The steam kept hissing somewhere.

"I was pretty excited my first time," said the Doctor, watching the boy. "Everybody always expects to faint, but hardly anybody ever does. You probably have thought of it. Well, you won't. As long as you're thinking *of* it, you can think *against* it. Keep your knees loose.—How old are you?"

"Nearly eighteen."

"I'd call you older, from your build. You look ready for medical college right now. Or, at least, you look more like twenty. How old do you *feel?*"

"I feel about nine and a half, right now."

"Nervous?"

"Yes."

"Stage fright is useful. I imagine a race horse always has stage fright. I bet a steam roller never does."

Bun laughed exaggeratedly, but he felt better.

He straightened up and faced the Doctor.

Peter saw his pulse beating below his breastbone; how powerful, how even, how rapid, how scared.

"Now we're reasonably free from infection. Put on your gown, there."

They got into their unpressed muslin operating dresses, tied the strings at the back of neck and waist, capped themselves and tied the gauze masks across their faces.

"You look like the Dean of the Medical Faculty himself," said Peter. "Let's go."

He walked to the swinging door of the operating room, and turned and kicked it open with his heel, and ducked through without touching it otherwise. When it swung this way, Bun caught it with his elbow and went through himself, into a new climate that smote him and choked him. The room blazed with white light, and yet it seemed misty with steam. He smelled the steam through his cloth mask, and it turned his stomach over. On the air was a heavy cloud of ether. He was not prepared for what he saw. The patient was already on the operating table. Nurses stood beside it. The anesthetist at the end of the table was dripping ether on to a cloth cone over the patient's face. The steam hissed loudly in here. He saw the nickel sterilizers in triple cylinders and the little flags of steam escaping from their cocks.

"Now, Doctor," said Peter Rush, turning to him. "Sister, this is my old friend Doctor McGinnis, from Detroit, just dropped by to see me, brought him along. Doctor, this is Sister Mary St. Francis, our head operating nurse.—How is everything?"

"Oh, yes, Doctor, splendid."

"Good.—Doctor McGinnis, will you just sit there, on that stool at the foot of the table? I believe you can get a good view there."

The steam and the ether and the sound of the steam were smothering him. He saw a nurse offer him a pair of rubber gloves on a towel, and he took them and turned away to put them on. He squeezed his eyes shut and bit his tongue. He was ready to die of sickness at his stomach, he thought. Then he heard somebody starting to whistle a tune, and he turned around, distracted and startled by such an odd thing at a time like this. It was Doctor Rush who came over to him as if to share a private joke. He leaned near and whispered,

"Don't you let me down, now, they all think you're Somebody.—So do I. Don't try to hold your breath. Now go sit down. You'll be fascinated in about two minutes.—And that's what I *mean*, Doctor," he finished in a jovial tone which everybody could hear.

Whistling again, the waltz from *The Merry Widow*, Doctor Rush took his station.

The anesthetist nodded.

There was a brief pause.

The steam seemed the only thing alive in the room.

"Um-h'm, Sister," said the Doctor, and the cloths were laid back, the patient's belly was exposed, now rapidly with never a second's space between one action and the next, the operating nurse swabbed the skin with iodine, and the fiery yellow stain spread so fast and so widely that no resemblance to flesh remained.

From his station at the foot of the table, Bun saw the skin tightened by rubber-gloved fingers that spread it smooth, and the knife in the other hand tossed once to feel the weight, the balance, and then the fingers taking a delicate grip of it, brought the blade down, and he wanted to look away, then, for this was the moment that he had thought to run away from downstairs in the hall, and the course from which there was only one direction to take, and that was ahead:

The Doctor turned his head slightly and looked at Bun. Bun caught the look. Something happened behind the Doctor's mask: an expression: it spoke clearly through his eyes, the little flickers of meaning which pass a disguise: they said, Hold on, now.

And so Bun did not look away, and the knife went, and went, and went, in short steps, and the incision was done.

He sat back a little, and then leaned forward again.

He forgot himself.

2

The sponges went in, and the lips of the layered incision were held back by the weighted nickel retractors. He saw veins and cords of white and of scarlet and faintly of blue. The hands kept weaving the fabric of the routine over and within the wound. The waltz from *The Merry Widow* kept up, with a perfectly even rhythm; it was even more serene than the cheerful melody of the steam in the white-tiled corner.

There was no tenseness among any of the workers at the table. They understood each other perfectly. Every gesture was answered with another. There was no drama visible.

The patient gasped softly.

The anesthetist leaned over and lifted an eyelid. Satisfied, he resumed the dripping of the ether, but with drops more widely spaced than before.

"Yes, Doctor, there it is," said Sister Mary St. Francis with almost a tender sense of congratulation. The appendix had been found, and the Doctor was now tying it off. His fingers were like a shuttle, not moving very fast, but with an evenness of pace that seemed the height of technical accomplishment.

The Sister handed over the forceps. The appendix was cut, and dropped into a standing basin. It stained the solution there pink. A few drops of blood appeared and were blotted with a patch of gauze.

For the first time Bun wondered if this were a man or a woman on the table. He knew they were nearly done. He wanted to speak but he couldn't think of how to say what he felt. He was filled with worship for the surgeon. He knew he had no way to mention it.

The basins were floating the cloth sponges now. The whole operation assumed a bloody aspect as the doctor made the retreat from the focal point. The steam hissed louder and the room turned hotter and the boy wished suddenly that it was not nearly finished. He was flushed, and in his belly was a burden of such deep joy, such a grasp of his bowels by the most hungry fulfillment, as he had not felt since he was a small child, lost among his toys on the floor of his room at home and surrounded by protection on all sides.

But the sutures were being made, and the retractors lifted away, and the ether cone was off the face at the other end of the table.

It was a woman; her face was white and her hair was bound within a muslin cap. Her eyes were caved with blue shadows, and her mouth was partly open, hungry for plain air. Her cheeks in their drugged relaxation sagged softly back toward her ears, and drew the expression of her face wide and helpless.

Now the surgical machine was humanly separated again, and at the sight of the woman's face, Bun came back to why this unearthly efficiency had been developed, and he believed that if he had seen her first, he could never have watched the operation upon her.

How can he do it, he wondered, watching the Doctor, and then he thought, Yes, but that's what you have to do, and now that it was over, he began to tremble. Nobody could see that he was trembling, it was inside him, along his bones, overwhelming him with significance now that all danger was past.

"There!" cried Peter, stepping back and hauling off his gloves which he dropped on the floor. He raised his arms and stretched, and yawned deeply behind his mask, and they all laughed when he did, and saw the yawny tears gather in his eyes which they could see, and they were relieved of the burdens they had carried so accustomedly.

"Come along, Doctor," he added, and turned Bun with his hand and led him with his arm back to the dressing room, leaving the nurses to remove the patient and clean up the room.

When they were alone again, he said,

"Good boy! I was very proud of you. You gave me a rough moment there, you looked sort of green, just once, but I knew you'd make it.—How are you?"

"Fine," said Bun, but his teeth chattered a little.

"H'ho! You worked so hard you've got a tiny bit of shock! Never mind. Next time that won't happen.—Did it interest you?"

Peter realized that his friend couldn't say very fully what he wanted to say, and so he offered him a cigarette. They both lighted up, and with the cigarettes in their mouths so they squinted out the smoke, they scrubbed their hands again, and made another date for a gall bladder operation two days later.

In a moment Peter was dressed and off downstairs to see the patient. Bun wondered if his interior trembling would stop soon. He stepped into the corridor and walked toward the elevator. He pressed the button and brought it up to the fourth floor. When it arrived, a nun in white uniform came out. It was Sister Mary St. Francis. He stepped aside for her.

"Oh, how do you do, *Doctor McGinnis*," she said, ironically lowering her eyes as she passed him, and for a moment he was dazzled by the possibility that he really *looked*—and then he flushed at her comedy, and rode downstairs.

But he refused to let himself feel foolish. He knew he had found where he belonged.

3

He was supposed to work in the store the rest of the afternoon. It was hard for him to go back there right away, he wanted to go somewhere, maybe down to the river, and be alone and savor what he knew. But without saying why he had to be away for an hour or so he had promised Rollie Glovers that he would return as soon as he could. He wondered if Rollie would notice anything. The trembling kept up, remotely. Perhaps it was not so much that he was trembling, actually, as that he felt a little weak when he stopped moving.

The drugstore was crowded when he got back. He had a glance of righteous reproach from Rollie who was gliding swiftly back of the counter to the prescription door. Rollie, like many pale, efficient people had the unearthly talent of making others feel gross and guilty. Bun hurried to the back room to put on his starched linen jacket with "Summerfield's" written over the pocket in green thread. Rollie was there explaining his order to the prescription clerk, and with no greeting, said to Bun,

"Large woman in straw hat by the cosmetics, first, and next, the young gentleman by the phone booth, we've had the rush of our lives."

"O.K.," said Bun, "I'm sorry. Is Dad here?"

He went out half an hour ago. He asked where you were."

"*Oh-oh,*" said Bun, meaning *Now I'm in for it*, and went out to wait on the customers.

He did his duty until half-past five, which was half an hour longer than he was supposed to work, since he was on again from eight o'clock until closing time today. Rollie noticed how he stayed over, and coming as close to an apology as anyone of his temperament could, he laid his hand on Bun and said,

"We would surely have been up the creek if you hadn't stayed a little extra, this evening."

"I'll be back a little before eight."

"Don't hurry. We can manage."

"I don't want for you have to *manage,*" said Bun, in revolt against the world of half-meanings and unspoken reproaches.

He needed more than ever to be alone, and it was getting toward twilight, the high yellow light of the sky would soon be a pale china gray, and then evening would sift in a vast draw of powdery darkness across from the mountains, over the mesa, down the lowlands of the town, across the river, and finally to the western profile of the last-lit sandhills beyond.

4

Suddenly he turned toward Borelli's.

He wanted a glass of beer.

He wanted to feel his body kindle as his spirits were kindled.

He walked out along Fourth Street, swinging energetically, because that way he did not notice the excited weakness of his limbs. As he walked, his thirst grew positive. He tantalized himself with how good the cold beer would taste, stinging his mouth with its golden shafts. A week ago, it would have been almost an adventure for him to go to Borelli's and hang around outside for a few moments, debating about going in or not, and wondering if there'd be any trouble about a high school senior getting an illegal drink of beer. It would have been something to tell about the next day when he saw any of the fellows.

But tonight this seemed a regular course to take. He felt years older. The Doctor himself said he looked twenty. Do you grow up in jumps, like this? he wondered.

He walked right in the door, and sat down at one of the round black tables, and waited. He heard a door open in the far side of the second room. Borelli himself came through.

"Hello, Mr. Borelli. I'd like a glass of beer, please."

Borelli gazed at him quietly.

He expected a boy's confusion after such a bland announcement, during Prohibition, and under age at that. But there was none. Bun simply smiled at him with a blue-eyed eagerness.

Borelli shrugged his shoulders at himself, and said,

"Why not?"

In a moment he was back with a tremendous mug crowned with live foam. As he set it down, he said, with the accents of one who is still no fool,

"Thirty cents, that'll be thirty cents."

"What're you doing," said Bun, fishing in his pockets for the money, "building yourself a poorhouse with hot and cold running water?"

He tossed the money out for Borelli, who took it away with

him, lamenting what a man would swallow for a few cents. The only thing in life that wasn't disappointing was the money he had in the bank, which would never lie to him, or cheat him, or speak so sassy to him, or run off to El Paso without a word like that girl last week, or make him feel guilty about anything, when he was trying to go to sleep. All he had to do to sleep like a brown baby was to think of the money in the bank, and his eyes would water without yawning, and his huge belly would rest like a fine melon on the mattress as if warmed and ripened by the sun.

The place was empty.

Bun took a drink.

It stung him exactly as he had expected, and tears came to his eyes at the tingle of his taste. He was suddenly and deeply at ease. He leaned back, spread his long legs out in front of him, and felt strength return. He drank about half the glass of beer, and the mild stimulus of it cured him of what had actually been a slight case of shock. He came back to himself, and felt like a full man. The marvel of what he had witnessed and survived in the operating room was something he wanted to consider, almost without thinking about it. Tomorrow, or sometime, he would tell somebody about it. If Martha were here tonight, he could have told her. He swallowed at the thought of her.

The room was important to him. In this room he celebrated his coming of age. The stained apricot-colored plaster of the walls, the ancient calendars, several of them with diamond dust flittered over their embossed welts, the naked electric globe, the bare boards of the floor, the warm evening outdoors over the river and the sound of traffic on the bridge out of sight; yes, his town was wonderful.

But (as in a parable of how briefly all things endure), Nick Borelli came in from the back room, smiling with secret purpose in his thick lips drawn down. He came around to Bun, following the outer tables, as if he approached with flattering fearfulness.

"Hi Bunny," he said.

"Hi, Nick."

"Glassa beer, eh?"

"Ye'."

"Purr' good beer."

"O.K."

"Like beer?"

"Sure."

"Atsa boy."

God, why can't I be *alone*, thought Bun. Why did he have to come in here fat/smooth/oily/mean.

Nick came and stood before him, seeking him with that same thick smile, and moving his hands in his pants pockets.

"Want some'n else?" asked Nick, finally, making a hint of a side-show hoochie-coochie movement with his thick, graceful legs and fat belly.

Bun frowned.

"Whatdya mean: I don't want anything."

Nick closed his eyes and rolled his eyeballs behind his lids, and smoothed his own belly with his short hands that were impersonating snakes' heads.

Bun turned hot, and stood up.

"Come on, I show you," said Nick, looking again. "Over 't the other house. Hot mamas just waitin' for *you*."

Bun choked on the smoke of an invisible fire. He braced himself on his sprung legs and hit Nick in the belly with his fist. Nick melted with comic swiftness. His face turned gray and he dropped to the floor, rueful and bewildered. He was like a child whose make-believe has turned pitiful and real. He was not angry; simply betrayed. He sobbed a couple of times and sat there. Bun strode out the door and walked back toward town.

It was much darker out.

The street lights going up to the mesa were coming to power against the dusk.

Why did I do that, Bun wondered.

He knew why, vaguely. Bun didn't consider himself a prig. But he had learned that afternoon a hard and triumphant lesson in what a man could do and he was dazzled by the things that lay waiting for him. It was the very glow in his face as he thought of these things that had attracted Nick to him first of all.

Walking up the long slope to the Highlands, Bun was sorry for what he had done to Nick. He remembered Nick's sleepy, confident face, and now it did not seem monstrous to him; only, before the astonishment of pain had flabbed down over it, full of some want.

It was a human claim, such as Bun was learning in all its forms. Some of them, like Nick's, were puzzling, and, unanswered, could only produce rage.

He reached the public library, and went in. He was full of splendid intimation. He recalled Martha almost sternly. Here he had met her almost for the first time. They had sat at the battered oaken tables and through each other discovered how people really were. Their minds had joined in thought and taken flight together. Imagine, he thought, how powerful their union was when it could actually produce a thirst for knowledge and a sense of pity! He was full of sharp longing for her when he looked around the reading room, with its silent readers bending over their books under the hanging green lamp shades. What clever things she had said to him here, and how grandly his mind had worked in response to her stimulus. Had anybody ever fallen in love before in a library? This large, brown, battered room, which had once been a schoolroom when the eighth-grade pupils had used the building? Never mind, it was almost like a temple to him. Too restless remembering her here with him, he could not sit down anywhere. He felt dammed up, ready to pour out his beliefs, his knowledges, his loves. He drifted to the bookstacks which were wooden ranges with long tunnels of black shadow between them. The librarian at the desk told him politely to turn on any lights he might need, and he nodded abruptly at her, remembering that she was Martha's friend, and afraid that she might ask him about her. He went down the aisle as far as he could get from the desk and the readers in the room, and pulled the string turning on an overhead light with a green glass shade.

He looked along at the book titles.

They were scientific books.

It was an astonishing coincidence.

Here was a book on physiology, and here was a large stout worn volume with a binding of rubbed calf and an old morocco label dyed red, with gold stamping that was still rich and clear. It said *Anatomy of the Human Body, by Gray.* He took it down. The binding was like an old door whose hinges were loose. He opened it and seemed to walk in.

In the brittle flyleaves there was much writing in rapid, sloping letters that had turned a faded brown. He looked for a name. On the title page he found it: "Edward W. Drew, M.D., Albuquerque, New Mexico, 1889." Why, he remembered old Doctor Drew. He was dead now. A funny old man, always driving a disgraceful ruin of a car with a canvas top and leather straps holding the top to the front mudguards. He was regarded as an "eccentric." In the growing town he had gradually been forgotten, until his practice consisted of fifty-cent consultations for poor Mexicans and desperate tuberculars living on the edges of town and of hope.

Bun turned the leaves.

His heart began to pound, though he didn't notice it, as such; he simply felt excited, and he knew why. Here was the science of the actuality of the afternoon. He leaned against the bookstack and turned page after page, staring at the engraved diagrams of *Gray's Anatomy.* His face turned dark red. His head swam. A lump came into his throat at the desire the pages aroused in him. He could hardly wait to *have* them, to know all that they held. The light from the overhead lamp poured hot and yellow down on him, his hair shone with light as he turned his head, his brows cast depthless shadows down his burning cheeks, he was carved out of the darkness by the empowering light over and within him, in the aisle of the old converted brick schoolhouse that served the town as library.

He was in a fury of creation, for he was inventing the future, with vows of himself, and it was a pledge of greatness which consumed him entirely, heart and all; he had forgotten Martha, for his true love now lay quietly before him in the scratched-up pages of old Doctor Drew's copy of *Gray's Anatomy.*

5

It seemed a long time afterward when he remembered that he had
to return to work at eight o'clock. He took the book to the desk
and checked it out, impassively discouraging conversation with the
librarian, who could not possibly understand what it held within its
rubbed leather boards. Old Doctor Drew! How wrong everybody
had been. He really hadn't been a walking cartoon at all, a sort of
comic spider who crawled along the streets in his rickety old car.
Bun walked downhill fast, apologizing in his thoughts to the long-
dead owner of the old book.

He would be a few minutes late again, but if Rollie so much as
looked anything about it, he would be forgiven tonight.

There ahead of him on the corner was the drugstore.

Hurrying toward it, he was smitten with a sense of recognition which made him smile and lift his brows. All his life he had
been looking at "Summerfield's" and it was now as if he were seeing it for the first time. The sight had a dazzling trueness about
it which seemed beautiful to him. In the darkness, the drugstore
flashed and shone with lights of many colors. The long sign over the
door spelled out the name in electric fights, and glimmered within a
border of running green and yellow globes. The immense windows
were like caverns exposing heaps of treasure. Huge jewels hung inside the panes, globes of peacock blue, and emerald green, and diamond yellow, and ruby red, the apothecary's signs. A high street
lamp on the corner threw a general glow over the white brick of the
store front. Over the front door a silver-bladed fan made the light
spin in midair. Beyond the windows in the lighted depths of the
store he could see the rows and rows of merchandise, the glass plates
of the show cases, the counters full of shining boxes, displays with
miniature electric signs, a profusion of fresh and gleaming wares
that sparkled with vitality and excellence. From a distance, the magazine rack inside the front door was like an oriental rug. He loved
the slick ink and the varnished colors of the covers. Behind the
soda fountain, these profusions and these lamps were doubled and
redoubled in the immense mirror which he had polished so many

times after school, earning his allowance, and as Mr. Summerfield
said so often, learning the value of a dollar. And far in the great
mirror were depths of gleaming darkness, the image of the night
outside, from which he was returning in such energy and prosaic
splendor.

XXXIX · THE TRIBUTARY

I

It was now full summer. The days were laden with the teeming scent
of the cottonwood trees, whose shade made great pools of coolness,
the only refuge from the heat. The nights lately were breathless.
Everyone spoke of it. They said the one thing they always had been
able to say up to now was that no matter how hot it got during
the day, the nights were always cool. Vast panes of glassy air waved
over the mesa and obscured the mountains. The river was bone-dry,
and its sandy bed was the color of bone in the light. The trouble
was, it didn't rain. Fields dried up, and the leaves hung down on
the trees, and tempers grew short, and hardly a cloud came up over
the mountains. At evening, the streets of town and the roads in the
country were fuller than ever of cars whose owners were out after
a breath of air. Yet as always, when people felt the same way about
a thing, in this case the hot weather, it was like a revelation of the
town's character; and people found their fellows to be patient and
resourceful, keeping humor alive in trying moments. They all knew
it was only a matter of waiting long enough. The cloud would come.

One afternoon it began to form.

They could all feel the light change, no matter where they were,
indoors or out. In the north, a black and blue sky began to gather.
The dusty green of the trees suddenly looked like bright new paint,
in the false twilight of the distant storm which made an immense
shadow all the way from the mountains at Santa Fe down the river
to Albuquerque, and below. People came into the streets and looked
to the north. The dark banks seemed to keep their distance, like

armies massing before a battle. The air was still, and still hot. The storm seemed to be holding its breath, way off in the darkened north; and so did the people; as if the release of the one would effect that of the other.

2

Peter came home a little past five in the car, and picked up Noonie and Donald to go for a ride.

"There is a perfect beaut of a storm coming up. I thought we'd all ride out the river road and see what we could see."

They got in with him in his great, open Packard, and he headed them out along the Rio Grande road where they were in the greenest of valleys. They could see the river bed, pale and dry beyond the ranks of trees at the bank. They passed houses of adobe whose walls looked almost violet under this slate-blue darkness. The sun was hidden. The warm air blew into their faces. The town lay to their right. As they drove, Don watched the silver water tank and the tall black stacks of the sawmill changing against the face of the mountains way back on the mesa. He saw a white blow of steam rising from the roof of the laundry against the day-black sky. It made him think of the inky satins and white ruffles in a picture by Anthony Van Dyck which he had looked at many times at home, in one of the books of culture kept behind the pongee silk curtains of the parlor bookcases.

"It is evidently not coming any nearer," said Peter.

"Peter," said Noonie, turning half toward him and putting both her hands on his sleeve.

He looked down, delighted by the impulsive and tender gesture. "*Yes,* Noon:"

But she looked at him with her mouth a little bit open, and shook her head. She looked back at Donald in the tonneau, a swift glance of reference, which her husband understood from long family habit of silent meanings before the child.

"Not now?" he said.

She nodded.

"I'll remind you," he promised.

It was a very little thing, this instance of a league of intimacy, even against his son, but it warmed his heart. He never let her know when he was observing her, but he saw with stubborn faith the slowly unveiling marks, week by week, of her returning self.

They were now in the land of ditches that were made for irrigation; but the ditches were empty, like abandoned roads on a half-scale map of an old battle, and the dried fields had the complexion of ruin over them. The big car rocked on the dried ruts of the road. He delighted in following every lane, every scratch that led to the remotest house. Everywhere was the hush before the storm. They saw Mexicans in doorways, watching the black north, and in their faces hope was again allied with patience.

At last a lane took the car where it could no longer go.

Noonie glanced at Don, and with a meaning which the father understood, she said to the boy,

"Darling, don't you want to get out and play around a few minutes?"

Donald assumed the look which always made her think of Wayne Shoemaker. It was the way the two of them looked when they were planning something together; an impersonal, unreachable look. She always felt "nervous" at it.

"I think not, thank you," he said, understanding clearly that a move had been made to get him out of the way for some exchange from which he was to be excluded.

She made a fleeting little shadowed smile at Peter, and it was like a sigh of resignation.

"Let's go back," she said.

He started the motor and began to back the big land-boat around.

And then a marvel occurred.

3

The sun came down below a hanging curtain of black cloud across the river, and shone with almost a wet gold light against the western face of everything in the valley. The trees and the houses were gilded in fire. Way to the north, where the sky had been blackening in tremendous shadow ever since midafternoon, the lowering sun now struck upon the bodies of the thunderheads and gave them glorious form out of the general dark. They climbed and bellied and towered, the fiery light, that would last so briefly, describing their cheeks and cheeks of curve and curve. It was appalling and wonderful. It was the golden promise made plain by the vanishing sun. Everyone who saw it could only stare at the magnificence of the apparition, and believe that no night could erase the memory, as well as the sight, of it.

They turned around and headed back to town as the sun went down behind the sandhills over the river. Darkness came like a hood after it. The lights of town were comforting as they came closer.

In the streets, between people, in the air, hung the suspense of weeks.

As the Rushes came into their house, the phone was ringing, and Peter hurried to answer it. It was a call. He had to go right on to the hospital. He kissed Noonie and said not to hold up dinner. It might take him half the night; an old man's case that had turned the way he had fought off, and yet expected. She clung to him a moment and shook his shoulders as if to say, Oh, why, why, why. And then let him go.

As soon as he was gone, she was ashamed of herself. Why do I always show him my worst self, she wondered, and then a wave of warmth swept over her, at what she believed for the future now, and she turned to find Donald. He was in the front room, reading with his book laid on the piano keys, and his elbows comfortably propped on the mahogany edge of the keyboard. She bent down and kissed him on the cheek, and left him forthwith. He watched her out of the room, astonished and charmed by something in her appearance. She looked so lighthearted, a new way for her to look. She was as pretty as he had always *wished* her to be. Knocking his book aside in a confusion of energy and sweetness, he ran after her and caught her, and hugged her, blushing furiously.

"Why Donnie!"—but she wisely said no more, and when he was ready let him go back to his book, after this burst of feeling, lately so unfamiliar.

As the Doctor had advised they did not hold up dinner. But the boy and his mother had it together almost as if it were a party. They didn't say very much to each other, but they behaved "something extra," as Donald said to himself. He was extremely courtly, he felt, and she was a dazzling beauty, quite like a lady in a book, and he was delighted to see that she had put on all her rings for him.

"Mother, isn't it almost too hot for all your diamonds?" he asked, meaning to be clever and very funny.

She waved them in the air with a theatrical gesture.

"My dear Lord Rendall," she replied, "I never notice them, I am so used to being crushed with jewels."

It was proper to the game that he should nearly die laughing at the very thing they were both pretending.

After dinner they decided to do their work together. She had her sewing box; he, his pad and pencil, and his water-color box too.

All evening she watched him on the floor, seeing the gray line of his writing on the pearl-gray paper with the blue lines on it as it spun some fantastic small life out of his imagination. He was at work on his novel, and though he did not speak of that, he did show her the drawing he made of Monsieur le Vicomte, when he had it done. A smiling and elegant creature, with mustaches and pointed goatee, a top hat, an "opera cloak" thrown back over one shoulder, and a slim long pistol held in one gloved hand. She admired it, wondering privately where on earth he had picked up whatever allusions to style there were in the picture—the hat, the cloak, the whiskers. But she had not gone to see the film of *Arsène Lupin* when it had been shown two years before at the old Crystal Theatre. Monsieur le Vicomte was a stylized transcription of a character in the movie.

The evening was deep and hot.

Where was the cloud?

Once or twice she went to the window and looked at the sky, but could see only darkness. No leaf flickered in any air. She put her fingers to her temples, and wondered why she didn't have one of her headaches. Her hair was damp upon her brow. She remarked aloud that she must look frightful. Donald replied that on the contrary, she looked prettier than he ever saw her. It was true. How ridiculous, she thought, but her heart made a beat that she felt in pleasure and gratitude.

Oh, yes, thanks, thanks, it said, not for her little boy's loyal compliment, but for everything large that it stood for.

It was too soon time for him to go to bed. For the first time in years, he let her come up with him, and when he was in bed, he wheedled permission to read for ten more minutes. She handed him the books he wanted; he asked for five, and made a bulwark of them alongside his covered legs. Five books! she scoffed, how could he read them all. He answered that he couldn't, but while holding one, he liked to know that the others were by him. She saw that they were, for him, alive. She left him to himself. She meant to go downstairs again and wait up until her husband came home; but suddenly she was overwhelmed with sleepiness, and she stood a second in the upstairs hall, listening for Cora and Leonard; but they must have gone, everything was quiet in the back part of the house. It was as quiet outdoors too, the darkness was a vast box in which nothing was happening under the heat. If nothing happened soon, she felt, she would almost have to clap her hands to make an event.

No, she could not stay up any longer. She went to the big front bedroom. The windows were open, but the filmy curtains hung listless. She didn't even turn on a light, but went to bed as quickly as she could, and with the feelings and comedies of Donald's evening still fresh in her like comfort itself, she fell asleep.

She was still sleeping when Peter came home, late and exhausted. He had worked for hours at the hospital. The old man was still living, but God only knew which way things would turn by morning. He had done everything possible. He kept very quiet when he found Noonie asleep, and got to bed without disturbing her.

4

He must just have fallen asleep himself when the crash came. The box of air over the town was shattered by lightning and thunder. It was a clap of thunder that must have taken the whole piled life of that thunderhead of the afternoon. "That first clap," it was later called by everyone who spoke of being awakened when the storm broke. Noonie sat up, and called out. He answered her.

"Oh," she said, and sank back again on her pillow, now that he was home beside her.

Then came the torrent, and the wind. The house was trundled by the storm. There came sky after sky of lightning, and whole avenues of the thunder's bombards. And in a trice, everything was drenched. Everything drank and was slaked. The powers of the heavens slit their hanging bellies and the rain fell in lakes. Its roar upon the roof, the streets, the ground, was tremendous. It made as much fear as it did joy. Now that delivery was come, save us, save us from the deluge!—this whisper of racial memory coursed in the hurried blood. But to be grasped all such natural forces had to come into scale with human beings, with a single one.

"Peter," she cried, and turned toward him. She was trembling. She sought him in the darkness, in that first moment of the storm's release. He comforted her, and they waited for the next crash together. When it came, he hugged her tightly, and when its echo caverned off up the street, he said,

"Just listen to it rain! We've waited a long time for this!"

She whispered that it made her afraid.

"There is nothing to be afraid of. I only hope it will rain all night. The lightning will spend itself soon. Then it will pour and pour."

They listened and waited tensely for the thunder, in the darkness, in which the cooled air moved over them.

But no thunder came yet, and she laid her hand on his cheek, and told him that what she had tried to say that afternoon, when Don would not leave them alone for a moment, was that after so many years, and all that fear, and helpless sorrow, now she had conceived a child again.

He laid his head heavily into the hollow of her shoulder and then they were both shaken again by a bout of thunder, and it seemed like their storm, come to tell them something, for the way all things took the meaning of their own lives once again.

His heart bounded back at the thunder like an answer. He exulted and felt confirmed. He told her everything she desired to hear from him, though with no new words to do it in. It didn't matter. She heard him truly. They lay listening to the rain in the darkness. The flashes were moving away now, and the thunder was rumbling farther away, over against the mountains. The downpour had turned steady, after the swiping gusts of the first wind.

A moment later the phone rang, and he said he had to answer it. She called to him as he went, to look in on Donnie, and see if he was all right. The call was from the hospital. A number of the patients were disturbed by the storm, but especially the old man he had been with all evening. The crashes frightened him. He was fighting the storm. What could they do? The Doctor authorized a weak dose of morphine. Let the old man sleep. Let him cheat the terrors of the storm that was walking tremendously back to the mountains. The nurse herself sounded grateful for a word of order, of decision, from the Doctor.

All over town there were minds awake with gratitude and alarm. Lights turned on for a little while as householders checked their property in the downpour. The earthen streets ran with little rivers. The night sounds of the city were engulfed by the washing of the rain. Nobody heard the switch engines plying the tracks… that sound which for generations had been woven into the texture of sleep in the wide valley. Was that a fire engine bamming and sirening its way up some street in the other part of town? The lightning had set something afire. Or did the rain ring with such portents upon the streets that all imaginations came alive to its power and promise?

Peter hung up the receiver and went down the hall to the sleeping porch where his son Donald slept. He cautiously opened the door from the hall, and let the light spill past him. The rain was misting in through the screens, but no stream blew upon the bed where the boy was sound asleep. He hadn't even stirred, not even the first clap had stirred him. He was sleeping almost energetically, his father thought, applying his whole self to it, as if to be suckled by dreams, to take huge restoration into his soul with his deep breaths. The bedcovers were like a relief map, a small mountain range made of the living hills and valleys of the young body. Like buildings built on that scrap of earth, five books lay scattered all about it. The whole sight was eloquent of a separate life. To see that it was safe was what the father went to do. He retreated softly back into the hall, and went back to the big front bedroom manned by love and thankfulness that his house was secure. It rained almost all night.

5

In the morning, he said he had a million things to do but even so, he stole a few minutes and drove out to the Barelas bridge to see if the river was running. Sure enough, when he got there, he saw the second life of the storm, coming down the river from all the tributaries of the hills, flowing under the bridge, bending superbly to the curve and the sand islands—a long run of water from the mountains brown with earth and bright with sunlight.

Afterword

THIS novel celebrates affirmations in life appropriate to different levels of age, and it speaks also of two backgrounds which correspond to those of my own life—the green country of my early memories of New York state, and the bare desert and blue mountain rock of New Mexico. The thread which weaves in and out of all these materials is the love of Peter Rush, the central character, for his native earth and its human history. How he sees these and feels about them provides the sustaining emotion of the book, with its several intertwined stories.

The contrasts between the life which I left in the East and that which I found in the Southwest were great. I have ever since belonged to both East and West, for different interests, which is primarily why I do not consider myself a "regional" writer.

I was born in Buffalo, New York (not Buffalo, Texas, as a German publisher reported on a book jacket). My father, of Irish parentage, and my mother, of German, made through intelligence and industry on his part and spirited charm on hers a pleasant place for our family. Talent ran through both sides, with aunts and uncles and cousins who could draw or paint or sing or act or write. Life had comforts and graces, in all the accepted values of those days.

Buffalo, like other provincial cities then, had a lively culture—many concerts by the great musicians of the time, a theatrical season sustained by touring companies of the greatest actors, a first-rate resident stock company, several good libraries, admirable museums, like the Albright—a general texture of cultivated social forms. As children we went to school at Miss Nardin's Academy, and swam at the Buffalo Club, and ice-skated at the Park Lake, and were sent weekly to Mr. Van Arnum's dancing school in the Twentieth Century Club ballroom where the boys wore patent leather pumps and the girls enormous satin sashes and hair ribbons and both wore white kid gloves. I was a violin student. Family tradition calmly holds that I got as far as the Tschaikovsky concerto, which I may doubt. Buffalo winters were fierce with blizzard or heavy with months of still gray light, summers were wilting with heat, and everybody went away—we, to a little island in an Adirondack lake. It was a sort of Scott Fitzgerald world for children—and in fact he had lived it in Buffalo only a few years before us.

The family destiny was suddenly changed when my father fell ill with tuberculosis. Doctors then ordered tubercular patients to high, dry climates. We came to Albuquerque, where we found very few of the flourishes which decorated the routine of life "back East." There was not even a violin teacher to carry me further into Tschaikovsky. In more serious wants, there was, for our family, no longer that sense of confident, ever-expanding achievement in the world's values which my father had worked so hard to obtain—so hard, in fact, that his effort cost him his health, and, too soon, his life. Other values must be found.

After a year or so of getting used to the swift and amazing change in the conditions of my boyhood environment, the values I began to absorb had to do with the vast land and its great river nearby, the mountains off there, and the golden sunlight that seemed to hold the past as well as the present in its power of revelation. Because the land was so vacant, and its forms so huge and abiding, it seemed that what men and women had enacted there long ago could still be seen if you looked hard enough with eyes closed, as it were. And if history did not tell enough about what people did in that land, then what they did must instead be invented. Among other of my fictions, *The Common Heart* illustrates this notion.

A novelist often imagines that persons whose likeness he draws from life are sure to be immune from recognition. I felt so about Mary Carmichael, my novelist in this story, who comes to stay in Albuquerque long enough for her and Peter Rush to fall in love. I did her portrait from an actual lady I knew slightly and respected fully as one of the best novelists of my time. None of the things told about Molly Carmichael in the book happened just so in real life to the lady I had in mind. Since I tried only to suggest her presence and her character in circumstances which I invented, I was comfortably certain nobody would recognize her. This lasted until the agreeable day when I first met the poet and critic Winfield Townley Scott in Santa Fe.

"Tell me," he said very soon after our introduction over lunch, "isn't Molly Carmichael really a portrait of ————?"—naming the lady I meant.

I have never known whether to be uneasy over his penetration or pleased at my success in catching someone to the life.

Made in the USA
Middletown, DE
17 May 2025